DIVINE PREY

PROPHECY OF POWER

CHRIS ANDREWS

CREATIVE MANUSCRIPT SERVICES

Divine Prey: Prophecy of Power

The Normagaell Saga book 1

A Veil of Gods novel
By Chris Andrews

ACKNOWLEDGMENTS

I honestly can't count the number of people who've had input and influence into Divine Prey.

Drafts have been read and commented on by family members, writing colleagues, work colleagues, my former agent, my former publisher, and friends.

Without their help, Divine Prey wouldn't exist as it does now.

I'm sure that if it tried to name everyone who deserves some measure of credit for this novel, I'd fail miserably. There are far too many.

Some people must be mentioned, however:

- My parents, who gave me every opportunity in life.
- My wife and children, who kept pushing me.
- The CSFG novel critique group for their incredible advice.
- Les Petersen, one of my greatest supporters and the creator of Divine Prey's cover art and map.
- Jo Clay, who provided astute advice and who also did the final proofread.

To everyone who's helped bring Divine Prey to life, named or otherwise, you have my greatest thanks.

Ellett
Kaijoosa
Simanode Mountains
Slaughter Bay
Leviathans Reach
Yaleeou
Delkoro
Sovereign Kingdoms
Tanceris Straights
Mistgrof Empire
Kenmoore
Fanolofyan
Free Southern Kingdoms
Gellont
Arachtigon

For my wife and children.

1

____

Three millennia, seven centuries,
and seventy-one years after the Seism.
The Season of New Life.
Prime Year of the Divine Lady Marnier du Shae,
Mistress of Healing, Goddess of Purpose.

Caroline stretched, ignoring the abbey's dawn bells for the first time in half a year. Although grateful to the Divine Servants for their care and discretion, she'd never had any desire to enter their ranks. Even so, her stomach knotted at the thought of returning home today. The Divine Servants were experts at healing bodies, but did not console hearts well. She needed friends for that, not religion, yet her friends could never know her shame.

Daughter, join with me.

Caroline stiffened and sat up, hoping she'd failed to notice someone enter her room. She gasped as warm light filled her, bringing with it a desperate need to join with divinity. She cried aloud, her fingers clutching the sheets as she broke out in a sweat. She couldn't breathe and didn't want to.

As divine light settled into her flesh she collapsed to the bed, every muscle aching and her skin coated with perspiration.

"My Lady, please don't ask this of me," she gasped despite wishing to feel the Goddess's light rush through her again. She lifted her bare arms. The outline of a luminous bell-shaped *alimoth* flower marked each wrist like an artist's sketch ready to be filled in. The flowers were the symbol of Marnier du Shae, Goddess of Healing. "I beg you," she whispered. "I didn't engineer this deception in your house. Please take your light back."

What else could it be but a punishment for her temerity? She'd come to the abbey under the guise of piety to hide an unexpected pregnancy and childbirth, and now she'd been marked as if she had truly sought Divine Service.

"Please," she whispered again, unable to take her eyes from the luminous markings. "Your abbey..." Was what? A convenience? She'd even lied to her best friends. If Caroline denied the Lady of Healing now she'd be denied the Higher Realm's graces her entire life. Yet if she accepted, the outlines would fill in and she'd be bound to serve the Goddess forever.

A blessing to anyone else, she couldn't imagine a worse rebuke, not even death. The luminous outlines were a punishment almost as harsh as the loss of her child. Fortunately, the King's Guard had arrived with orders to return her to Fandelyon City. She could be mounted and out the gates before a Divine Servant noticed her markings and forced her to confront her calling.

Her hands trembling, she threw her heavy covers aside. The cold hardwood floor felt smooth under her bare feet. She removed her yellow nightgown, pulled on her warm grey riding dress and boots and threw her royal-blue travel cloak around her shoulders.

Her clothes were tight, but there was no time to get them altered. She'd worn only the order's pale yellow robes since last autumn and she'd grown an inch taller in that time. Wider too, thanks to her child.

Footsteps approached along the corridor as she tied her curly red hair back. She tried to show only but the grace of a princess as the novice Bharise stopped at her open doorway, the young woman's olive skin and dark curly hair setting off her pale robes.

Caroline caught her breath when she noticed the shimmering *alimoth* flowers on the insides of the young Servant's wrists, something she'd never been able to see before. A nightmare. It *had* to be.

"Everything's prepared, Your Highness," Bharise said, staring up at Caroline's face as if she noticed something different.

Caroline felt her cheeks flush. The girl knew somehow. "Thank you Bharise. I'll be down in a moment." As the acolyte's footsteps retreated, Caroline buried her face in her spare riding dress to smother her growing distress. She needed someone to talk to; the closeness of her sisters.

"It's ironic, don't you think?"

Caroline jumped, a loose strand of her curly red hair drooping over her face. She dropped the dress on her bed as the abbey's High Priestess entered her room in a swish of richly embroidered golden robes. Easily a foot shorter than Caroline and perhaps half her weight, Tarine's presence nevertheless intimidated despite her years. Her grey hair and carved staff of office made her even more imposing, as if she were looking for an excuse to it as a weapon on someone.

With her mother's clan heritage Caroline had always been tall. Now she stood a head above almost everyone, even most men, yet still felt like a child as she confronted Tarine. "Ironic?" Caroline almost stammered as she stuffed the heavy dress in her travel pack, making certain her sleeves didn't slip and expose her wrists.

"How you came here under the pretext of finding your calling?" Tarine glanced pointedly at Caroline's wrists, her expression suggesting Caroline was no more worthy of Divine Service today than she'd been half a year ago. "Did you even pray to our Goddess while you were here, guile aside?"

Our Goddess. The words felt like a slap. "Of course. Devoutly." What woman wouldn't beg the Goddess's blessing while pregnant?

Tarine showed her own wrists. Like Bharise, a single bell-shaped *alimoth* flower glowed with divine light on the insides of each.

Caroline kept her eyes on the swarthy woman's face. Only three Servants knew why she was here, and Tarine was one. "I've imposed upon you too long, High Priestess."

Tarine's eyes narrowed. "You're ready for your journey?" The words were cold. Precise. Angry even.

Caroline felt her cheeks flush with shame, but was grateful the woman didn't force the issue. "Yes High Priestess. Thank you for your patience and the kindness you've shown me."

Tarine produced a tight smile, her skin crinkling at the sides of her mouth if not her eyes. "Unlike some Gods, our Divine Lady isn't biased toward age, station or gender when offering Service, but neither does she grant her favours lightly."

It was another opening, a chance to acknowledge her divine marks without being called out. "High Priestess, please understand that this abbey only holds bitter heartache for me." Humiliated, she revealed her luminous *alimoth* outlines. "I'm not prepared to accept these. They're a punishment."

"They're *never* a punishment!" Tarine said with the harshness of a slap, but quickly composed herself. "I'll pray to our Divine Lady. Perhaps she'll give you the time you need to accept her offer." She sounded as if the words were forced.

"I shall pray for the same," Caroline whispered. She'd always assumed that if she were ever called to Service it would be the Divine Lady Kindra du Erim, Protector of Warriors, or perhaps one of the Elemental Gods such as Haram du Heth, Lord of Fire. She couldn't remember a time when she hadn't loved watching fire dance in a fireplace.

"Before you depart you should know that Lady Rhonda duPrey also discovered the healing flowers on her wrists this morning. She has accepted her calling and expects to return to begin her training this summer. Her flowers are fully formed, not outlines like *yours*."

Caroline dropped her eyes. "Rhonda will make a wonderful priestess." And she would. She had a gentle nature, as did her younger sister Kirsty. She would be well suited to the Goddess of Healing.

Tarine stared as if measuring Caroline's words, but finally seemed to accept them as intended. "Rhonda's loyalties run deep. She's only leaving because she was asked to remain with you."

"I made no such request. Who asked?"

"Our Goddess."

Our. "But..."

"The Divine Lady speaks to all of us at the moment of our choosing. You'll eventually have to make a choice; walk the Divine Lady's path or step from it forever."

The choice was easy then. "High Priestess-"

Tarine threw her staff on the bed and grasped Caroline's hands, squeezing painfully. Although there was conflict in the priestess's expression, Caroline had never seen her shirk her duties to her Goddess. "I understand your doubts, but She won't give you another chance if you deny Her."

For a heartbeat Caroline considered refusing anyway. The woman clearly wanted Caroline to refuse Service despite the words, yet to deny the Goddess in her own temple... She couldn't do it. "As you wish, High Priestess. *May peace and health always be yours.*" Caroline's *alimoth* outlines flared warmly at the ritual blessing, divine light passing through her to the High Priestess. Caroline gasped and pulled her hands free as Tarine's eyes widened. Only devoted Servants could invoke the Divine Lady's blessing.

Taine backed a step, confusion and doubt in her expression. "I... I must pray for understanding. Perhaps you're being called to greater things than this abbey."

With her body still flushed with divine warmth from the invocation, Caroline picked up her pack and swept out of the room, wishing she could leave her fears with Tarine's shocked stare.

Within the hour she was a mile along the road toward Fandelyon City in the company of her friends Rhonda and Kirsty duPrey, all three escorted by the King's Guard. Behind them rode two maids, a hefty Servant devoted to Kindra du Erim, and the duPrey brothers sent to chaperone them. Overcast and gloomy for the most part, Caroline suspected it might rain despite the occasional patches of sunlight. The clouds were certainly getting heavier.

"How are you?" asked Kirsty, the younger duPrey sister and Caroline's best friend. Although pale-skinned like most nobles, she had dark hair like a commoner, but straight. Almost blue-black. Little Raven, her siblings called her when they wanted to tease. They hadn't seen each other in months due to Caroline's *illness*.

She kept her eyes forward as she didn't how to reply without revealing her heartache over giving up her child, but tried a hesitant smile. No doubt she'd have similar trouble keeping the secret from her sisters when she got home. The number of nights she'd woken up crying, a phantom baby in her arms... She took a calming breath, slowly releasing it. "I'm fine, Kirsty. Fully recovered. Truly." She'd wanted to die, at first, but only cowardly izzen chose that path. She reached out and took Kirsty's hand. "Your presence helps."

Her baby would be long gone from these parts, a month old now. For the first couple of weeks Caroline had fantasised about seeking out the child and running away with him or her, perhaps to live among the clans. She was sure to have kin there if she could find them, but after watching Tarine swear an oath of secrecy to her Goddess, Caroline was certain the priestess would neither divulge the child's location nor Caroline's indiscretion.

Caroline stared ahead, blinking to keep tears at bay. Best not to think about it. Obsessing would only lead to more heartache.

"But you were sick for so long. The High Priestess said you only began to recover a few weeks ago. Are you sure you're well enough to travel?"

Lying to her friend didn't come as easily as she wished. "High Priestess Tarine is cautious. She probably made it seem a worse illness than it actually was." She'd almost died, certainly, and for days afterward had muffled her sobs under her sheets, wishing she had. It shouldn't hurt so much to lose something she'd never held.

Wind caught Rhonda's long honey-coloured hair, but the older girl didn't pull her hood up to protect herself. She had a distant look, as if she'd rather be somewhere else. Back at the abbey, no doubt.

"High Priestess Tarine said you plan to return," Caroline said, hoping to change the subject. "That the Divine Lady marked you?"

Something like fear passed across Rhonda's features, but it was gone in an instant. Rhonda held up her wrists and her sleeves fell back a little. She stared at her *alimoth* flowers as if she wasn't sure she'd made the right decision. The fully formed flowers were clear to Caroline, and very lifelike.

Kirsty frowned. "I wish I'd been called," she murmured, staring at Rhonda's wrists as if wishing she could see the divine marks too.

Despite the wistfulness, Caroline heard the hurt in Kirsty's voice. Rhonda was tall, graceful and confident, and now she'd been called into Divine Service. Kirsty, prettier except for her raven hair, was small, timid, and awkward, younger than Rhonda by more than a year.

"You're expected to make a sacrifice when entering a Divine Lord or Lady's Service to show your dedication. What was yours?" Caroline asked.

Rhonda paled, her posture stiffening. "Nothing I wouldn't give a thousand times over."

Lightning flashed bright and thunder pealed across the sky like a God crying out in anguish.

Elias watched the valley from the edge of a cliff, turning his ears back and forth as he listened for anything out of place. The final leg of his journey had taken him into the mountainous lands between three small human kingdoms, reason enough to concern any izzat. Humans weren't the cause of his unease, however.

Something was wrong. Something of magic.

Storm winds swayed the tree tops like wind-swept grass as his cloak whipped about his legs and threatened to push him over the edge. He backed a step as the wingbuds on his shoulder-blades tightened in anticipation of a flight he couldn't take.

He caught movement a mile away; a group of mounted humans travelling through the forest. About fifty in all, most wore chain shirts and carried lances. Soldiers meant nobility, possibly even royalty in these parts. The coincidence was intriguing. He cast a near-sight spell to make the air before him work like convex glass and picked out five nobles and a small entourage among the soldiers, including a rather hefty warrior-priest judging by his dark grey robes. Half the soldiers rode ahead, lances resting in stirrups. The rest followed the nobles.

Elias's sense of foreboding grew as he watched, although nothing suggested the humans were responsible for it. He crouched and placed his longbow behind him, the wind blowing under his cloak. It left him cold, reflecting a chill in his spirit he'd been fighting since leaving his homeland.

The very air seemed to resonate with anticipation. It was nothing obvious, nothing aggressive, but it made him restless.

Distant thunder echoed across the valley while dark clouds on the northern ranges shed heavy rain. The humans turned north again toward the lowlands of Fandelyon, but nothing in that direction pulled at him either. He reworked the near-sight spell to gain more detail. Four of the nobles wore a standing bear embroidered in white, while one of three girls bore a crimson wyvern embroidered in golden thread.

As he watched the wind whipped her hood back, revealing the red hair of a clanswoman, though curly like a lowland peasant. His wingbuds tightened with a chill of recognition. He would have staggered if he'd been standing. Her soul resonated in tune with his own. It was instant recognition on a near-divine level.

"Princess Caroline," Allyn said.

Elias almost jumped. He stood up to cover his embarrassment. He hadn't heard his teacher approach. Why did his soul recognise hers? Had they met in a previous life?

Allyn's emerald eyes reflected his amusement at catching his student off guard, his angular face softening. Elias wasn't sure how old his teacher was, but he was rumoured to have been there when the unicorn was slain by the faspane two hundred millennia ago. Only one unicorn remained now, his people it's guardian. If it was killed magic would fade from the world.

If Allyn really was as old as everyone said, the years should have bought wisdom, yet most of the time he acted like a curious teenager.

"She bears a royal wyvern on her cloak," said Allyn.

"So does every soldier and both maids. She could be a noble come to marry one of Fandelyon's princes." His wingbuds tightened as he watched her. "I recognise her soul Allyn. There's no attraction," he added a little too quickly. The girl was human, after all. "Merely recognition."

Allyn raised an eyebrow as if he'd heard the lie. "Perhaps she was once born an izzen? If so, she's fallen a long way. Whatever relationship you had must have resolved itself in a previous lifetime if it's mere recognition you feel."

Elias wasn't sure he wanted to voice his next concern. "Yet still, could we be... soulmates? I wouldn't know what that feels like."

"If I were to guess, I'd say your soul is very new, so it's unlikely. Most soulmates know each other for many lifetimes before taking the eternal commitment."

"You think my soul's new? Aren't new souls usually born among mortal creatures?"

"Most people are born with a history. It's as if they've come to their new lives knowing they should be doing something, but clueless about what that might be. You're waiting for something, not chasing something, which suggests newness."

"My grandparents are soulmates. Could that have something to do with it?"

"Like?"

"Resonance from them? I don't know. Did they tell you how they came to bind themselves to each other?"

Allyn's narrow eyes watched the valley. "No, but their souls are old. Ancient. They were soulmates in previous lifetimes."

"I thought they were newly bound in this lifetime?"

"Queen Sellendria once told me she knew your grandfather was her soulmate the moment they saw each other in their youth. Their souls have history."

That didn't help. "Despite my apparent newness, is it still possible I could have a soulmate from a previous life? I must have been born before to be izzen in this life."

"When the Gods create a new soul, they create it from the essence of life itself, drawn from the Void. Sometimes though they create twin souls - a single soul divided into two. Perhaps you've seen your soul's twin?"

"Twins?" Elias pushed hair back from his face. The Gods had a sense of irony if his soul's twin was human. Best to change the subject. "Perhaps the girl down there's not Princess Caroline. Maybe she's clan born and on her way to marry one of the King's sons? A treaty of some sort?"

"Fandelyon's heirs are barely fifteen. They won't be marrying for a few years yet. That's got to be their older sister."

"But-"

"Most nobles this side of the Temern Straight are blonde, the descendants of the invasion thousands.of years ago. The clans arrived from the same sinking continent, but they took to the mountains and stayed apart, fighting fiercely for their independence. You know the King married a woman of clannish descent. Queen Lynn. That has be their eldest daughter."

"If our souls are twinned, the Gods have a wicked sense of humour. I can feel the connection pulling at me, even at this distance."

"Then you should avoid her. If you bind yourselves together, you'll die when she dies."

He'd already considered that. It scared him more than anything else ever had, even the prospect of his upcoming test. Shifting forces touched him again, teasing him toward the valley. Like earlier, it felt magical. "Something's not right."

"Really?" Allyn asked with feigned innocence. "If you figure it out, come and tell me. I'm going to finish my meal."

"You know? What is it?"

The wind pushed Allyn's long pale hair back, revealing high cheekbones and a sharp jawline. He grinned, acting the teenager again. "You need the practice. Don't forget your wards."

"Why not just tell me?"

Allyn gave the question serious consideration before answering. "I suspect the Gods are paying close attention to events here, most likely manipulating our Realm to deliver new elements into their game. I can sense *Quala Umitha* stirring against the edges of our Realm as our reality bends under their influence."

"The course of the future is being altered? Now? Could it be Noramgaell?" The thought made his heart start pounding. Fear or anticipation?

"Perhaps. The final battle between the Gods is closing in. Only Marnier du Shae and Marak du Tren remain in the contest, though the others will be attempting to exert influence and gain concessions for their followers."

"So it's not a coincidence that I've just found my soul's twin?"

Allyn shrugged. "Seek your own answers. I have none."

As Allyn left, Elias sent his magical senses questing so fast it made him giddy. He paused to re-orientate himself, before forming a magical net over the entire area and sending his Sight into it. When his vision adjusted he saw magic, life itself, illuminating the world. Wherever it pooled, magical creatures congregated like animals around a waterhole.

Elias adjusted the net to screen out the natural magics, looking for subtler energies. Human auras glowed dully, while further back along the road heavy patches of magical energy clung to the ground like mist.

Were the faspane up to something? He and Allyn had seen far too many signs of their mortal cousins. He searched again, but each time he came close to pinpointing the magic's source, it slipped away as if never there.

Curious, he reworked the net to resonate against directed energy. Between one breath and the next, his net illuminated with power. He stiffened and cried out as sparks showered the air around him and his chest cramped. He fell gasping to his knees, the icy wind blowing his cloak over his head. He gulped for air and fought down the initial power flow, but another surge tore control from his grasp.

Like mist before the wind, the barriers between this world and the Higher Realm wavered. His vision twisted in nauseating slowness as he beheld the edges of *Quala Umitha,* a vision of eternity only a God's mind could fully encompass and influence. To Elias, it was a revelation of infinite possibilities bound within the Fey Realm.

Billions of probabilities hit his overextended mind, each a potential future. He tried to force the visions away, but they changed again and again until he could barely tell them apart; an unbearable wall of pain.

A single vision cut through the others; a man standing beside a pool of rippling silver – the Silver Well containing the Power of Ages. Phoenix, Marak du Tren's Champion, held a ball of liquid power from the pool.

This was a prophecy. If today's events failed to lay a new course Phoenix would gain dominance over the Silver Well. The prospect was even more terrifying than the faspane invading his homeland.

Drawing on all his strength, Elias desperately constructed a ward to act as a block between his mind and *Quala Umitha.* Although the pain eased and his senses cleared he could feel the power mounting on the other side.

He opened his eyes, shoulders tight with tension. He had to survive and warn Allyn. Trembling as power trickled through his ward, he yelled and slashed at the link with all his remaining power, crossing his forearms as he invoked a desperate warding.

Lightning born of twisted magic struck and threw him hard against a tree. Energies arced about him, and then dissipated into the ground.

2

Elias groaned and gingerly stretched his bruised limbs as the breeze ruffled his hair. The air stank of burned wood and lightning. It could have easily stank of his own burned flesh if he'd been less lucky. The pine where he'd been standing still smoked, its side charred. Several coin-sized patches of glazed rock provided evidence of the power he'd unwittingly unleashed.

There was too much magical resonance to detect anything else. He couldn't even sense *Quala Umitha*. Hopefully it had withdrawn back into the Fey Realm where it belonged. Head pounding and his bottom lip sore from where he'd bitten it, he stood and focused his thoughts before sending another net out, this time fully warded against a backlash.

He found the mist-like energy again, slightly stronger where the humans were, though still spread wide and difficult to centre on. He'd missed the obvious. "You idiot," he muttered to himself. He'd missed it because it was impossible, or should be.

He finally recognised an unconscious energy dispersal, all that prevented a latent sorcerer's power from building into something dangerous.

It didn't make sense. There was enough energy being dispersed for two or three novice izzen, and no creature had that much power, particularly not a human. They'd lost their magic when they'd lost their immortality, or so the legends went. It would take hundreds of humans, thousands perhaps, to produce that much latent magic.

He released his net, running his fingers through his hair as the implications sank in. The significance of it so close to Noramgaell had unsettling consequences. The final battle between the Goddess of Healing, Marnier du Shae, and the Paladin of War, Marak du Tren, must be closer than Allyn thought. One of the Gods had gambled a lot on a single human by investing them with so much power.

Still mulling the implications, he picked up his ghostwood longbow and followed Allyn's barely discernible tracks to a sheltered copse of trees, the wind there hardly strong enough to tousle his hair.

"Setting wards against unexpected surges isn't such an issue anymore, I take it?" Allyn asked with a disarming grin. Despite the criticism, Elias saw concern and relief in the sorcerer's eyes.

"You knew," he said. "There's a human down there with more magic than even you and I possess together."

Allyn gave a slow nod. "As unlikely as that seems."

"What the seers said about Noramgaell is true then? The Gods really are drawing humans into conflict." A rune-carved ghostwood staff lay on the ground beside their packs. Allyn casually picked it up as he stood, but Elias read suppressed excitement. He should have taken more notice of his teacher before.

"With training, someone in that party could be very powerful." Childlike eagerness coloured Allyn's voice, making him seem as young as his features. "The faspane have aligned with Marak du Tren whether they know it or not. Someone down there could be the key to tipping this war toward Marnier du Shae."

"We can't go after the human," Elias said. "The faspane are too close and their wizard will have noticed the magical resonance."

Allyn gave Elias a hard look he hadn't seen since his early tutelage. "The decision's mine, not yours."

"The Queen and Council gave us *both* a task. Investigating humans isn't it."

Allyn's hard look melted into a grin. "I suspect the Gods are laughing at you just now, daring you to ignore their influence."

"The faspane..."

"Have no real chance of finding us. They'll be seeking the human too, which is as good a reason as any to interfere."

"Interfering would be reckless." Curious, Elias walked back to the cliff, hoping to discover more. Allyn followed. The wind was picking up with the fast-approaching storm.

"The feeling of being drawn to the valley is far stronger than your connection to your soul's twin, isn't it?" Allyn asked. "I feel it too."

"All I'm sure is that there's war and death surrounding at least one person there, probably all of them. If we get involved it could cost us our lives." Not that Noramgaell or even his upcoming test offered better prospects.

"Are you planning on living forever?"

"Yes."

Allyn grinned as if he'd just heard idiocy. "We're immortal, not eternal."

"You're so ridiculously old you can hardly comment on such issues."

"Yet I'm still not eternal."

It wasn't an argument he was likely to win. "The power I felt from the latent was different compared to our own kind. Raw."

"Someone down there has been touched by one of the Gods, and I don't mean as a Divine Servant. Marnier du Shae has upset the balance and so the other Gods are taking advantage of their freedom to act."

"Marnier du Shae can only be responding to Marak du Tren's gift of eternal life which was given to Phoenix."

"For which we've helped the shivras create the *Sword of the Sun*. No. The Gods act through us, they cannot affect anything directly. It would have taken Marnia du Shae millennia to invest that much power into a single human. She's been very subtle. Most likely, the other Gods have just found out."

"Perhaps there's a new alliance between Gods?"

Allyn's ears lifted as if he hadn't considered that. "You saw something within *Quala Umitha*, didn't you?"

Elias nodded his head. "Phoenix at the Silver Well. He intends to master its power."

"Then we must find the human Marnier du Shae favours before the faspane can kill him or her. They may be the key to stopping Phoenix."

"It has to be Princess Caroline. The coincidence is too convenient otherwise."

"I agree."

Elias sighed. "You're going to defy Queen and Council and go after her, aren't you?"

"Of course."

Why did Elias always feel like the adult? "We're supposed to meet Dobbin, not investigate latent human sorcerers. And don't even consider invoking my bond to you. We have a sacred duty to Queen and Council."

"Then I suggest you break the bond. You've been capable for years."

"Our laws demand the bond remain so long as you're my teacher."

"Then act like a student and respect my decision."

"But..."

"We'll meet Dobbin in plenty of time. This will only take an hour or two."

Heavy grey clouds moved across the valley, mottling the forest with patches of sunlight. Something glinted within the trees north of the nobles' party. Elias cast his near-sight spell and picked out a man wearing chain mail and a plain white tabard darting through a clearing. A mile ahead of Princess Caroline's retinue there were more glints of chain mail and halberds on both sides of the road. They greatly outnumbered the forty soldiers guarding her.

"Ambush," he murmured.

Allyn frowned as he cast the same spell, squinting through the slight distortion. "I estimate a hundred men." He grinned and slapped Elias on the back, almost toppling him over the edge. "Let's see what's going on."

Elias grabbed the sorcerer's cloak. "That's a battle you're about to drag us into."

Allyn glanced at Elias's hand on his cloak as if amused. "And?"

Elias let go and Allyn walked away. Back at the clearing Elias watched restlessly as Allyn gathered the remains of his meal into his backpack. Elias crouched before Allyn. "Don't do this. Please. It's dangerous."

"Of course it's dangerous, but it's also exciting, isn't it? We'll get to Dobbin's cabin soon enough and we can provide plenty of distractions if the faspane show up."

Elias could almost feel divine will pulling at him. "But..."

"I only want to see what's going on."

"Why do I doubt that?"

Allyn grinned. "Because humans with great power don't exist, and that human's got far too much for any race, mortal or otherwise," he said. He stood and slung his backpack across his shoulder and picked up his staff. "Follow or not. If not, I'll see you at Dobbin's cabin."

"One exists," Elias said under his breath. He almost felt his fate tangling with a Gods-determined misadventure. "Promise me we're not getting involved. Allyn?"

❧

Caroline tried to ignore the warrior-priest Tarion Hunthres, but he had a habit of prodding the same part of her shoulder when he thought she wasn't paying attention. It felt bruised already.

As her sleeves were a little short and she didn't want him to see her *alimoth* flowers, she kept having to pull the sleeves down. At any moment he might catch sight of the flowers, and then he'd never leave her alone. By the way he watched her she suspected he knew anyway.

Thunder rolled across the sky and she welcomed it, but he continued the moment it passed. "You see, they clear the trees all the way to the bridge and half a mile on the other side to stop outlaws and clansmen from bottling caravans there. With enough warning, travellers can take a chance at running." He almost quivered with excitement for the subject.

There wasn't nearly enough space to turn a wagon packed with goods and try running, but no one could argue with a priest. She'd discovered that over the past six months. She glanced back at Rhonda and Kirsty, but their expressions suggested they were taking delight in her predicament.

Traitors, she mouthed at them with an overly-dramatic glare. That only set their grins wider.

Heavy drops of rain began thumping down, driven hard by gusting winds. Caroline pulled her hood further forward and turned away from the priest, as much to stop the rain hitting her face as to avoid him.

Tarion's voice picked up to contend with the rain. "Ahh, the damage storms can do to civilised roads," he began, but stopped as he had to shield his face with his free hand. Ahead, Captain Bastion raised his hand to signal a halt. Caroline followed his eyes and nearly cried out in surprise. Soldiers in plain white tabards and chain shirts were charging on foot from the trees.

"What's happening?" Kirsty cried from behind, her horse skittering in reaction to her fear.

"Ambush!" Captain Bastion yelled. "Present lances and face the enemy!"

The soldiers lifted their lances from their stirrups as dozens of men with halberds ran across the clearing. "For glory!" one man yelled, and the others took up the cry.

"Captain, we need to retreat!" Tarion yelled above the storm. The priest stood up in his stirrups and looked back the way they'd come. His eyes widened.

Caroline followed his gaze. Behind them, half a dozen men in white tabards had ran from the forest to scatter caltrops, nasty four-pronged spikes with one point always facing up. The horses would be crippled if they tried to retreat.

"We're trapped!" Caroline said, trying to hide her fear. Her words were overshadowed by a peal of thunder.

Caroline let the reins slip a little through her fingers to gain enough slack to shield her eyes from the weather. Her free hand held her hood tight. Her heart raced with the need to flee.

Bastion threw his cloak off broad shoulders. "Rear ranks circle forward and protect the Princess. Front ranks with me!"

"Fandelyon!" his men cried and spurred their horses into action, forming a single line as they charged across the mud-soaked grass. Soldiers circled forward to protect Caroline.

"Bastion must have seen the men behind us. Bloody good commander, Bastion," said Tarion. He kept a hand on the hilt of his longsword, though Caroline doubted he'd used it in years. "There'll be a trap further up the road, too."

"Will our soldiers be overcome?" Rhonda asked.

"Of course not, Lady duPrey."

Caroline glanced at the priest in surprise. Tarion was clearly not above lying.

"We should risk running!" said Jonathan, one of the duPrey twins. "Before they surround us."

"No!" Tarion yelled, glaring the younger man down. "There's a bridge ahead. There'll be an ambush there."

"Into the woods?" asked Jared, the other twin.

Tarion shielded his eyes. "We may have to. Let's see if Bastion can clear the way first. The other side is too steep."

The enemy commander shouted something. The charging men stopped and formed a ragged line across the grass. With varying levels of skill they lowered the tips of their spiked halberds and braced the butts under their feet. Charging horses churned up grass and mud as the riders lowered their lances as one. The two lines closed amid yelled battle cries.

Caroline almost felt the collision as the steel-tipped lances punched through chain shirts. Lances shattered and men screamed in agony, some thrown back a dozen feet. Barely relieved at the small victory, she wiped rain from her eyes as two horses impaled themselves on the halberds, throwing their riders. Another riderless horse bolted for the trees.

Her soldiers reformed their line and reared their horses before the enemy, the trained animals lashing out with hooves while their riders drew swords. Caroline held her breath as her soldiers began fighting with swords and shields, slashing at any enemy within range.

One of her men toppled from his saddle with a cry of pain and she had to fight the urge to yell for help.

"For Fandelyon!" Bastion yelled to rally his men, the Captain's blade slashing before his mount's hooves lashed out once again. "Forward," yelled Bastion, and they began pushing double their number toward the trees.

"Captain Bastion, ware!" shouted Lieutenant Crace. The urgency in the yell was enough to catch Caroline's attention. He'd been left in charge of defending Caroline, and judging by his expression wished he hadn't been.

Bastion glanced over his shoulder and cursed so loud Caroline heard him over the battlefield. "To the Princess. Enemy at the rear!" Bastion yelled.

"Where?" cried Kirsty, looking back down the road.

"From the woods on the other side. We're trapped." Caroline said as she followed Bastion's gaze, dismayed. Too late for Bastion and his men to get back in time, about fifty men in white tabards were running to attack the rear guard from the opposite line of trees. She turned to see Bastion deflect a swing from an axe-headed halberd with his shield and thrust back. The man stumbled backward but recovered.

"What are you waiting for Lieutenant? Attack them!" Jared yelled.

Crace focused on Jared, anger and determination on his face. "This is a trap, Lord Jared. There will be more soldiers lying in wait. Even running is a risk. We need to draw them out first."

Caroline looked about. More? Their numbers were already overwhelming. "Is there anything we can do to help?" Caroline asked more for Kirsty's sake than her own, knowing the answer already. The raven-haired younger girl looked ready to panic. Caroline turned her horse back and took Kirsty's hand. "We'll be fine," she said softly, leaning close. "They want us captured, not killed."

Tarion looked around, assessing. "If we get the chance to run, you all need to be ready to take advantage of it. Understand?"

Lieutenant Crace pointed to three of his men. "Stay inside the circle. Protect the Princess and nobles with your lives."

Caroline sat straighter, trying to show confidence for Kirsty's sake, even though she felt none. It was the only gift she could offer her friends. The rain pelted harder before the rising storm winds, intensifying in proportion to the fight and forcing her to wipe her face with a wet hand.

"Lances down," the Lieutenant yelled. "Prepare to repel the enemy." Water blew from his lips.

Caroline's soldiers shifted their lances to the on-side and lowered them against the charge, giving themselves a free hand to draw swords. The enemy slowed to smash the lance tips aside, but as soon as they passed the long weapons Caroline's soldiers dropped them.

"Horse assault!" Lieutenant Crace yelled. The horses jumped forward and reared, hooves lashing at the enemy. Men fell with cries as swords and shields began striking and deflecting the halberd's axe-heads or counterbalancing spikes.

On the field Bastion's battle was precariously balanced.

Blocked by the new attack, he yelled, "We're nearly there. Form two lines. Rear line defend, front line attack and crush the enemy against our circle." Half his men turned and began pushing toward her circle again, forcing enemy soldiers to defend from both sides. Bastion's men eventually closed around a small group of eight and slaughtered them, the last slipping in the mud to die screaming under a hoof.

The riders joined ranks and the circle quickly expanded. The united field helped Caroline's defenders hold their own even as it allowed the enemy to spread out so more could attack at once, their ranks still three deep beyond her horses.

A blunt finger jabbed Caroline's shoulder. "Make sure you stay in the centre," Tarion said, nodding to Rhonda, Kirsty, and their twin brothers as well. "The whole lot of you."

Where did he expect them to go?

Kirsty and Rhonda flinched as a man broke through only to be cut down a yard away. Even the twins paled. Soldiers were missing, Lieutenant Crace included. Caroline found his body on the ground, his neck and chest bloody. She had to turn away.

Lightning lit the storm-darkened highway and for the first time she understood how many men her soldiers faced. Too many.

Rhonda screamed as a broken halberd spike flew past her head and dropped into the mud, startling Caroline and Kirsty's horses. Caroline had to release Kirsty's hand to grip her reins tighter, settling her horse. Lightning lit the road again and she saw fresh men in white tabards running toward the fight from the direction of the bridge. Thunder smashed across the sky and the rain fell harder, but not hard enough to keep Caroline's sinking heart afloat.

"We're all going to die," Jonathan whispered.

"No. Captured and held for ransom," Caroline said. She took Kirsty's hand again and squeezed. "That's the worst that will happen. Understand? We'll be locked away until our fathers raise enough coin to free us. We'll be fine. Move your horse closer to your brothers. They'll protect you and Rhonda."

"And you," Kirsty added.

"Of course," Caroline said with a forced smile. The brothers were merely along with Tarion to ensure their sisters and Caroline were properly chaperoned, though she was sure Bastion wanted them out of any fighting. If the fight got to them they were already lost.

She looked around. The circle seemed smaller, more familiar faces missing; Greyloft, Anhers and Rhion among them.

Caroline cringed as Bastion cut down a man who broke through during a coordinated charge, his halberd useless when Bastion got inside his guard. "Don't let that happen again!" Bastion yelled. He continued to ride back and forth, shouting orders emphasised with the point of his sword. "Use the horses' hooves if they get too close. You're the King's Guard, not common soldiers!"

Bastion glanced back toward the nobles, swore and then turned away. He shielded his eyes with his hand as he scanned the battle. His expression didn't invite conversation. He bellowed three names, and the three soldiers inside the circle answered. "I have a plan."

3

―――――

Elias and Allyn slipped to the edge of the trees, hardly wet as minor wards repelled most of the rain.

Amid battle cries and the clash of sword against halberd, the mounted soldiers held back well over double their own number. Bloody bodies sprawled across the green spring grass between the road and the trees, and just as many lay on the mud-churned road. Horses were down too, one still kicking and trying to stand. The ground appeared as red as it was muddy.

Elias grasped Allyn's arm. "Looks like we're too late to warn them."

Allyn shook water from his hair. "I still want to find the one with power. We might be able to help."

Elias winced as a rider on the near side of the battle took a cleaving blow to the chest. As he fell the horse bolted, knocking several men aside and dragging its rider by the stirrup down the road, the body leaving a trail in the mud.

The men in white tabards on the opposite side of the circle moved back to regroup and then charged in a line, the spiked tips of their halberds dangerously sharp. Two slipped and went down, but the rest met the horsemen together.

Elias nudged Allyn as a cold feeling came over him. "Ready yet? My wards are reacting. The fight's attracted the faspane." They couldn't be any more than a couple of hundred yards away.

Allyn shook his head.

Elias turned his attention to the brutal fight. It could spill into the woods at any moment and he didn't want to be caught distracted. "A few minutes more, then we have to go. Even if you pinpoint them, how could we possibly help?"

Allyn shrugged, concentration on his face. "String your bow. We might need it," he said.

"If you get us into trouble..." he said under his breath, but removed the bow's protective sleeve. He didn't need Allyn's urging to defend himself.

Allyn pushed a branch aside. "There's got to be a ward involved. Without getting closer there's no way I can study their auras with enough depth."

"A hundred auras all flaring with violent emotion isn't ideal either. Focus on the princess. It's got to be her."

"I can't get a clear view of her. We need to do something."

Elias tried to hold back his growing tension. "It's a pitched battle. There's nothing we can do without risking our lives and our mission."

Allyn grasped Elias's shoulder. "I know, but whoever it is could be important to us. You know that. If Marak du Tren wins Noramgaell our people will be destroyed."

He glanced at the battle. "Without intervention from the Higher Realm Fandelyon's soldiers will all be dead and the nobles too, most likely."

"Have you considered *we* may be that intervention?"

"Yes, and it should scare you as much as it scares me."

"Think of it as a game where they don't know we're involved. That gives us an advantage."

Shouting increased as the north of the circle opened and three soldiers charged the attackers. Lances smashed through chain mail before the riders' swords hissed free of scabbards. A man jabbed his halberd at a charging soldier, but the rider veered and ran him down.

The three slashed at their enemies until horsemen at the open ends of the circle kicked forward to surprise them.

More halberd-wielding men circled, but another group of horsemen charged, forcing the attackers to defend. For one brief moment Elias wondered if the attackers would charge the broken circle. It was the obvious flaw in the plan. Instead, they tried to hold them back. Their plan wasn't to kill, but to subdue.

Elias watched closely as the Captain of the Princess's guard raised his sword. "Forward!" Three more men charged, opening the way for the royal party who rode immediately after.

"Stop them, stop them!" a man in gilded armour shouted as he ran from the tree on the opposite side of the road. Another man in a white tabard followed close behind, sword unsheathed as if expecting to fight. Several of the closer foot soldiers whirled and threw their halberds.

"Don't harm the Princess! We need her alive!" the man in gilded armour shouted, but chaos erupted and all further commands were lost in the noise and rain.

Lightning momentarily illuminated a field of devastation as more men swarmed forward, whirling and throwing their halberds. A soldier and several nobles fell from their saddles. Elias found himself anxious to see who was hurt as the remaining soldiers and nobles pulled up, adding to the confusion. No more halberds were thrown, but the princess and at least one other noble were down.

The confusion aided the mounted soldiers who had remained to delay their enemies. They charged now, slashing at unarmed foot soldiers and killing a dozen in the chaos. They formed another protective circle around the nobles, but in moments were surrounded again.

"Nice try, but too late," Elias said. "There's still too many foot soldiers. They'd need to kill another ten or fifteen to make any difference." Every instinct told him to stay. Twin-souled or otherwise, he began to understand why soulmates among his people rarely left each other's company. The fear of not being there to protect each other must be overwhelming if this is what he felt for a girl he'd never met. A human girl, at that.

"Let's get further up," Allyn said. "They've moved too far for me to work properly." Without waiting, he hefted his ghostwood staff and ran into the trees. Elias followed, wishing he didn't feel just as keen. When they emerged near the road again it was too close.

The white-tabarded men had regrouped in several clusters around the soldiers. On command they charged on all sides. The horsemen closed ranks to form a tighter circle and keep as many of their enemies out of the attack as possible.

Blood stained the surcoat of one of the noble-born young men, but he remounted and sat straight without assistance. One of the maids was dead. A fallen soldier remounted, but had a cut to his forehead and looked ready to fall again. Blood marked the shoulder and face of one of the ladies who had to be helped to mount before a soldier, the man supporting her as she slumped against him. Only the red-headed princess seemed unhurt, much to Elias's unexpected relief. Her horse was dead though.

Another soldier helped her onto a riderless horse with a shove to get her into the saddle, the strain clear on his face. She was considerably bigger than him. Her pale legs stuck out from her soaked skirts as she sat astride rather than side-saddle.

Allyn touched Elias's arm, startling him. "You were right. It's the Princess. She used her power without knowing to protect herself. Otherwise she'd be dead from the halberd that hit her horse. If they try to get through again, assist them." Allyn indicated Elias's longbow.

"Are you sure it's her?"

"Not entirely, but she has a strange aura. It can't be anyone else."

Elias focused on the girl, and for a long moment he saw nothing unusual. Abruptly her spirit flared like a sun among the stars, radiating emotion and latent power far greater than any other person on the field. Allyn must be blind. But then he looked away and she disappeared from his mind's sight. "I've never seen a ward do that before. You can penetrate it, but only if you know to look."

"Look beneath her emotions. Everything else is masked. She

couldn't have done it on her own, not untrained. There's got to be a ward hiding her from casual sight. We have to get her away."

Elias felt caught between fear and curiosity. "If we do, it's going to cause trouble. We can't kidnap a princess and expect no repercussions. "

"But she has power! As much as the most gifted izzen of legend. More. She's been gifted by a God."

Elias's protective wards flared freshly and he saw movement on the opposite side of the road. It wasn't wind or rain. "The faspane are watching," he said softly, indicating the trees on the far side with his bow. "They must know we're close. No magic. I'll keep an eye on them."

The foot soldiers regrouped and charged the riders once more, several slipping in the mud. The mounted soldiers repulsed them. Just before the next charge, Elias noticed the Princess's soldiers moving to try another break.

Allyn said, "Ignore the faspane. When you see a weak spot in the attackers' line, hit it. Make sure the princess goes into the trees over here rather than down the road."

Elias heard a woman scream and saw Princess Caroline clutching her shoulder, blood seeping through her fingers and mingling with the rain running down her cloak.

Elias pulled an arrow from his quiver, suddenly sure this is what he had been called for. Born for. He knew it within the depths of his being. The Goddess of Healing was making a play at power and he was part of it.

He nocked the arrow and drew to his cheek, the bow's magic tingling his fingertips as he counted to ten and let fly. The arrow did not arc. It flew flat with the power of a catapult. It struck a man in the back, smashed through his chain mail and slammed through the man beyond him. A third man, ready to swing at a horse, jerked and crumpled from the same arrow. A hint of green energy discharged around their wounds. Hopefully none of the nearby faspane were gifted with magical sight.

Another man in a white tabard turned to see what had happened and a horse kicked him in the head. Elias released another arrow, the force of its strike throwing a soldier into the man before him and killing them both. He drew again, counted to four and let fly, the arrow punching through a man's neck.

It was enough to create a small gap in the fighting. Fandelyon's Captain yelled an order and the circle opened, allowing four soldiers to charge out ahead of the royal party. More followed. Others kept enemies from chasing them.

As the old priest went down on a thrust intended for a soldier the remaining maid fell screaming from her horse, her cries stopping as she struck the ground. The princess reigned in her mount to help the maid, but a soldier yelled and slapped her horse's rump, forcing her into the trees.

Allyn touched Elias's shoulder. "Keep as many foot soldiers here as you can. The Princess's men can't afford this again."

"No problem, as long as they and the faspane don't see me."

"If they do, lead them in another direction. You'll be able to lose them in the forest. I'm going to follow the girl and try to separate her from the rest. Catch up when you can."

"Good luck," Elias said as Allyn departed. He drew another arrow and let fly at a running man without waiting for the bow's magic to give it power. The man fell.

He held the next arrow for a count of eight before letting it fly. It struck the enemy commander. The arrow punched through his gilded breastplate and threw him into the tree behind him, pinning him there. Elias drew another arrow to his cheek, allowing the magic to build for several seconds.

He released, and two more men died. Unfortunately, he'd chosen front-runners and those behind took notice. A good number turned and charged at him. "And curse me for stupidity." He shouldered his bow and ran.

4

———————

Caroline rode as hard as the trees, brush and uneven ground would let her. Her injured left shoulder and short stirrups slowed her, her back jarring with each stride. She barely kept her balance with the unsure grip of her calves. Others carried injuries, some much more serious than her own, but she could only assume Captain Bastion kept up the pace in the hope of resting some distance from the road.

Poor Tellise. Her maid had fallen, trampled. Thank the Higher Realm Caroline wasn't bringing her baby home... She glanced at her wrists. Perhaps the Goddess of Healing really did have her best interests at heart.

They slowed for a deadfall, changing direction a few yards beyond it as thick bushes and a nasty slope barred the way. A low branch slapped Caroline's shoulder and she cried out, struggling to hold onto the saddle with her good hand. As soon as she righted herself she kicked her horse up the slope again, grimacing at the chafing on her thighs and knees.

"Hard eastward at the top of the slope," Captain Bastion yelled.

Caroline cantered the last few yards up the hill before pulling up. No one turned. Instead, they went straight down the other side. She

30

slapped the reins on her horse's neck and it jumped forward, making her grip its mane with her good hand. She held tighter as the horse slipped on mud and debris, each time barely regaining its footing.

She sensed her horse begin to balk at a fallen tree trunk, but she forced the animal to jump over it. She fell hard against its neck when its hooves hit, the impact jarring her shoulder. She cried out and came close to toppling off, clinging desperately to the mane before righting herself. She wasn't sure if it was tears or rain on her face now.

Everyone waited at the bottom of the slope where Caroline pulled up behind Jared and Jonathan. Jared looked pale.

"Jared?" she asked. The twin gave her a brief nod over his shoulder.

Feeling no better, she held her aching shoulder. The bleeding had mostly stopped. The rain hadn't, though the full brunt of the storm had passed.

With numb fingers she managed to adjust one stirrup as Kirsty, the soldier holding Rhonda, and the rear guard caught up. Rhonda looked ready to pass out, a nasty bruise already showing on her forehead from her fall.

"Are you okay?" Caroline asked Rhonda, wondering if she should ask a reprieve from Captain Bastion. Rhonda looked her way, but couldn't seem to focus.

"Forward!" Captain Bastion ordered.

"Hold tight, Rhonda. The Divine Lady of Healing is looking after you," Caroline said as she kicked her horse into a canter. They rode over the next rise, turning at the bottom. They slowed to follow a freshly flowing watercourse for a few minutes, and then moved into the trees again.

Her shoulder ached deep inside. When Rhonda and the soldier supporting her caught up, Caroline found her friend unconscious, slumped but held upright. The guard's nickname came to her. Grimms. "Is Rhonda..." she couldn't say the last word. *Alive.* A sickly feeling filled her stomach, and she didn't know whether it was a reaction to the fight or Rhonda's condition.

Kirsty appeared close to tears. "Rhonda was marked by the Divine Lady of Healing. Surely She'll protect her?"

Grimms nodded. "She'll be fine, Lady Kirsty. She passed out, is all."

"Attention," Bastion called. "We'll try and go more quietly from here. If anyone gets separated, head for the main pass but stay off the road for as long as you can. If you're threatened, try to get into the next valley instead. There's a clansmen's village there. We've had no trouble from the clans for several decades and they seem to be on good terms with King Phillip. They may even help if offered gold, but should at least let us pass without trouble. For now, we'll go north-east and swing north-west within the hour."

They started out again. Caroline rode behind Jared and Jonathan, holding her horse's mane and letting it pick its own path. She listened for the men in white tabards, wishing she knew who they served, but heard only the gradually easing rain. She turned in her saddle and found Kirsty crying softly as she rode ahead of her injured sister.

"Kirsty," she whispered."

"I'm fine, My Lady," her friend said with a sniff before touching her nose to the back of her left arm. "Honestly."

Rhonda remained slumped, her wet hair plastered across her face in water-dark streaks. Caroline slowed her horse and took Kirsty's hand. "I'm sure Rhonda will be fine. A night's rest and she'll be telling us *we* look terrible." Kirsty smiled a little, but her expression was edged with fear.

"Time to move faster," Bastion called.

Caroline let Kirsty's hand drop and followed Bastion's lead. They rode at a fast walk while the gloom deepened and the cold of evening began to bite. Everyone kept their hands close and their wet cloaks drawn tight.

Stiff with tension, soaked through and shivering, Caroline listened for danger. There was an abbey devoted to the Divine Lord Toram du Grah a few miles north of where they'd been attacked, but she guessed trying to get to it would be too dangerous.

"Hold!" called Bastion. Caroline stopped her horse and wiped her face with icy fingers. The rain had eased, but the trees continued to drip.

Their path led onto a stone outcrop, but part of it had broken away to create a drop of fifteen feet. Water collected at the base, rippling with heavy drops from the trees. Flowering redberry bushes full of thorns overgrew the left slope, preventing them going around. They would have to cross here or double back and find another way. Bastion spoke. "We'll cross in single file. We can't afford to let those bast..." He glanced at the ladies. "Those men catch up again."

It looked like a perfect place for an ambush. Caroline stared at the drop. "The outcrop's too narrow," she said, her voice too weak to carry to any ears besides her own. Shivering, she sneezed drips from her nose. Bastion signalled a man forward. Caroline watched anxiously as the soldier moved his horse onto the outcrop. The shod hooves rang on wet stone but the rider passed without mishap.

As the next soldier rode across Caroline caught Rhonda's hand and gave it a slight squeeze. Rhonda opened her eyes, clearly disorientated as she looked about. Rhonda's brothers and Kirsty quickly surrounded them. "Rhonda," Caroline said, relieved her friend was awake.

"Princess," Rhonda murmured, holding up her free hand. Her sleeve slipped back, revealing a luminous flower. She smiled and gave Caroline's hand a slight squeeze. "She promised it wouldn't hurt, and it doesn't."

"What do you mean?" she asked as Captain Bastion ordered Jared and Jonathan to cross.

"Promise me you'll protect her," Rhonda whispered.

"Who?" Caroline asked.

"Grimms, you'd better cross now with Lady Rhonda," Sergeant Graden said.

"No," Rhonda said. "Not yet." She gripped Caroline's hand tighter.

Grimms nodded to Caroline. "Why don't you cross, Your Highness?"

"Protect Kirsty. Promise me you'll look after her. Always."

"Of course," Caroline said. "I have to go now," she said as she disengaged her hand from Rhonda's.

It was only a short walk, no more than twelve feet, but a sense of fear settled over her as she nudged her horse onto the broken outcrop. Her horse's hooves seemed to ring out on the stone louder than any previous horse, and an eternity passed before soft earth muffled the sound. She trotted her horse the last few steps, hoping no one could see her hands shaking or hear the pounding sound her pulse made in her ears. Despite the chill and wet clothes, perspiration coated her upper lip.

"Lady Kirsty," Bastion said, indicating the younger girl should cross.

Kirsty raised her chin, clearly frightened, but Rhonda gripped her sister's arm. "Wait. Let me go first."

Bastion gave Grimms a nod, and the soldier kicked his horse into motion.

"Forgive her," Rhonda said to Kirsty as they clattered onto the outcrop. "You're her strength." They'd hardly taken three steps when the horse slipped.

Caroline's heart skipped a beat.

"Rhonda!" Kirsty cried as the horse fell, its legs still struggling for footing.

Grimms tried to throw himself and Rhonda clear, but as the horse went over and they fell beneath it. Rhonda never made a sound, but the soldier cried out before water engulfed him and the horse's body crushed them both.

Water splashed nearly as high as the ledge. Caroline felt frozen in place while the pool settled. Only part of the horse's chest and the soldier's limp arm and leg remained visible.

"Rhonda!" Kirsty screamed again.

Two soldiers dismounted and made their way down to the pool. "Quickly!" Caroline cried. "Please!" She stared at the luminous markings on her wrists. What was the point of Rhonda entering Divine Service if a Goddess couldn't even protect her?

She took a deep breath, preparing to speak the words revoking her calling, but hesitated. Once revoked, she'd never be able to return to the Divine Lady's graces. Not in this life, at least, and maybe not in any other. She wiped her eyes dry and buried her wrists from sight, not that anyone else here could see her markings now.

Rhonda must have been told this would happen, and she'd accepted her fate regardless. The sickly realisation made the situation worse.

If Caroline denied the Lady of Healing now it would be a poor way to repay Rhonda's sacrifice. The scriptures were always talking about Divine Balance and how the Gods couldn't intervene without keeping it. She wiped her eyes clear again, determined to ensure Rhonda's death meant something.

Someone chuckled from the trees beyond the basin. Caroline looked around as an izzat stepped into sight. His long dark hair, shot through with grey, was plastered to his head and held back in a ponytail to reveal tall, pointed ears turned forward for listening. Dressed in dark brown leathers, the hilts of his sword and dagger had been bound in black cord to avoid catching light. His green eyes and high cheekbones stood out. Everything else about him blended into the gloom. He lifted a crossbow and aimed it at Kirsty. Caroline caught her breath. A slip and she'd be dead.

"I overheard one of your enemies. They seek the girls."

He had a thick accent Caroline had never heard before. He raised his crossbow slightly, the bolt now aimed at Kirsty's throat. Kirsty sat rigid, shaking slightly but not looking away.

"If you throw me enough gold I'll let you all pass and confuse your trail. If you don't, I'll kill this one myself."

"May the Gods strike you!" one of the men called. Halfway to Rhonda, he drew his sword. A bolt thumped into his ribs. He cried out and toppled, his body splashing into the pond. Caroline caught Kirsty's eye and saw her own fears reflected.

"We'll be okay," she tried to reassure her friend.

Another man began to ride between Caroline and the izzat, but the izzat shifted his crossbow, stopping him. The bolt hadn't come from him. "I'll kill the girls first, and I've more than enough friends to help me." The soldier stopped, jaw clenched with anger.

"Your gold, including all the jewellery the girls are wearing."

Caroline touched her throat as she caught a nod from Bastion. Too cowed to protest, she pulled the necklace her mother had given her free from under her clothes and lifted it over her head. The round ruby was polished flat, the middle hollowed out. A fine circle of gold edged it and joined it to the chain. A ransom for any noble, and then some.

She looked up at the sound of a thump, surprised to see a yard-long arrow through the izzat's stomach. Something green flickered around the wound, like strangely-coloured lightning. The izzat's crossbow fell from limp fingers and he collapsed to his knees, a hand grasping the arrow. Caroline glanced around, but none of her soldiers had a bow. They appeared just as confused.

A voice she didn't recognise shouted from the trees. "Cross! There's more faspane around."

An arrow whizzed over the party, flying high into the trees. Someone screamed and crashed through the branches before hitting the ground with a solid thud. She couldn't see where the izzat fell, but heard a moan.

Fire erupted well off to Caroline's left and someone screamed. Her skin crawled with goose bumps.

"Izzen!" Someone yelled the word in the same accent the first izzat had used. Izzen killing izzen? It made no sense, but people were crashing through the woods in almost every direction.

Soldiers surrounded Caroline and Kirsty. "Where's the bowman?" Caroline cried.

"Do as he says," yelled Bastion as he signalled his men across the outcrop. "Get over here! We can't be divided."

"It could be a trap," one man yelled. The soldiers on the other side hesitated.

"Cross! Now!"

Another scream broke from the forest, but Caroline heard no bolts. It seemed to be a signal. One soldier spurred his horse past

Kirsty and clattered over the outcrop. Another man nudged Kirsty's horse with the flat of his sword. It jumped ahead, forcing Kirsty to hold the saddle as it crossed. Caroline held her breath until Kirsty arrived safely. The younger girl rode straight to Caroline, her hands shaking and her face white.

Caroline gripped her friend's hands. "We're okay. Bastion will keep us safe and we'll come back for Rhonda."

The surviving man who'd gone to retrieve Rhonda and the fallen soldier ran back to his horse. The next horse and rider to cross slipped but recovered, and the rest made it, amid yelling and another cry from the forest.

"Forward," Bastion yelled. Caroline slipped her mother's necklace back on and spurred her horse into a dangerous canter. Kirsty rode close behind her, crying Rhonda's name over and over.

The underbrush thinned for a moment before thickening, forcing them to slow to a trot until they were able to canter again. Holding on as tight as she could, Caroline bent low in her saddle, her eyes on the soldier before her. Something whizzed by and she heard someone nearby crash to the ground behind her.

Kirsty! She glanced back, but her friend was safe, riding a couple of lengths behind. Caroline's pulse threatened to pound her into unconsciousness and fear told her she'd never get home if she stopped. She let her horse choose its own way, her biggest concern holding on. As the column thinned, she lost track of everyone but Kirsty. She hoped her war-horse knew where it was going.

It wasn't long before her pace slackened off, the overworked horse tiring. Caroline tried to focus on the forest and on making sure Kirsty stayed behind her, just as Rhonda should be. She suppressed another pang of grief.

She slowed to a walk and stopped as Kirsty pulled up beside her, followed by a soldier bleeding fiercely from a gash across his forehead.

"We better keep moving, Highness," the soldier said. "Quietly. No telling if those cursed izzen are about." He glanced around nervously. "These aren't mountains to be lost in. There's snake people who'll drag you off to their caves, clansmen, outlaws, bears, wolves, and who knows what else?"

"Can you give us a moment, please? Lady Kirsty's distraught and we all need rest, the horses included."

He scowled, clearly unhappy. "Of course, Highness."

Caroline reached for Kirsty's shoulder as the younger girl wiped tears from her cheeks. She didn't even look up. If they weren't in so much danger, Caroline had no doubt she'd be crying herself.

A rock cracked against another.

"What was that?" Kirsty asked, looking around.

"I heard it too," the soldier whispered. He drew his sword with a quick hiss.

Caroline tried to look confident for Kirsty's sake, but her horse put its ears back and shifted sideways. "Let's get moving," she said as evenly as she could. The click and rush of a released bolt preceded a thud. The soldier's horse screamed and stumbled to the ground.

Caroline cried out as another bolt slammed through the saddle by her thigh. "Kirsty, go!" she yelled, and threw herself clear of her falling horse.

5

———————

Caroline slammed into the ground, her breath knocked from her. The world went black for a long moment. Distantly, she heard someone cry out in pain. She tried to stand but only staggered and collapsed again. Her face pressed against wet forest litter.

"Kirsty," she whispered as she struggled to get her arms under herself and breathe again. She was still winded and her injured shoulder ached.

Someone caught her arms below her shoulders and helped her up. Strong hands. Her one remaining soldier. Still a little unsteady, she turned, seeking Kirsty. Wide-set emerald eyes above high cheekbones regarded her, while soft-looking ears turned back and forth. An izzat!

He smiled.

She screamed.

He clapped a hand over her mouth. "Quiet! There are more faspane around."

She thrashed until she broke his hold. "Don't touch me!" She spun and ran, only to collide with Kirsty. Caroline hit the ground atop her friend, the younger girl crying out as Caroline's weight crushed her. She rolled off her friend but stayed protectively close.

"Princess, he saved us," Kirsty gasped. "He saved us! You passed out."

The izzat, his long blond hair pulled back at the nape of his neck, leant casually on his staff. Caroline did her best not to look scared. The clearing was silent. The trees loomed. He wore the leathers of a hunter or woodsman, but his only weapon was his walking staff.

"He's an izzat!" Caroline hissed loud enough to regret. The izzat's ears turned, the inhuman movement defining their differences as much as the emerald of his eyes. This one barely looked older than she did, though he was a few inches taller. Otherwise, he could pass for human on a dark night.

She struggled to her feet while keeping an eye on the foul creature. Its skin paler than in the stories she'd heard, considering they lived beyond the northern deserts.

"My Lady, he helped," Kirsty said as she got to her feet. "He... killed the others. Made them..." She shuddered and turned away. "You really did pass out. I thought you were dead."

Caroline's head began throbbing. She risked a brief look around. There were two bodies at the edge of the clearing, daggers in their chests. Nearby lay two of their three horses and the soldier, all dead. A dagger protruded from the guard's neck, blood visible around it. She still couldn't remember his name.

Caroline's hands shook as she turned to the izzat. "Please leave. We don't need your help." She glanced at the bodies again. "Anymore." His ears stood up and she backed half a step, pulling Kirsty with her.

"His ears move," Kirsty whispered, clearly intrigued.

"At least you're capable of acknowledging my help," the izzat said without any accent. "That's a start. My name's Allyn." He pointed with his walking stick. "Between here and your soldiers are about two dozen faspane." At her look of confusion he added, "Your people ignorantly call them izzen. They're not. They're the mortal descendants of my fallen brethren."

Mortal descendants? "All izzen were cursed by the Higher Realm at the dawn of creation."

He gave her a sardonic smile. "To the west are the men who attacked you. You're cut off from help." Caroline backed another step, keeping Kirsty behind her and forcing her friend to back away with her. The more distance between them, the better.

His left ear moved, angling toward the trees, though his unsettling emerald eyes never left her face. Moonlight pierced the branches, but it wasn't enough to drive the shadows from an izzat.

"The izzen are fallen creatures," she recited. "Punished by the Higher Realm's hand for sacrilege. Izzen have no chance of rebirth." Her whole body was shaking, and not from her cold wet clothes.

He sighed. "The Higher Realm punished only those who sought dominance over divine power, and they're long dead. Their descendants, the faspane, are no more or less evil than your kind." He looked around as if he could see well in the gloom. "My student is confusing your trail, but you'll need to come with me. I'll see you to a Fandelyon outpost." He held out his free hand.

Caroline felt her scalp prickle and the hair on her arms and neck stand up. She could have sworn she saw a greenish light surrounding him from the corner of her eye. "I'll risk the forest," she said. "My soldiers will come for me."

He frowned, though it seemed more in curiosity than irritation. For a moment, she thought he was about to argue, but he inclined his head. "As you wish."

She hesitated, surprised. "You're letting us go?"

"Hide then. Wait until dawn before looking for your soldiers, remain quiet, and keep to shelter as much as possible."

"I thought..." What? He wanted her dead?

"I'm not going to force you to come with me. That would hardly inspire trust."

Caroline took Kirsty's icy-cold hand for comfort. She wouldn't trust him until he was out of sight, and probably not even then.

Allyn touched his forelock. "If you need my help, speak my name thrice. I'll hear if I'm not too far."

Caroline felt another chill and fought down fear. Again, she thought she saw something from the corner of her vision, but there was nothing there when she tried to focus on it. "Goodbye."

He gave her a long look, but inclined his head. "As you choose." He strode into the gloomy trees.

"My soldiers are coming for us," Caroline said, shivering as she realised how cold she was getting. She waited a long moment before checking on the fallen soldier.

"What if those faspane people kill them? Allyn said they were following and there's more of them. There's also the men who attacked us at the road. We don't even know who they were. Shouldn't we call Allyn back? He said he can get us to safety." Her breath frosted in the air as she wrapped her arms about herself.

Caroline closed her eyes, wondering if Kirsty were right. "I... don't know, Kirsty. The scriptures say izzen are evil."

"But he saved us."

"To what end though?" She met her friend's eyes. "Do you believe he has no agenda?"

Kirsty looked away.

Caroline placed her hand over the fallen soldier's face, closing his eyes. She felt guilty for not remembering his name. "I'm sorry," she whispered. His face felt cold already. "But thank you. I'm sure you've earned some respite in the Higher Realm and a better life in your rebirth."

She drew the man's dagger and began digging at the dirt, despite the pain it caused in her shoulder. Kirsty knelt beside her after pulling a stirrup from the dead horse, and for the next hour they carved out a shallow grave amid the leaves and tree roots.

By the time they rolled the poor man into the hollow and covered him up, Caroline couldn't help the tears on her face. They weren't just for the soldier, but for all those who'd died at the road and since, and particularly for Rhonda. Who else had died today to keep her alive? How many more soldiers had since fallen? Were Kirsty's brothers still alive?

She knelt beside Kirsty when they were done, her hands and

dress filthy, and put an arm around her best friend's shoulders. "I'm so sorry, Kirsty. This is my fault. If those soldiers hadn't been after me, Rhonda and everyone else would still be alive."

"It's not your fault. Please, don't ever say it is."

And yet it was. If she'd accepted her calling and stayed at the abbey, or never got pregnant, or... There were too many possibilities. She could imagine her next-oldest sister, Stephanie, scolding her for thinking like that. She'd probably have said much the same as Kirsty, if harsher. "I hope your brothers are safe," Caroline said.

"They're impulsive, but not stupid,' Kirsty said. "Captain Bastion will look after them."

Caroline's stomach growled. "I wonder what my sisters are eating tonight? Roasted lamb spiced with herbs shipped from across the Temern Straight would be nice."

"Food at the abbey was plain."

Caroline smiled. "Plain?"

Kirsty couldn't help a timid smile of her own. "Yes. Plain."

They remained where they were, an arm around each other for comfort and warmth. The cold was beginning to make Caroline's back and shoulders ache when Kirsty finally shuddered, grieving with a torrent of silent tears. Caroline held her tight, unable to bury her own grief or the tears that came with it, only it wasn't just for their situation or the people who'd died, but also the baby she'd lost.

It was a long time before the clouds broke. Unfiltered moonlight flooded the trees. Kirsty's tears stopped, but neither girl moved. Caroline wanted to talk, but couldn't find the words to begin. Her breath created plumes of mist. The temperature dropped as moonlight took hold of the night. Shivering uncontrollably, she stiffened when leaves rustled.

"What was that?" Kirsty whispered, eyes puffy from crying.

Caroline watched the moon shadows, expecting Allyn.

"I heard a noise."

Another rustle sent dread over Caroline. Something scraped against bark. It might have been the breeze blowing a branch, if there had been a breeze. "Do you see anything?" Caroline whispered. Kirsty shook her head.

Caroline nodded in the opposite direction. She stood stiffly and drew Kirsty to her feet. Getting home suddenly seemed an impossible task.

"Run."

6

———

Hands trembling, Elias held his breath as he slowly drew an arrow to his cheek and released it, the gloom hiding him as much as the forest. The faspane across the gulley grunted and fell to his knees, clutching the arrow buried deep in his stomach. Elias held still, expecting an alarm, but the warrior only stared at the fletching as if trying to make sense of it.

Cautiously moving from cover, he drew and nocked another arrow.

The wounded warrior still appeared surprised as blood soaked into his leathers. When he saw Elias, bow drawn, his expression turned to utter dread. "Please."

Elias relaxed the bow's tension and pointed the arrow at the ground. "May your journey be swift, and in your rebirth may your soul find immortality," he said in Faspaneth.

The warrior closed his eyes, clearly relieved. Grimacing, he drew an ornate, thin-bladed dagger from his belt. He raised the weapon to his chest, carefully positioning the tip between his ribs. When he looked up again, Elias saw grim determination. He gave Elias a nod, uttered a brief prayer, and with a single thrust drove the thin blade into his heart. He gasped, staying upright for a moment before toppling to his side, his final breath fogging in the air.

Elias looked away. He'd killed humans earlier and even put a few arrows into some faspane, but he'd never actually been this close when they died. He felt... dirty. He spun at the sound of a footstep and drew the bow's string to his cheek, but relaxed the tension almost as fast.

Allyn moved like a shade from the shadows, gazing at the dead faspane with a hint of unease. "We're only a mile from where I left the girls. I'd hoped most of them," he indicated the faspane with his staff, "were following the soldiers and they'd be safe."

Elias crouched beside the body. Allyn stopped beside him. "Most are. They're spread thin from what I can tell, chasing a dozen trails." Elias swallowed queasiness and ripped the bloodied arrow from the faspane's body. He held it up, checking for damage in the gloom as he tried to appear nonchalant. He told himself it was just like ripping an arrow from an animal. Only it wasn't.

Allyn glanced at the arrow with similar distaste. "Killing isn't something I've ever gotten used to," he said softly. "The older I get, the harder it is."

Elias wiped the arrow on the faspane's shirt, pausing at the sight of the sun-lines around the faspane's jade eyes. His cheekbones weren't as high as Allyn's and the face was a little more rounded, but still close enough to be related. "Strange how they still look so much like us. It's the similarities more that the differences I find disturbing."

"It must be terrible having both a mortal body and soul, knowing your rebirth depends on taking your own life."

Elias remembered the faspane's dread as he'd faced him. "He thought I might kill him outright. Can't say I wasn't tempted."

"Why?" The tone was neutral, but the word burdened. "He's just a warrior. Can't fault him for that."

"A warrior whose ancestors slayed a unicorn and tried to use its power to challenge the Gods."

Allyn shifted his feet, staring into the trees. "For them, this is what

Noramgaell's about. Their mortal souls. They're easily manipulated on the promise of regaining what they lost."

"You believe they're that simple? They have oracles just as we do. They know we're after the *Sword of the Sun*. They still want power. Dominance."

"Perhaps some do."

Elias pulled an oil-soaked rag from his pack, thinking about his vision. "Regardless, some of the Gods must be using them," he said. He began rubbing his bow down.

"Probably. The faspane knew to be here just as we were. They were trying to get the princess to remove her jewellery. Something she's wearing must be masking her aura. Did you notice anything? They'd have singled her out and killed her when they had the chance, otherwise," Allyn said.

The skin over Elias's wingbuds tightened at the thought of the human girl. "No. I was keeping an eye on the faspane. Hopefully she'll be safe enough where she is." Cursed with empathy for the girl, he wanted to see her to safety.

"We were drawn to her and the faspane would have been, too. Marak du Tren wants war sooner than Marnier du Shae and he's pushing her to act. If the faspane unite under Phoenix they'll be unstoppable, so he's pressing while he has the advantage."

Dobbin's cabin suddenly seemed a long way off. "Do you think we've crossed into Noramgaell already?"

Allyn gave him a worried look. "Not until Princess Caroline assumes the mantle of Marnier du Shae's Champion or, if she passes the choice on, until someone else accepts. We still have options and so do the faspane."

"They'll run themselves into graves before giving up on her now. Us too, most likely."

"At least we're approaching Noramgaell," Allyn said. "Finally."

"Finally? You want this?"

"I've been waiting for it since the unicorn was slain."

"That was two hundred thousand years ago!"

Allyn gave him a sad look. "It's the source of our curse and burden. Worse, I'm the last who remembers, the last never to be tested."

"I haven't been tested yet." He'd been preparing to face his test when ordered to accompany Allyn.

"Perhaps Noramgaell will be your test. You could ask the Queen, King and Council to rule on it."

"If I survive Noramgaell." He met Allyn's eyes. "If we survive."

"I've lived long enough. I'm more concerned about Princess Caroline."

"She has to choose her own path. Even the Gods can't force her into their causes."

"I know, but she's alone and vulnerable. The faspane won't give her the option to walk away knowing she's Marnier du Shae's choice."

"How do *we* know for sure? She has power, but that confirms little."

"There's no way to know, but when I began to lay a follow spell on her, I felt her power concentrating as if to repulse me. She's not completely latent and I dared take the spell no further."

"How could she repulse anything without training?"

Allyn leaned on his ghostwood staff. "I wish I knew. She'll have to face it within the next few years and she won't be safe until she's mastered her magic, if then. If the faspane get her..." He lost his distant look. "I thought we'd done our duty in helping her get away, but I suspect we have further obligations here."

Elias had the same feeling. "We're here for the *Sword of the Sun*," he said, regardless. "Perhaps if we keep an eye on her overnight her soldiers will find her in the morning."

Allyn dropped his gaze, clearly avoiding eye contact. "Perhaps you should go to Dobbin's cabin. I'll be there in the morning."

Elias sighed. "What aren't you telling me, Allyn?"

Allyn shrugged. "It's fate. We're in the midst of divine influence and I'd bet my soul we still need to help her."

"Don't speak like that!" Elias said. "Ever."

"I made a mistake in leaving her. I have to go back and convince her to come with us. I think we were put in her path to do more than save her. We need to teach her. Guide her."

"Even if you had the time to train her, the humans in these parts would kill her for her abilities. And us. She'll never lead her people into Noramgaell. They won't accept her."

Allyn shrugged. "I have to do this. It *feels* right."

"What? That's... Marnier du Shae must have other plans for the princess. She can't be the Champion you think she is."

"She won't use the call spell I keyed to her voice," Allyn said, doggedly pursuing his ill-conceived notion. "I have to go after her. Help her."

Elias sighed, resigned to his teacher's stubbornness. The only other option was to send a message to the Queen and Council in the hope they would order Allyn to continue their original mission, but that would take too long. He'd be better off helping his teacher and contacting them later, if necessary. 'Fine, but considering she's already turned you down, why don't you let me go?"

Allyn gave him a measuring stare. "You want to help her, or kill her?"

"That's not fair!"

A slow grin crept across Allyn's face.

"And it's not funny. I thought you were serious," Elias said.

"You're right, though," Allyn said. "She might respond better to you, particularly if she recognises your soul. Go. I'll keep the faspane away and set wards at Dobbin's cabin. I should have enough sense of the girls' auras to allow them through. How are you going to convince her to come with you? Caroline believes we're faspane. Her people are unaware of our existence."

Elias grinned as an idea came to him. "If she refuses I'll make her more scared of the forest than she is of me."

His teacher raised an eyebrow. "I suspect she'll surprise you. She's determined to follow her own ignorance."

The thought of a little fun lifted his spirits. "I doubt she's that sure of herself. See you soon."

Allyn touched his forelock as Elias shouldered his bow and ran, following Caroline's tracks to the clearing. He chased off a lone wolf feeding on the carcass of a horse. It gave a few half-hearted snarls before running northward, leaving the feast. Within the moonlit trees he found the bodies of two faspane, both dead by their own hand. Allyn's work, no doubt. Surprisingly, there was a mound of dirt in the middle of the clearing, freshly piled. It had to be a grave.

Elias examined the area more thoroughly, finding the girls' tracks leading in the same direction the wolf had taken. So much for scaring them silly. The wolves had probably done it for him. He hoped they knew how to climb trees. Concerned, he followed the tracks and quickly picked up those of nearly four dozen wolves, all heading in the same direction. A growing sense of unease gripped him. There were far too many wolves for a single pack.

He opened his senses and felt something unnatural stirring in the air, yet it passed over him as if he didn't exist. He dug deeper, immersing his mind in the problem, and discovered lines of force more complicated than anything he could produce. It seemed to be a temporary effect bound to a single creature, stirring restlessly as if it had a life of its own. It carried the signature of a wolf as it spilled its malignant array of threads through the trees, ready to ensnare.

Impressed, Elias widened his senses. The spell was deliberate, powerful, and huge, stretching from mountain peak to mountain peak. "Some sort of a wolf call?" he whispered. He followed the lines of force to their origin a mile away, where he encountered the twisted pattern of a mind's aura, warped from human to animal. "A werewolf?" he said in disbelief.

He glanced up. Full moon. "By all that's holy..." The Gods truly were conspiring against the princess.

7

———

Caroline ran as hard as she could, holding Kirsty's hand as they struggled on the uneven slope. Kirsty stumbled and nearly fell. Caroline barely kept her feet trying to hold Kirsty upright.

"Another wolf! Hurry!" Caroline hissed as she dragged Kirsty into a run again, her breath frosting in the air and her icy wet skirts hampering her stride. The full moon illuminated patches of ground through the spring canopy, but not enough to see anything but moss-covered trees. They desperately needed to find somewhere safe to hide.

A wolf cut across their path and both girls cried out and stopped. Caroline pulled at Kirsty's hand. "This way. Hurry. Hurry!" Almost twice Kirsty's weight, she had no trouble dragging her friend into motion again, snapping a dead branch from her path before plunging through a tree-fern's fronds.

"Wolf ahead!" Kirsty cried.

Caroline turned across the slope again, gripping Kirsty's hand as much to keep upright as to ensure they stayed together. Caroline had a feeling the wolves turned to keep pace with them. A quick glance found movement to either side.

"The wolves are herding us like sheep," she said, almost breathless. She couldn't think of a way to escape them.

Caroline forced herself to keep running, stumbling over every uneven patch of ground, deadfall and rock. The wolves turned them away from trees they could climb and rock faces they might be able to use as shelter.

Caroline stopped. She doubled over and wheezed. Her side ached, forcing her to keep a hand on it. "They're wearing us out." Wolves howled close by, showing themselves briefly and disappearing back into the moon shadows.

Caroline heard something and spun, her right foot slipping. She fell, her hand pulling from Kirsty's. "Help!" Caroline screamed as she tumbled, breaking saplings and ripping her skirts as she rolled down the slope to stop in a gully beside a thick tree trunk and a trickling stream of water. Her knuckles bled. She pushed herself to her knees, desperately looking for Kirsty. "Kirsty?"

"My Lady!" Kirsty screamed. "Watch out!"

With a quiet snarl, a dark wolf crashed into Caroline, the impact throwing her sideways and exploding the breath from her mouth as she hit the ground. She raised her arms over her face, expecting pain, but the wolf only kicked once, and then lay still. Caroline opened one eye. The beast lay across her thighs and hip, a three-foot arrow buried in the base of its neck. Dark blood stained its fur. Shaking, Caroline found she didn't have the strength to push it off.

A huge izzat with ice-blue eyes stopped beside her, gripping a longbow. A shock of recognition passed through Caroline, almost as if she knew him.

She cringed as he hauled the limp wolf off her with his free hand.

"So you wouldn't go with Allyn, huh? Lucky I came."

"Your eyes..." she whispered. He didn't have emerald or jade eyes like any other faspane, but pale blue like a shivra or human. He was big enough to be half shivra. He dropped the wolf beside her. Caroline leaned away from both him and the wolf, the warmth of the animal's blood soaking through her dress.

The huge izzat ripped the arrow free with a sickening sound. "My name's Elias," he said as he rubbed the arrow's head on the animal's fur. "You're coming with me." He returned the arrow to the quiver at his hip and reached for her.

"Please!" Caroline said, but he hauled her to her feet like she was a child. By the Higher Realm he was big, as big as any clansman. Caroline crossed her forearms in a gesture to ward off evil, but that only made him grin.

Wolves howled, very close. Panicking, she struggled in his grip and tried to push him away. Kirsty stopped against a tree a few paces away, hands to her mouth.

Elias let her go. She stumbled and almost fell. "There's a werewolf controlling that pack. The wolves are herding you toward it. You need to come with me."

"But-"

"Do you want to die?" He reached for her hand as a wolf leapt. Elias side-stepped and slammed his bow into the wolf's neck, crushing its windpipe. The wolf flipped backwards and dropped at his feet as another hit his back and knocked him sprawling to the ground. Caroline backed away as he slipped his dagger from his belt, but the animal kept its distance.

Elias spun and slashed as another wolf came at him, slicing its neck open. He twisted and stabbed the next wolf in the chest as it sprang. It still crashed into him, one final snap of its jaws catching his arm. He grunted, jabbed his thumb into the wolf's soft cheek and forced its mouth open. He pulled his knife free and shoved the dying animal aside before picking up his bow. The string was broken.

Caroline grabbed Kirsty's hand and dragged her into a run. Saviour or otherwise, he was still an izzat.

Behind them a high-pitched yelp cut off short. The sound spurred her on. She caught a glimpse of movement in the moon shadows to their left. "Wolf," Caroline said. "Only one." Yet one was enough. It was too much for the younger girl. Kirsty stopped running and began to cry. "Not now, Kirsty. Come on!"

Another wolf casually loped toward them, bigger than any other wolf she'd seen. "It's got red eyes," Kirsty whispered, horror in her voice. "It's the werewolf."

Caroline stared in shock at the creature's unnatural red eyes, feeling strange to be so calm, but better death than capture by an izzat. The wolf tensed to spring. "Go!" Caroline yelled and shoved Kirsty aside, ensuring her friend had a chance as the beast hit Caroline full on.

The impact smashed her off her feet, the werewolf tearing at her left arm before she hit the ground. They tumbled down the wet gully, rolling uncontrollably over each other and dislodging mud, rocks and debris before thudding into a rock banked with deadwood. Caroline struggled for breath as fresh blood warmed her injured shoulder. Coughing, she looked around, but saw nothing. The huge werewolf was gone.

She pushed onto her knees and gripped a thick branch, certain it hadn't left her for good. Intelligent red eyes appeared in the moonlight as the creature moved into view, circling a dozen yards away and growling softly. Playing with her. Caroline's heart pounded as she stood on a painful ankle and hefted the branch, her bleeding arm close to her side. She took a step toward it. "Get away from me!"

As if commanded, the beast turned and bounded back up the hill.

She didn't realise its purpose for a moment. Oh no. "Kirsty! Run!" She limped after it, but the massive wolf turned and leapt. Caroline's fear and instinct came together and she swung her branch, striking as the werewolf hit her. She tumbled back, losing her grip on the wood as her head glanced against something.

Barely conscious, she could do nothing as werewolf stood over her, moonlight shining silver on its damp fur. It looked insubstantial, like a ghost or a dream, until hot saliva drooled on her face. Too hurt to feel panic, she could barely focus on its face.

It lunged. Teeth punched through her neck. She screamed in pain, then in agony as it tore. Warm blood sprayed. Hers. She tried to swallow, but her mouth fell open as her head lolled.

The last sensation she felt was its weight on her chest, the werewolf's warmth almost comforting.

8

Elias sprinted around a tree and dove over the werewolf, driving the silver-tipped arrowhead through the creature's ribs and snapping the shaft as momentum carried him past it. He rolled to his feet and came up with his knife raised, but the creature collapsed across the girl. Breathing hard, he spun, ready to defend himself from the circling wolves, but as one they broke and ran into the dark trees, the spell broken.

"Caroline!" the raven-haired girl cried, running forward as blood pumped from the princess's throat. Elias got there first and hauled the dead werewolf away as Caroline choked on her own blood. "We have to help her," the other girl cried as she dropped to her knees beside the princess, reaching out but not quite touching.

Something crystalline glinted in the moonlight beside the princess's head, half buried under the dirt and debris. As if guided by divine inspiration, Elias brushed the dirt away from the palm-sized white stone. "A healing stone," he whispered with awe. "A God really is looking after this girl." It just might be enough to save her. He pressed the stone to Caroline's bloody neck.

Agony shot through him as her pain surged through the stone. He cried out, tensing as his hand went numb with cold, but he didn't withdraw it.

Caroline's back arched as healing energy rushed into her body, repairing her torn flesh as he watched. Her heart stopped and she slumped, dead, the magic far more powerful than her body could take.

"Breathe," he whispered, certain he was watching her die, the connection to her soul dissipating. The pain he felt through the stone began to ease. He pressed the stone harder and sent his own power into it, and with the jolt of magic their souls connected, drawing her back.

Only a soulmate, or a twinned soul, could draw another soul back to its body once it had left. A divinity must have foreseen these events and planned for it.

Fresh pain surged into him and Caroline gasped, her back arching again as she took a deep breath. For a brief moment he caught flashes of her past lives, hundreds of them. Thousands. She'd lived as almost every type of creature possible – animal, izzat, shivra, everything except faspane. And then the connection was gone, hidden again as her soul fully re-joined her body.

He almost collapsed.

"Is she going to be okay?"

Elias struggled to look up. He'd forgotten the other girl entirely. "Maybe."

Caroline coughed blood from her lungs, the dark liquid running down her chin and cheek, and then her head rolled to the side, unconscious. At least she was breathing again.

It took him a moment to regain his strength. He hesitantly drew on his magic again to activate the stone's healing power. Healing energy flooded Caroline's body once more, but rather than healing her remaining wounds, the stone attacked the curse spreading through her flesh. For a moment the curse retreated, pushed back by what Elias could only describe as pure light, and then the healing stone went dark and Elias found he had nothing more to give.

Elias slumped, removing the stone from her exposed neck and severing the connection to the princess.

"Is she okay?" the other girl asked, hope in her features. "She doesn't look okay. Her neck's still bleeding."

With an aching hand Elias touched the stone to Caroline's neck again. He stiffened as her pain surged back through the link.

Her wounds were only just closed, her life still desperately fragile, but it was the curse that made him shudder with revulsion. Dark, malevolent, and soul-corrupting, it was infusing her flesh and altering her body.

"Why did the stone go black?"

Elias dropped the stone as he met the girl's eyes, her expression desperate, devastated, and heartbreakingly hopeful. He thought he understood that hope, but he had to kill it. "She's a werewolf now, assuming she survives," he said, reaching for the knife at his hip. "I have to-"

"You can't kill her," she said, dropping to her knees and gripping his forearm to still him.

He drew the blade anyway, but she remained protectively across her friend, trying to push the blade away. He tried to speak gently. "Girl, I tried, but she's cursed. We have to allow her to pass on. I'll send her to her rebirth before the curse can corrupt her flesh and she takes unnecessary guilt and grief into her next life."

"No. She's my friend!" She held on tight despite the bloody mess, futilely trying to dissuade him.

"And she'll do terrible things she won't remember." He tried pressing the blade to the princess's bruised and bloody throat, but the smaller girl put her arm in the way.

"Give her a chance. Please."

He stared at Caroline's unconscious face, her soul almost resonating in tune with his own. She wasn't quite his soulmate, but he couldn't deny the connection. "Girl, please. I've no desire to harm you too."

"My name is Kirsty, not *Girl*. Lady Kirsty duPrey, and the person you're about to kill is Princess Caroline duFandelyon. She's my friend. She has a family. Parents. Siblings."

"Kirsty..."

"Yes, and this is Caroline. Please, please don't hurt her. I know I'm not strong enough to stop you, so I'm asking. Please give her a chance." Slowly, pleading with her whole body, she released the princess and sat back on her knees. "Please."

Elias held the knife steady, staring at the princess's bruised and bloody face. The flesh of her neck had barely knitted together. Clear fluids seeped through.

"Please."

He sighed and reluctantly sheathed the knife.

"Thank you," Kirsty whispered, gently placing fingers on his wrist. "Thank you so much."

Uncomfortable, Elias pulled his bloody hand away and picked up the healing stone, but didn't dare touch the girl's flesh with it again. He knew what he'd feel. He slipped it into a pocket inside his cloak. "Take my bow. I'll carry your friend."

He slipped one arm under Caroline's neck and the other under her knees, her curly hair cascading over his arm, damp and limp, like her body. He grunted as he stood. She was considerably heavier than he'd expected. Soft living had given her plenty of excess weight, but she was also solid underneath it.

"If she's not able to fight off the curse, I'm going to have to kill her. Understand?" They began walking. Kirsty lifted his bow and ran to catch up, the weapon considerably taller than the girl. "Keep the tip down, not up," he said. "It'll only catch on trees otherwise."

She lowered the tip as she walked, casting anxious glances at her friend. After a while she spoke. "You believe you made the wrong choice?" she asked, almost timid now she wasn't fighting for her friend's life.

He stopped, a little surprised that she'd even found the courage to speak to him. "Against my better judgement, I'm carrying a half-dead werewolf princess through unfamiliar mountains with a human girl I don't know. But no, I thought the day was going to include this when I woke, and I'm happy I was right. This is the right choice."

His sarcasm made her smile. "You had your own reasons to save her, didn't you? You came after us. Why?"

He studied her unexpectedly gentle eyes, surprised by her insight. "I thought you humans were supposed to be afraid of my kind? And magic."

The girl glanced away, timid once again. "I didn't really believe in magic until now. After seeing what you did, it can't be a bad thing, can it?"

He considered her words for a long moment. "You're a very rare creature, Kirsty. She's lucky to have you." He began walking again, and Kirsty almost had to run to keep up.

"So why did you save us?"

He adjusted Caroline's weight in his arms. Holding the princess this close felt right, her body warm against his chest. "Because the Gods never do anything by chance."

9

———————

"It's been days," Elias said, pointing north. "We have to get to Delshear before they change their minds about the sword. You know what shivras are like."

"You saved her life and now you want to abandon her?" Allyn asked.

Dobbin interrupted. Even seated, he was huge. "What exactly are we like, mongrel?" he asked in his clipped shivra accent, his voice gravelly from years of yelling orders as a soldier.

"Dobbin, this isn't your business."

The shivra's bushy eyebrows came together. He stood from his chair, towering over Elias by eighteen inches. Corded muscle pressed under his shirt. "Is that so? I say the girl still has a chance, and yer in me home, after all."

"Please," Allyn interrupted, "Both of you."

The shivra gave the sorcerer a long look before dropping back into his stuffed chair.

Allyn visibly relaxed in Dobbin's rocker. It was so big, he almost looked like a child in it. "I told you, Elias, I'm not going on without her."

Elias tried not to let his anxiety show. "The curse may not have taken her yet, but she's not recovering either," he said. He was surprised she'd even survived this long. "Letting her pass on is the best thing we can do for her."

"She'll survive this."

Elias crossed his arms. "That's not comforting." It really wasn't. Not if she was a werewolf.

Dobbin's chair creaked as he leaned forward. "I have to admit sorcerer, I don't like it either, Gods' willing or not."

Elias turned an ear toward his unexpected ally, but watched his teacher. "Even Dobbin agrees."

"Agree isn't the right word, but ye both know she'll be more trouble than we can handle. Ye can't control a supernatural beast no matter what ye think."

Allyn stood and began pacing. "This isn't resolved. The Higher Realm is guiding our steps. Neither of you can abandon her any more than I can."

Elias raised his eyebrows at the challenge. "Of course I could. No God determines my fate." No Princess either.

"Where would you go?" Allyn asked with an amused grin. "Well?"

He hadn't thought that far ahead. "Um, I'll get the sword and return it to our people as *we* were tasked."

Allyn gave Dobbin a sidelong glance, amusement growing. "The shivras will hang you on sight without Dobbin as escort. What say you, Dobbin?"

Dobbin gave a non-committal shrug. "The message said to escort Allyn. I didn't even know he had a mongrel apprentice. Most like they'll take ye for a faspane despite yer baby blue eyes."

He couldn't tell if Dobbin were joking or genuinely insulting him. "I'm not an apprentice, Dobbin. I'm a student. And don't call me a mongrel again. I may not know my father's lineage, but I couldn't have been born if he weren't izzen."

Dobbin inclined his head. "Sorry. I didn't realise ye were so sore about it."

Elias turned to Allyn. "I still say there's no point in waiting."

"And I say there is. Go tattle to the King and Queen if you wish, but I'm staying."

"Tattle?" Elias clenched his jaw. He wasn't being childish. He was being sensible.

Allyn crossed to the window and pushed the shutters open to allow in more light and fresh air. Leaning on the sill, he spoke as if to the breeze. "If it were your mother in there Elias, would you let her go so easily?"

"That's hardly fair."

The bedroom door opened and they turned in union. The little human girl, Kirsty, walked out, rubbing her face with one hand. Her long dark hair was tangled from sleep and her dress, though washed and stitched, remained stained. She kept her eyes on the floor. She was such a slight thing. Why she'd been caught up in Caroline's destiny, only the Gods could say for sure.

Dobbin stood and touched his forelock, as did Allyn. Kirsty acknowledged them all with a timid smile. Barely more than half Dobbin's height she looked like a child. He guessed they all did in Dobbin's presence, even though Dobbin was exceptionally short for a shivra. Most of them grew to eleven feet or more.

"I take it you heard our discussion?" Allyn asked.

Without looking at the sorcerer, she nodded.

"My apologies if we've upset you. How's your princess?"

Kirsty's shoulders hunched slightly. "The same."

Allyn glanced at Elias, then Dobbin. "I'd best check on her."

"Don't ye worry, lass, she's a fighter, that one." Dobbin said as Allyn left the room. He met Kirsty's eyes, but it was the huge shivra who looked away, cheeks flushing above his short blonde beard. "To speak the truth, I expect she'll live." He paused, glancing at Elias. "Even if I'm afraid of it."

Kirsty climbed into the rocking chair Allyn had vacated. It dwarfed her even more. "Can Allyn help her? Can either of you?" she asked, as she pulled her knees to her chest like a child might. She was talking about magic.

"Not I," said Dobbin.

Elias crossed the room and sat on the hard corner stool. "I don't know, Kirsty. I doubt it. None of us are healers. With preparation we might have been able to stop the curse taking hold, but I think it's too late now."

"What's going to happen?"

"If she lives?" Dobbin asked. Kirsty nodded. "She'll be a werewolf, most likely. The curse will take her on the full moon and she'll remember nothing of it. Until then she'll... become harder to live with, maybe even drive people away, probably in an unconscious attempt to protect them from herself." Kirsty's expression didn't change, though her posture slumped ever so slightly. "Whatever she says or does from now on, don't take it personally, even if it seems that way. She won't know she's a werewolf or be likely to believe it if anyone tells her," Elias added.

Kirsty held his eyes for long seconds before dropping her gaze to the wooden floor, her expression pained. Elias tried to suppress the sympathy he felt for the dark-haired girl. He couldn't afford to get involved in their lives, not with the connection he had to the red-haired girl.

"Allyn said something about a destiny. A Champion?"

Dobbin cleared his throat. "The problem is that while an event may be certain, such as Noramgaell, the means to it and its resolution aren't. Allyn believes Caroline could be the person who'll unite yer people against the faspane. It may be true, but if she dies beforehand the task will fall to another. Nothing's set until she accepts."

"She's awake," Allyn called from the other room.

Elias exchanged a glance with Dobbin before following Kirsty in. They found Allyn sitting on the edge of Dobbin's huge bed, Caroline's bruised and torn body under the blankets.

"Caroline? Can you hear me?" Allyn asked.

The girl winced, turning away from Allyn's voice despite her heavily bandaged neck. Allyn placed a hand against her cheek. She slowly turned in his direction, but seemed unable to focus her eyes.

Elias moved closer. Caroline's face was badly bruised, and freshly formed scabs marred her cheeks and forehead. His wingbuds reacted at the sight of her, and he had to turn away or risk going to her. He couldn't allow himself to care. "Perhaps in your next life," he whispered under his breath, so no one else could hear.

"Caroline? Can you hear me?" Allyn asked again. The princess swallowed and tried to speak, but her face contorted in pain. She licked her lips. "Elias. Get her some water."

"I'm a servant now?"

Kirsty flashed him a dark look. "I'll get it," she said as she left the room. She certainly had nerve, timid though she seemed. What had the princess done to earn such loyalty and fierceness from so quiet a friend?

"Caroline, do you understand me?" Allyn asked. She didn't respond. He touched her cheek again, his fingers gentle. "Caroline?"

Kirsty returned and handed Allyn a shivra-sized clay mug. Allyn raised Caroline's head slightly and poured a little water onto her lips. The princess flinched, but opened her mouth for more. He poured another trickle, splashing as much on her face as in her mouth. She swallowed, coughed and winced, then swallowed again. She licked her lips dry.

"More," she whispered. Allyn dribbled another mouthful. She closed her eyes after swallowing it. "Fresh air," she whispered. "Smokey."

"I've got it," Elias said. By the time he opened the shutter Caroline was unconscious again.

"That's got to be a good sign," Allyn said.

10

───────

The following day, Elias, Dobbin and Kirsty watched Allyn examine the bloodstained bandages around Caroline's swollen neck. Dark bruising showed above and below. Allyn carefully unwound the bandages, revealing torn and bruised flesh. Clear fluid seeped from scabs that barely held skin together. The wounds looked as if they could be pulled apart with little effort.

"Only the Gods know how she survived this," Allyn said.

Elias felt a flush of guilt. "The Gods and me."

"Huh?"

"He did something after he killed the werewolf," Kirsty said, looking at Elias as if she'd expected him to have said so already. "I thought Caroline was dead, but Elias held something to her throat and she started breathing again." Allyn glanced at Elias, ears lifting in curiosity.

Elias tried to hold back the memories as he reached into a pocket. As soon as his fingers touched the smooth stone, he sensed echoes of the pain and suffering he'd felt when he'd healed Caroline. "Here," he said, shuddering as he passed the flat, palm-sized black stone to Allyn.

Allyn examined it in the morning light, his eyes widening as his ears fell back. "Where did you get a healing stone?" he whispered. He turned it over in his hands. "It's completely discharged."

"It was white before," Kirsty said. "It was on the ground beside her."

Allyn raised his eyebrows. "On the ground? The chances..." he glanced skyward, "Marnier du Shae has to be looking out for the girl. We're on the right path."

Elias tried not to recall Caroline's ripped and bloody neck. "The werewolf had torn her throat out. Blood was gushing with each heartbeat. By the time I saw the stone and got it to her neck, I..." He paused, taking a moment to calm himself as the traumatic memories became too vivid. "Her heart had stopped and I swear she'd crossed over. Only divine intervention could have helped her."

"Or a healing stone," Dobbin added. Allyn sat up a little straighter, but said nothing as his ears half lifted.

Elias continued. "The stone turned so cold I almost dropped it. My hand still aches with the memory of using it, but by the time it discharged she was breathing again." He didn't want to mention that their souls had connected, and that, as much as the stone, had bought her back.

Dobbin whistled softly. "I've only ever heard one likely story about a healing stone. I didn't believe they existed."

"I've never possessed one," Allyn said. "Though I've seen a few. How did you recognise the stone for what it was? You've never seen one."

He shrugged. "I just knew."

"What was it like?" Dobbin asked. "Using it, I mean."

"Horrible."

"Come now," Dobbin said. "Surely it was marvellous?"

Elisa tried not to let them see how much it affected him. "I felt her suffering through the stone as well as her ebbing life-force. I suffered as she did. I swear I could feel the foulness of the lycanthropy seeping through her flesh. When the stone ran dry I added all the magic I had, but it wasn't anywhere near enough."

Allyn offered the stone back to Elias. "No. Keep it." Elias said. "I don't ever want to touch it again. If you can find a way to recharge it you may yet cure her."

Allyn pressed it to the princess's cheek. He pulled it back an instant later, swallowing hard. "I understand, Elias. The poor child is suffering tremendously." He took a deep breath and released it slowly.

"Can ye feel the curse in her? Through the stone?" Dobbin asked.

"Like pain," Allyn acknowledged. He stood. "Thank you. I can recharge it, but short of intervention from the Higher Realm or a Pool of Radiance, it'll take longer than her lifetime and a good deal of my focus."

"May I?" Dobbin asked. Allyn handed him the stone. Dobbin held it reverently, the black stone small in his huge hand. "Legend has it that one of these can return ye to youth. Just carrying it with ye will keep ye young."

Elias laughed in genuine mirth, breaking the tension. "You don't even have any grey in your beard. Perhaps it's me who should hold onto it. Sleeping on your wooden floor is killing me."

"Perhaps yer right." Clearly reluctant, Dobbin passed the stone back to Allyn, who pocketed it. "We should let the lass rest. Our talk isn't helping her."

"I'll keep watch," Allyn said.

Allyn emerged from Caroline's room late that afternoon.

"Ye look tired," Dobbin said. "How is she?"

Allyn rubbed his face and sat in the huge rocker across from Elias. Kirsty stood near Dobbin's round table, barely able to see over it. "She's failing. I'm not a healer, but I doubt she'll make dawn." He pulled out the healing stone, staring at it as if wondering how to recharge it sooner.

"It could be for the best, despite what Marnier du Shae may wish," the shivra said with a reluctant glance at Kirsty. He didn't look happy about it. Elias wanted to echo the sentiment, but whatever plans the Gods had they hadn't considered Caroline's needs. If nothing else he didn't want to see her suffer any longer, particularly after what he'd felt through the stone.

"Hardly charitable," Allyn said.

Dobbin held up his hands, palms outward. "I was thinking of her welfare, sorcerer. Have ye given any consideration to the child's future? She can't return home."

"Perhaps that was the plan," Elias said. They both looked at him curiously. "Another God's plan, I mean. One of Marnier du Shae's opponents. If Caroline can't return home to unite her people, she can't be a Champion. More than likely, Marnier du Shae will be forced to seek a replacement for the princess."

Allyn closed his eyes and rested the back of his head against the chair, his ears falling back. "I'll not abandon her if that's what you're suggesting."

"I'm not," Elias said. "I'm suggesting that if she survives, we'll need to see to her welfare."

Dobbin ran stubby fingers through his short blonde beard. "What about the full moon? Someone's going to have ta cage her, and probably against her will."

Elias watched his teacher closely. Allyn's expression suggested he'd been thinking much the same thing. "We'll offer all the help we can, even if that means taking her back to our own people."

The shivra leaned forward. "And if she refuses yer help?"

Allyn glanced at Kirsty, who stared at her feet. "Let's not dwell on that."

An uncomfortable silence pervaded the room. Dobbin eventually slapped the table, making everybody jump. "Hungry?" he asked. "I don't have much, as I've been expecting ta move on, but yer welcome ta what's here."

"Good idea. Kirsty, a woman's touch might make Dobbin's cooking palatable, and I'm sure he'd appreciate the help." He stood. "I'd best remain with Caroline."

"Can ye cook, lass?" Dobbin asked as Allyn left the room.

Kirsty glanced at Allyn's retreating back. "No," she said softly.

"Hah! Me neither. I was hoping ye knew how to bake a pie. Looks like stewed goat again. There's some spuds in that cupboard. Wash 'em and dice 'em up small. I'll start with the meat."

"I'll be outside," Elias said. "If there's any faspane about, I want to know."

Outside, the fresh mountain air carried a hint of wood smoke, yet despite an hour of searching with both magic and mundane skills, Elias couldn't pinpoint any of the faspane. They were masking their auras somehow.

He renewed his wards to react in their presence and searched for another hour before finally giving up and returning to Dobbin's cabin. The smell of stewed goat filled the room. Dobbin and Kirsty, looking like an adult and child from behind, were busy adding spices to the meaty stew. Kirsty barely reached Dobbin's waist. She wouldn't be much more than a tenth his weight.

"Anything?" Dobbin asked without looking up.

"Possibly." He made for Caroline's room. Kirsty and Dobbin followed. Allyn, kneeling beside Caroline's prone form, looked up as he entered. Elias spoke softly. "The faspane haven't left the area, which bodes poorly. I didn't see any, even with farsight, but they're close. They'll likely find us despite your warding."

Allyn pulled the blanked down to expose Caroline's bruised and torn neck. "There could be a problem. See this necklace?" Allyn asked, pointing to the circular ruby on a gold chain, the centre of the stone worn away. It rested on the blanket over her chest.

Elias stared in surprise. He vaguely remembered it from the forest. The faspane had been trying to make her remove it. How could he have forgotten it... unless it had an inattention spell on it? No, it had to be more than that. Allyn had bandaged Caroline's neck several times and missed it even then.

"Have you ever seen a stone like it?"

Elias leaned closer, seeing the hollowed out ruby for what it was. "How did she get hold of a faeriestone?"

Dobbin gently touched it with a thick finger. "By the Gods, the ruby alone would be worth a king's ransom."

"She's been wearing it the entire time," Allyn said. "It's more than just a faeriestone."

Elias stared at the priceless jewel. "The fey don't let too many faeriestones slip past their notice. Not real ones. Are ye sure it's honest? Any jeweller worth his trade could have hollowed out the middle."

"It's Queen Lynn's," Kirsty said. They all looked at the young girl. Dropping her eyes, she continued. "Her mother gave it to her before she left, for good luck."

"More than good luck," Elias replied. "If it's real, that is. It must be, or charmed in some other way. I didn't notice it when I healed her. I should have seen the chain, at least."

"Same as when I was bandaging her neck," Allyn added. "I'm guessing it's why we couldn't penetrate her aura."

"Who'd be stupid enough to steal a jewel like that from the fey?" Dobbin asked.

"It's not stolen," Allyn said. "That's the strangest thing. It's attuned to her."

"Ye mean it was gifted?" Dobbin asked. "To her mother first, then the princess?"

"Doesn't make sense," Elias added. "The fey are capricious."

Allyn shrugged. "Humans with power don't make sense. Neither do healing stones appearing when you need them, nor *Quala Umitha* making an appearance unbidden. We all believe the Gods are involved, right? The question is, which ones? The Lady of Healing and the Paladin of War, certainly, but what of the others? What influences are they exerting?"

"Which other God might have sent the werewolf after Caroline?" Kirsty asked.

"Gods have foresight, but the possibilities change every time one of them alters events. Either Marnier du Shae foresaw the possibility and reacted when it became clear, or other Gods contrived both the healing stone and werewolf," Allyn said.

"To gain influence over Caroline, and through her, Marnier du Shae?" Elias asked. "They may seek to influence the outcome of Noramgaell."

"Possibly."

"What about the humans who attacked her retinue?" Dobbin asked. "And the faspane just afterward? More interference?"

"More than likely. The Gods are vying for position. We're their game pieces."

"There's only two possible candidates," Elias said. "The Lady of Healing or the Paladin of War."

"Yet they all have agendas," Allyn said. "They all seek to leave some legacy in our world when the final battle is done."

"We have to help the lass," Dobbin murmured. "Particularly if she's Marnier due Shae's Champion."

"I still don't understand," Kirsty said. "Aren't the Gods united on everything, influencing only their own domains?'

Allyn slowly shook his head. "The Gods agree on rules, nothing more. One of those rules is the appearance of cooperation. They don't want factions tearing the world apart. Another rule is that they can only alter events through influence or agreement, not direct action. Marnier du Shae may want Caroline as her Champion, but Caroline has to agree."

"It would have taken Marnier du Shae centuries to create this situation," Dobbin said. "Millennia maybe. The moment the other Gods saw her plans come together, they would have reacted, doing whatever they could to influence events to their own ends."

Kirsty spoke quietly. "My sister was marked by the Lady of Healing the night before we departed her abbey. Rhonda only left the abbey because her Goddess asked her to." Kirsty held her chin up, clearly holding back painful emotions. "Does that mean Rhonda took Caroline's place in some foreseen accident?"

"Possibly, although the Gods rarely act so obviously. Your sister must have been very brave if she accepted such a fate," Allyn said.

Elias glanced at Caroline. If their souls had been forged from the same spark, what was the plan behind that? Surely it had to be for more than saving her life in the forest.

Allyn grasped Caroline's faeriestone, closing his eyes. Arcane energy crackled across the sorcerer's knuckles.

"Best I can determine, the faeriestone's been empowered to

protect its wearer. It seems to have a few other qualities too, but they're subtle. I'm guessing they're nullifying her aura and hiding the stone from casual view. With study I might be able to determine what else it does, but it's fey magic."

"Is there any doubt Marnier du Shae contrived to get it to Caroline? Why else would the fey give away something so precious?" Elias asked.

"I suspect the Goddess wanted to keep Caroline hidden, but the other Gods forced her hand."

"If the fey gave that stone away, then Marnier du Shae must have offered them something very valuable in return," Dobbin added.

"Probably a promise not to cast them from the universe if she wins Noramgaell," Elias murmured.

"Any idea how Queen Lynn got hold of it?" Dobbin asked Kirsty. Kirsty shrugged.

"It is definitely gifted," Allyn said. "It wouldn't be attuned to Caroline otherwise."

"Maybe the protective spells can help neutralise the curse."

"I suspect they're already trying to shield her from it, but that's not something they were designed to do. If the stone's keeping the curse at bay, she can only heal naturally. She isn't strong enough. She's dying."

Elias stared at the girl's seeping injuries. "Death may be the only gift Marnier du Shae can bestow on her just now," he said softly, his tone betraying regret he'd meant to keep secret. "A werewolf's going to do the Goddess little good."

"The healing stone?" Dobbin began.

"It's spent," Allyn said.

"I channelled all my energy through it and it wasn't nearly enough," Elias added. "Whatever we do, we need to hurry. The faspane will find this cabin soon. Can we assist the stone's spells in some way?"

"Three forms of magic contesting for the same body? We'd kill her."

"Remove the stone," Kirsty said, her voice barely above a whisper.

"Then the curse will possess her," Dobbin said.

"My sister sacrificed her life for the Goddess of Healing. If Caroline dies, her sacrifice will mean nothing. Remove the stone."

Elias glanced at Kirsty with respect. She was probably the only one of them who saw the matter clearly. "Dead girl or living werewolf, make your choice, Allyn." He didn't dare voice the decision he hoped his teacher would make, and the one he feared.

11

———————

Mist covered the forest, luminescent with the full moon's light. Somewhere deep in the damp trees a wolf howled, the sound muted by fog. Glancing around in the hope there wasn't another wolf nearby, Caroline shivered as much with cold as with a feeling she'd been here before. Her last memory was with her escort on the way home to Fandelyon City. Where was her horse? Her friends? Her guard?

She jumped. Further up the slope, an animal moved through the mist. A wolf, as dark as the fog was pale. Caroline held still but the sudden thump of her heart must have given her away. The wolf stopped, raised its nose and sniffed.

Cautiously backing a step, Caroline looked around, but found no refuge. A quick prayer to the Higher Realm brought neither assistance nor inspiration. If she prayed to Marnier du Shae, would the Divine Lady intervene on her behalf? What would be the cost? Gods never offered anything for nothing and always got what they wanted first.

She backed another step and bumped into a tree as the animal turned toward her, its eyes the colour of rich blood. She felt more than heard the low growl it made. She backed around the tree, hoping to get the trunk between herself and the animal.

Close your eyes.

Startled, she looked around but saw no one. "What?" she tried to say, but her throat closed on the word.

Close your eyes or I'll kill you.

Panic rising, Caroline spun and ran, only to slip and tumble down a steep slope. She dropped over a small ledge and landed hard. Miraculously unhurt, she pushed herself up, but cried out as the wolf collided with her. They rolled and... she sat up in bed, breathing hard, perspiration sticking her hair to her face.

She put a hand to her throat, confused. It took her a moment to recognise the nightmare and let it fade. She was in her own room at Kirrilee Palace, the familiar smell comforting.

"Shush," her mother said. Caroline jumped, but relaxed as Queen Lynn held her close, as she'd done so many times before. Caroline let herself be drawn into the fresh scent of her mother's hair.

"Did you have one of your nightmares again?"

Caroline nodded.

"The one where you die by fire, or the one about the wolf?" the Queen asked.

Caroline took a shuddering breath. "The wolf."

Lynn kissed Caroline on the temple, her hand on her daughter's cheek. "Don't worry, perhaps it'll get you next time."

Caroline glanced at her mother, uncertain she'd heard correctly. "What?"

"What's the matter, dear?" Lynn asked as Caroline pulled away.

It was no longer her mother. It was a wolf. "No!" Caroline cried, struggling from the blankets and out of her bed. She backed to the wall as the wolf watched her with unnatural red eyes, the stone cold through her nightdress. "What are you?"

Your defences are finally gone. Come now, close your eyes and this will all become a half-forgotten memory.

Caroline ran for the door, but the wolf leapt as she went through. They crashed to the rug, her elbows losing skin as she hit.

"Caroline!" Daniella screamed. Her youngest sister stood at the far end of the corridor, the wolf between the two girls. Fumbling in fear, the six-year-old girl tried the door beside her, but it was bolted from the other side. "Don't let it get me!" Daniella cried.

Choose, said the voice in her mind. *You or your sister.*

"Run, Daniella!" Caroline cried as she struggled to her feet. Daniella backed away, hands out as if she could calm the wolf.

Close your eyes, Princess.

"Run Daniella!"

Do it now or I'll kill her!

Intuition prickled. "This isn't real," she said with realisation. "It's another dream."

It's real, the voice said. For you.

Before she could turn, it ran at her. Caroline stumbled and tripped, hitting dirt where there had been floorboards before. Bright sunlight blinded her as mailed fists grabbed her tunic and pulled her into a tent. She struggled, but guards bound her hands with thick rope. "What-"

A backhanded blow struck her face, almost knocking her out cold. Her knees collapsed and her vision darkened. The men holding her dragged her to her feet. Blood ran from her split lip, and it tasted good. Bruises she didn't remember pained her muscles and she felt welts and cuts on her back from a whipping. "Where-"

Another blow broke a tooth. She spat it out with a cry of pain as he knees collapsed. Someone grabbed her hair and pulled her head up. She blinked tears, trying to make out the blurry faces. They were nobility for the most part by the way they were dressed, but none she recognised.

A fair-haired man gave her a half-bow. "Your Imperial Majesty. We have a verdict. For your heretical crimes we sentence you to death by fire." He glanced at the men holding her. "Take her out."

"No!" Caroline cried. Her worst fear.

Someone hit her in the stomach. Unable to breathe or even stand, they dragged her outside and chained her to a thick wooden post, hands above her head. They piled wood around her, enough to cremate ten people. She raised her head, trying to focus. Before her, a crowd of soldiers and nobility cheered. Hundreds. Thousands. She was in the middle of an army.

A priest in the red robes of the God of War spoke. "Do you renounce your sins, Empress Caroline duFandelyon? Answer carefully. Your soul depends on it."

She couldn't focus on him, but he sounded familiar. She spat blood in his direction, though most of it dribbled down her chin.

The priest spoke. "History should have remembered you as a great leader. Instead, you'll die despised and hated."

"Light it," someone said. Soldiers thrust their torches into the kindling. Smoke wafted up. The dry wood caught, and in moments she felt its heat. She struggled against the chains, cutting her wrists in a frenzy to get free as heat scorched her clothes. She screamed, twisting as the flames burned. Thousands of soldiers cheered.

Fear hid the pain as blood ran freely from her wrists. "Help! Please!"

Close your eyes.

Naked flame touched her and she screamed in agony. Skin blistered and her clothes burned, cauterising her bleeding flesh. She tried to scream but the heat and smoke seared her lungs.

Close your eyes and I'll take the pain away.

She lost all strength amid agony she'd never believed could exist. She could smell her own flesh burning.

Close your eyes. Surrender. I can take away the pain. Close your eyes!

"No!" she choked. She gasped one final whisper of defiance, but the agony was too much. She closed her eyes.

Darkness swallowed pain. The nightmare quickly became a lost memory.

12

———

Firewood clattered to the timber floor. A door slammed shut.

Caroline sat up, heart pounding as heavy boots thumped in her direction. A draft from the open window tickled her naked back as the footsteps stopped outside her door. Terrified, she lay back and pulled the blanket up to her chin before the door cracked open. A weather-beaten shivra with a close-cropped blond beard peeked through. Small for a shivra, though broad across the shoulders, she doubted he'd be much above eight feet tall. Certainly not nine. Most shivras she'd met were at least ten or eleven, and the women taller again.

Only a shivra, thankfully. "Who are you?" she asked. The draft carried his scent, the same scent pervading her blanket and bed. She could smell Kirsty also, and two other people she didn't recognise, one of them quite pleasant.

The shivra raised bushy eyebrows and pushed the well-oiled door fully open. "I'm Dobbin of the Five Peaks," he said in a deep, abrasive voice, a grin splitting his beard. "Ye'd be Princess Caroline." Caroline stiffened when he mentioned her name, but realised Kirsty would have told him. "It's good to see ye looking healthy." He entered the room.

It wasn't until he moved that she realised how solid he was. Muscle stretched the shirt across his chest. He had the physique of a soldier used to heavy work, or perhaps a blacksmith. "Where am I? Where is Kirsty?"

"Safe, lass."

Lass? "I expect to be addressed as 'Your Lady,' 'Princess,' or 'Your Highness'."

He frowned. "Use that tone with me again and I'll give ye a hiding ye'll never forget. Understood?"

Shivras were generally even-tempered, but only to a point. "You're right, master shivra. Please forgive my abrasiveness. So I'm a hostage then?"

His brows met and he seemed somewhat surprised. He stared for such a long time she thought he wasn't going to reply. "No. Yer not a hostage. Ye were hurt. Yer not far from where ye had the accident. We're a couple of valley's south of the high plains of Fandelyon."

"What accident?"

"I'd best leave explanations to those who were there. I'm no good at telling tales. Not while sober, anyhow."

She could wait for answers. "Where's Kirsty?"

"Coming, lass. Don't fret."

She would have to put up with 'lass' for a while, it seemed. Surprisingly, it had a familiarity she liked.

Distantly she heard someone walking toward the cabin. Soft steps, probably a small woman, yet it was a male voice accompanying them. Her frown deepened when a second man spoke, but they were still too far away to make out the words. "Two men are approaching, but I can only hear one person walking. The steps are from someone small and light."

Dobbin raised his bushy eyebrows. "I can't hear a thing. Not unexpected, considering. That'd be Kirsty ye can hear walking. The voices would be Allyn and Elias. They rescued you."

"Why can't I hear them walking?"

"They spend a lot of time in the forest. They're quiet." His expression suggested he wasn't being entirely truthful and his scent changed too, confirming her suspicions. She followed their progress to the cabin, but even when they arrived she could barely hear any tread but Kirsty's.

"She's awake!" Dobbin yelled. Caroline almost jumped out of her blanket, naked and all.

Kirsty squealed and ran through the doorway, nearly bouncing off the powerful shivra on her way through. "My Lady," she said, sitting on the oversized bed and pulling Caroline close. "You're well. Thank the Gods!"

Doubt assailed Caroline. She didn't feel as if she'd had an accident or even been sick. When the younger girl sat back, tears gleamed in her eyes. Kirsty smelled freshly bathed, yet stains marked her dress and whole sections of her skirts had been mended or completely torn away. "Kirsty, what happened to your dress? Who did this stitching? They should be scolded."

Dobbin chuckled, "Then ye'd better scold Kirsty. She washed and stitched it herself. No maids here."

Kirsty let go and sat back. "You don't remember, do you?" Kirsty's disappointment tainted the air like bitter herbs, yet she didn't drop her eyes as she studied Caroline's face.

"Remember what?"

"I told you she wouldn't remember," someone said from the doorway. "How's your hearing? What about your sense of smell? Do you feel stronger?"

A thrill of fear jolted through Caroline when she saw the izzat. He was taller than most men, but frail-looking beside Dobbin. Very young, too. Just out of his teens. She growled a warning.

Kirsty grabbed Caroline's hand. "My Lady. It's okay." Caroline glared at the izzat, teeth barred, unable to believe her friend was so calm. If he tried to touch her she'd bite a finger off. "Princess, please. They saved us!"

A larger izzat walked in behind the first, fully a head taller and far more solid, though still no match for Dobbin. Although they both looked quick and agile, the bigger izzat seemed to have shivra-like strength behind him, whereas the other had the wiry build of a boy.

She met the big izzat's eyes and could have sworn she recognised him from somewhere, though she couldn't remember the time or place. Rather than the emerald or jade eyes common to male izzat, his were ice-blue and far too... human. He returned her gaze with a look of... expectation? Knowing? Familiarity? All of them, or perhaps fear. He smelled... Her heart began to race with desire. What was happening?

"Ye two look like ye each just found yer long-lost love," Dobbin said, following Carline's gaze to the izzat, who abruptly turned away.

Was her expression that transparent? "Your eyes," Caroline whispered to the taller izzat in the hope of hiding her unexpected reaction. "Are you half shivra?" It took a moment before she realised Kirsty's hand was squeezing her shoulder.

The izzat stood at about six and a half feet tall. Strong, like a smith, yet lithe. His features, though fine, were blunt compared to the smaller izzat. A mongrel, then. He had to be. Was he half human or shivra? She couldn't tell from his scent. It was unique. Dobbin stepped forward, breaking her focus. "Princess Caroline, may I present Allyn and Elias." He pointed to each as he said their names.

"Dobbin, I don't doubt your... integrity, but they're izzen," she said.

"I told you she'd be trouble," Elias said to Allyn.

"I've heard the same said about you," Allyn said.

Dobbin chuckled while Kirsty's scent changed. Her friend smelled offended, of all things.

Elias frowned up at the shivra. "How'd you like a fatter nose?"

"Come outside and I'll find ye a stump to stand on so ye can try."

"Caroline," Allyn began. "Two nights ago a group of humans attacked your soldiers. Many of you escaped into the forest where a band of faspane..." She must have looked confused. "You mistakenly call them izzen. They attacked you." He sounded as if he'd explained such things before. "I think they were after you specifically. Do you remember?"

Caroline glanced at Kirsty, uncertain. Kirsty offered an encouraging smile. How could her friend smell so calm? "Vaguely. Did you say two nights?"

Allyn held up her mother's ruby necklace, and she stiffened. She wanted to demand he return it, but didn't have the courage. "Two nights. Almost too late I remembered they wanted you to remove this. Although the stone is beautiful, its purpose is actually a protective device. Among other things, it helps hide your aura."

She almost made a sign against evil at the implication of magic, but suspected he'd only laugh. The divine marks on her wrists didn't seem such a burden right then. She glanced at the luminous flowers for assurance, feeling oddly comforted by them.

Allyn continued. "I believe they wanted to be sure of who you were before they killed you."

"I believe him," Kirsty said. "They're not the izzen we know about."

"What do you remember after that?" Allyn asked.

She put aside her doubts and searched her memory, finding it clouded in fear. "We fled and got lost. I think my horse threw me." She struggled for recollection. "I must have hit my head. Why have you got my necklace?" Allyn crossed the room and passed it to her. She examined it before putting it back on, cautiously keeping an eye on him at the same time.

"Amazing," Elias murmured. He seemed to be watching her, but not looking at her directly. More... something about her.

Allyn said, "I removed it to save your life. A werewolf attacked you."

She laughed. "A werewolf?" His scent told her he believed what he'd said was true. They all did, even Kirsty.

"Do you see any of us sniffing the air?" Elias asked.

"I'm only checking your scents. You all believe this madness, don't you?"

Allyn raised an eyebrow and exchanged a glance with Elias. "You can smell emotions?" Elias asked.

She frowned. "Of course. Can't everyone?"

"No," Dobbin said. "Apparently some werewolves can though."

"Some werewolves?" She couldn't quite hide the disbelief in her voice.

Allyn cleared his throat. "The stone gave you the strength to resist the curse, but not defeat it. You were dying, Princess."

Caroline read Kirsty's face and found no deceit. Kirsty must believe them. "You're lying and you've somehow convinced Kirsty of it."

Elias stepped forward and she instinctively leaned away. "The curse hides your memories and twists your thoughts. Would you normally doubt Kirsty?"

Would she? She wasn't sure.

Kirsty twined her fingers in her skirts. "It's true, My Lady. A werewolf nearly killed us both."

Liar, Caroline thought, but immediately felt chagrined. How could she think such things about Kirsty? She needed time to think everything through. "Leave me please. All of you.'

"Allyn said the curse would influence you and try to drive me away once you recovered." She reached out and took Caroline's hand. "Is that what you're doing now?"

"Of course not." She needed to get away from them all and take Kirsty with her before they corrupted her further. She tried not to glance at the window or otherwise give away her intentions.

No one moved. Why weren't they leaving? "What else?"

13

———————

"Kirsty, could you please get the Princess's dress and cloak?" Allyn asked.

Caroline kept her eyes on the shorter izzat, curious despite herself, while Kirsty rummaged through a huge chest at the end of the shivra-sized bed. The younger girl held the dress out to Caroline. Caroline gasped. "By the Higher Realm. What happened?" Despite washing, the echoes of bloodstains remained and new stitching couldn't hide the rips and missing fabric. Kirsty's dress was in far better condition.

"Kirsty, perhaps it's time you left," Allyn said.

Caroline scowled at the izzat. "Kirsty will leave when she's ready. Not before."

"We're wasting time," Elias said. Kirsty's smell changed from apprehension to fear, her expression reflecting it.

"Kirsty? What's going on?"

Kirsty dropped her eyes.

Elias spoke. "You're not going to believe us without proof, maybe not even then," Elias said as he unrolled a strip of oiled cloth to reveal an arrow and a dagger. "Are you?"

The sharp smell of the weapons sting the back of Caroline's nose and throat. She swallowed, wondering what poison they'd been coated in. The reek of the weapons overpowered the other smells in the room.

Allyn took the weapons from Elias. "I take it you're aware that only silver, fire, dismemberment or magic can kill a werewolf?" Allyn asked.

She glanced at the weapons, forcing herself to open tense fingers before raising her chin. "Any harm visited upon me will be avenged many times over." It was a ridiculous, empty threat and she could see he knew it.

"We intend no harm," Elias said.

"Please," Kirsty said, squeezing Caroline's hand. "It's only a test. A demonstration."

Allyn held both weapons out for Caroline's inspection. They seemed unremarkable except for the stench. "The dagger is simple steel, but the arrow-tip was dipped in silver," Allyn said. "All I ask is that you allow a nick from both. If I'm right and you're a werewolf, the cut from the dagger will close over and heal within minutes while the nick from the arrow will remain as if a normal cut. If I'm wrong, I'll apologise."

Caroline glanced from face to face, heart pounding with unfounded fear. It was just a nick, after all, yet it seemed far too significant. The weapons could have been poisoned. "I will not submit to this."

"Lass," Dobbin said. "We're not giving you a choice."

Allyn looked over the arrow very carefully. "Child..."

"I'm a woman. Do not call me a child." A woman with a child of her own, somewhere. She wished she knew where.

A frown creased Allyn's forehead and removed the boyish cast to his features. For a moment, he seemed far older than he looked. "My apologies, Princess, but I can't permit you to leave here ignorant of the danger you present. Take the test or... Take the test. Please."

Caroline looked from Allyn to Elias. The mixed-blood izzat kept his eyes on the ground. Kirsty stared at the floor as well, terror in her scent. Terror?

She stared at Allyn. "If I don't take the test?" Were they going to kill her?

"Would you have taken it a week ago? Would it have mattered then?"

"Fine," she said, "but you nick yourself first." He wouldn't likely poison himself if that's what they'd done to the weapons. "After that I'll take your test."

"Deal," Allyn said.

She glanced between them, surprised. "But it's poisoned. It has to be. I can smell it."

"There is no poison. Only silver. Kirsty, can you smell anything?"

"No," her friend said quietly.

"Dobbin?"

"Me neither," Dobbin said.

Allyn knelt beside the bed and nicked a finger with each weapon, drawing a bead of blood on each. The scent of his blood bloomed in the air like a rose ready for picking. She took a deep breath, trying to remember when she's smelled anything so good despite the taint of poison. She waited for the poison to take effect but he merely wiped the metal clean, polishing it on his cloak.

"Satisfied?"

Uncertain, she held out her hand. "Let me see the arrow." Allyn handed it over. It reeked, but she couldn't see anything on it. It was freshly polished too. It stung her nose, regardless. She gave it back to him.

Allyn handed the arrow and dagger to Dobbin. "I'm assuming you don't trust me or Elias, and I don't want to give you any reason to disbelieve the results. Should you wish, Kirsty can do it. Otherwise, Dobbin should suffice."

Kirsty shook her head. "Not me. Please."

Caroline watched Kirsty carefully. Her friend truly believed it all. She could smell it above the silver.

Dobbin pushed past the izzen and knelt beside her. "No games, lass. No poison. No deceit. All ye smell is silver. Yer hand?" He held both weapons in his right hand, his left hand open to engulf hers.

This close, his smell was particularly strong. Not entirely unpleasant, but musky. "The Higher Realm has touched you all with madness," she whispered.

"I agree that the Gods had a hand in pushing us together," Allyn said. Elias shook his head.

She put her hand in Dobbin's huge meaty palm, the luminous outline of the *alimoth* flower on her wrist a painful reminder of why she'd gone to the abbey and why she was here now. Perhaps now might be the right time to accept her religious calling.

"My apologies if this hurts, lass," Dobbin said as he placed the dagger on the bed and held the arrow like a woodcarver's tool.

"Just hurr- Ow!" She snatched her hand back. Her middle finger bled from a small nick. She could smell her own blood and the sharp reek of what he claimed was silver. "You should have warned me." A drop of red slid down her finger. She stuck the finger in her mouth and sucked, nearly choking on the taint of silver.

"Taste good?" Elias asked, eyebrows raised.

She removed her finger and stared at him with impotent anger. "No." She held her hand before her eyes. A fresh trickle of blood appeared. "Happy?" she asked, showing them. Her finger throbbed, the cut stinging as if the weapon had been heated over a candle.

"Not yet," Allyn said. "Dobbin, the knife."

"Yer hand, lass. Last nick." Grudgingly, she held her hand out again. He took another finger and made another cut.

"Ow! Could you make it any bigger?" The shivra released her finger and she had to resist the temptation to suck the blood from it again. The gash was twice as long and deep as the first. She could smell the blood again, but no taint this time. It didn't sting nearly as much.

She wiped her finger on the palm of her other hand. The blood didn't re-appear, and she felt a disturbing rush of fear. She squeezed it. A hint of blood marked the wound, but it didn't flow again. It had already closed over and stopped bleeding, while the smaller nick from the arrow still produced a trickle.

The strength slipped from her. "What sorcery is this?" she

whispered. Her hands trembled, the marks given her by Marnier du Shae proving no comfort.

"I remember seeing you get wounded while escaping the soldiers at the road," said Elias. "How's your shoulder?"

Caroline had forgotten. She flexed her shoulder. No pain. She touched it. No wound, no tenderness, and only a fading scar. She couldn't stop the trembling.

Allyn said, "Elias, we should check for faspane. Try farsight again. They can't all be shielded. If you find nothing, take a walk and see if anything's disturbed. Dobbin, can you go with him please? You know the area."

They nodded and left the room. "What's farsight?" She glanced at her rapidly healing finger before meeting Allyn's inhuman stare. Green eyes, vaguely like her own, but ever so much greener.

"What you do from here is your choice," Allyn said. "I offer my help freely and without reservation, but you'd best make your decision quickly. The faspane are still looking for you and no doubt the curse will try to shadow your emotions again."

"Faspane," she whispered, beginning to believe him.

"Yes. Like us, they etch or dip their weapons in silver, as it's the only metal that easily harms magical creatures." He paused, waiting for her to meet his eyes. "And cursed ones." He left, closing the door behind him. Caroline stared at her trembling fingers. The one cut with silver still throbbed. How could it be a trick?

Her entire future seemed to be falling apart. Visions of her family torn to death come the next full moon haunted her. She wanted to deny it, but she'd be lying to herself. Had her senses always been so sharp? Surely she'd always been able to smell this well. "By the Gods, what have I become?"

A hand touched her shoulder and she nearly cried out. She closed her eyes, taking a deep breath. "Kirsty," she said. "Aren't you afraid of me?"

What she wouldn't do for her mother's comforting presence just then. Her mother always knew what was wrong. She usually had some idea things would go wrong beforehand.

Kirsty touched Caroline's chin, lifting the princess's face to meet her eyes. "I remember the first time I came to court. My sister and brothers were teasing me relentlessly, along with a dozen other noble children. I was in tears. You were the only person to stand up for me. You ordered them away and took me to your rooms."

Caroline frowned. "I don't remember. We must have been young."

"Very young, Highness. It may have meant little to you, but I've never forgotten." She looked down, her eyes distant. "The other night in the woods, the werewolf charged us. I doubt you remember, but you pushed me out of the way, putting yourself in its path. I owe you my life. More than my life. You sacrificed everything for me. You could have tried to run and perhaps saved yourself. Instead, you saved me." Kirsty took a shuddering breath. "Thank you. I wasn't sure I was going to have the chance to say that, you were hurt so badly."

Caroline pulled her friend close and held her tight, enjoying her rich smell. "I did that?" she asked. "I find it hard to believe the slightest part of all this."

"Allyn said it's unlikely your memory will return. The curse is very powerful. It distorts your past, makes you think you've always been... well, the way you are now. It hides the truth from you."

"What else did he say?" she asked as Kirsty sat back. "Is there a cure?"

"He doesn't know."

Softly, she asked, "Is he a wizard?" She touched the stone dangling from her neck. He'd said enough to imply it.

"I've seen no proof, but he's mentioned terms like *farsight* and *wards* several times, and I've heard them all discussing magic as we would talk about dresses. I also saw a stone heal your flesh."

Caroline held Kirsty's gaze. "Allyn's not to be trusted. You understand that, don't you? None of them are, not even the shivra."

Kirsty looked at the floor. "Of course, Your Highness." Her tone and scent said otherwise, but Caroline let it go.

"Have they mentioned my soldiers, or your brothers?"

"Elias said a group had gotten away safely, but he couldn't name any of them."

"Bastion will have kept your brothers safe. We need to find our way to safety as soon as possible. Do you know where we are?"

"Generally. After Elias saved us we walked for hours through the night. Elias carried you the entire way. He's very strong." A hint of a smile quickly disappeared from Kirsty's expression as her eyes found Caroline's. Her smell changed too. It was something akin to pleasure, though deeper than a fleeting emotion.

Caroline didn't like it. "Help me dress. We're leaving. We can't in good conscience use any more help from practitioners of magic."

14

————————

Caroline stiffened as Allyn walked into the room. She tried hiding her reaction by smoothing her skirts. She didn't want him to realise she felt fear and revulsion at his presence.

"You're looking well," Allyn said.

Caroline avoided his emerald eyes as Kirsty came to stand by her side. Did the izzat never blink? "What do you want?" she asked, before realising how rude she sounded. "I mean, how may I help you?"

"Can we talk? Privately? I'd like to show you something."

Kirsty gave Caroline an inquiring glance. Caroline nodded reluctantly. Her friend slipped past the izzat without any scent of fear and closed the oversized door behind her, leaving Caroline feeling trapped with a creature she'd been taught to fear.

While Allyn appeared young enough to be inexperienced, she suspected he was much older than her. Shivras aged slowly. Izzen probably did too. He could be older than her father. Judging by the way Elias and Dobbin deferred to him, he was probably a lot more dangerous than the fragile youth he appeared to be.

"The path home?" she asked and almost bit her own lip in annoyance at herself. "I'm sorry, Allyn. My manners aren't at the forefront of my thoughts today."

He smiled, and it seemed genuine. "I will help you get home if that's what you want."

She considered her chances without him. Despite what she'd said to Kirsty, she had to admit they weren't good unless they received help. "I do. Thank you."

"The Gods work in subtle ways, do they not?"

She almost reached for her wrists to hide her *alimoth* flowers. "They do. What was it you wish to discuss?"

"Elias believes your souls are linked in some way, that perhaps yours is a twin to his own."

She couldn't help showing surprise. "I don't understand. How could a soul have a twin?"

"You recognised him the moment you saw him, didn't you?"

"No. I mean, I've never seen him before."

He gave her a searching look which suggested he recognised the hidden truth. She felt herself flush. "Felt something, then. What you're probably not aware of is that your soul is far older than his."

He couldn't possibly know that. "No one remembers their past lives."

"Yet the signs are obvious when you've been alive for as long as I have. Your soul is ancient, I'd wager. You've been reborn many times."

She crossed her arms. "What's your point?"

"My point is that you can't be connected given the difference in your past lives. At least, it's very unlikely. There has to be another reason."

She shrugged. "Such as?"

"Elias may have been born to protect you. A Champion's protector, if you like."

"Champion?"

"I believe Marnier du Shae wants you as her Champion." Allyn said. "You've heard of Noramgaell?"

Everyone had. "The final battle. Of course." She'd read about it in the scriptures. "It's said to be the time when the Gods will battle among themselves for the right to guide this world to enlightenment.

It's supposed to be a contest of some sort to prove which divinity is the most deserving."

"It's a little more than that, considering Normagaell has been playing out for millennia. Whenever two Gods challenge each other, both sides need a Champion."

Both? There were twelve Gods. "I haven't heard this."

"Which brings me back to my theory that Marnier du Shae took a spark from your soul and used it to forge a new soul."

It took her a moment to see the connection. "You mean Elias?"

"You feel an attraction to him, don't you?"

"There is no attraction."

He smiled, revealing a hint of mischievousness. "Perhaps not in a physical sense."

She sighed. "Is this all you wanted to talk about?"

"I suspect Elias was born to be your guardian in this life. He's connected to you, just as you are to him."

"I'm sorry, Allyn, but although I believe you mean well, I don't believe you."

He shifted slightly, blocking the way to the door. "Hear me out. Please."

She glanced at the door. "You're blocking my way."

"I'm sorry." He moved aside, his open hand showing the way past him. "You're free to leave, but please hear me out."

With the way clear, she felt slightly more at ease. "Okay, but please make your point."

"Thank you. The Gods recently delivered four affinities into this world. Your people are the current pawns in the battles between the Gods. The most monumental events in history are due to divine struggles, and they sometimes come with gifts."

"None of this is in the scriptures." She'd read enough holy books in the last half year to know.

"That's because the Gods prefer to let us think they're unified, but they're not. Two hundred thousand years ago our world had two unicorns. One died at the hands of the faspane, the opening volley in the battle for this world. Ebonair du Sai lost that gamble, taking him out of contention for control of this universe. There have been many more such contests. For example, twenty thousand years ago the faspane tried to kill the remaining unicorn. My people held them at bay. Another gamble, removing another God from contention."

"I don't want to be rude, but I honestly don't believe you."

"I understand," he said. "I'm only asking that you listen. Fair?"

She acknowledged with a nod. "Fair."

"We're approaching the final clash between Gods. Only Marnier du Shae and Marak du Tren remain in contention for this world. The conditions are agreed upon. When they're met, the battle will pit humans against faspane. Either the Lady of Healing or the God of War will claim this world, depending on who wins."

She stared, looking for deceit, but found none in either his expression or his scent. "Go on."

"Elias and I are on our way to collect the *Sword of the Sun* from the shivra citadel Delshere. It's the only weapon capable of killing Phoenix, Marak du Tren's Champion." He gave her a pointed look.

She tried not to show her unease. "I'm not Marnier du Shae's Champion."

"Yet you are a sorceress."

"I'm no such thing!" She forced down enough anger she wanted to slap him.

He held his palms apart and greenish lightning arced between them. She backed away.

"Magic," she whispered in fear.

"In the same way only Divine Servants can see divine light, only the gifted can see magic."

"There was nothing there," she said a little too quickly, realising he'd see the lie from the fact she'd reacted.

Rather than showing anger or irritation, he laughed. "I suspect Marnier du Shae made many concessions to the other Gods in order to deliver such a talent to you. It might explain the necklace as well. Do either of your parents have any... gifts?"

She stared at him defiantly, but his expression said he knew the truth and wasn't judging her. "My mother," she conceded. "She often knows things before they happen."

"And your brothers and sisters? Do they possess magic like you?"

Like you. The words made her feel sick. "I don't know," she said honestly.

"I see. Marnier du Shae is backing your people, yet they're greatly outnumbered and lack magic, not that the faspane are particularly gifted. However, the conditions for Noramgaell include four affinities to help even the battle for your people: earth, air, fire and water. I suspect you've received one of those gifts." Green fire erupted above his palm and she almost jumped. Goosebumps settled across her skin. "My guess is that you were gifted with an affinity for fire."

He took a scrap of cloth and held it to the greenish flame until it caught fire. He blew it out, leaving smoke curling toward the roof and making the room stink. "Put your hand in the flame."

"No!"

"Then put it as close as you can until you can stand it no longer."

"I can feel its warmth from here, thank you."

Again that humour returned in his eyes and smile. "Humour me. Please. I won't move the flame. I promise."

Opening and closing her fists in indecision, she finally nodded, determined to prove him wrong. That, and she was a tiny bit curious. She reached out until she felt heat against her fingertips.

"Closer."

She gave him a look, but inched her fingertips forward. The flame was hot enough to sting, but not really painful. It was like touching metal left too long in the sun. With surreal fascination, she slowly moved her fingertips into the flame. "I'm not burning," she whispered. She didn't know what it meant except that he hadn't lied about the affinities. What other truths did he know?

"Gods rarely show their hands when they're vying for the fate of the world. It's not surprising you're ignorant about all this." Allyn took the piece of cloth and put it to the flame again while her fingers were still there. It caught immediately.

Caroline snatched her hand away in sudden shame and fear, her entire childhood beliefs defied. Everything she'd been taught was wrong. "I don't want to be the pawn of a Goddess."

He smiled, revealing too-sharp teeth. "About three thousand years ago Marnier du Shae backed your ancestors to defeat what was then the most powerful human empire in the world. Mistapol. The Divine Lady Kindra du Erim, Protector of Warriors, lost that gamble despite the odds. It was thanks to the influence of another God who offered a concession to the leviathan who rules the mermaids. You're not safe from divine influence, and won't be until you help Marnier du Shae win Noramgaell."

"You're suggesting other Gods want me dead?"

"Dead or incapacitated. Threatening you is a means of forcing Marnier du Shae into offering concessions if She wins Noramgaell. They all want to leave legacies. You've been given magic *and* an affinity. More than likely, Marnier du Shae has gambled everything on you. Absolutely everything. You must lead your people to victory or they'll perish."

"She gambled poorly."

"Would you be insulted if I agreed?" Allyn asked.

She raised her chin. "I'm not prepared for any of this."

"I understand, but you need to know the *Sword of the Sun* is the only weapon capable of destroying Phoenix. It's a weapon of fire, which you're immune to. It was created for Marnier du Shae's Champion. Can you see my point now?"

She gave him a level stare. "It can't be me. I'm not even a legitimate child. My father and mother met when she was a commoner, herself the bastard child of a clansman she'd never met. She returned to Father after I was born and begged for money to raise me. He married her instead, but because I was born prior to their union my seven younger siblings stand between me and the throne. I have no intention of killing them off in order to serve in Marnier du Shae's game."

"You believe Marnier du Shae will give you a choice? She contrived to give you magical powers well beyond anything any other human has, as well as one of the four affinities. No doubt it's what tipped Her hand to the other Gods. She needs your loyalty. We all do."

"I'd rather die than harm my family for Her purposes."

"Then She'll find another way to put you on the throne."

"Get out!"

15

———————

Elias shoved the huge door open and walked into Dobbin's cabin. "We have to go."

Allyn walked out of the bedroom as Kirsty walked in, frowning like he'd been slapped. "Faspane?"

"Many. We should thank the Gods for giving us this much time." Elias ran his hands over his bow, checking for wear and damage as Allyn returned to the bedroom. The string was showing some signs of wear, but not enough to be concerned with.

"Don't you knock?" the princess said coldly from the bedroom.

"We're leaving," Allyn said as he stood in the doorway. "There's a band of faspane nearby. Are you up to travelling?"

She gave a dramatic sigh which grated on Elias's nerves. "If I must."

"Good. We'll be spending several nights in the mountains. Dobbin should have some spare gear."

"Gear? We're not packhorses."

The image of Caroline loaded up like a mule made Elias grin. He chuckled.

"I heard that!" Caroline called from the other room.

"Everyone carries their own gear," Allyn said.

98

Elias put his bow aside as Dobbin burst into the cabin and stopped a few feet from Elias. "What's with the sudden running?" he asked, red-faced and out of breath.

Ally leaned through the bedroom door and spoke to Caroline again. "You and Kirsty will need something more appropriate to wear." Allyn crossed to the kitchen and began rummaging through the cupboards.

"Curse all izzen," Dobbin boomed as he finally stood straight. "Never make up yer minds about anything and now yer rooting through me foodstuffs as if they were yer own. Why the hurry all of a sudden? This place is warded, after all."

"I told you, Dobbin. Five miles in that direction there's about forty faspane and they're heading this way," Elias said.

"Pigswill! Me wards will keep 'em away."

"They know what to look for," Elias said. "Besides, we've been in this smelly hole long enough." He opened a cupboard, pulling out a clay jar filled with jerky. Behind it was a sack of pine nuts.

"Smelly hole?" Dobbin asked, voice rising. "That from a lanky excuse for a beardless gnome!"

"Can I have a piece of jerky?" Caroline asked as she left the bedroom, eying the jar.

Elias raised an eyebrow. She must have smelled it. She couldn't have seen inside. "Your home is rotting," Elias said to Dobbin as he threw a strip of dried meat to Caroline. She caught it, grinning at the feat as if she hadn't expected it.

Dobbin's teeth grated. "I just told ye there's no threat, ya fool. Me home's obscured. If ye somehow managed to get close enough despite the aversion spell, ye'd walk into the wall and not even see what ya hit until afterward."

Elias stuffed the food into a sack and passed it to Allyn before grabbing his quiver. He pulled a string from his belt pouch and strung his bow. "They know we're here, Dobbin. Their wizard must be able to sense traces of your magic. No doubt he's using the wards here to find us. Your magic is as subtle as a cudgel. Your mother should have taught you better."

"Shivras use magic?" Caroline asked, halfway through a bite of jerky.

Dobbin looked from Caroline to Elias. "Don't ye bring me mother into this!"

Elias grinned. "Of course not. I'll catch up. I'm going to play *forest wraith* for a while." Outside, he jogged a few miles before finding tracks. He drew an arrow. Time to slow them down.

～

Back in the bedroom Caroline lifted her chin as Dobbin looked her and Kirsty over. "Of all the shivra luck," he muttered. She couldn't help but feel insulted.

He opened the chest and began pulling clothes out. "Here," he said. When they hesitated, he raised his voice. "Quickly! Are ye deaf? We've little enough time as it is. If yer embarrassed, I'm leaving the room anyway, but get 'em on now." He threw trews, a woven belt each, two shirts and woollen pullovers at their feet. "Yer own boots will do." He threw them a pack to stuff their dresses in and left the room.

Caroline looked at Kirsty and decided to do as told. Magic-wielding faspane outweighed any other concerns. Caroline picked up a pair of baggy trews and pulled them up under her torn skirts, lifting the bodice to belt them. They were huge. The ends of the woven belt hung nearly fifteen inches below her waist. Kirsty's hung nearly a foot further.

Caroline unlaced her bodice and pulled on a shirt that, although made for a shivra, seemed ridiculously baggy even then. She laced the front closed and knotted the hem below the waist to stop it looking like a short dress. Kirsty did the same, and then they put on their own cloaks. She felt like a child dressing in adult's clothes as she rolled the shirt sleeves back, hesitating when she exposed the divine markings on her inner wrists.

"I suspect we'd be better off in our dresses," Caroline said. She felt absurd, the trews so baggy they'd probably fall down despite the belt.

Kirsty, shorter and slimmer, looked ridiculous. She smelled embarrassed.

When they returned to the other room Dobbin cut off the excess length of their baggy trews at their ankles. He belted a double-bladed half-moon axe on his left hip and a war hammer for balance on the right, both protected under leather covers. They were so big Caroline doubted she'd be able to lift either with both hands. He slung a three-foot wide banded wooden shield over his back and then nodded to Allyn, who threw him a pack, slung another across his own shoulders, picked up his walking stick and opened the door.

Dobbin opened another chest and pulled out three canvas rolls with blankets inside, each tied at both ends with a single cord so it could be slung over their backs. He handed one to each of the girls and kept one for himself. Caroline hefted it. It weighed a good ten pounds and was probably wide enough to sleep two humans.

"You can't expect us to carry these," she said. "They weigh more than Kirsty."

"Fair enough," Dobbin said. He pulled his weapons free and held them out to her. "Why don't ye take these and defend us instead?"

She gave him a look. He gave her a wink and pointed to the rolls. "Take 'em or leave 'em, but don't expect anyone to do it for ye."

Caroline slung her roll across her back and Kirsty did the same. "Good," Dobbin said critically. "Comfortable?"

"No," Caroline replied honestly. The cord cut uncomfortably into her shoulder.

"Ye'll get used to it." He followed Allyn out.

"Come on," Caroline muttered to Kirsty as the younger girl stuffed their dresses into a backpack. "First chance we get we're taking whatever assistance anyone offers." Outside, they waited while Allyn finished speaking in some foreign, lilting language. Goosebumps covered Caroline as he spoke and she saw something greenish from the corner of her eye.

Between one heartbeat and the next the cabin disappeared. Caroline stared, mouth open.

"Wow!" Kirsty said with awe in her voice.

Allyn stepped near and Caroline had to resist the impulse to step away. She was still feeling angry with him. "I want you two to follow quietly. Faspane can hear nearly as well as animals and they'll have trackers. Elias will confuse our trail, but you've got to be as quiet as you can. Let's go."

Caroline shared a look with Kirsty. What choice did they have?

Kirsty leaned over a rock and dry-retched. Caroline put her arm around her friend's shoulders and held her hair back until the fit passed. Kirsty wiped the corner of her mouth with the back of her hand, breathing heavily. She hadn't actually vomited, at least.

"I'm going to tell Allyn to slow the pace."

Kirsty took Caroline's hand. "I'll be fine. I just need water."

"Dobbin!" Caroline called. "Kirsty needs water."

"Be quiet," Dobbin hissed as he backtracked and handed Kirsty his oversized, leather-wrapped water flask. Kirsty had to hold it with both hands, and even that looked like an effort. She took a big gulp, dribbling water down her chin and neck. "Don't ye understand what'll happen if those faspane catch us?" He was almost half again Caroline's height and carried enough muscle to outweigh five or six big men, yet he smelled scared.

"I'm sorry. I'm not used to this. I thought they were a long way away," Caroline said

Kirsty took another sip and handed the flask back. "Thank you."

Dobbin took it and proceeded to trudge on after Allyn. Two mountain peaks rose before them, a hint of snow on the summits. Allyn seemed to be heading for the pass between them. "Caroline!" Allyn called, though somehow not loudly. "I think you'll want to see this. Kirsty, you too, if you can be quick enough."

Allyn stood a hundred yards up the trail in a position to view the valley between a couple of massive ghost oaks, their bark going grey with the approach of summer. "Come on," Caroline muttered. "I'll help you."

Kirsty shook her head. "No, you go, My Lady. I'll be there shortly." Caroline pursed her lips, ready to insist. She didn't want to leave her friend alone. "Really. We shouldn't irritate anyone offering help just now, particularly an izzat. Who knows how we'll end up if he abandons us?"

It made sense. "Okay, but call if you need me." She gave Kirsty's shoulder a squeeze and ran up the hill, one arm holding her breasts as she passed Dobbin. When she arrived Allyn pointed between the trees.

"That spot is where Dobbin's cabin is hidden. The faspane have arrived, though you probably can't see them."

"Where?"

He pointed. An intense chill stung her skin a moment before a flash of greenish light made her squint. A ball of flame erupted from the forest, forcing her to turn away. The earth shuddered, the sound slapping her hard in the chest as it half-deafened her. She felt it, even though it was two miles away. She squinted until the worst of it passed.

"By the Higher Realm, no," Allyn whispered as he stared in shock.

Dobbin stopped beside them, breathing hard. The shivra looked shaken. "What did ye do? Me simple wards could never have caused that."

Allyn continued staring. He hadn't turned away like Caroline and Dobbin. Hadn't even squinted. "That wasn't supposed to happen. You vested far too much power into your wards over time, Dobbin. How many crystals did you use?"

The shivra shrugged. "A few dozen. Forty or fifty perhaps."

"Foolish." Allyn rebound his hair at the nape of his neck to keep it from his face. "I was watching with near-sight. The wizard had his apprentice take your wards down. The kid messed everything up. If they'd gone about it correctly it would have taken them hours to figure out no one was there." He scanned the area surrounding the cabin. "Now the kid is dead and nine warriors with him. The rest won't stop until we're dead now, or they are. We're going to have to move quickly."

Dobbin grabbed Allyn's arm before he could turn. "What aren't ye saying, sorcerer?"

Allyn scowled, but his expression quickly relented. "Never kill a faspane outright. Ever. Not unless they come at you first."

"Why?" Caroline asked. Smoke billowed upward now, carrying ash into the sky. Her whole body resonated to what she could only assume was magic, as if sensing the destruction.

"Only ritual suicide will ensure their rebirth. Otherwise their souls dissipate like mist burned off in the morning sun."

"And you just killed nine of them?" Caroline asked, trying to hide her shock.

He gave her a look which denied all responsibility. "No, the wizard's incompetence did, but they'll blame us."

She realised what she had to do now. "Thank you for your help," Caroline began as politely as possible. "But we'll make our own way from here. I can no longer condone an association with practitioners of magic."

He gave her a sardonic look. "Princess, you *radiate* magic, probably more than your entire race combined."

Involuntarily, she glanced at her wrists as she remembered the demonstration in the cabin. Could the curse have made her forget so quickly? "I don't have to give in to it."

He sighed as if dealing with a child. "Magic is the glue that binds the soul to the body. It's what keeps you alive, you and every other earthly creature in this world. Your soul in particular draws more magic into this wold than any human has a right to."

She shrugged. As long as she didn't use it, it didn't matter. "I don't want it."

"You believe the faspane care what you want? They've probably been hunting you for months."

"Then someone better tell Marnier du Shae. She can find another Champion and release me from the obligation."

He looked heavenward, clearly trying not to let annoyance get to him. "She will if she has to, but that won't stop the faspane killing you to make sure you never fulfil your potential."

Caroline had no answers to that. It made her feel lonely and vulnerable. "I just want to be a normal girl," she said in a soft voice.

He took her shoulders and met her eyes. "You are a normal human girl, but you also emanate enough magic to make an izzat sorcerer jealous. You're also a normal girl attuned to a fey jewel who happens to be a werewolf. Mostly though, you're a normal girl with a Gods-granted destiny." He leaned closer, speaking softly. "You felt that chilling sensation when the cabin exploded, didn't you?"

She stiffened, but there was no point denying it. "Yes."

"Ask Kirsty if she felt it. Do you honestly believe there's no reason the faspane would want you dead, considering what *they* know about you?"

She looked away. "Perhaps I could use your help," she murmured.

"Then let's go."

Kirsty had paused about half way to them and was now doubled over again, perspiration dripping from her face. "We can't go yet," Caroline said, "Kirsty needs to rest."

"Why don't ye bite her?" Dobbin said with a cheeky grin. "Ye couldn't have run half as far as her a few days ago."

She gave him an unimpressed look. "I don't think so."

"I'll carry her," Allyn said. As he went to Kirsty, Caroline turned back toward the former cabin. Smoke and ash billowed high. She felt closed in, constricted, yet unwillingly curious as she watched. It seemed the cabin's smoke carried her freedom with it.

"Caroline. We're ready." Allyn had Kirsty slung over his shoulder like a sack of grain.

"Put her down immediately! I'll not have Kirsty carried like a prize of war."

"Dobbin, break the trail please. Caroline, follow." He winked as he walked past, as then whistled as if calling a dog. "Come on."

"Oooh!"

16

———————

Sheltered within the shadowed undergrowth, Elias crouched over the bloody body of a faspane, the dead warrior's hands loosely curled around the hilt of the ceremonial dagger buried in his chest. Elias's arrow to the faspane's groin had spilled a lot of blood, forcing the warrior to take his own life before he bled out.

He hadn't raised an alarm, at least. He'd seemed more afraid of dying by someone else's hand than his own. Small luck, considering Elias had no more arrows and the faspane had snapped his last one as he fell.

Elias quietly drew his dead foe's sword. The length of the blade was beautifully etched with family symbols, the etching filled with silver and polished back. A weapon for killing magical creatures; slender and double-edged, not that he'd ever had more than simple training with swords. He preferred the bow and staff. His only other option was magic, but with a wizard nearby he'd be risking an all-out duel of wills, suicide with warriors so close.

He held still as several warriors moved through the trees, brushing against leaves. A flock of sinuous horse-sized reba dragons flew above the trees, heading toward the western desert. Their sleek bronze wings sliced silently through the air as they glided on updrafts. The males displayed iridescent blue scales on their chests, a challenge to anyone brave enough to take them on.

He caught movement to his left, a warrior crouching about twenty yards away. Elias stayed still, barely breathing as the warrior rose to look around. Leaves rustled just behind Elias. He tensed, ready to swing his new weapon, but relaxed when a bird jumped between branches. Reassured, he turned back to the dead faspane, closing the warrior's eyes. "May your rebirth be swift," he whispered. "And in your new life may your soul find immortality."

He half stood, careful not to be seen. Any number of faspane could be within crossbow range. He moved a few dozen feet ahead, hoping to find a clear path through their search. His stolen blade scraped a naked rock and his pulse thumped. He crouched again, knuckles white around the hilt. He felt jumpier than the day he'd left for his first hunt. A drip of nervous perspiration ran down his temple and cheek and he wiped it away, a curse from his father's heritage. No other izzat he knew perspired.

A boot scuffed the earth maybe fifty yards ahead of him. He risked a look as the faspane ducked behind a stone outcrop, a lock of dark hair still showing. Elias dropped down again as another warrior brushed against leaves somewhere to his left, less than thirty yards away. Too close. He turned his ears back and forth, listening. There were more about. They must be getting confident, or were perhaps hoping to flush him out.

Behind and to his right he heard three moving together; the sound of a snapping twig, a sigh of breath, someone scratching an itch. Surrounded. If only his wingbuds would let him fly.

He guessed about fifteen warriors still pursued him. He'd led them back toward the road, but that was all. As soon as he lost their attention they would pick up Allyn's trail again, and they could easily cover two or three times the amount of ground the girls were likely to make.

Click. He dived sideways as a bolt slammed into the tree he'd been using for cover.

A shout went up, answered by others. He swore as he scampered for the cover of shrubs but there were too many surrounding him now. In desperation Elias chose the closest warrior he could see and called in Faspaneth. "Fallen One! Single combat, or are you a coward?"

They all stopped. Silence. They had him trapped and they knew it, but he'd slighted their honour. It was a gamble, but other than running and hoping to break through their trap he had no other option. His heart pounded as he waited.

"Brave enough to fight a coward who hides behind a bow," the warrior called back. Silence descended on the forest again as the others held their ground.

Elias released his breath. "What weapon do you choose?" he called, knowing the answer already.

The faspane stood up so Elias could easily see him. Mousy brown hair. Jade, overconfident narrow eyes. The faspane lifted his blade, his eyes sweeping the forest. "My sword, the weapon of my soul. Choose your weapon. No magic."

Elias grimaced. Magic was not an option anyway. He didn't have the means or the time to enchant a sword and he needed to conserve his energy in case he came across their wizard. If he'd managed to kill even one who'd had a crossbow, he wouldn't need to do this. Maybe. "The same. Faspaneth rules of combat? Will your companions allow me two minutes if I win?"

The faspane smiled a lazy smile as he shook his head, confident now. "Izzat, no. A slow count of ten."

Two minutes was enough for him to disappear into the forest, and they'd know it. Ten seconds wouldn't give him much more than a hundred yards, but he doubted any of them would be able to keep up. It should be enough. "Swear by it," he called.

The faspane nodded, kissed his naked blade and spoke formally. "I swear by the Gods, my sword and my rebirth. Our contest shall abide by the formal rules of combat." He searched in Elias's general direction. "Your oath?"

Nothing to do but agree now. "I do so swear by the Gods and my immortal soul to abide by the same rules." Not even any magic to charge his muscles with speed and strength. He was at a serious disadvantage.

The faspane pointed his sword at a yellow-tipped needle palm perhaps forty yards away. "Meet me in the clearing, *noble one*," he said, adding sarcasm to the words. "The war band will honour our agreement."

~

Caroline forged ahead of the others up the steep mountain track, despite burning legs. She paused, breathing hard. She needed distance. Time to think. A flask of wine. By the Higher Realm, she needed some way out of this mess. With every moment her thoughts grew darker and she could almost feel the insidious curse clouding her judgement and influencing her outlook. She walked on.

She fought the curse, but it was hard. She pictured herself running from them all, even Kirsty. It was probably the best thing she could do. Run and hide from everyone and everything. Yet the more she thought about her situation and everything Allyn had said and shown her, the more ridiculous it seemed. "It's the curse," she whispered to herself as if saying it aloud helped. "It's poisoning my thoughts and trying to make me forget."

Yet she couldn't quite convince herself. Was it an elaborate trick? She'd put her hand in the flame after all, but what if that were an illusion? Magic. What if Allyn had put a spell on her to make her believe his lies? Kirsty too.

"I am a werewolf," she said under her breath, though she didn't want to believe it. Everything was too convenient.

She paused, leaning on a huge ghost oak. "It's all true," she whispered as if repeating a mantra. "Don't let the curse win." They were trying to help her. It was the curse making her think like it was all a lie. It had to be. The cloth had burned. Her hand hadn't.

Illusion. Tricks.

"No. It was real."

She continued, no longer sure what to believe as she ducked a low branch. Her foot knocked a small rock and it bounced down the mountainside until flowering thornberries caught it twenty yards down in a small ravine. The trail was at its steepest yet, forcing her to work harder to get to the next turn. Once there, she paused to catch her breath and wipe the perspiration from her upper lip and brow. After a few deep breaths, she began again.

Anger welled up unbidden, it's focus on Allyn. It didn't feel like the same anger like when one of her brothers annoyed her. This was darker. Malevolent. Murderous. He'd tricked her...

"No."

Was the curse even real? She couldn't tell, but she could hear Allyn and Dobbin a good way back down the trail. What were they talking about?

Her shirt snagged on a branch and she pulled it loose, but as she did the bedroll on her back caught. "Someone should burn this rotten forest down," she said. She tugged at the bedroll but it remained stuck. Twisting, she ripped the green branch away. A thrill of fear raced through her as she overbalanced and tried to grab something. Anything. And missed.

She smashed through a thicket of leaves and saw sky. Her back slammed hard into the ground, knocking the breath from her and causing a small avalanche of broken branches and leaves. She slammed head first into a thicket and cracked the back of her head on a branch as thick as her arm, the sudden stop almost knocking her unconscious.

She lay there, caught in branches as she stared at the scattered cloud passing overhead, her eyes going blurry. Struggling to remain conscious, she carefully crawled back up the slope to the narrow path using the trees and shrubs for hand and footholds. Her head hurt like it had been split open. At the narrow path, she collapsed a few feet from where she'd slipped.

She must have dozed off, because a splash of water to her face brought her awake. Pain throbbed in her head and her neck hurt. Allyn, Dobbin and Kirsty watched her anxiously.

"Are ye okay, lass?" Dobbin asked.

"Where am I?" She grasped Kirsty's hand as memories of a ride and chase in the forest overwhelmed her. There was a full moon and wolves. "Help me sit, please," she whispered.

Dobbin and Kirsty pulled her up. She sat shaking and staring at memories. The werewolf. Her throat getting torn out. "I remember," she whispered. The curse had made her forget about her lycanthropy, and was turning her against the people trying to help her.

"My Lady, are you okay?" Kirsty asked, her voice formal as if afraid.

Caroline focused on her friend. Kirsty's real face superimposed over the memory of Kirsty in the forest, absolute fear in her eyes. Fear of a werewolf. "Stay away," Caroline whispered. She struggled to her feet, holding onto a tree trunk for balance. "I'm so sorry," she said as more memories blinded her.

She pressed her palms hard against her temples. "I remember the run and chase through the moonlit forest, and Elias fighting a wolf."

Kirsty moved forward to offer comfort, but Caroline backed off, putting a hand out to ward her friend away. "No," she said. "Just... No."

Another memory struck her like a crossbow bolt between her eyes; Allyn, when he'd offered to help her and Kirsty. *Before the werewolf.* An offer she'd refused. Was it possible that Marnier du Shae had sent him? If so, everything resulting from her refusal was her own fault. "Divine Lords and Ladies," she whispered. She'd put herself into this situation; her distrust and fear.

Unable to stand the pity on their faces, she ran up the path as fast as she could, hardly conscious of the ache in her head or the weight of the canvas roll still across her shoulders. It was all her fault. If she'd accepted Allyn's help she'd have been safe. Kirsty too. She'd endangered not only her own life with her ignorance and prejudice, but everyone's.

She hated herself.

17

Elias waited, still hidden, as the faspane he'd challenged performed some sort of rite of death. It mostly involved ritualistic singing and mock stabbings. Seven warriors stood in a loose circle around his opponent, all of them watching. The rest remained hidden, but he'd marked only two.

The faspane bowed to each point of the compass, dropped to his knees and mock-stabbed himself yet again. Elias winced. He'd witnessed the real thing and the dagger looked very sharp. The faspane followed the mock suicide with a rather tuneless song, the words so badly mumbled Elias had no idea what they were. He'd heard some faspane believed that performing these rituals just before risking death would protect their souls if they died from the event. It might be true.

He glanced at his unstrung bow, unsure what to do with it. He couldn't hold on to it during the fight and he didn't trust the faspane to leave it alone. Still, he had no other choice. If he left it where it rested there'd be little chance it would still be there afterward. Assuming he survived.

Elias hefted his blade, holding it uncertainly. In this fight he would be relying entirely on his natural speed and strength. He glanced at his opponent again, doubting it would be enough. The warrior looked like he'd had more duels than most human freebooters.

"Izzat fool. Are you ready?"

Elias took a deep breath, trying to bolster his courage. He knew what they'd be thinking. Elias stood a head taller than the tallest faspane there, and was as broad across the shoulders as any blacksmith. Though most faspane were lighter built than an average human, they usually outweighed their immortal cousins.

"I'm ready," he said in Faspeneth, smiling with false courage as he stepped into the clearing. He dropped his bow at the edge and hefted his sword. He removed his light cloak, dropping it with his bow. He had arms a shivra would be pleased with, but the faspane didn't seem concerned, particularly not his opponent. He shrugged to adjust his sleeveless shirt as he swung the sword back and forth.

His opponent's expression changed to a sneer. "So mongrel, are the izzen now mortal?" His sneer became a confident grin. "Was your mother a bear or a shivra?"

"Izzen, body *and* soul."

The faspane lost his mocking expression at the reminder his own soul wasn't immortal. "What do you call yourself, mongrel?"

Elias tried to look confident. "Your opponent. You?"

"Thule."

"Thule, are you a coward or do we fight?"

"The bear wants a brawl?" One faspane called from the edge of the clearing. "Pity he'll only get the edge of a blade."

One faspane stepped forward, this one with a hint of grey in his hair. "I'm Kaibahr. It's my duty to oversee this duel and ensure honour is kept. Are you the sorcerer who laid the trap at the cabin?"

"No, and there was no trap. Your wizard's stupidity caused that, so take revenge among your own. Are you going to challenge me next?"

"I won't have the chance. Begin!"

Elias barely caught his opponent's thrust. Metal slid along metal as he barely turned Thule's blade away. He wanted to swear but had to parry instead. Faspane may stick to the rules, but it didn't mean a fair fight. He caught the next two swings before trying one of his own, more to test his sword than to wound his opponent. Thule changed his posture in response, aware of Elias's speed and strength, but seeming more relaxed than he had been a moment ago. Elias hid his irritation. His lack of skill must be showing.

Thule circled to force Elias to turn; another distraction. Several more faspane emerged from the trees, filling in the circle at the edges of the clearing and cheering for Thule. Elias didn't expect any to interfere directly as honour would keep them from going that far, but it didn't stop jeers and insults.

Thule swung, but Elias slapped his blade away. "You fight poorly, half-blood," Thule said. "Your father must have been a shivra goat herder."

Half the faspane laughed, but Elias tried not to react. Anger wouldn't help. He blocked a swing but Thule dropped the tip of the blade and cut upward. Elias jumped back, the edge of the sword almost opening his groin.

Thule grinned. "No matter your tainted lineage, your ancestors betrayed our ancestors. Cowards, all of you. Your kind should stand up to the Higher Realm, not cower before the Gods and beg forgiveness."

"We retained our immortality. How did your people fare?" Elias had to jump back or get skewered. A blade through the heart would kill him as easily as any faspane. He kept his own weapon low in a two-handed grip, even though the hilt wasn't quite long enough. He had no ridged arm-guards or leather armour like his opponent, making his only defence speed and strength.

Someone called from the side. Kaibahr's voice. "Izzat, you have more hair on your arms than a sheep. Is your back likewise furry?" Elias's fingers whitened around his blade. He had very little hair on his arms, but izzen had none.

Thule swung and Elias easily caught it. They exchanged several quick blows before they separated to circle. A flush in his cheeks showed Thule's efforts. Elias felt his own brow growing damp from tension. Thule stopped circling left and moved right. Elias took advantage and struck.

Thule backed up and Elias pushed, keeping the faspane on guard and forcing him to turn in the undergrowth beside the clearing. The war band scattered to allow them room, but Thule managed to avoid tripping and circled back to the centre of the clearing. He took several nicks to his upper left arm and one light slash through the studded leather protecting his chest, until a high swing forced Elias away.

Elias took the moment to wipe perspiration from his face while keeping his eyes on his opponent. The war band had fallen silent, more enthralled with the fight now than with heckling.

Breathing heavily, Thule flexed his injured arm before circling again. Thule yelled and leapt forward with a huge overhead swing. Elias slapped the sword away, but Thule forced Elias to defend again and again. They circled, clashed, attacked and circled. Thule began to push him harder, outclassing Elias.

Elias watched the faspane's face. Thule must have realised Elias had more stamina, strength and speed, though Thule retained the advantage thanks to his skill. Both needed to finish it quickly. Elias swung hard, knocking Thule's blade down, but the warrior countered and Elias barely twisted away.

Nicks and cuts bled on Elias's arms and chest. He barely remembered taking any of them. They were beginning to sting more from his sweat than anything else. His own attacks inevitably met his opponent's blade, or swung through air. Strength and speed weren't compensating. Desperate, he realised he may not survive this fight.

Thule slashed low and Elias blocked, but Thule used Elias's sword to turn his own upward, slashing Elias across the right shoulder. Elias grunted and backed away as blood ran freely from the deep gash. The wound began to throb.

Thule attacked again and Elias barely defended. Blood ran over half his arm and dripped to the ground. If he didn't do something quickly he'd be dead before he had the chance to run.

A look of victory crossed Thule's face. In a gamble chancing all, Elias waited for the next attack, blocked high and moved under the strike, bringing his knee up into Thule's groin. Thule grunted and dropped his sword, grappling Elias and dragging him down. Elias's shoulder struck the ground and he cried out, pain momentarily blacking his vision as he sprawled.

Thule reached for Elias's sword, his teeth gritted in pain, but Elias staggered to his feet, wrenching his blade away. He put his sword's point against Thule's neck. "Take your dagger and drive it through your heart or I swear I'll kill you myself," he said. The tip of his weapon drew a fine line of blood on Thule's neck.

Gasping for breath, hatred marred Thyle's expression. Defying the fear in his expression, Thule drew his dagger and placed the tip over his heart, gripping the hilt with both hands. "This is courage," he whispered as his eyes locked on Elias's, jaw clenched. He grunted as he drove the blade home, his face losing all colour. A slow sigh escaped his lips and then the warrior's head lolled.

Kaibahr entered the clearing, but the rest of the faspane remained where they were, silent. The faspane leader had trouble taking his eyes from his dead companion. "From the time you leave this clearing, izzat, you have until the count of ten. If you escape us, I suggest you don't try the sword again. Thule was one of our weakest. Most others would have killed you in the opening clash." He touched his forehead, then his heart. "From one warrior to another, for daring a weapon not your own."

Elias dropped his sword and clutched his aching shoulder. Blood still flowed. Too much. He glanced around the circle of warriors, eager to begin the chase. He should never have tried this. He would have been better off using his ghostwood bow as a staff rather than matching swords. Kaibahr was right. He would need more training if he expected to survive another sword fight.

He glanced into the trees, wondering if a count of ten would be enough. Even reinforcing his muscles with magic would be unlikely to help him in so short a time, and he didn't know how many remained in the forest. He staggered to his bow and picked it up with his good hand, leaving his cloak. It would only slow him. The warriors parted for him as he charged his muscles with all the magic he could deliver, and then sprinted.

Trees and brush rushed by as he counted. Three. He changed direction as soon as he was past the first dozen trees, keeping his head down in a vain effort to get out of sight. Five. The thick undergrowth both helped and hindered. Even if he managed to get away they would be able to track him by his trail of blood.

Seven. He ran past a surprised faspane who'd been keeping watch further out. He put his bow under his bad arm and used his opposite hand to keep pressure on the wound. Eight. He doubted he'd made a hundred yards.

Ten. He couldn't keep sprinting even with magic assisting him, but ran as best as he could. For an insane second he wondered if Caroline and Kirsty had felt this way when the wolves were chasing them.

Somewhere ahead a river raged with the spring melt, but with blood pumping from his arm and his head beginning to grow dizzy, he couldn't tell how far. Too distant to be any use. He slowed to a desperate jog, breathing hard, the sounds of pursuit clear. For the first time in his life he felt mortal. They were going to catch and kill him.

He needed more magic to keep running, but he was already growing weak. A warrior ran out of the foliage, sword whistling.

Elias ducked and punched hard, connecting with the faspane's jaw. The impact jarred his arm as the warrior fell. He desperately called more magic and directed healing energy to flood into his wound, but healing of any kind took massive amounts of strength. It barely stopped the worst of the bleeding.

Drawing on all he had left, Elias continued running. Pushing himself in such a bad condition would have consequences, but it allowed him to continue for two, maybe three minutes, all the while leaving a clear trail for them to follow. When he stopped for breath, he couldn't move his right arm at all and he'd tapped all his magical strength. He had nothing left but what magic he'd stored in a couple of crystals, and they'd require time and focus to use.

The sounds of running were getting closer, the warriors making no effort to keep quiet. Grimacing, he took a deep breath and staggered on. Faspane shouted, probably trying to make him run himself to exhaustion. No doubt they could see him. If he could get to the river it might carry him away to safety, or at least give him a chance. The sound of rushing water was loud now, but he still couldn't see it.

Something struck his left side and he sprawled on the ground, a fist-sized rock bouncing beside him. He winced with pain but staggered to his feet regardless. At least they'd thrown a rock and not a dagger. Toying with him.

Two warriors walked toward him, one holding a hefty branch. The sounds of more warriors told him the others were closing. Elias backed away, trying to heft his bow in defence. More warriors emerged from the trees, forming a loose half-circle and forcing him back through thickening undergrowth until water roared just behind him. He glanced back at a gorge a dozen yards from his heels, deep and rocky.

He backed all the way to it. Another step and he would fall thirty yards to the icy river's rapids, the white water slowed only by a few deeper pools gouged from the rock. The river would not carry him to safety. It would kill him.

The closest warrior taunted him, "Try it. Jump. No one could survive that torrent."

"He doesn't look confident now," another called. "How does mortality feel?"

A rock struck his shoulder and he grunted. There had to be a way out. Eight faspane surrounded him, tormenting him with their jeers. "You're going to die slowly, mongrel. Your magic killed some of us today. They never had the chance to take their own lives. For that, we're going to roast you for days and leave you for the animals, still breathing."

"We'll gouge your eyes out and break your knees and fingers," another said. "You'll beg us to end you."

"You'll scream when we charcoal your feet in the fire, izzat. We'll catch your friends first so they can watch you screaming." They crowded closer.

"We'll slit their throats and make you watch them bleed out, one at a time."

Elias's heels brushed space. Thirty yards to white water and a quick death. He dropped his bow over the edge to ensure the weapon would be lost. No faspane would ever use it.

Several warriors laughed at his defiance. They were almost close enough to grab him. Better a quick death, he decided. He leaned backwards to a thrill of vertigo and weightlessness.

"Grab him!" Hands reached - and missed. For a heartbeat he looked up at angry faces staring in disbelief, and then icy water swallowed him.

The cold shock almost made him gasp. He curled up as water churned over him, holding him down. He quickly lost the air in his lungs and panicked as the current finally swept him over rocks. He gasped air before white water washed him under again. It slammed him against boulders the size of carts, sucked him under and washed him around fallen trees.

He surfaced a dozen times, spitting and coughing water, each time barely catching a breath before being dragged under again.

He struggled for as long as he could, but his remaining strength quickly failed and the river carried him to oblivion.

18

Caroline's head pounded and perspiration ran down her face as she pushed herself to keep ahead of the others on the steep track. Hunger gnawed at her, but she couldn't face backtracking to ask Dobbin or Allyn for something to eat.

She stepped onto a protruding boulder and kicked a stone from the path, watching it fly into the undergrowth and disappear. She felt like that stone, out of control and at the mercy of others. It was a feeling she hated and didn't want to experience again.

She wasn't even sure if she should go home. It's what she wanted, but possibly the worst thing she could do to her family. Although at least there, she could lock herself in the dungeons over the full moon so she couldn't hurt anyone.

She trudged on, staying well ahead of her companions in case she said something she regretted under the curse's influence. Not that she was cranky at anyone but herself and her Goddess. The thought pulled her up hard. She didn't want to think of Marnier du Shae as her own Goddess. She hadn't made the choice to become a Divine Servant. She suppressed irritation that she didn't even know her own mind anymore. Walking on, she was determined not to dwell on it.

The Goddess's light within her was like the curse, clouding her thoughts and judgement.

How long would it take before the curse made her forget the things that mattered most, or the Goddess twisted her loyalties? Would they drive her to abandon the people helping her? Would the curse and Marnier du Shae work together and make her attack her family after she arrived home?

She tried taking a calming breath, but the anger remained. At least the scrapes on the back of her left hand were almost healed, a reminder she wasn't normal any more. Perhaps not even human. She pushed a tree-fern frond from her path as she moved on. Even the bruises were fading. Supernatural healing would be a wonderful gift if she didn't have to turn into an animal every full moon and kill people.

She wiped perspiration from her forehead and shrugged the bedroll against her back. The weight made her shoulders ache, but it also kept her feeling normal, so she welcomed it as she trudged on as fast as she could.

If Elias had gotten to her sooner she'd never have been bitten... She paused, wondering if that was her own thought or the curse's influence. If she'd accepted help though...

"Enough!" she hissed aloud.

She couldn't afford to dwell on it if she wanted to stay sane. She touched her mother's ruby necklace, her fingers tracing the circular shape. She imagined she could sense the magic in the ruby now, like a subtle tightening on the skin of her fingertips.

Bitterness returned. Allyn should never have removed the necklace. If she'd been given more time to fight the curse... "Stop it!" She grasped her head, wishing she could pull the angry thoughts out. "This in not Allyn's fault."

Every curse had a weakness, didn't it? She would discover hers. Yet if the curse took her and she hurt or killed someone, would Allyn kill her with the silver-dipped arrow? Would she want him to? Yes. She'd ask him to do it if it came to that. She'd demand a promise.

With the breeze at her back carrying a hint of smoke from Dobbin's cabin, she climbed onto some boulders embedded in the side of the mountain where the path turned back on itself, breathing hard.

Although she couldn't see most of the path, the track zigzagged its way down the mountain. It was barely three inches wide in places, rocky and muddy and overgrown. One slip would kill her. Caroline gingerly touched the back of her head where blood still matted her hair. It throbbed.

Disjointed memories of what she'd heard in Dobbin's cabin returned unbidden. Had Elias argued with Allyn to kill or abandon her? She clenched her fists in annoyance. Darker considerations fought to the surface, like the magic tainting her soul.

"Twice cursed," she murmured. "I need the wisdom of a temple." She glanced at her wrists. Did she dare enter a temple now? Even Marnier du Shae's? Perhaps the Divine Lady had been trying to protect her from this all along, presenting better options she'd failed to accept.

Could magic be exorcised? Could the curse?

Down the mountain, Dobbin and Kirsty were breathing hard enough to draw attention from the Gods. She spotted them a little over a hundred yards down, travelling slowly. On a path like this it would take them a while to reach her.

There was a comfortable looking ledge a few yards beyond the boulders, almost as if it had been made for travellers. She began to make for it, but hesitated. Something seemed wrong. It appeared too comfortable, as if boulders had been arranged on purpose. The stones before the ledge were too level, as if they'd been dressed and placed. There was no dirt between them, no grass or shrubs to deny easy access to the ledge.

She sniffed, and even though the breeze was at her back she recognised a hint of reptilian musk. She backed up a step, fear rising. Simorath snake people. She'd heard a childhood story about simorath traps designed to ensnare unwary travellers.

She backed another step, heart beating faster. The snake people weren't likely to attack a group, but a young girl, alone... She jumped down from the knee-high boulder to the path as rocks grated. A simorath burst out of the ground, short sword in hand. She cried out as it landed on the boulder before her. Smaller than a man and scaled all over where mail didn't cover him, it grabbed at her with a free hand, but suddenly stiffened and crumpled to the ground, a bolt in his back.

A faspane beyond the ledge stood up in surprise before anger coloured his tanned face. The simorath had prevented his kill. Another simorath catapulted out of the ground and almost rushed at Caroline until he saw his dead companion. The faspane drew a long, slightly curved blade.

Two more faspane moved into view above Caroline, crossbows steady on her. Trembling, she didn't dare call for help in case she drew her friends into the double trap.

Another simorath catapulted out of the ground, the creature dead before he hit the path with a bolt from one of the other faspane.

Caroline cried out as the faspane with the sword jumped over the trap and cut the other simorath down. He picked up first simorath's short sword and levelled at her. "Fight," he said with a thick accent. He tossed the simorath's weapon at her.

Shocked, she fumbled and dropped it at her feet, almost cutting herself.

"Pick up. Fight." He pointed to the blade with his own sword.

She glanced at the two faspane above her. One still had his crossbow on her, the other was reloading. "But..." Shaking, she picked up the wicked looking short sword and tried holding it with both hands, but the hilt wasn't long enough.

"Fight!" He slapped the blade with his own, almost knocking it from her hands. "Fight." He pointed to himself with his free hand.

Shaking, she nodded. What else could she do? She swung, but he knocked the clumsy blow aside with enough force to sting her hand. The sword thumped to the dirt path.

"Shameful."

She cringed as he raised his own blade to kill her just as two more simoraths catapulted out of their trap. One died on a crossbow bolt, but the second simorath fell before the faspane.

The faspane cut the creature down almost without effort. The distraction was enough. Caroline charged him, jumping up onto the boulder to try and knock him from the path.

He must have seen her because he twisted and used her momentum to shove her past him. She hit the ground a foot from the simorath trap, skinning her palms on rough stone. The hole was gone now though. "Better," he said.

He let her get to her feet, a dead simorath between them. She snatched up the creature's sword and raised it as the faspane approached. He smiled as if in approval, his own sword level.

She backed half a step, and then another, but stopped there. She had to be at the edge of the trap. The faspane gave her a slight nod. "Good fight, now. Honourable."

Given her choices, she decided on the one that would appeal the least to the faspane. "You lose," she whispered. Making the faspane come after her was the only way she could protect Allyn, Dobbin and Kirsty from a similar ambush. She stepped back and the boulder gave way.

She gasped as she dropped through the trap, landing hard and falling to her side. The sword clattered on stone as she lost it. The boulder silently moved back into place eight feet above her, leaving her in complete darkness. The rank smell of living creatures pressed in on her, along with the reek of blood. Boots moved in the dark. Many of them.

"Stay back!" She tried to stand as one of the simoraths hissed a command, but they rushed forward and cold hands grabbed her, pinning her arms behind her back. They dragged her over to the wall. Chains rattled as they prepared to restrain her. Fighting panic, Caroline struggled until one of them twisted her right arm back so far she almost screamed.

Light burst into the cave from above. The faspane she'd faced before fell in. He landed cleanly and cut down a simorath and then another before, rushing at Caroline. A dart hit his neck as a simorath crashed into him, but he knocked the reptilian creature aside and took a moment to pull the dart free. More simoraths rushed him. He swung to keep them back and tried for Caroline again, but they surrounded him.

The boulder closed in the roof, enclosing the cave in darkness.

A simorath cried out. She heard a scuffle, ending with a human-sounding grunt of pain. A body collapsed to the dirt and silence descended.

The smell of faspane blood filled the air.

Simoraths hissed in their own language, sounding angry.

Blinking in pitch dark as if it would clear her vision, Caroline tried to lift her head. A scaled hand pushed her face into the dirt. She struggled until manacles clamped around her wrists and ankles. They quickly locked the two chains together, ensuring she couldn't even stand.

"What have I done?" She should have chosen a quick death from the faspane.

Kirsty picked her way past a broken stone face as she moved into a small forest of tree ferns, their spring fronds three yards across. The previous season's fronds hung dry and brown, hiding the upper-half of the trunks. Something moved on her arm. She squealed and slapped it away.

"I thought Caroline was the princess," Dobbin said from behind her.

Kirsty took a deep breath to steady herself. "Where is Caroline?" she asked, looking ahead. "I haven't seen her in a while."

"Not too far," Allyn said. "Leave her be, she needs time to think."

Dobbin shaded his eyes. "Can ye see her, sorcerer?"

Allyn squinted, his expression slowly changing to a frown. He closed his eyes for a few moments, and didn't seem happy when he opened them again. "She's gone."

There was a long silence before Dobbin swore. "Snakeheads! Their filthy sliths are breeding at this time of year."

Kirsty felt a cold shiver despite the heat of exertion. "Simoraths?"

"We'd better find their cave. Fast. A nest of hatching sliths can devour a horse in hours. By dawn there'll be nothing left of her but polished bone."

Caroline lay on her stomach, her face resting on hard-packed dirt. Everything ached and the air smelled acrid. Darkness was total. She couldn't tell if her eyes were open or not. Every time she tried to move the chains clinked, her wrists and ankles still locked together behind her back. She was helpless to do more than lift her head.

As near as she could tell she'd been alone for hours. They'd taken the body of the faspane out some time ago, probably to feed their sliths, and hadn't been back. She could still smell his blood. The smell of it made her hungry, which in turn sickened her.

Alive, she had a chance, at least. If only she could break the chains. She tried, and only bruised herself. The best she could hope for now was slavery.

With the growing instincts of a werewolf, her body told her the sun had set. Perspiration coated her wrists, but the cuffs were too tight to slip, even with the moisture.

She spat dirt as a distant door creaked open, the sound of its hinges strange after so much silence. She held her breath as a claw scraped on stone somewhere down the corridors, the sound echoing. She pulled at her chains, the clinking making her cringe. What would they do to her?

Sibilant voices echoed through tunnels, raised in disagreement.

The arguers stopped just outside the room, the sounds of their disagreement muffled behind a door she couldn't see.

Caroline pulled uselessly against the chains until they cut, not caring now how much noise they made. She caught her breath and stopped only when she heard a brief struggle outside the room, followed by a body crashing into the stone wall. A moment later one of them ran off, their chain armour jangling. Silence returned, save for harsh breathing outside the door. Whoever was out there drew the bolt back and shoved the door open. The rattling chains cut into her wrists and ankles, but she didn't care. She pulled harder, her skin growing slick with what she thought was sweat until she caught the smell of her own blood.

Lantern light almost blinded her. She squinted and could just see.

The creature said something in its sibilant language as it slunk into the room like a thief preparing for murder, reeking of musk and dirt. Except for the wide mouth and hairless, finely-scaled green skin, the snake-man could almost pass for a small human on a dark night. A cloaked human with no whites in its eyes.

It knelt beside her, its breath reeking of the fresh meat it must have just eaten. She struggled harder despite the pain, desperate. It spoke in her language. "We would have sold you for slave, but need fresh meat to feed hatching sliths. Pity. Red hair humans are valuable."

Sliths? Gods, no. She pulled at the chains until she cried out in pain. Her wrists felt like they were dislocating. The simorath opened its wide mouth and fangs dropped down.

"No, no. Please. Sell me as a slave. Please!"

One cool hand pushed her face into the dirt floor while the other gripped her elbow in a painfully strong hold. She struggled with a cry of fear and jerked as the simorath bit her arm. The pain lasted only a moment before numbness spread.

Sweat broke out in rivulets on her face. "Please..." she begged as if the bite could be undone, but it seemed even lycanthropy couldn't save her now.

Her entire body felt numb by a count of twenty and though she kept trying to struggle, the sound of the chains fell silent. A moment later she heard a final rattle; her body twitching in reaction to the venom, but by then she couldn't feel anything at all. She wasn't even sure if she was still breathing. The simorath removed the chains to flopping sounds; her limbs hitting the ground.

She couldn't scream. She couldn't do anything but stare.

19

———

Caroline heard a soft rip as if slightly damp parchment had torn. A lantern by the door shed just enough gloomy light to reveal hundreds of translucent, soft-looking eggs stuck to the floor and walls, each about the size of a thumbnail. A tear filled her eye and blurred her vision, but she couldn't blink it away. She desperately looked around for the source of the tearing sound, wishing she could move even a little.

The room reeked of acrid mucus from the sticky silk protecting the eggs from small insects which seemed attracted to the smell. More food for the grubs later, she guessed. Dozens of crawling insects had been caught already.

She'd watched the dull brown two-legged slith laying them, its thick body like a fat see-saw dipping up and down, swinging its stumpy tail back and forth as it carefully placed each egg before weaving a fine silk over each cluster. Within the translucent shells and sticky silk she could see pale grubs curled around themselves. She suspected there were hundreds more eggs beyond her sight.

A paralysed clansman lay on the other side of the chamber, staring back at her with drool pooling around his slack mouth. His face was as expressionless as hers must be, even half-hidden by his shaggy grey beard. His older eyes betrayed fear, the stoicism of his people ruined by the knowledge he would soon die here, eaten alive. Paralysed like her, there was nothing he could do. Dressed in family colours of greens and reds, he was certainly not a Fandelyon man. Not that it mattered. She'd help even a faspane avoid such a fate if she could. Even if they were rescued, there was no cure for simorath venom. They'd just take longer to die.

Perhaps he thought her a clanswoman because of her red hair. If not, would he help a Kingdom girl? It didn't matter. The venom ensured neither would move when the grubs began eating them. Hopefully she would bleed out and die quickly.

The clansman's eyes examined her hair as if trying to place her, before moving to an egg barely six inches from his face. A moist, fat slug slowly emerged and began eating the soft eggshell under its protective layer of silk.

Morbidly watching the pale grub, Caroline felt guilty relief that it was closer to him than her. She couldn't find the will to look elsewhere. At least for a few minutes more, she could tell herself someone would rescue her and everything would be okay. She imagined she could feel the venom in her veins, numbing her muscles. She wished she could feel anything, even her own breath.

She wanted to curl up against her mother's warmth and close her eyes and not have to endure this torture, but the conjured image didn't last for more than a moment against the reality. Why not just slit their throats?

Desperately, she closed her eyes and prayed to Marnier du Shae for help, for anything, even a quick death. As the final words left her thoughts she felt a hint of her breath on her lips. A thrill of hope rushed through her. The sensation, barely perceptible, renewed itself with the next breath.

Despite everything she'd heard about simorath venom having no cure, she felt sensation on her lips. Elated, she offered another prayer of thanks, begging the Higher Realm for more sensations across her entire body.

When feeling returned to her limbs she would crush every egg and the disgusting slugs they held. She tried to move her lips. Nothing. She waited a minute, another. The feeling didn't spread. She remained immobile, unfeeling except for the hint of breath. Across from her, the slith grub had eaten over half its shell. The clansman couldn't seem to focus on anything else.

She closed her eyes. No miracle then. The Higher Realm wasn't going to save her.

It must be the lycanthropy slowly purging the venom from her body. Too slowly. She desperately waited for the tingle in her lips to spread to her cheeks, her jaw, anywhere, but what little hope she had died at the sound of a slug tearing through an egg behind her. One miracle wasn't enough, if she could even call it that. The curse would take far too long to save her. Days or even weeks perhaps. The slith grubs would have eaten her by then.

Instinct told her the night was more than half past and the moon up. Maybe eight hours had passed since the simoraths had caught her. Hundreds of grubs would soon be crawling over her like maggots. She'd be nothing but bones by dawn.

She prayed for an answer but felt no inspiration, even though she could distinguish the scents of dozens of simoraths who frequented this part of their tunnels. Even if she escaped this chamber, she'd have to get past them. Further away there would be hundreds more simoraths and more sliths than she wanted to think about. Even if her friends knew where to find her, Allyn and Dobbin couldn't get past them all, probably not even with magic.

If only she knew how to use her own magic, or even what she could do with it. Just now she was desperate enough to risk her soul for the use of magic that might help.

She hesitated at the thought of a darker possibility. If she could make the curse work faster and force it to change her, she might survive. Would it force Marnier du Shae to withdraw her blessing if she did? Would she care?

Refusing to give in to something so dark and evil was commendable. Encouraging it was possibly more evil than the curse itself. Perhaps a painless death was the only miracle she'd be granted, and yet, deep inside, she couldn't accept that either. Another egg tore. She found it a few feet from her face. The sight of the wet slug gave her all the incentive she needed to try.

She willed the curse to take her. Nothing. No inspiration, no feeling, no sense of what to do.

Change, she shouted in the depths of her mind. *Take me!*

Seconds passed. She began to panic. She could see one of her hands from the corner of her eye. No twitch, no movement, no fur. She tried to remember her battle with the curse but found nothing to help her.

The moon was up, no longer completely full, but present and seemingly as aware of her as she was of it. Or at least her strange new werewolf senses told her so. She concentrated on the moon. Perhaps if she tricked herself into believing it was full...

The moon is full, the moon is full, the moon is full...

She let the thought consume her. The moon was waning, but only just. She focused on it and pretended she was basking in the sensation of its full presence. She imagined it glowing orange as it cleared the horizon between two mountain peaks while she stood facing its light.

Something very much like a shiver passed through her, less a physical sensation than a stirring presence buried deep inside. Hope surged. She focused on the feel of the moon at its fullest when it would draw her darkness to the surface. She silently called on the moon's energy to take her in its grip and crush her body to its will.

The dark presence within stirred again, but quickly subsided back to dormancy. The curse seemed to be a conscious presence, still too immature to rise up and consume her. It must be protecting itself by denying the change. Her body, however, felt the curse's power. Her heart, dulled and slow from venom, throbbed. For a second her vision darkened as she felt a surge of blood pound through her ears. It was working. Her legs twitched.

Again, she said to herself. She focused on the moon, imagined it large and full, barely above the horizon. Her heart throbbed again.

Blood surged, scouring the venom from her veins. Another strong beat. Another.

Her face tingled and she felt the fine hair on her arms prickle with gooseflesh. She kept the vision of the rising moon in her forethoughts, imagining she bathed naked in its light. The curse, a malevolent presence hiding in her mind like a malignant growth, began to wake. She felt it like a physical part of her body. Opening herself to the imaginary full moon, Caroline shuddered as it took her in its grip. She heard a whimper as her breath came faster and her heart thumped harder. Perspiration rolled down her cheek.

She felt it.

Sensation swept through her like a cold shiver as overwhelming rage and bloodlust welled up. If she hadn't been paralysed, she would have lunged at the clansman. The rage turned inward, the room darkened and the curse drew her into a dream.

She stood on the edge of a cliff while a wolf pup struggled to its paws a few feet away, snarling. Although it was as awkward in its youth, it stood almost as tall as a grown wolf.

"Fool!" the wolf said. "You'll destroy us! Let me sleep."

Caroline stiffened as the wolf took a step toward her, its movements as unsteady as the first steps a human toddler might take.

"On your knees," the pup said.

Caroline saw a silver collar and chain on the rock, the long chain buried in the stone as if dipped in water that had frozen over. "No."

"Kneel. Now!" the wolf snarled. "Before we're lost! I must finish what you've began." The wolf took another unsteady step forward, but Caroline had nowhere to go.

"I won't be chained," Caroline said. "Not to your will."

The wolf snarled. Muscles bunched as it leapt at her throat. She braced herself and struck back, surprised as she knocked the wolf away as if slapping a puppy down. It rolled, snarling, and struggled back to its feet.

Inspiration gripped Caroline. The curse truly was immature and its weak manifestation proved it. That's why it had suppressed her memory. It needed time to mature. She grabbed the collar and ran at the wolf, pinning it to the ground.

"No!" it howled. She forced the silver circle around its neck. It kicked and struggled and tried to bite, but she held it down and locked the collar into place. The chain held it to the cliff.

The world shifted.

Caroline screamed in agony, or thought she did. Pain shattered her body's immobility and she flopped like a newly landed fish, crushing eggs and shredding sticky silk. She gasped and stiffened as her limbs cramped. She struck out, smashing dozens more slith eggs with a swipe of her arm, an arm covered with thickening hair.

Divine Lords and Ladies, what had she done? Her newfound fear submerged under a wave of primal anger and hatred while heat flushed her body. She wanted to bash her way through the door and kill every simorath she could find. Her body tossed violently, crushing dozens more slith eggs.

A sudden thirst for blood and flesh had her thrashing again. She needed to feel reality, cold stone against her fingertips, anything, but her hands wouldn't flex. Another wave of bloodlust shoved her against the edge of sanity. The moon's influence drove her flesh now and it was all she could do to hold onto consciousness.

She howled as her ribs cracked and bent before reforming. Thick hair erupted all over her body while her muscles cramped. She couldn't breathe. Pain became her entire existence. Caroline felt her skull almost shatter as her jaw dislocated and extended. She drew a breath and screamed in agony, the sound transforming into the howl of a wolf. The moon continued its destructive pull, reforming her from human to animal. She curled into a ball, her muscles and bones an agony of fire. She writhed, wishing the sliths would eat her.

The pain eased as the heat of the transformation dissipated and she lay on her side, her breath coming in short, sharp pants. An ache lingered, but nothing like it had been. After a moment she lifted her head to sniff the stale air, recognising simoraths and sliths and butchered animals and people. Her sense of smell had been good before, but now an entirely new dimension had opened. The entire world was made of scent.

She kicked her torn and useless clothes clear of her body and gained all fours, squishing a slith maggot under her front right paw.

Caroline turned her ears at a distant whisper of footsteps. Someone far away was running toward her cell. She instinctively bared her teeth, her hackles rising. They'd heard her screams. Her howl. She cocked her head. Tough, bare feet and clawed toes. The sound of chain armour. A simorath. She snarled again, backing away from the door.

The man across the room stared in terror before his eyes rolled back into his head and he lost consciousness. He smelled like rotten flesh already, a stench her own body was scouring away. It would be a mercy to kill him, but she didn't want to kill a human. A simorath, though. That was different.

The door burst open and an unarmed simorath stepped, big mouth agape.

Oh, sweet joy! She leapt.

20

There'd be a frost tonight, Kirsty guessed, her breath visibly wafting before her. She tried to pay attention as Dobbin stood motionless near a cluster of boulders, but it was already closer to dawn than the previous nightfall. Despite exhaustion, tension kept her awake.

"I think I've found the mechanism," Dobbin murmured, his gravelly voice barely carrying. He bent over, fingertips lightly brushing the place where two boulders met. His breath formed huge plumes in the still air. "Let's hope she hasn't been poisoned."

"With enough time I can deal with the poison," Allyn said, the words a relief to Kirsty. "Let's just get her out."

Clouds shrouded the moon, making it difficult to see much more than shapes in the dark - certainly not an entrance to simorath caves. Kirsty shivered. Every time she thought of what Caroline may be facing she felt a little more fear and a little less hope. Every moment might be the extra second they needed to save her, and until now they'd found no trace.

"If sliths are hatching, we may be too late already," Allyn said softly.

Tension tightened around Kirsty's ribs. Dobbin shot her a quick glance as if her reaction gave her away, but he turned back without comment. They were treating her like a child.

"No need to waste more time, then," Dobbin said. "Let's get in there."

"Is it a door of some sort?" Kirsty drew the courage to ask. She expected a key or lever would be needed to open it.

"A trap, lass." Dobbin pointed at the place he'd touched. "Gap there - slight draft coming from within." His finger moved. "Rub marks there and there. The problem isn't finding it. It's figuring out how it work without setting it off."

"I'd assumed a simorath had grabbed Caroline and hauled her off," Kirsty replied.

Dobbin shook his head. "Cowards set traps."

"What now?" Allyn asked.

Dobbin considered the trap for a long time. "We'll have to trigger it, preferably without getting caught."

"Any ideas? This is your area, not mine."

Even in the gloom, Kirsty could see the concerned look Dobbin directed at Allyn. "Unfortunately, there may be no other way than risking ourselves - not from the outside."

Allyn's ears dropped as if he hadn't expected that answer. Kirsty's heart sank almost in time with Allyn's ears. "Is there any way to trigger the trap and jam it open? Say with a stout branch?" she asked.

Dobbin shook his head. "Possible, lass, though I'd hate to rely on the branch. Probably get crushed."

"I could try to force it open with magic, but with faspane so near..." Allyn trailed off, obviously not liking his own idea. He glanced toward Kirsty, his expression hidden in the dark. He'd probably just remembered human aversion to magic.

Kirsty looked down with fresh tension. Magic evoked all sorts of emotions she didn't want to embrace, mostly fear and excitement. Her curiosity that disturbed her. She wanted to know how it worked and was afraid to ask.

"Risky," Dobbin said.

Shivering with disquiet, Kirsty sat and pulled her knees under her chin. "Would they really feed Caroline to sliths?" she asked. It was both disgusting and frightening. The fact it was Caroline made it much worse. Caroline was her princess, her friend, and the only person who'd ever taken a real interest in her and treated her with respect. The izzat and shivra turned toward her as one, their expressions difficult to see. She suspected neither wanted to answer.

Dobbin sighed. "Any other time of year I'd say they'd be selling her to slavers. Early spring though, their sliths are breeding. They care more about their sliths than gold."

She shivered again. "But..." She didn't know how to say it. "Why people?" Speaking Caroline's name aloud would make it too real.

"Sliths like fresh meat, lass. The fresher the better. Insects, animals, birds. Whatever. Snakeheads chain serious lawbreakers and enemies prone to the ground in breeding chambers, and make other prisoners watch them being eaten alive. When merciful, they paralyse the prisoner instead."

The thought of anyone being eaten alive made her nauseous. "But there's still time, isn't there?" Even if Allyn could deal with the poison, saving Caroline would be much easier if she weren't paralysed.

Dobbin nodded. "Of course, lass. Of course."

Allyn's eyes lingered on Kirsty's a moment longer, as if gauging her reaction.

"Stealth's our only chance," Dobbin added. "And springing a trap won't achieve it. There could be hundreds of snakeheads in there."

Hundreds? They needed an army or a better way in. They needed Elias at the very least. She wished she weren't so useless. She'd even use magic herself if it would help Caroline. She sighed and looked back down the dark path, hoping to see Elias. She could barely see to the bend, while the nearby trees were shadows against a greater darkness.

"You've a better option?" Allyn asked.

"No."

She saw a flash of teeth as he grinned. "Then we'll spring it."

Kirsty thought she saw Dobbin shake his head. "Opening it's easy. Keepin' it open's the trick. I've seen a few traps like this. There'll be some hefty counterweights involved. Unless ye've got a big rock that ain't going to block the entire hole, we're in trouble."

"Then it's got to be magic. If I bind it open rather than force it, it will create a lot less resonance. But that will mean you'll have to trigger it."

The shivra nodded without hesitation. "If it'll give the lass a chance, I'll do it. But yer going to have to follow me real quick."

Kirsty sighed with a nervous sort of relief. At least they had a plan, even if it did involve magic. She stood up, feeling better, but didn't approach.

"Wait until I create the binding, and then spring the trap on my mark." Allyn slowly moved his hands apart. Kirsty found herself holding her breath, expecting to see something spectacular. "Now," Allyn murmured.

Dobbin jumped onto the fissure. It didn't even begin to take his weight before he disappeared with a gasp. Kirsty almost cried aloud with surprise. A moment later a flash of light stole her vision. She covered her eyes with her hands until the bright spot dimmed. When she peeked again she was alone. The sounds of a scuffle reverberated from the hole, quickly followed by the crack of something like a skull hitting stone.

Silence.

The trap was still open, a gaping, horrible crevice in the rocks. She could see the hint of a glow emanating from within. She blinked a few times, but the glow remained. Apprehensively, she moved closer, peering over the edge.

Thick, meaty hands reached through and gripped the edge of the rock. She squealed and jumped back, almost stumbling. Dobbin's head popped up through the hole. He grinned. "All's safe for now, lass. Jump in and I'll catch ye." He winked, let go and disappeared.

A wolf howled somewhere deep in the tunnels, the sound echoing. Silence again. Kirsty cautiously glanced into the hole. A dimly glowing lantern rested on the floor near a wall. Dobbin and Allyn stood near it, peering through a doorway.

"Better yet lass, stay up there," Dobbin whispered from the gloomy hole. "Keep watchful though."

She was relieved she didn't have to follow, but guilt consumed her. She leant over the hole, hoping not to disturb the magic holding it open. Beside Allyn and Dobbin's dimly illuminated forms, she could see a heavy wooden door and a simorath slumped against the wall. Another simorath lay underneath the first.

She jumped as the wolf howled again, its cry echoing through the tunnels. She wondered if it were one of the captured animals used to feed the sliths. It sounded like it was in pain. Allyn and Dobbin disappeared through the dim doorway, both so quiet she couldn't hear them.

She watched for a long time, changing position several times to relieve tense muscles and trying not to worry about Caroline, Dobbin and Allyn. The danger they'd put themselves in... She'd make sure Caroline knew what they'd risked for her. The wolf howled several more times as clouds moved away from the moon, covered it again, and then moved away once more.

Distant, echoing footsteps reached her. Someone running. She cringed away from the hole as the sounds drew nearer. Heavy footsteps. Hard breathing.

Two figures burst into the room below, easier to see with the moon exposed. Allyn, with Dobbin hunched to keep from belting his head on the roof. Caroline wasn't with them. Running footsteps followed. Many footsteps. Kirsty's heart fell and she felt tears building. Caroline was truly lost to them.

Dobbin shoved his huge axe into his belt and stopped under the hole. "Allyn, quick. I'll give ye a boost!" His moonlit expression abruptly changed and he ducked. Kirsty didn't know if she'd seen fear or surprise.

A huge wolf's head burst through the hole, paws scrabbling for purchase. Kirsty screamed and jerked back. The wolf began to slide, nails scraping against rock. It couldn't quite pull itself out. Its green eyes caught hers, desperation on its face as if pleading for her help.

Instinctively, she reached out and grabbed handfuls of fur.

Instead of biting her, the wolf continued to claw itself out. She pulled, her strength barely able to make the difference. Abruptly the wolf came clear, shoved from behind, and Kirsty fell back to the path. She lay, breathing hard. When she looked again the wolf was gone. Her heart pounded. Caroline? They were her green eyes without a doubt.

Dobbin's upper body burst through the hole and a moment later he swung his legs up and over, nearly crushing her as he stood and got his bearings. He knelt, his head and shoulders disappearing into the hole. "Grab me a hand ya stupid bleeding pixie!'

Kirsty heard scuffling noises and scrambled out of the way. Dobbin's huge muscles bunched and he hauled Allyn half out of the hole as Allyn cried out in pain, kicked at something, and then came free as Dobbin pulled him the rest of the way out.

"I got bitten," Allyn gasped, clutching his calf.

"Close the bleeding hole!" Dobbin swore. "We can cut yer leg off later."

Allyn said something and Kirsty heard the rock crash into place.

Dobbin drew his axe again and pulled his shield off his back. "Kirsty, help Allyn. Get him as far up the path as ye can. There'll be dozens of snakeheads bursting out that hole soon. Go now!"

21

———

Fresh air washed over Caroline like warm sunlight on a winter's day. She breathed it in, rich and forest-scented, free of the suffocating stench she'd almost died in. The world seemed luminous with the scents of trees, flowers, dirt and animals. She could almost see individual odours. And her strength! She'd never anticipated the incredible freedom of running on four legs, her tail a perfect balance. The world felt new. Alive. Everything felt surreal, yet she felt *good*! Some small part of her knew she shouldn't, but oh! Breathing fresh air had been a desperate wish only a little while ago.

Yet she reeked. She shook, trying to remove the stench of the caves from her fur. The smell clung like a repulsive cloud.

The sound of a brawl in the cave spurred her into motion. She sprinted up the path and turned as it cut back above the trap, pausing well above Kirsty and Dobbin as the shivra reached into the hole. Below, Dobbin stood ready while Kirsty helped Allyn hobble away. Tiny as Kirsty appeared next to the izzat, he seemed grateful for her assistance, resting an arm across her shoulders for balance even as he leaned heavily on his staff. He shuffled like he'd been crippled, his right leg dragging.

She could smell them all distinctly. She shuddered as the icy burn of the poison paralysing Allyn's leg reached her. He mustn't have caught more than a scratch of venom or he wouldn't be able to move at all. She breathed in again. Their scents were more individual than their faces, though Allyn's scent remained subtle despite his wound. She turned her nose at Dobbin's sour odour. His smell pervaded the air like mist from a waterfall, as strong as freshly turned compost. He needed to bathe.

The rock before Dobbin grated. Her ears pricked up, a rather strange sensation. She wondered if Allyn and Elias felt something similar when their ears moved. Standing almost twenty yards directly above Dobbin she had a perfect view of the rock dropping down on a hinge of some sort, the same rock she'd stood on.

Caroline instinctively tensed as a simorath catapulted out of the hole, thrown up by others below. She jumped again as Dobbin's huge axe met the creature while it was still in the air, cleaving through its chest and throwing the body back to collide with the next one being catapulted out. Both tumbled into the hole, the second hissing.

She cheered, but the sound came out like a strangled whine, reinforcing the reality of her situation. The smell of blood wafted on the air, an intoxicating wine. She wanted it the way old Lord Vannenbalm seemed to need his wine. Worse. Much worse. She wanted flesh.

Dobbin stood ready again, his huge axe held high. Another simorath sprang from the hole and Dobbin swung, the sound sickening as his axe cleaved into the creature. He cursed as the body stuck on the weapon, forcing him to kick it free. Another scrambled from the hole and ducked under Dobbin's late swing as the limp body tumbled back into the hole. Before the shivra could swing again, the simorath charged, forcing him to lower his shield.

The simorath feinted left and dodged right, but Dobbin smashed the creature aside with the shield. It tumbled down the mountainside, but it had given two more the chance to make it out of the hole. They came at him with curved, wicked looking swords about a third the length of Dobbin's axe.

Dobbin retreated a step, his axe smashing a blade aside. The second creature risked jumping against the side of the mountain and springing back at Dobbin, but the shivra dropped his shield again and threw the simorath back toward his companion.

The scent of blood enriched the air, thick and fresh and as sweet as honey. Her stomach growled and she salivated, finding it difficult not to join in.

Several more simoraths scrambled out of the hole, forcing Dobbin further back. Six now, all lined up to attack. She heard him cursing, but couldn't make out the words. He kept his shield low. Twice as tall as his opponents and weighing more than any ten together, she could see he wasn't going to be able to hold them all back. There were already too many.

Two more scrambled out and moved down the mountainside as two others began climbing up to outflank him. The rest pushed along the path and still more climbed from the hole like ants. Dobbin hit one with his axe and the creature tumbled from the path, crashing loudly before something solid stopped it. Dobbin swung again, missing this time, but forcing them to keep their distance. He began cursing again, the words in another language. His own, probably.

Caroline counted a dozen simoraths. Her hatred resurfaced, strong and deep, fed by their treatment of her. The face of the man she'd shared a cell with flashed into her mind, but she backed away from the blinding anger his memory created. It would only take a single bite to incapacitate her. Dobbin, Kirsty and Allyn might face the same fate.

Despite Dobbin's size and skill, the simoraths climbing the side of the mountain would outflank him soon, forcing him to give more ground. She had to help. She heard herself snarl, a quiet sound compared to the chaos below.

Dobbin yelled something and stumbled back from a blade that nearly opened his leg. He didn't look hurt but his face was flushed. She smelled his desperation and a hint of fatalism. She understood his intention. He didn't expect to get away. He was willing to die to ensure Kirsty and Allyn had a chance. He'd risked his life to save Caroline as well.

Anger and bloodlust swamped her, fuelled by hatred, hunger, and loyalty. It was a suicidal gesture, but she sprang at the two climbing upslope. The leap carried her the full distance and her jaws caught the closest simorath's arm before she body-slammed the other, throwing them both from their feet. Tumbling, she felt another impact as they collided with a third creature, but it barely slowed her fall.

She rolled a dozen times before scrambling to a stop against a sapling, miraculously unhurt beyond a few bruises. She stood, realising she still held an arm in her mouth. Just an arm. The sound of tumbling bodies continued down the mountain. She resisted the urge to bite harder. Hungry, hungrier than she'd ever been in her life, she dropped the arm. She should feel sick, but it felt *right* and the torn flesh tasted delicious. She wanted more.

Bloodlust welled and she scrambled up the side of the mountain, her thoughts driven by the taste of flesh. She pinpointed the simoraths by sound and smell before leaping with a snarl and catching one from behind. She bit and crushed his skull like an eggshell and tossed the body aside just as quickly, the taste sending a quiver of joy through her.

A simorath jumped at her. She caught him by the throat and bit, decapitating him. The parts dropped to the path as others screamed and came at her, swords swinging.

She tore into them. Bliss! She barely noticed when the last one fell. Delicious blood soaked her muzzle and head and her fur was ripe with it. She picked up a still moving body and shook it until she heard bones snap and it went limp. She released the warm flesh with a snarl, its heart now silent, yet she was quivering with the desire to keep killing.

Silence. She looked around for another simorath, but only Dobbin stood near the turn in the path, shield and axe held ready. What a challenge he would be, but as the bloodlust eased she felt sick for even considering the thought.

He looked both relieved and fearful, his axe high and his shield low, his skin no longer flushed, but pale.

"Dobbin?" she asked, realising too late the sound came out as a growl. She took a step toward him, but he tensed, raising the axe marginally higher. She wanted to growl her frustration, but no doubt he'd take her growl badly. Despite all the warm flesh she resisted the desire to eat. Even famished, she didn't want to risk Dobbin's opinion of her falling further that it had already.

She sprang up the side of the mountain, not bothering with the path in case Dobbin took a swipe as she went by. He called something after her, but she didn't turn. She passed Allyn and Kirsty's scents but continued on, not daring to consider what they might think of her with blood on her muzzle and fur. Her hunger pinged freshly at Kirsty's delicious scent, but she managed to ignore it.

A dozen yards past them, she caught another living scent, a simorath. How she knew the creature was alive she had no idea, but it had quietly climbed up the side of the mountain while she'd slaughtered the others. She stopped, smelling venom and wood oil. Circling, she found the creature crouching beside an old pine tree, dry needles coating the ground. A female, judging by the smell. She had a crossbow aimed at Allyn.

Caroline growled loud enough to attract attention. The female turned with a start, her big eyes widening. A sense of satisfaction flooded Caroline, distilled entirely from the fear she'd caused. With the weapon safely off Allyn, she sprang. The creature was too surprised, or scared, to act.

Caroline struck full on, crushing the creature's neck in her jaws before her paws hit the ground again. She left the body where it was, not wanting to let bloodlust overpower her again. Instinct told her it was just fresh meat, but she doubted Allyn and Kirsty would consider it that way if they caught her eating.

She sprinted up the mountain, desperate to get away from the scent. It took a couple of hours to make the top of the pass. Once there she stopped amid ancient and twisted pine trees, panting. Snow-spattered twin peaks stood like sentinels to the east and west, the snow rapidly giving way to spring grasses.

As her pulse slowed she noticed a twinge of pain in her side and another along the back of her neck to her ear. Her hind leg throbbed, too. Hidden under the smell of simorath blood, she'd missed the scent of her own. Strange how she hadn't felt any pain during the slaughter. The wounds were closed already, but became more painful now she'd noticed. She walked on.

Far across the valley stood the last mountains between her and the lowlands of Fandelyon. They were smaller than the ones she stood between now. She longed for home, to crawl into her own bed and curl up. She would be happy to curl up anywhere just now. Hunger, however, kept her prowling.

She picked her way around the side of the west peak, until she found an outcrop of rock. It formed a cliff taller than the mighty trees that gripped the mountain below. She stopped above the tree-line, but below the snow-line. Somehow, everything felt *right*.

The scent of human habitation rose on the breeze and her stomach growled with renewed interest. Something about the human scent appealed far more than the flesh of simoraths. She suppressed a desire to investigate.

A long way below she saw a moonlit village, nestled against the mountains near a river. Traces of wood smoke rose from smouldering hearths. Patchwork farmland spread away from the village, filling the entire valley floor. It was one of the clan villages closest to the lowlands of Fandelyon.

Her stomach growled again, driving her to action. She moved back into the pass, discovering a new scent. She tracked it and soon saw a pink-eared rabbit with most of its white winter coat unshed. It was eating grass beside a weather-rounded rock. She allowed her instincts to take her downwind, and with preternatural skill had it kicking in her jaws before it even knew she was there.

Its scrawny body barely touched her hunger. She caught one more, and again it wasn't enough. Restless, she roamed until the waning moon began to close with the horizon. As the sky began to brighten she found the path again and lay near it, falling into an exhausted sleep before the sun touched the peaks.

She woke as she transformed back to human form, the sensation as pleasant as turning into a wolf was painful. Bright sunlight warmed her chilled, pale skin. Smiling, she curled closer into herself, and for the briefest moment she couldn't remember where she was. It wasn't until she noticed the long pink scar on her leg that memories rushed back. The taste of flesh had been sweet.

She ignored the stirring bloodlust and concentrated on the refreshing feel of the dew glistening on her skin. Refreshing, but icy. She shivered again, realising just how cold she was. Frost covered the rocks and grass surrounding her. As the bloodlust subsided, she found herself too tired to care about the cold. She put her arm over her face. Exhaustion pulled her back into sleep.

It was midmorning when the heavy tread of a shivra's footsteps woke her. She sat up with a start, expecting to see Dobbin a few feet away, but she remained alone on the mountain pass. She cocked her head. It was Dobbin's tread without doubt, but still some distance off, the sound of puffing accompanying the footsteps.

She relaxed. The breeze felt especially soft on her face and body, lifting fine strands of her hair and tickling her neck with them. It brought the smell of grass, pollen, and far off wood smoke, stirring her hunger again. Somewhere to the north she caught the song of a bird, and closer, a rodent scurrying through grass. Closer yet, insects buzzed among spring wildflowers. She smiled, feeling awake for the first time in her life. How could she have ever feared this?

As Dobbin neared, the breeze turned, bringing the scent of stale blood on his clothes. It smelled much the same as the blood on her skin. He smelled exhausted. She felt disappointed when the breeze turned and carried his smell away. His smell was comforting, though not particularly appetising. Not like Kirsty's. She tried not to think about that.

As he came into sight, she could see the exhaustion on his face, the creases in his forehead, the tightness of his bearded jaw and clenched teeth. His heavy breathing. She doubted a whole day of rest would be enough. She sat up and brushed grass from her skin, suddenly realising her eyesight seemed muted. Dull, compared to how sharp it had been at night. It didn't bother her. Her sense of smell more than compensated.

Dobbin stopped a dozen yards away with a gasp, quickly followed by a muttered curse. He'd only just noticed her.

"What?" she asked. "The blood will wash off. Hardly any of it's mine." She considered that for a moment. It didn't sound like something she'd normally say. Rather than rephrase it, she decided to tease him. "I could lick it off, if you like?" Although she was teasing, the thought was thrilling. He looked her over, his stance tense, a hand on his axe. She pulled her legs tighter to her chest, preferring not to let him see her fully naked.

"What?" she asked again, her sense of playfulness ebbing. She watched the familiar features of his face and could smell as well as see the tension about him.

"Are ye sane, lass?"

Perhaps the joke about licking herself wasn't her best. "Do I look insane?" she asked.

"Yer eyes are so dark a brown I'd almost call 'em black. Last night, while ye were tearing those snakeheads apart, they were as green as the sea ever can be. Almost green enough to pass for an izzat. Are ye sane, lass?"

Dark brown eyes? "I'm sane, Dobbin. Very." She watched, just as wary until he moved his hand away from his huge axe.

"Mind if I borrow your cloak? I'm a little bit naked."

22

———

A brief shimmer marked the appearance of two young women on a mountain's ledge. One had rare blonde hair and appeared about nineteen. The other had long white hair and seemed a few years older.

"That's them," said Kimbriel, the blonde woman. She pointed to a shivra, an izzat and two human girls in the pass across the valley.

"How long has it been, Kim?" Ellie asked as she looked around. "I don't recognise these lands and I grew up near mountains."

Kimbriel didn't take her eyes off the group. "The lands you remember sank a few millennia ago. The entire continent is now scattered islands."

Ellie turned, surprise showing. "How is that possible?"

Kimbriel shrugged. "War. The shivras and simoraths fought over a crystal, a gift from the Higher Realm. In the end they both lost, shattering the world with the destruction of the crystal." She glanced into the distance as if she remembered the submerged continent, or perhaps the war that caused it. "It's the reason the descendants of your people hate magic so much. The islands barely support a few dozen fishing villages now, all struggling to make a living from the cold sea. The rest migrated here. Everything you knew is gone."

The group across the valley distributed food and began eating. Ellie pointed. "And those two girls are descended from my people?"

"Yes. Their ancestors sailed north and conquered these lands from the Mistapol Empire in a Gods-inspired war."

"Which one do you expect me to betray? Who dies?" There was bitterness in Ellie's voice.

Kimbriel pursed her lips, as if she didn't like Ellie's tone, but she kept her eyes on the group. "The girl on the left," she said softly.

Ellie watched them. "I still don't see why it has to be this way. If it's merely about ensuring..."

"It's not."

"Then what? I can do this task without harm. The Higher Realm doesn't need the girl."

"The world has moved on, Ellie. The task is no longer yours."

"Perhaps if I'd known I'd been set a task..."

There was an awkward silence, after which Kimbriel's tone softened. "Perhaps she'll survive. You did."

Pain crossed Ellie's face again. "She's a child, Kim. Innocent."

"So were you."

"But I can protect her!"

Kimbriel watched the group for a long time. "I'm sorry, Ellie, but you quit this world, leaving nothing but your Covenant. Now it's time to break it. She's the cost, the first of many to pay it no doubt, but necessary. Putting yourself in her place will achieve nothing."

"I'm fine with achieving nothing." Ellie's voice regained its bitter edge.

"I suspect you'd regret that even more. The Higher Realm wants this resolved. It's been too long already. The Gods are growing restless."

"There has to be something else I can do."

"Of course, if you're willing."

"Anything."

"Pass your Covenant to me and take *my* part in Noramgaell. I'll accept your burden, gladly, if you take mine."

Ellie looked away, shuddering. She shook her head. Kimbriel

touched her arm. "We all have our place, Ellie. That girl has a part too, but she can't play it without your leave."

Ellie stared at nothing. "I... I can't. She'll die in agony. Alone."

"Alone? No one demands she die alone." Kimbriel gently squeezed Ellie's arm. "You have to fix your mistake. The Gods demand it. *All* of them."

Real hurt flashed across Ellie's face. "Mistake? Saving innocent girls? Am I being punished for compassion?"

"You're being given a chance to fix things."

"Fix things? How many girls have I saved? Thousands! Hundreds of thousands!"

Fury crossed Kimbriel's face. "You saved none, Ellie, not one! It should have ended with you. That girl will die because of you! It wasn't your compassion that created the Covenant but your anger and hatred. *Your compassion* would have avoided this." Her voice dropped, the heat leaving it. "Your task now falls to another." Almost whispering, she added, "And to as many as it takes."

Ellie's shoulders slumped. "I tried to make things better. How will doing this help? What will it achieve?"

"I don't know, but every time I've worked in direct opposition to the Higher Realm I've ended up worse off. If you don't believe anything else I say, trust that."

"You mean you don't know what will happen? Please don't make me do this, Kim. Not on faith. I need to know it's going to mean more than the deaths of thousands of girls."

Kimbriel sat, crushing the new grass and wildflowers beneath her, her arms drawing her knees to her chest. Ellie knelt beside her, resting on her heels. "Do as you will, Ellie. You know I can't force you and neither can the Gods. It'll go worse, though."

"The choice is mine? Honestly?"

"Of course. But this will be resolved. Compassion is the key here, and I suspect the Gods are giving you some just now."

"Making me do this is *not* compassion!"

"Giving you the chance is."

They glared at each other, but it was Ellie who turned away first.

"The Gods could have taken this out of your hands, Ellie. If they're forced, to I can guarantee you'll live with regret for the rest of your life. That girl will face a worse fate if you deny her, and so will many others."

"I only wanted to help."

"If you break your Covenant and it means a million girls die horrible deaths, then it'll be better than any alternative you could hope for. We have to work *within* the Higher Realm's plans. This will be your only chance. Take it."

Ellie's tears fell freely, each tear becoming a tiny diamond before striking the grass. Within moments, there was a small pile of tear-shaped jewels. "Trust you or the Gods?" Eyes bleary, Ellie wiped her tears away. "I *did* the right thing. I can't do what you ask, Kim. I swore."

Kimbriel glanced across to the opposite pass. "Perhaps you're wrong. Maybe she'll shoulder your burden and carry it better than you ever could. The Gods are never cruel, even if it appears that way sometimes. There's a plan here. Have faith, Ellie."

"Faith in that girl?"

"Yes. And faith in me. You know I wouldn't ask if it weren't for the best."

Ellie closed her eyes and let out a long sigh. More tears fell, tinkling as they struck those already on the ground. "Okay, but only because *you* ask, Kim. The Gods can..." She let the words trail off, perhaps not prepared to insult the Gods aloud.

The mixed group across the valley stood and began making their way northward toward Fandelyon.

Kimbriel squeezed Ellie's shoulder. "Thank you. You have a long journey to make. You'd better get going. Remember, once you dissolve the Covenant you can't interfere. You have to let her fulfil her own fate. Stay with the girl if you like, tell her stories, comfort her in whatever way you wish, even hold her hand as she dies, but don't *do* anything. You can't participate. This is no longer your world and breaking your Covenant is the only part you have in this. Promise me, Ellie, please."

Ellie bowed her head even further and wiped tears away again.

"At least tell me her name. If I'm going to be responsible for her death I should know her name."

"Promise first."

Ellie took a long, steadying breath. "I swear I won't interfere, no matter how much I think the Gods need a good kick in the... I do, however, reserve the right to offer whatever comfort and advice I deem fit."

"Thank you." Kimbriel glanced across the valley once more. "The child's name is Kirsty. Kirsty duPrey."

23

—————

Elias woke, painfully cold. He shivered and winced at a deep ache throughout his entire body. The filtered brightness above stung his eyes, but he concentrated on it regardless, trying to decipher the moving colours. Leaves, stirring to a gentle breeze. Small leaves. Draping willows.

He belatedly noticed the sound of a river and water lapping across his chest. Most of his body remained submerged. He'd been caught by tree roots, his bruised body washed up in a back-eddy. Face-up, fortunately.

He had to get out of the water before the cold drove him unconscious again. He moved, but gasped as pain shot through his side and shoulder. He ground his teeth, holding still until the pain subsided. A wound in his side ached, taken while travelling the rapids no doubt, but the cold had stopped the blood.

Wincing, he grasped a thick tree root beneath the surface. Holding it with aching fingers he closed his eyes and felt for the energy moving through the tree, the slow pulse of its life. Slipping into a trance, his heart slowed to match the flow of the tree's sap, thriving with spring. Directing a trickle of magic into the tree, he blended it with the sunlight the leaves absorbed to capture the sun's full spectrum of energy. The connection established, he teased a little of the tree's newfound strength back into his own body.

Time passed, his awareness limited to the movement of the sun across the sky.

When he sensed his worst wounds healing, he opened his eyes. It was well after midmorning, the sun approaching its zenith. Taking a deep breath he found the pain diminished and gingerly sat up to examine the gash in his side. It remained closed, but felt like it could tear open at any moment.

Like a decrepit drunk, he crawled from the icy water, soft mud squishing between his fingers. He didn't make it far before collapsing onto long spring grass, trying to remember when he'd kicked his boots free or struggled out of his cloak. No, he'd left his cloak at the clearing.

The smell of grass was as refreshing as the mottled sunlight on his back. The light breeze carried wood smoke and the smell of baking bread. Hunger forced a groan from him, tempting him to merge with a tree until completely healed rather than risk moving through human territory while wounded. Merging with a tree would take days he couldn't spare. He had to find Allyn and get to Delshere. He had to stop Phoenix.

He pushed himself to his feet, swaying until he found his balance. Beyond the rise was a ploughed field, the crops just beginning to sprout. Far across the stone-walled paddock, a young human farmer with a shock of red hair pulled out weeds. Further away stood a round house of mortared stone with a thatched roof. Smoke wafted from its chimney and several cows milled nearby.

"Persistence pays off," a self-satisfied voice said from behind.

Elias started. It took him a moment to recognise the language as Faspaneth and the voice belonging to the leader of the group he'd faced. He tried to remember the faspane's name. Thule? No, that was the warrior he'd killed. Damn. What was it?

He turned to find a crossbow aimed at his heart. The warrior sat on a fallen tree about fifteen yards away.

"Persistence is a *good* quality," Elias said, implying 'good' was something a faspane had no use for.

The warrior's half-smile came nowhere near his eyes. He indicated Elias's battered body with the crossbow. "I've been told to take you alive if possible, or bring back your body otherwise. I've also been told to give you a message and let you continue on to Delshere."

"Why do you believe I'm heading for the citadel?" Elias asked. Who would have given the faspane warning?

The warrior smiled again, and this time it seemed genuine. "Disobeying either command could see me dead. Not pleasantly." He didn't seem perturbed by the prospect.

Defenceless and exhausted, Elias shrugged. "If you intended to kill me you wouldn't have waited for me to recover. What's your message?"

The warrior smiled again. "True, izzat. I found you hours ago."

Elias grimaced. If he'd crawled from the water earlier, or fully merged with the tree... "How did you get here? Crossing those mountains in a night should be near impossible for a mortal."

The warrior frowned, his knuckles going white around the crossbow. "Remind me again of what my people have lost, and I'll see you dead and suffer the consequences. I have many reasons to kill you, izzat, and only one to leave you alive."

"And that is?"

Making sure Elias understood the significance, the faspane said, "Phoenix seeks the Silver Well. I want you to stop him."

Taken aback, Elias stared for a long moment. "Why betray him? I thought he was your prophesied leader?"

The warrior snorted. "Leading us on an ill-fated quest against the Gods with nothing but a promise of immortality will only deliver grief. As much as I despise your kind, I'd rather see him destroyed."

"And he can only be killed by the *Sword of the Sun*," Elias whispered. The faspane inclined his head. "Who commanded you to let me get to the citadel?"

There was something in the faspane's expression Elias couldn't read. "Phoenix."

"Phoenix? But..." Elias tried to see the reason, but exhaustion sapped his concentration. "What for?"

"I don't know. He's playing his own game. Your coming was also prophesied, as well as the red-haired human girl's."

Elias felt a sudden protectiveness toward Caroline and had trouble keeping a threat from his voice. "You were sent here to kill her." So many coincidences had aligned that only the Gods could be influencing them.

"Yes, but nobody foresaw you with her. Except Phoenix, and he wants her dead. You need to stop him reaching the Silver Well."

"The Well's been lost since the Crystal Wars, thousands of years past now."

"Our prophecies claim he'll find it. Be there when he arrives and kill him. Stop the war before it begins. Challenging the Gods again will only see my people suffer more." The faspane glanced away from the river, frowning. "It looks like we've attracted that human's attention."

The farmer was walking in their direction. The warrior stood and backed off before jogging upriver.

Elias pondered his latest misfortune as he began staggering in the opposite direction, still too badly hurt to move faster than a walk. He quickly realised he'd never get away. He spotted a small tuft of fur caught on a thornbush and knelt beside it, pulling it free. Rabbit hair. Desperately tired, he nevertheless took a single strand of hair and called forth as much magic as he could. In an instant the hair flashed into the appearance of a fully-grown rabbit made of light. He attuned the spell to Allyn's aura and entwined it with a message.

"Go," he said, exhausted. The rabbit bolted off along the river.

As the lean farmer stopped at the top of the rise, shock and surprise crossed his face.

"Lovely day, isn't it?" Elias said.

24

U nder Dobbin's huge cloak, Caroline wore her torn riding dress, but the cold mountain air seeped through regardless and the icy dew made her bare feet ache. She pulled her knees to her chest, making the cloak bulge. The movement dislodged crumbs from a hard biscuit Dobbin had given to her, all that remained of her meagre breakfast.

"Perhaps you should tell us what happened," Allyn said. He watched her cautiously, almost as if he expected her to turn rabid and attack. "I don't think anyone's ever done what you did."

Caroline glanced at her wrists, a little surprised the *alimoth* outlines were still there. It was reassuring to know the Divine Lady of Healing hadn't withdrawn her offer of Service, despiteCaroline's desire not to respond in kind. "I'm not going to bite anyone," she said.

Kirsty moved closer, showing her trust. "I know," Kirsty said. Caroline smiled and took her hand. Kirsty had helped clean the blood away using a rag and some water from Dobbin's flask.

"Not today, perhaps," Allyn said.

Caroline gave him a look. "Or tonight."

"Trust me, please. Explain it."

Everyone expectantly watched her. Dredging up the memories,

she shuddered. "Sliths were hatching. They were going to eat me alive." She felt Kirsty's hand tighten and squeezed back, but couldn't find the courage to meet anyone's eyes.

"Then what?" Dobbin prompted, his expression concerned.

"My only chance was the curse. The simoraths had paralysed me." Remembered fear began to choke her voice, so she took a deep breath before continuing. "The curse wasn't mature but I drew it out. It was like fighting a person. It was still weak and I chained it. Literally." She lightly tapped the side of her head with two fingers. "In here. In the prison it intended for me." She didn't feel anywhere near as strong now as she had last night, but that could be to do with the change of form. Or moonlight. "I'm sure I can change when I want to now." It was tempting. Even now she wanted to feel the curse's power.

"What about the full moon?" Allyn asked, sounding cautious.

"I don't know," she admitted in a whisper. Could she resist the full moon? She could sense it even now. By Allyn's expression, he didn't like the answer. "I'm fine. Really. Besides, Father can ensure my safety and that of everyone else."

"Perhaps." Allyn glanced at Dobbin and Kirsty. "We should get moving."

Caroline stood with everyone else, tired but at least alive. She shrugged to get her torn and crumpled dress comfortable. It seemed so loose now. She'd lost a lot of weight since the ambush on the road. She didn't have any spare boots, either.

"Are you really okay?" Kirsty asked. Her voice betrayed exhaustion.

"Yes. I just wish we were home," she said, although she had mixed feelings about that. She desperately wanted to see her mother and sisters, but feared what she might do come the full moon. "Or safe back at the abbey." She tried not to breathe in Kirsty's too-human scent. Her friend smelled good in the way a pie smelled good. The bloodlust from the previous night stayed away, fortunately. Hopefully it was only something that happened when she changed form.

Last night's scrapes had already healed, an indication she was a little more, or perhaps less, than what she used to be.

About half an hour into the walk Allyn paused. "We're going to have to hurry to stay ahead of the faspane," he said, his foot still dragging.

"And the simoraths?" Caroline asked.

"Keep watching for them. For any danger. It's all we can do." A sheen of perspiration gleamed on his brow, the stink of poison in it. He wiped it away and stared at his finger as if he'd never seen perspiration before. "Considering the trail we're leaving, we'll be easy to track, and there's only so much I can do to disguise our passage."

Everyone was in danger because the faspane wanted Caroline dead. It made her feel sick. "Just get me home. The sooner I'm there, the safer everyone will be." Everyone except her family. She'd have to figure something out to keep them safe.

"What are you planning on telling your parents?" Allyn asked, almost as if he'd been reading her mind. He was breathing hard, as hard as Kirsty, and poison-laced sweat dripped from his face. She hadn't seen him perspire even when climbing the mountain yesterday.

"I don't know." That was a conversation she'd like to put off indefinitely. "Where's Elias? Shouldn't he have caught up by now?"

"Still delaying the faspane, I suspect."

"Suspect?" She couldn't help the twinge of concern in her voice. She didn't know why, but she really didn't want to see him hurt.

"He's alive."

"How can you be sure?"

"It's something between izzat."

"Magic?" she pressed, trying to keep her tone neutral.

He gave her a look, his too-green eyes piercing. "Another day."

They walked on, the leaf-filtered sunlight warm enough despite the cool mountain air. She tried to enjoy the rich scents of spring. Each flower's perfume was quite distinct, though she couldn't name a single flower she'd seen. The trees and shrubs had their own unique smell, even among the same species. Like people.

Did izzat have similar senses? What about faspane? Could they track her by smell? She couldn't even begin to identify all the animals, birds and insects she could smell.

"Hurry up," Allyn called as she delayed. He was barely twenty yards further along the trail, and moving fast even though his limp was getting worse.

"I don't know how long I can keep walking," Kirsty said quietly to Caroline. "I haven't eaten properly in a full day and we barely slept an hour last night."

"Lean on me," Caroline said. The slight girl smiled thankfully and together they made their way down the trail. Kirsty barely weighed anything. "I still find it impossible to believe you're not afraid of me," Caroline said.

"Should I be?" Kirsty asked.

"Yes. You smell really good. It scares me just being so close."

"Really? What about Allyn and Dobbin? Do they smell good too?" She seemed more curious than afraid.

"Not so much. But I can smell the people in the valley." It was a distant thing, like catching the smell from a baker's shop every now and then. "Humans smell so much better than izzen, shivras, simoraths and even animals."

Kirsty sniffed the air. "Sometimes, I can smell a little wood smoke."

"I can smell three hundred and seventeen people." Caroline's stomach rumbled at the additional scents. "Breakfast time. Bacon, boiled and scrambled eggs, pies and pastries, toasted bread, porridge, honey, preserves, milk, tea. More." None of it smelled as good as the people.

Kirsty's stared in amazement.

"I can smell everything, Kirsty, even how people are feeling when I'm close enough. I can smell Allyn's pain and the taint of poison causing it."

Allyn leaned heavily on his staff, leaving a track a blind hunting dog with manure up its nose could follow. He seemed to have lost his coordination, tripping over everything and staggering against trees.

"Time for a break," Allyn said, breathing hard.

"Allyn's hurting more than he'll admit," Caroline murmured to Kirsty as the two young women leaned their shoulders against each other. Kirsty closed her eyes and seemed to fall asleep. Dobbin sat on the trail a few yards further on, while Allyn limped to a tree. The izzat sat and rested his back against the trunk like it was a drunken friend.

"Ye look like yer doing alright, lass," Dobbin said to Caroline. His cheeks were flushed as he looked her up and down. He smelled tired, though he kept it from his expression.

Caroline shrugged. "We're going downhill."

Dobbin raised his chin. "I'm a little unfit, but I'm guessing I could still have run ten times further than ya before yer run-in with the werewolf. More."

She smiled. "At the abbey I'd go red in the face climbing a staircase."

"Looks like that curse has become a boon, then."

She turned away, not wanting to mention Kirsty's enticing scent or the smells of the village and its people. "Not that much of a boon." Only the Higher Realm knew how she'd cope when she returned to Fandelyon City. If she got there. "I never thanked you for coming after me. All of you."

"Ye did yer share."

She wanted to accept the camaraderie, but if she hadn't got into trouble there'd have been no need. She'd still have a chance of fighting off the curse, too. It had changed her. She felt it, the process complete now. Instinctively she knew she could never return from that and wasn't sure she wanted to. The strength, the sense of power... Caroline distracted herself by watching Allyn. He remained with his arms about the tree. The longer she watched, the more she felt something wasn't right.

She noticed goose bumps on her arms. The hair on her neck stood up and a nervous energy made her restless. He had to be using magic, although she couldn't see anything. It disturbed her to admit she even knew, and she couldn't escape her ingrained response that magic was evil.

Magic had sunk her ancestors' homeland and shattered the world. If she learned to use it, would it keep her from entering the Higher Realm and being reborn? Was that the test Marnier du Shae had set for her? What of the curse? Did it taint her soul as well as her body? Marnier du Shae's luminous flowers remained, but she couldn't be sure.

The goose bumps didn't leave until Allyn stood. A look passed between him and Dobbin, with Allyn giving a slight shake of his head. What could that mean? What had he been doing with his magic?

By mid-afternoon they were almost down to the valley floor, but Allyn's condition was no better. He stank of pain. It was like following a wounded animal.

Allyn said, "We'll follow the valley west, away from the river, and keep to the trees until we can swing around to the next pass."

Was there a slur in his voice? Caroline glanced around, but neither Kirsty nor Dobbin seemed to have noticed.

"Shouldn't we wait for Elias?" Kirsty asked.

The izzat shook his head. His expression betrayed concern. Dobbin dropped his voice. "Did ya catch anything?" He glanced at the girls with an expectant, almost guilty expression. Was he hinting at magic?

Allyn shook his head slightly. "He's alive."

Dobbin grunted. "The sooner we get beyond all this, the better."

"Why are you so concerned for Elias?" Caroline asked. "Do you think he's hurt?"

"That's none of your concern," Allyn snapped, his voice edged with pain.

Taken aback, it took Caroline a moment to find a reply. "I want to know."

"You're going home, not with us. Unless that changes, mind your questions." His expression abruptly softened. He closed his eyes, pinching the bridge of his nose with his thumb and forefinger. "I apologise, Princess. I'm not myself. This damned poison..." He massaged his lame leg. "We'll discuss this later. I promise. Fair?"

It was probably the best she was going to get. "Fair."

Through the trees a patchwork of farmland lined by rock walls was visible through the trees. They began making their way around the valley. It took much longer than it should have, as Allyn couldn't climb and found it difficult getting around obstacles. He stopped occasionally, dropping to one knee and touching the ground. Caroline felt goose bumps each time.

"What are you doing?" she finally found the courage to ask.

"Ye can sense that?" Dobbin asked. "Can ye see it?"

She nodded. "There's greenish glow if I don't look directly. Can you?"

Allyn and Dobbin shared another look. "I'm confusing our trail," Allyn said. "Healing the forest of any damage we've done in passing, while nullifying the impressions our auras leave on the ground."

Magic. It didn't hurt so much now to admit it. She glanced the way they'd come. "I can still smell our trail," she said, concerned. It was as clear as a path would be to her eyes.

Allyn grimaced as he stood. "I doubt the faspane have such refined noses."

Close to dusk, they began arcing around to the north. Caroline's stomach growled. She hadn't eaten more than biscuits and water since dawn, but wasn't game to ask for anything, though Kirsty had twice asked Dobbin for biscuits in the last hour.

"We're going to need shelter," Dobbin said, shrugging the tension from his shoulders. "I suspect the wind'll cut through this valley like a storm tonight. We might even get rain."

Allyn nodded. "And I need to rest."

"That snakehead poison stronger than ye thought?" Dobbin asked.

Allyn nodded. "Fighting it off is draining almost everything I have." He lent back against a huge tree, closing his eyes while Kirsty and Dobbin sat on a log. Caroline felt goose bumps and that nervous tension again, and it remained until Allyn opened his eyes several minutes later.

A sickly sweet smell drifted in the air. She turned around to find a tree covered in masses of drooping pink flowers a long way up the slope. Perfume.

"I wouldn't be resting under there," Dobbin said as he followed her gaze.

"Why not?" Not that she would. The perfume made her throat ache.

"Dryad tree. Get close enough, they'll lull you to sleep and you'll never wake up."

Curiously, a rabbit hopped out of the underbrush next to Allyn. The izzat reached for the creature, but a flash of light made Caroline squeeze her eyes shut. When she looked again, the rabbit was gone.

"What was that?" Caroline asked nervously.

"Trouble," Allyn said, emerald eyes watching the forest in the direction of the village.

Dobbin cleared his throat. "About a mile northwest of here, there's an old clansman's house. We'll find warmth and a break from the wind, if not protection from rain."

"Lead on Dobbin," Allyn said. "We'll need time to collect wood before it gets dark."

Caroline glanced at Kirsty, but her friend only seemed concerned with moving. She put a hand on Kirsty's shoulder. "Need help?"

"I should be helping you," Kirsty said as she got to her feet. She sounded as drained as she appeared.

The sun had dropped well behind the mountains when they arrived at what had once been a rounded house. Part of a wall had collapsed and trees grew between what remained. The roof was decades gone.

Kirsty collapsed to the ground without bothering to clear forest debris or spread her canvas roll, but Caroline was too tense to rest. What did Dobbin and Allyn know? Were they all in immediate danger from the faspane? What happened with the rabbit?

"Dobbin," she said. "Allyn and Kirsty are not up to collecting firewood, so it falls to us." Dobbin turned sharply, clearly surprised, and Allyn paused in clambering over a broken rock. "What?" she asked.

Allyn spoke. "What princess offers to collect firewood when only days before would not have lifted a hand to dress herself?"

Darn. She thought she was being subtle. "The sort who turns into a wolf?"

"A wolf that needs a bath," Dobbin said with a wink at Kirsty. The younger girl tried hiding a smile before turning away.

"I don't smell," Caroline protested, feeling betrayed as she resisted an urge to lift an arm and sniff. Kirsty, grinning, refused to look her way.

Allyn gave her a speculative look. "I told you she was sharp, Dobbin," Allyn said.

"That doesn't explain how she knows."

"She doesn't. That's why she wants to get you alone." Speaking to Caroline, Allyn said, "Elias sent me a message earlier."

Caroline tried not to react. "How? Magic?" She was sure of it. A week ago she would have expected to see anyone burned for just the suggestion, and now she was in the midst of it. Despite everything she'd seen and done in the past few days that told her magic wasn't as bad as she'd been taught, she still couldn't stop her instinctive fear.

"Elias has been taken captive by the clansmen of this valley. He's injured and weak. They'll probably kill him once they get themselves organised."

"How do you know?"

"I'll teach you, if you like," he said.

She stiffened. "No. Thank you." Yet she wanted to say yes.

He smiled, perhaps seeing the conflict on her face. "Unless Dobbin and I can help him..."

A memory from her time in Dobbin's hut returned and she spoke without thinking. "Elias wanted to leave me for dead," she said, and then regretted it.

Kirsty looked up. The sudden pain in her friend's face made Caroline wish she'd cut her own tongue off. How had she missed it? Kirsty had a crush on Elias. The thought of Kirsty with the izzat inspired instant jealousy and Caroline had to stop herself from snarling. What was wrong with her? She didn't even like Elias in that way, yet the thought of someone else with him...

Allyn spoke coldly, and Caroline had no doubt she deserved every nuance. "He also saved your life, Princess, and he's only where he is because he was hindering the faspane for you. Dobbin and I will be leaving around midnight. Get some rest while we're gone. If we don't return, get Kirsty home. It's the least you owe her."

His tone cut her deeper than she'd have thought possible. She felt something shatter deep inside, something profound. She blinked tears. She was spoiled and selfish and she hated herself.

"I'm sorry," she whispered, too quiet for the words to carry. She wasn't sure she even said them aloud. She glanced at Allyn's lame leg, desperate to make amends. He needed her. "Who's going to help you? Those clansmen won't have any trouble catching a cripple."

Allyn's expression unexpectedly turned dark with anger. His knuckles clenched around his staff and he spoke coldly. "We asked for no help and expect none. Go collect firewood like the good little princess you are." He paused, continuing when she didn't speak. "And while you're looking for wood, take care, for I don't expect you to give any."

She turned to Dobbin, not sure what she expected. He avoided her gaze. She couldn't look at Kirsty, unable to endure seeing pain on her friend's face.

She ran out of the broken house, sprinting up the slope as hard as she could. She didn't know how far she ran, but when she stopped she had a pain in her side and could hardly breathe. She found a damp log and sat on it, unable to push away the memory of Allyn's cold expression. Wind blew her hair into her face. Fresh tears ran down her cheeks.

On the wind-torn mountainside, the enormity of what had happened to her finally shattered her composure.

As the rising moon buried her first twilight as a werewolf, Caroline's composure shattered under a torrent of tears.

25

Elias woke to a kick to his stomach. He gasped and curled up to protect the wound in his side. Two men, one almost big as Elias and the other bigger, grabbed his arms and hauled him out of the hut. He struggled to get to his feet. They dragged him as he stumbled.

"Where are you taking me?" he slurred, a fat lip and swollen jaw preventing clear speech. They didn't respond. He wasn't even certain they spoke the same lowland language as Caroline and Kirsty.

They stopped in the village square where they'd built a pyre from heavy timber and dried branches. Anything unwanted that would burn had been added, including old clothes and even the legs of a broken bed.

He tried pulling his arms free, but another punch to the stomach buckled his knees. They dragged him, gasping, the rest of the way. One of them pushed him hard against the timber post, while the other used coarse ropes to keep him upright. They bound his wrists behind the post, joking in their own language and laughing.

After a few more ropes, the men moved back, still joking with each other. They clambered down through the brush and wood before piling more into the gap that had let them through. They threw more over the top until it was all the way up to Elias's waist.

He pulled at the ropes but they only cut into his skin. Elias charged his muscles with all the magic he could and strained, but after a few seconds he gave up. Slumping into exhaustion, he resorted to the only option he had left. Speech. "I'm not your enemy," he said, his jaw aching. Neither of the men bothered looking up. "Surely one of you understands me? I'm only trying to get to Delshere. Send a runner. The shivras are expecting me."

One man took out a small flask and sipped. The bigger man picked up a branch as long as his forearm and flipped it, catching it in his other hand. He put a finger to his lips, indicating quiet.

"Look. My eyes are blue. Izzen don't have blue eyes, do they? I only need-"

The man threw the branch, catching Elias on the shoulder. Elias gasped in pain as blood began trickling down his bicep from the wound.

"Quiet, or we keep playin' tis game," the man said in an accent not dissimilar to Dobbin's. "Lots of wood to trow." He picked up another chunk the size of a boot.

Elias lifted his chin. "Please, I..." The chunk glanced off his forehead and almost knocked him unconscious. He slumped, only the ropes keeping him in place. "I shas... I swas..." Blood trickled down his temple and past his ear to follow the line of his jaw.

He tried to speak again, but the words came out soft and slurred. If Allyn and Dobbin didn't rescue him soon, he wasn't sure he'd last long enough to be burned alive.

~

By Caroline's best guess it was about midnight as she followed her own scent back to the dilapidated stone house, carrying no firewood. She really did need to bathe. She reeked of sour sweat and stale simorath caves.

A cold breeze cut through the valley and pushed her hair and cloak about, the air laden with smells from the nearby village and carrying hints of cooking spices from as far off as the Mistapol

Empire. Every so often, she caught a hint of Elias and her pulse quickened, a sensation she wasn't comfortable with.

Hungry, tired, and shivering, she hugged herself for warmth as her friends' scents grew stronger. She found Kirsty curled up in her huge canvas roll, asleep beside the glowing coals in the ruined hearth. Allyn sat against one of the small trees within the walls, his eyes closed and his breathing regular, if shallow. His ears stood tall as if listening for danger.

Caroline's scalp prickled and goose bumps crawled across her skin. What magic could he possibly be doing while asleep? Was he really asleep? She had an urge to poke him to see how deep his trance was, but she didn't want to disturb him further.

Something moved to her left. She jumped, her heart racing as Dobbin stepped out of the shadows with his huge hammer in hand. He frowned, but as he was downwind she couldn't catch his scent to tell if he was angry with her still.

"Is it time to save Elias?" she asked.

He gave her a searching look. "Thereabouts." He indicated Kirsty. "Look after yer friend while we're gone. Allyn believes many more of the faspane will have crossed the pass by now, so ye might see danger."

"I-"

"Leave at first light if we don't return. Walk all day and night to get across the last pass if ye have to. I doubt ye'll be safe until yer surrounded by yer own people."

Home. She badly wanted to see her parents, sisters and brothers. Brother, she amended. Just Phillip. She could go a lifetime without seeing Aaron. "I'm in Elias's debt, Dobbin. Allyn's too. And yours." She raised her chin. "I'll do whatever I can to help."

His frown deepened. "We're not going to slaughter clansmen if that's what yer thinking."

"I've cried my last regrets. I am sorry... more than I'd like to be. How can a werewolf help?"

Dobbin stood still for such a long moment she thought he'd ignored her, but eventually he nodded. "I'll probably need to carry

Elias, depending on how badly hurt he is. I can't carry both him and Allyn fer long, or even one with any speed."

"You want me to defend Allyn?"

"Allyn needs time to heal."

Fear caught her heart when she realised what he was asking. "You want to go without him?"

He put a calloused finger to his lips. "Aye."

Fresh fears almost choked her voice. "I'm... different when I change."

"I saw the bloodlust," he acknowledged. "Do ye think ye can avoid attacking me? Ye hauled it back last night."

"Only because you kept your distance."

"Then I'll keep me distance. Kirsty needs sleep, and if yer not going to stay with her then Allyn should. The sorcerer's disguised our trail with magic and set wards to warn of any unexpected approach. Without a wizard, the faspane can't come within a few hundred yards of this place without us knowing."

She shivered at the mention of *wards*. "Magic. It's a part of me, and I hate even knowing that. I can sense him using it, even now."

"Magical resonance. Nothing lives without magic Princess, including yer ignorant priests." He glanced at Allyn. "The sorcerer's drawing strength from that tree he's leaning against. An izzat trick. Says it works best in sunlight."

Always magic. "If he has to use magic then I hope it helps," she said softly. "I want him to be well again." It didn't hurt to say it as much as she expected it to. "How do we save Elias?"

He grinned, all enthusiasm now as he ushered her away. "Firstly, I'm going to place a second ward around here to give Allyn and Kirsty a little extra protection."

He could use magic? Of course. She'd forgotten. Shivras obviously didn't let it be widely known. She swallowed her fears and refused to allow a lifetime of ingrained mistrust show on her face. Not sure she was doing the right thing by her soul, she said, "How can I help?"

"Ye can't, not untrained. The ward I'll set creates a flash of light ye can't see, but so bright it'll blind ye for hours. Darklight, it's called. A shivrad trick. I'll need ye to change form too, now or after I cast the spell, but not during. I don't want ye distracting me."

"I think I can do that, but there's another problem. I can't understand speech when I'm a wolf. I couldn't understand you last night, at least."

"Really?" Dobbin sucked air through a gap in his teeth. "Then we'll work around it. Scout ahead. A wolf can move largely unnoticed, though I'm not so sure about a thumping giant monster like yerself," he added with a grin. She tried to give him a look, but her own grin slipped through. It felt right to be on good terms with him again.

"Steer me away from any danger until we get ta the village and again on the way back. Secondly, watch me back when I enter the village, but don't let yerself be seen."

"What are you going to do?"

"Walk in and demand they hand Elias to me, fer justice."

"And you expect them to?"

He chuckled. "No. But I'll spin some tale about wrongdoings. On the assurance I'll get ta witness the execution, I'll share a flask of brandy with 'em. Spiked. A few minutes later, I'll grab Elias and run."

"I can't kill anyone if something goes wrong. I mean, I don't want to." Even now, Kirsty's scent teased her in a similar way to Elias's, though it didn't have nearly as much influence over her. It seemed stronger now night had fallen.

"Ye killed snakeheads and stopped at me."

"People don't smell the same as simoraths. They smell... far more tempting." She tried not to look at Kirsty. "I don't want to risk you or Elias." The occasional sensual hint of Elias on the air made her feel both embarrassed and hopeful at the same time.

"Then ye'd better scare 'em good, cause if I can't get Elias to safety, me and him are both dead come dawn and ye'll have to tell Allyn." He softened the words with a grin, but she felt the sting. He was relying on her and he needed her to know it. "I'll be setting that ward now. If ye don't want ta stay..."

She shook her head. "Its fine," she said, trying to mean it.

Outside the walls he sank to his knees and closed his eyes, lightly touching the tips of his fingers together. Caroline felt a familiar prickling on her skin. This time, a chill ran down her spine and her hair stood on end as well, much like a storm approaching.

Dobbin moved his fingers apart and a shimmer appeared, incandescent, but no colour she could name. It formed insubstantial threads, like spider silk. It was beautiful, much like her *alimoth* flowers.

Not wanting to intrude on what felt like a private moment, she turned, but found she could still see the energy with her mind. Why now and not before? The answer seemed obvious; because she'd accepted it.

Dobbin flexed fingers of pure power as he wove the energy into a circle tinged with incandescent violet and a hint of green at the edges. He threw it outward like a fisherman's net, spreading it thin on the ground. It covered maybe thirty yards in every direction around the house. She felt every manipulation he made and idly wondered if she could do it with practice.

He touched the magic with fingers entwined in power and the energy changed to a darker shade of violet. He made one last manipulation and the energy disappeared from her mind's eye altogether.

She opened her eyes, staring in wonder. So that was magic? It was beautiful. "I-I should change, need t-to take my clothes... to-"

Dobbin wiped his forehead with the back of his sleeve, breathing hard. "There's some rocks downaways. Catch up when ye can."

Once alone, curiosity caught her. Looking around to ensure she wasn't being observed she fell to her knees and touched her fingers together as Dobbin had done, searching for that tingling feeling that gave her goose bumps. Deep within she felt an answering response, a sense of energy, like lightning flickering through her soul.

The marks on her wrists flared. It scared her, and yet the thrill of doing something she knew she shouldn't was a thrill she understood. It was the same thrill which forced to come to the mountains in the first place, to have an illegitimate child.

She took a few deep breaths before teasing forth the lightning.

"By the Divine Lords and Ladies,' she whispered, her hands trembling as incandescent power arced between her fingertips, ready to be used.

She thought she could do what Dobbin did, or at least some of it, but for anything more she would have to watch and learn. She released the power, and lightning dissipated into her skin, leaving her bones thrumming. Goose bumps covered her, much more than from just the cold. She felt... alive.

"Intoxicating, isn't it?" said a female voice.

Caroline squealed and fell back, the dangerous thrill of using magic turning to fear. Guiltily, she looked up.

A short blonde woman regarded her, her scent mimicking flowers but unnaturally different. She appeared only a few years older than Caroline, but her eyes seemed old. Perhaps that's what Allyn meant when he'd said Caroline had an old soul. This woman must, too.

"I'm Kimbriel. Sorry about startling you." The young woman was pale like most nobles, and slender, her hair falling to her waist. "Lost for words? How rare."

Sarcasm from someone she'd never met? "What do you want?" Caroline got to her feet. She stood head and shoulders above the woman, but it didn't make her any more confident.

"You've had a hard time this last week, both you and Kirsty," Kimbriel said. "Your choices have bound her destiny to your own. That's unfortunate for her."

"Leave my friend alone," Caroline said, the woman's words sounding close to a threat.

"I'd never harm so beautiful a soul." Kimbriel inclined her head in the direction Dobbin had gone. "You've a true friend in that shivra. Perhaps one day you'll have the chance to repay that friendship."

Caroline shivered as if the words were prophecy crawling across her skin like gooseflesh. "What do you want?"

"Things weren't supposed to be this way Princess. My efforts to groom... more appropriate candidates have failed."

Groom candidates? What did that mean? "Are you a...?" She couldn't say it. God?

Kimbriel laughed, but there was a bitter edge to it. "Divinity? No. But I did place the healing stone Elias used to save you. Hardly the actions of a God. More like their fool. Now I'm trying to smooth over some of the unforeseen consequences of my own actions. Your survival is going to affect a great many things. It's already messed up quite a few of my plans."

Caroline pulled her cloak more tightly around herself, feeling the need for protection. "Which God or Goddess do you serve?"

"Serve? I'm here to talk about you, not discuss Gods. There are werewolves on many worlds, in many universes. Some are even bred for specific traits. You though, you're like none of them; completely feral, yet largely in control of yourself. You'd be unique even if it weren't for your incredible magical power."

Many worlds? Universes? Who was this woman if not a Divine Lady?

"I'm here to offer you advice and a gift. Two gifts, actually. The advice; don't change form during daylight. You'll be stuck like that until the next full moon. The moon pulls at you, certainly, but day and night regulate your form. You can force the change in daylight, but you'll upset your body's balance. Only the full moon will reset it. That's the advice. Now, touch my hand." Kimbriel held out her own, palm up as if something rested on it.

"I don't need your gifts," Caroline said. It had to be magical. There was nothing there otherwise.

"Really? You'll want these. I promise. There's only one condition."

Caroline met the woman's eyes. Hesitantly, she reached her trembling hand out, but kept it above Kimbriel's, afraid to touch. "What's the condition?"

"If Allyn finds out about me because of you, you'll lose my gifts." She winked. "Can't let him know I'm around just yet."

"What does Allyn know of you?" Caroline asked.

"Just keep this secret for a couple of weeks."

Caroline hesitated, considering. "So long as it doesn't harm my friends or family."

"Fair enough. Now touch my hand. You need to signal your

acceptance." Caroline's touched her cold palm to Kimbriel's warm skin. Nothing happened. "Like them?" Kimbriel asked.

"What?"

A smirk crossed Kimbriel's lips. "You will. The first will only work once, the second you can use as often as necessary. Remember though. Don't tell anyone."

Caroline turned her hand over to examine her palm, but there was nothing there and she'd felt no magic.

Shock crossed Kimbriel's features as she stared at Caroline's wrist. "Marnier du Shae marked you?"

Kimbriel caught Caroline's hands. Marnier du Shae's luminous flowers were clearly visible. Caroline pulled her hands back. "You can see the marks?"

Kimbriel met Caroline's eyes. "Why would she mark you? You're to be her Champion, not her Servant."

Caroline took half a step back under the woman's intense stare. "I don't know. I don't want any of this."

"You obviously haven't accepted her invitation into Service. Smart girl. Don't. The Goddess of Healing doesn't like conflict. I knew she'd gifted you, but what's her purpose in marking her desired Champion?" Her voice trailed off at the last as if she were talking to herself.

A shimmer marked the air and between heartbeats, Kimbriel disappeared like a mirage.

Caroline stood still for a long moment, wishing she had some idea what had just happened.

26

———

Before Dobbin became curious Caroline stripped and dropped to her knees, trying to find the courage to face her new nature. Her fey necklace dangled, but somehow that felt right.

"Now," she whispered as she pictured the full moon and its pull. Nothing. She concentrated, trying to remember the moment she'd changed in the simorath caves. She'd had to trick herself into believing it. She closed her eyes and focused, letting the feel of a full moon rush over her. Heat swept outward from her centre, a thousand times faster this time. She gasped and collapsed face-first to the ground, shuddering as if having a fit. Pain flashed through her like the stab of white-hot iron. When her vision returned, she found herself on her side, panting, the breeze ruffling her thick fur.

She moaned, aching all over, and it took several seconds to regain her equilibrium. She stretched as an unnatural hunger infused her with dangerous desires, driven by the smell of human habitation.

Ignoring her new needs, she found Dobbin's trail and quickly caught up, letting him see her but keeping her distance. He didn't smell as good as the people from the village, but good enough to make her stomach growl. Considering how easy it had been to get lost in the violence, keeping her distance seemed wise.

Scouting ahead, she kept her nose to the ground as the gusting breeze brought ripe human scents from the village. She paused as she noticed something... Elias. Snarling, she almost rushed ahead. Almost. She wasn't sure how she stopped herself, but the need to tear into him was almost overwhelming. Something about his scent stirred up dangerous desires, whether she was in the form of a human or wolf.

In the hour it took Dobbin to reach the village, she crossed faspane scents several times. She continued with more caution, but never saw them. When fields and cattle became visible through the trees she stopped before Dobbin, making him pause. He watched her, a hand on the haft of his axe. Despite the embarrassment nakedness would bring, she focused on becoming human again so she could tell him about the faspane.

Nothing happened. She growled in irritation as wind ruffled her fur. Perhaps she needed to relax? She imagined the moon setting, sinking below the horizon in the dawn light. Nothing. She finally gave up in frustration and moved from Dobbin's path, hoping he'd taken the warning.

He probably thought she wanted to eat him.

The complex human smells thickened at the outskirts of the village, including a tantalising hint of Elias. She trembled with a need she didn't understand, but managed to keep herself from charging ahead. The aromas of last night's cooking overlapped the tang of a smithy and other small industry.

As Dobbin neared the first homes, Caroline dropped back, shy of his heavy steps. She kept to the shadows as the shivra trudged up the muddy road between round stone houses toward the open village square, his casual stride suggesting ease though he smelled tense. Firelight flickered from an open hearth in the square, the flames guttering. She kept back as Dobbin approached two men with long braids in their red hair and beards. Dobbin hailed them. They jumped and reached for weapons, the firelight putting them at a disadvantage.

She had rarely seen clansmen, though her father had been

negotiating with the clans for her entire life and her grandfather even longer. Both men were pale enough to pass for nobility, yet they wore leather breastplates, padded tunics and heavy, double-edged swords. Round shields lay nearby. The two men seemed as fierce as they were big, but the shivra dwarfed them and at least one of the men was considerably bigger than Elias.

Beyond the two guards, she saw a figure bound to a post amid a mound of dry wood. Elias. He didn't look up at Dobbin's approach, though she could see his shallow breathing.

The wind abruptly changed, swinging around from Elias's direction and bringing his undiluted, pain-filled scent. She gasped. Kirsty smelled delectable, but this close, Elias's scent multiplied that a thousandfold. She began shaking, savagery rising, snarling as the village faded to an insubstantial ghost of its real presence. Desire, hunger and bloodlust took her.

White light seared her vision along with Kimbriel's scent.

Magic held her in place. Kimbriel's gift. She looked around in confusion. Elias still smelled incredible, but her mind was clear. She should run, get away from him, but she needed to protect Dobbin. Uncertain, she felt Kimbriel's magic fading and her concentration dissolving with it.

She needed a distraction. An image of an ebony-skinned young man came to her. Lutaicus Tee Lubao. A year ago she'd dreamed of him, sought his attention, and finally found herself alone with him on the last day he'd been at court. His face remained fresh in her memory, warm and gorgeous, his skin such a rich mahogany he didn't seem real. A little shorter than her yet powerfully built, he'd leaned close in that little alcove while she trembled, his foreign looks and smile as devastating as his first touch. She'd kissed back, risking everything a moment later as she led him to her rooms.

She'd had no idea then how much it would cost her. She blinked the memory away. If it hadn't been for Lutaicus, she'd never have come to the mountains, never been attacked by a werewolf or felt a desire to tear a friend apart.

She stared at Elias, bound to a post and completely helpless. And for a heartbeat she didn't care. She wanted him so much more than she'd wanted Lutaicus. She wanted blood.

The wind washed his scent solidly into her face, but this time it wasn't caution or rational thought stopping her. The smell reminded her of... Shock overpowered her bloodlust. It couldn't be. His scent was similar to Allyn's, but tantalisingly human as well. Human!

His blood, sweat and pain mingled to produce a temptation only the Higher Realm could have created for her. She wanted to howl as bloodlust rose like storm winds, sweeping aside the last of Kimbriel's magic.

Before it consumed her, she caught her breath and sprinted to the edge of the village. Unwilling to leave, she jumped onto a stone wall to watch between the houses. Her pulse pounded as Dobbin poured the guards a drink and another for himself. The wind brought the drink's smell to her, brandy infused with a herb extract. The smack of it was almost as overwhelming as Elias's scent, its sickly sharpness providing a desperately needed distraction.

Stupidity must be a clannish trait for they drank it all, and in moments collapsed. She wanted to move nearer, but dared not. Just a single breath of Elias's unbroken scent might overwhelm her. She remained still as the shivra cut Elias free and hauled his limp body across his shoulders.

Dobbin jogged down the muddy road, stopping only when she unintentionally snarled. The shivra backed off instantly, but she didn't look at him. Only Elias. Even holding her breath, she could taste his pain. The snarl became a growl as she took an involuntary step forward. She wanted him more than she'd wanted anything in her most spoiled mood.

Dobbin returned the way he'd come and disappeared around a house, fortunately downwind. She didn't know what she'd have done if he'd tried to walk past. It took only a moment of honesty to realise she did know. She'd have killed him. Killed them both, and then slaughtered the village.

She jumped down from the wall and ran through the fields until she reached the forest, staying upwind a good hundred yards as

Dobbin emerged and made a break through the farmland. A few minutes later she heard an outcry from the village. Dobbin's pace increased until he reached the trees.

She fell back and hid among bushes, listening to clansmen gathering and milling about. It didn't take them long to find the trail by torchlight. The ground was soft and Dobbin's tread heavy. The first three clansmen ran past carrying torches and swords, their long braids and thick beards as unwashed as their clothes. Four more quickly followed, with others shouting from the village.

Elias's unique scent tantalised her still. She felt possessive, some instinct to protect what was, or should be, hers. Big as he was, Dobbin wasn't particularly fast and she needed to distract them. She picked a man near the back of the group and sprang, pulling him to the ground.

Lingering traces of Elias's scent infused the clansman's clothes and she couldn't help herself. He screamed as she savaged his arms and chest, knocking his shield and sword aside as if they were toys. She tasted his blood, but managed to stop. She held back the killing bite, then felt her curse pouring into him. No. She couldn't allow it. Committed now, she had to kill him.

A flash of white heat filled her once again, Kimbriel's second gift. Caroline jumped back, snarling. The curse hung between them. She could pass it on, or not. Bloodlust at bay, she drew the curse out of his flesh as if pulling free a barbed arrow.

The clansman yelled and took a swing, his sword almost catching her across the face. She jumped away, belatedly noticing the other clansmen running to defend the man. She loped off, letting them chase her for a while before circling back.

It didn't take long to find Dobbin. Another group of clansmen had surrounded him, torches and voices raised. Dobbin stood with his battleaxe in one hand and his shield on his opposite arm, his back protected by a tree. He'd dumped Elias on the ground. The clansmen were yelling, pointing at Elias with their swords. Dobbin spoke something back.

She caught Elias's scent again and couldn't help a snarl. The menace in it broke even her own deadly focus. She fought the bloodlust down, yet couldn't entirely suppress the desire to kill him. One clansmen cried out and fell as Dobbin bashed his arm with the flat of his battleaxe.

Three clansmen watched the shivra while the others spread out, yelling and waving torches to scare her off. The excitement drove Caroline's killing lust. Before she lost control, she darted into the forest and moved silently around the clearing, picking her moment before leaping from the dark trees and crashing into two of the three men surrounding Dobbin. Before the third could react, Dobbin's shield cracked his head and the man crumpled.

Caroline sprang at one of the remaining five. Her weight carried him to the ground with a thump and she disappeared back into the darkness before the other four could swing.

Shouting grew louder. Behind her she heard Dobbin hit the two she'd knocked over. More shouting. She moved from the shadows and the men moved closer to each other, wary of both Dobbin and her. Dobbin's voice added to theirs and he pointed several times at Elias.

A clansmen yelled back, a huge fellow with a red beard and brown hair. Another raised his voice above the rest, a command by the tone. They stopped arguing, pressing at her as a group with only a single clansman facing Dobbin now. Caroline growled to catch the attention of the man watching Dobbin and Dobbin clubbed him. She snarled again, backing away.

Dobbin dropped his weapon through the loop in his belt and hauled Elias to his feet, lifting him over a broad shoulder. Caroline kept the clansmen's attention by pouncing on an unconscious man. Sudden hunger at his smell nearly crippled her. She gripped his throat as a warning to the others, salivating at the salty taste of his skin. The clansmen raised weapons and moved forward, but stopped as she growled. Dobbin turned and ran.

The clansmen began arguing among themselves before edging away from each other, circling her. She growled another warning as her canines sank into the man's flesh. She moaned at the tang of blood, shuddering with near-ecstasy while the curse began infusing into the man. Just a little pressure and a gentle pull and his throat would come away.

Kimbriel's gift remained and she used it to pull the curse back, the sensation like drawing a barbed shaft from flesh until pain shot through her stomach. Her jaws clenched, crushing the clansman's neck. Blood sprayed.

The man had buried a dagger deep into her stomach. Fury overwhelmed her as another clansman slashed his sword along her ribs. Another came at her, rage on his face. She dodged a swing and tore his leg off at the knee before killing two more, despite the agony of the blade still embedded in her intestines. Pain finally overwhelmed bloodlust and she ran away, keeping her left hind leg off the ground. Every jolt was agony.

She limped through the dark trees barely faster than they could run, trying to put distance between herself and the remaining men while hoping they would never find her in the darkness. Pain shot through her abdomen with every step, but the sounds of shouting fell further and further behind. Dizzy and almost unable to continue, she slipped under a fallen tree laying across a small gulley. It wasn't far from a dryad tree with drooping flowers, giving her some protection with its proximity.

Ignoring the sickly sweet smell and keeping well beyond the reach of its branches, she worked her way into the thicket until the hilt snagged, the blade cutting her insides. She yelped in agony. Caught, she hesitated, fearing more pain, but there was no alternative if she wanted to survive. She took three shallow breaths and twisted hard. Her entire focus became pain as the blade sliced her open as it pulled free, cutting through her insides and opening her up further, blood and gore spilling to the leaves as she collapsed on top of it.

27

Caroline dreamed of pain, cold, a sickly sweet perfume, and a miserable dawn full of rain. A breeze touched her and the rain became dampness on her skin. Shivering consumed her, pushing away sleep until Dobbin's scent flooded her senses. His presence brought more pain, mottled sunshine and a gentle rocking motion.

Later she dreamed of a deliciously warm bed with heavy blankets, and eventually another moonrise.

She woke to the gentle sensation of dawn, the fog of her dreams slowly lifting. Two concerned blue eyes regarded her from above a fat shivrad nose and a close-cropped beard. She smiled. "Dobbin." Her whispered word echoed a little. The air was warm and rich with wood smoke and her friends' scents, along with old, lingering traces of other shivras. "Where are we?" she asked. A domed, smooth-cut stone roof rose high above her.

He returned her smile. "A hidey hole. I brought ye here. Took me half a day to find ye, too. I thought ye dead at first, that maybe ye'd been stabbed with silver. Cold, miserable, wet morning it was. Clansmen everywhere. Was a clever plan to hide so near a dryad tree. The clansmen weren't keen on lookin' too closely. Mind, ye were almost too close yerself. The dryad might have left the protection of her tree and dragged ye into her abode if she'd been desperate enough."

"Thank you for risking your life to help me."

Dobbin's scent pervaded the room, masking Allyn and Kirsty's. Even Elias had been here, the lingering traces of his presence igniting her senses and quickening her heartbeat. She thanked the Higher Realm her sense of smell was somewhat dulled in human form, or at least her reactions to it. Allyn must be right. They did share some sort of bond. Her heightened sense of smell confirmed it.

"Might have been better if I had died," she whispered. Safer for Elias, at least. When she was human, he smelled good in a nice way. As a werewolf, he inspired near-uncontrollable bloodlust. Compared to the anguish his scent brought her in that state, birthing a child was joyful. She quickly buried thoughts of her lost child and replaced them with visions of her sisters' faces at home, but the regret and heartbreak. She doubted the wound would ever close.

"Yer in no danger of dying, not now. Ye saved me life again, lass. I'm in yer debt."

She shook her head a little. "Never you, Dobbin. No tallies, okay? If anything, I'm in your debt. How long since we rescued Elias?"

"Two nights ago. Ye must be thirsty? Allyn said yer not to swallow more than a little. Just enough to wet yer mouth."

He supported her head as he held a clay cup to her lips. The water was fresh and cool, and very satisfying. "You shivras make really good water."

He chuckled. "Ye can have some more in a few minutes. I need to clean yer wound first and bandage ye up again. Allyn thinks ye'll be fine by tomorrow."

She remembered her entrails spilling. Had he pushed them back in? She shuddered at the thought. Her stomach felt tender, but hardly what she might have expected. She placed a hand on his thick wrist. "Dobbin?"

He paused. "Aye, lass?"

"Next time you're fighting someone, do yourself a favour."

His eyebrows lifted. He smelled offended, though it barely showed in his expression. "What's that?"

"Don't get gutted."

His laughter boomed, echoing around the room. The smell of tension left him, replaced by his normal scent and a mighty grin. "Aye. Good advice that. Can ye move so I can bandage ye properly?"

She allowed him to help her sit on the oversized bed, pulling a blanket across her lap and keeping an arm across her exposed breasts. It hurt, but not too badly. "I seem to have made a habit of this," she said. "How many times should I have died in the last week?"

"A few. Like I said before, the curse seems to be a boon. I'd almost swear Marnier du Shae is using it ta look after ya. Can ye sit a little straighter?" When she stiffened her back, he examined her bandages, gently probing with his huge blunt fingers. For someone so big, he was incredibly gentle.

"I smelled faspane when we were rescuing Elias."

He paused in unwinding a bandage. "Go on."

"They're not going to leave me be, are they? They'll keep searching, even if I stay here for a month. They'll try to stop me getting home."

"Very likely."

She sighed. "Everything's different now. Everything." She was being forced into a life she didn't want, all because of a conflict among the Gods she wanted no part of.

He gave her a cautious look. "Some oracle must have told them ye were in the mountains, but the mountains are big. Don't fret. They could be scattered over a hundred square miles and more."

"You should all leave me. Save yourselves." It was the only gift she could offer.

"Ye don't abandon yer friends, no matter what."

She placed a hand on his. She doubted she'd ever had any real friends besides Kirsty and Rhonda. "Do you realise what Father would do if he walked in on us like this?"

"Lucky I'm bigger than him." He continued stripping the soiled bandages.

"You know what I mean."

He failed to hide a smile, but didn't look up. "Aye. I can guess. Probably about what I'd do if I found a lad courting me daughter without her mother in attendance. Break every tooth in the fool's head, and maybe a few bones, too."

She glanced at him, wondering if he actually had a daughter. "Father would hang the man if he caught him." Memories crept up, drowning her attempts at a lighter mood. Lutaicus Tee Lubao, perfect mahogany skin and thick, curly black hair. By the Divine Lords, he'd had the most glorious smile. Fortunately, he'd returned home across the Temern Straight before her indiscretion had been discovered.

Dobbin peeled the last layer away, the bandage sticking to her skin. He dragged a bowl of warm water closer and dipped a soft cloth into it. "I'd not go that far." He paused, his mind obviously elsewhere. "Well, I doubt it." He began wiping the dried blood away. Gentle though he was, she tensed a few times. He paused whenever she cringed, but she just nodded each time for him to continue. He remained quiet until he finished cleaning and dressing her tender, scar-puckered stomach. It took a while.

"What should I do, Dobbin? Do you think I'll be okay at home?" It wasn't really a question, more an expression of her own doubts and concerns. "What of my sisters and brothers? I'd never wish any harm on them, yet my presence would put them in danger."

He examined the bandages. "I'm not sure what else ye could do. The izzen will return home when they're done at Delshere and ye can't remain with me. I've no idea where I'll be, considering me home's burned. Besides, there's a Goddess requiring yer services."

A Goddess she wanted to despise, even if she wasn't sure it was deserved. "Distract me, Dobbin. Tell me about Delshere. Perhaps I'll get to see it one day." In truth, all she wanted to do was track down her baby and find somewhere safe to raise it. Him or her? She didn't even know that much, though she'd asked. She took a deep breath, hoping to avoid tears.

He wrung the cloth out, red water cascading. The smell of her own blood didn't inspire bloodlust, fortunately. "Delshere," he said, his eyes far away. "I haven't seen it in a decade. Longer." He remained motionless for such a long time she thought she'd upset him. She began to feel uncomfortable and pulled the sheet around her shoulders.

When he finally spoke, his tone was full of fond memory. "Delshere's something to behold indeed. It's a lone mountain rising out of a valley, yet small enough ye could walk around it in half a day or less. It's surrounded by a massive wall of stone with huge gates facing north and south, and two smaller ones in between to keep the balance. In all of history it's never been taken. Never even been breached. Enchanted it is, built by the ancients thousands of years ago. It's an entire city atop a mountain, and deep within, too. In times of trouble it can hold every shivra from every village and farm, and have room for more." He sighed. "The izzen don't appreciate it, but then they're izzen. Maybe when I return I'll stay."

"Why did you leave?"

His expression lost its fond look. "Stubbornness, I suppose." He shrugged as if it no longer mattered. "Traditionally among shivras, it's considered a wife's duty to birth a dozen sons before a daughter. Sons are... they look after the family with their lives if necessary. The best make good mates and protectors. They honour the people. Me wife though, she's a strong-headed woman. It's part of her attraction. I should have seen it as a warning even before she offered me her heart. She birthed a daughter first. Humiliated me. Humiliated both of us, and the child. Poor girl will have to live with it. Can ye imagine a girl with no brothers devoted to protecting her?"

Caroline's jaw dropped. "It's not your wife's fault."

He frowned. "Yes it is. She *chose!*"

"You can choose?" she asked, wonder clearly evident in her voice. "How incredible such a gift would be."

Dobbin took a deep breath. "I lost me temper frequently after that, and much of me social standing. It says something when a daughter's born before sons. I swore if the next child was a daughter I'd leave her, though I didn't say as much, just stupidly demanded a son. She took it as a challenge and birthed us another daughter. I left Delshere that same day."

Caroline felt lost. Shivrad culture wasn't what she expected. "It's your wife's duty to obey you," she said.

"Pfft! Yer expected to devote yerselves to each other, and we did for a time. Obedience plays no part and it seems respect doesn't either. Fools both. Me too old and set in me ways, her too young and proud. Me first daughter, she'd be nearly grown now. I can only guess what she looks like. Beautiful like her mother, no doubt, and probably just as head strong."

Memories flashed through her mind despite her resolve never to recall them; a final scream of agony, a moment of pure exhaustion and silence, and then the first whimper of a newborn and an incredible desire to hold it, a desire she'd never fulfilled. It left something hollow inside her and she hadn't been able to fill it since. Nothing ever could.

She wiped a tear away. A month afterward, she'd mounted a horse and rode away, having never heard the baby cry again or even seen its face. More tears fell. She ached with guilt and resentment. She took a deep breath and tried to bury the feelings. She hoped never to find them again.

Dobbin, at least, could see his children if he chose. "Let's hope your wife loves your daughters," she murmured, unable to hide her resentment. Dobbin stiffened.

She immediately regretted her thoughtless words. "Oh, Dobbin. I didn't mean it like that. It was petty and unkind. I was angry... angry with... someone else. I'm so sorry." She felt more tears gather, this time because of her own stupidity. "Please forgive me?" She could clearly smell the anger. "Please?"

"Yer wound's mostly closed up, though still weeping a little," he said tersely. "If ye weren't a werewolf... Ye need rest. Allyn and Elias won't be fit to travel before tomorrow, and I doubt ye'll be either."

She felt worse. She'd rather have seen him get angry. "Dobbin, I... Please. I didn't mean what I said. You've no idea how much I regret it. Honestly. I..."

He held up a hand. "I recognise stretch marks when I see 'em. It didn't take more than a moment to understand what ye meant, though it hurt anyway. Ye delivered a child ye had to give up. We all know. All of us except Kirsty, of course.'

Caroline felt shock and surprise like a cold pit churning in her stomach. "You knew? Of course. Why else would a girl get parcelled off to an abbey in the mountains?" Ironically, her parents had told everyone she'd gone to discover if her calling was for a religious life. She glanced at the divine markings on her wrists.

"Oh, Dobbin." She began crying again. "I'm so sorry."

Dobbin helped her lay down and pulled soft sheets over her before leaving. She sobbed for a long time and stared at the roof for hours more, refusing to answer Kirsty's gentle enquiries.

When Elias came to thank her for helping rescue him, she rolled over and pulled the sheets up over her head until he left.

Queen Lynn woke doubled in agony. She lay on her side in bed, clutching her stomach. Warm blood soaked into her nightgown and seeped through her fingers, the last vestiges of a nightmare still clinging to her mind. She took short sharp breaths until the pain began to subside. Sweating with fear and pain, she struggled with the sheets and pushed them aside, managing to sit up.

Perspiration and the cool air gave her goose bumps as memories of the nightmare slowly subsided. She shivered in the darkness until a sound startled her; her husband softly snoring beside her, oblivious.

For minutes, she could do nothing more than endure the broken dreams resurfacing in her mind. Just a dream, she tried to tell herself, and wished she believed it. A nightmare really, about a wolf, though it had started with her daughter. Like so many of her dreams, it was far too cryptic to be useful. She woke from dreams as often as not, but they were rarely so real or immediate. The pain had almost gone now, but the blood remained. That manifestation was real, at least.

They'd received word that two days ago. Caroline had been lost to an unknown enemy in the mountains. If her daughter lived, a ransom would be demanded. And paid. The dream, or nightmare as it seemed to be, told her Caroline lived. She hoped nothing more of it was true.

Carefully so as not to wake Phillip, she left the bed, lit a candle from the coals of the hearth and carried the light to her sitting room. There she lit more candles, allowing the silver mirror to reflect her tired and worried features. She had lines at the corners of her eyes and around her mouth, and a hint of grey through her red hair. A few strands, but grey nevertheless. She didn't feel old, but her body was showing it.

She undid her nightgown's laces and let the bloody garment drop to the floor. Despite eight, children her body was nearly as slender as it had been when she'd married. Only now it seemed... softer. Facing the mirror again, she found no wound from the dream, only the marks given her by childbearing.

She turned away and tipped cold water from a pitcher into the basin and splashed her face, and then dipped the hem of her nightgown in and used it to wash the blood from her stomach and hands. She shivered, but not from the cool air.

The dream hadn't been a foretelling. It had the feeling of immediacy. There was often danger in her dreams, but those which foretold the future always came too late or were too cryptic to help.

Like her husband's death. She only ever remembered one thing; her husband with an arrow through his thigh. The dream had the feel of death, but no matter how she strained to remember, she couldn't recall a time or place. Still, she knew what it meant. She'd known it before she'd married him. They'd had many good years together, more than she'd expected, but events were stirring and she doubted there'd be many more.

When it happened, she'd have to leave this place. Not yet, though.

She took a deep breath, steadying herself, and tried to put it all from her thoughts.

She donned clean clothing, blew out the candles and let the fire consume her bloody nightgown before quietly returning to bed. She avoided the cold, sticky blood on the sheets as she slid over against her husband.

"Another dream?" he asked, startling her.

"Yes," she whispered.

"Tell me about it."

Cringing, she pulled away. "Can it wait for morning?"

He sighed. "Come dawn, you'll put it off until noon, at noon you'll promise that night or the next day, then later again. I know you too well, Lynn. Tell me."

She rested her head on his pillow and slid her hand over his bare chest. "I dreamed of Caroline and a wolf, both badly hurt. They were in a forest. She may have been trying to fight it off. I remember little else." As much as she wanted to say more she dared not, for when the wolf got stabbed so did Caroline. She hoped she would never understand it.

Exhaustion quickly drove her to sleep and nightmares returned. This time she saw izzen from her daughter's eyes, and izzen frightened her more than any wolf could.

King Phillip lay awake wondering what his wife had not told him. She moaned in her sleep, restlessly shifting beside him, and it continued over the hours until dawn seeped through cracks in the shutters. She'd been trembling when she'd returned to bed, which told him her nightmares were worse than she'd claimed. There were a few dreams she refused to tell him about, but when she'd dreamed of death in the past she'd shown only regret that it had to be. This one wasn't death, but it had frightened her.

He contemplated getting up, but his touch seemed to calm her. Even so, it wasn't long before she was kicking the blankets off, her body sweaty and hot. He closed his eyes, wondering what this new dream was.

It had been three years since she'd woken and told him her sick mother had died. Officially, they'd had no word until the passes had cleared and a rider could get through the mountains to the same abbey they'd recently sent Caroline to. That had been a terrible winter for Lynn, knowing without being able to say a word to anyone.

Somehow, Caroline had known too, but thankfully the girl had enough sense not to speak of it. It was one of the few times in her life she'd shown good judgement. The girl was ruled by her emotions most of the time. If only she was as sensible as her younger sisters.

He stared at the roof until Lynn slept peacefully again, yet he remained as tense as the one time he'd ridden into battle.

28

Caroline woke well before dawn, her memories bringing on crippling shame. As tears threatened, she stared at the cut stone roof while wishing she'd learn to avoid speaking before thinking, a bad habit she seemed exceptionally good at. She covered her face with her hands and lay there for a long time before. She truly did have the gift of stupidity when it came to conversation.

Still ashamed but unable to put up with her own company any longer, she shoved the sheets aside and found neatly folded clothes on the rug near the bed. Kirsty.

She peeled off the bandages to find her stomach healed. The puckered scar had lost some redness. She examined her leg where she'd been cut while killing the simoraths. Only a fading scar remained.

Bending gingerly, she picked up the clothes left for her; practical wear, unflattering men's clothes, tough, but better than the torn riding dress she'd been forced to wear until now. She put her face to the cloth and breathed in her friend's scent before holding them out. The clothes, made for a shivra, had been altered.

"Blessings on you, Kirsty," she whispered. She stiffened as her *alimoth* flowers flared, ready to bestow a blessing she couldn't deliver without Kirsty nearby. After a few seconds the light faded from her wrists, the blessing lost.

"I'm not even a Divine Servant, My Lady," Caroline whispered. "Why allow me to convey your blessings? So many others are far more worthy of your attention."

As expected, no answer came.

After dressing, she opened the door to the rich smell of stew and the scent of burning pine. Her stomach growled. Despite feeling ridiculous in men's clothes she followed the rich smell past a dozen doors at least twelve feet high, all expertly set into smooth stone walls.

At the end of the corridor she found another walkway going left and right. The way left disappeared into darkness, so she followed light to the right. It lead her into a gathering room furnished with four huge chairs made for shivras and an open fireplace in the centre.

She felt like a child as she stopped by a chest big enough to serve as a table. Furs and old tapestries of shivras decorated the walls, and dusty rugs covered the floor. Lingering scents of the shivras who'd used this room remained.

Dobbin stood by the hooded central hearth, staring into the fire. Her stomach growled again at the smell of stew, or perhaps at Elias's lingering scent. "Good morning, Dobbin," she said hesitantly. She hoped he wasn't still angry with her, though she couldn't imagine why he wouldn't be. She needed to make up for her poorly-considered words. She removed her ruby necklace. It was the only gift she could offer besides another apology.

He jumped in surprise, looking up. "Ye shouldn't sneak up on a shivra like that. It's not polite."

She tried a smile, hoping his poor mood was due to the early hour. "Just wake up?"

He returned his attention to the fire. "I'm not used to being so cooped up. Feelin' alive, I see?"

"Yes, thanks to the curse. And you. It was a mortal wound, true?"

"Without a doubt. Ye seem to have had the rough end of it lately."

"You barely know me, yet you care. Thank you. I'm so sorry about what I said yesterday."

He made a dismissive sound. "Do ye feel up to travelling today?"

"Not really, but some food and drink might help." She glanced at the stew. Rabbit seasoned with dried herbs by the smell. "May I?"

"Of course. There's a jug of water on the chest to yer left."

"Thank you." She poured some water, the clay cup huge, and sipped slowly. It sat cold in her stomach. Dobbin ladled out stew in what would be a child-sized bowl for shivras.

"Allyn wants to be gone soon. If yer not up to it, I'll carry ye."

"Carted about like a sack of grain? I'll walk even if my gizzards spill out. Again."

His face grudgingly split in a grin. "Ye would, too."

"Where are we? Exactly?" She examined the chiselled walls and roof. Smooth enough, but not polished.

"A cavern built and maintained by my kind for emergencies such as this. They're peppered throughout these mountains. This one sits in the south side of the pass leading to the lowlands of Fandelyon and the Senbow River."

"Really?" She glanced around again. "Who knows about them? My father?"

He handed her the steaming bowl, wishing she knew the names of the herbs he'd used when making it. "No, lass. Only shivras. And if ye all weren't so hurt as well as having faspane running after us, ye'd never have found out about 'em either."

She felt offended. "But these mountains belong to my father."

"Pfft. Clansmen and simoraths live in 'em, shivras mine 'em despite yer knowledge, and trappers wander through 'em without acknowledging boundaries. Just because yer great grandfather claimed 'em doesn't mean yer father owns 'em. No doubt Kenmoore claims much of 'em too. Yer father may garrison a few fortresses and valleys along the trade routes, but it wasn't more than half a century ago clansmen controlled the same fortresses. A century before that some of those fortresses belonged to Kenmoore. A few thousand years ago they all belonged to Mistapol."

"Do you remember that?"

He snorted. "A few shivras are close to a third of that age, but only a few, and they're decrepit beyond usefulness. The izzen though, they remember. Allyn, anyway. Not Elias."

"Oh." Just how old did a shivra live? "How is Elias? And Allyn, of course."

"Elias is much better this morning, though still not entirely well. The izzen are doing their tree-healing thing outside. Allyn claims he'll be able to walk properly today. Would have been already if he'd been able to focus entirely on healing, instead of watching for faspane."

Caroline ate half the stew in silence. "Dobbin, I need you to return home with me." It surprised her how much courage it took to say those words. The thought of seeing her parents again brought both longing and dread as she wondered what she would tell them. "Please?" Simply facing them after her indiscretion would have been hard enough. Now... She waited, but his expression and scent told her nothing.

She continued in a rush. "I don't know if any soldiers from my retinue made it home, and I can't tell Father that Kirsty and I walked out of the mountains alone. He'll never believe me. What's more, there's a traitor in the Kingdom. How else could those men have known where I'd be? I need your help. Please. Come with me. Make Father see you helped. It will avoid some unpleasant explanations." She thought of her mother, who always seemed to know everything, even things it wasn't possible to know.

"Lass, we're not planning on entering yer Kingdom beyond the first guard post. I'll have ta drop ye and Kirsty there. I'm sorry."

"I..." How could she explain? She wanted to go home, but... "I'll have to tell him I had help. What if Father decides to send soldiers to look for you? What if I make a mistake? I'm clearly an expert at saying stupid things. Or Kirsty? I don't doubt her, not at all, I'd trust my life to her, but the slightest slip will see soldiers searching the mountains for you all. If you're there, it'll be much easier."

Hearing a sound, Caroline spun and found Kirsty standing in the room's entrance. How she hadn't heard or smelled Kirsty earlier, she didn't know, but her friend's expression suggested she'd been listening.

"Join us, lass," said Dobbin. He smelled slightly embarrassed. "There's hot stew in the pot if yer hungry."

Caroline took another mouthful of stew. It was getting cool, though still much better than anything else she'd had in the last few days.

"Thank you," Kirsty said, crossing to the fire. She was growing gaunt, her cheeks hollow and her body too thin. She must have lost four or five pounds in the last week. More.

Dobbin grabbed a bowl and slopped gravy over the side as he ladled stew in, handing it over without wiping it. "We were discussing the remainder of yer journey."

The younger girl looked down. "I understand." She sounded unhappy.

"What's the matter, lass?" Dobbin asked.

"Nothing, Dobbin." Kirsty glanced at Caroline again. "Just tired." Their eyes met for a heartbeat before Kirsty looked away. She seemed... resigned.

Elias! Kirsty didn't want to go home at all. She wanted to stay with Elias. The thought of Kirsty and Elias together nearly brought a growl to Caroline's throat. She checked her emotions, determined not to think like that. There was something between herself and Elias, but she didn't know what it meant beyond Allyn's unhelpful explanation.

"Don't fear, lass. It's almost over. Ye'll be safely home soon, both of ye."

Caroline closed her eyes. They were exactly the words Kirsty wouldn't want to hear. Nor did she, unfortunately.

"My duty is to my Princess." Kirsty stared at her stew, but didn't eat. She appeared even more miserable.

Fighting irrational emotions, Caroline crossed the room and put a comforting arm around the younger girl's shoulders, guiding her to a seat big enough for them both. Kirsty smelled good, much better than the stew. Certain she was going to regret the words, Caroline gripped Kirsty's hand. "I have to return home and you need to tell your parents what happened to Rhonda. She needs a proper burial."

Kirsty's expression fell further. "Truly." She smelled dangerously depressed.

An infatuation with an izzat shouldn't be encouraged, her own desires included. "Dobbin, will you take us all the way home? Please?"

He shifted his feet, chewing on the inside of his cheek. "I'll get the izzen. Let's see what they have to say." He left the room. A moment later, rock grated. Caroline felt a draft of cool air before the rock grated again.

"So, you want to chase after Elias," she said, making sure it wasn't a question.

Kirsty stiffened, but kept her eyes down, her expression pained. "I didn't think anyone knew, My Lady."

"Even if he'd take you, would you honestly go with him back to his homeland, wherever that is?"

Kirsty lifted her chin slightly. "Am I really that obvious? I think about him constantly. If he asked me, I suspect I'd agree to do anything. He's immortal, you know?"

"Immortal?"

"Allyn told me. Wouldn't that be wonderful?"

Caroline had to suppress another wave of irrational jealousy at Kirsty's yearning tone. "Your feelings are not obvious and I doubt Elias knows. Dobbin certainly doesn't. It's irrelevant, though. We have to return home. We have responsibilities."

Kirsty morosely stirred her food. "I know."

"I need to get away from him too, Kirsty. Something about his scent compels me to act... in ways I shouldn't. I nearly killed him the other night when we went to save him. As a werewolf, I go crazy with bloodlust in his presence." She waited for Kirsty to react, but her friend kept her eyes down. "It's worse when I'm human, like now. It's not bloodlust I feel when I smell him."

Kirsty glanced up. "What?"

"It's lust."

Kirsty frowned, and almost began to say something, but remained silent.

"It's something about his scent. It creates... desires in me. I can barely control myself around him, human or werewolf."

If anything, Kirsty became tenser. Slowly, deliberately, Kirsty nodded. "I understand. Thank you for telling me." Hurt acceptance wasn't the reaction Caroline had been expecting. She felt worse and tried to think of something to ease her friend's pain.

"Still, I'm a werewolf. Maybe I won't be able to stay at home. If I'm forced to leave, I promise I'll take you with me if that's what you really want. We'll look for Allyn and Elias. If we find them, you can stay with him if he'll have you." By the Gods, the words almost choked her. "Please don't expect him to though."

Kirsty's scent filled with hope. "Honestly?"

Caroline bit her lip. "It'd be stupid, but yes. Just promise me you won't hate me if we can't go after them, or if we do and he refuses your company."

Kirsty looked aghast. "Never, My Lady. Best friends. Always."

Caroline hugged her. "Always." Somehow, she felt like a traitor, only she didn't know who she was betraying.

29

Rock grated again and another draft of cool air washed Elias's scent in. It was enough to increase Caroline's heartbeat and fill her with unwanted desire. She concentrated on breathing normally, hoping the sensation passed as the izzen entered the room. Elias stopped before the central fire and she was shocked to see his face was badly bruised, all because he'd tried to help herself and Kirsty. She almost went to him to gently touch his skin and sooth the bruises. The way he walked suggested he remained sore all over, and a different desire overcame her as she considered what he'd look like without clothes.

Allyn also headed for the fire. Caroline stood and moved away. Elias had smelled good at Dobbin's cabin, but after fully transforming into a werewolf, it was as if he'd been made just for her.

"Dobbin says you wish to be escorted to your father," Allyn said as he warmed his hands.

Caroline struggled to pull her attention off Elias, grateful for the distraction. "Yes." Fortunately, Elias didn't look up. She'd have died of embarrassment if he'd caught her staring. She'd desperately wanted to tear Elias apart the other night, but this human desire was far worse. Unless she got used to his scent she'd find herself in bed with him.

"And after that?"

She barely avoided a glance at Kirsty. "We'll be safe."

She noticed the human cast to Elias's features now; the pale blue eyes rather than emerald or jade, the softer, rounder set of his ears, and his lower cheekbones and squarer jaw.

He met her eyes almost as if he'd known she was watching him, and frowned. "Why are you staring at me?"

Something clattered. She blinked, realising she'd dropped the stew. "Sorry," she muttered. Why didn't everyone else see he was partly human? He was much bigger than Allyn and the faspane she'd seen, though that might mean little considering she'd seen so few. She'd thought he might have some shivrad heritage, but he smelled nothing like Dobbin. She'd seen clansmen who were just as big. Bigger. Almost compelled, she stepped over the bowl with a silent promise to clean it up later, moving close to the fire. He smelled so *good*.

"What?" he asked again, his expression genuinely curious as he met her eyes.

"Caroline, what are you doing?" Allyn asked, taking half a step forward.

Did he recognise the wolf rising up within her? Desire gripped her almost as strongly as her murderous instincts the other night, only this time she didn't want to fight it. "Your scent, Elias... it's unique," she whispered, her voice suddenly raspy.

She took a deep breath to try and calm herself, but it only created a desire to press her face against his skin. She broke out in a sweat. Almost against her will, she reached out with trembling fingers and ran the tips along his jaw line. Stubble! She dropped her hand in surprise. The stubble was soft and he'd shaved close, but it was still there.

Elias frowned, touching his jaw. Sudden realisation crossed his face and he swore under his breath.

"What?" Allyn asked, clearly curious.

How had Elias managed to keep that secret from Allyn? "Your smell is exquisite, Elias. There's nothing like it."

He looked afraid of her. No, of what she knew. "Keep your lycanthropy to yourself," he said, clearly trying to protect his secret.

"Lycanthropy?" The word felt like a challenge. "No. I smell what you are."

"Izzen." The word came out, hesitant. Fearful even. The fear ignited her predatory instincts. She moved within inches and, though tall herself, she barely reached his chin. She hadn't realised just how big he was until now. His scent saturated the air like a heavy rain and she couldn't help but reach out again. "Enough," he said, backing half a step, but only a half. She could see it in his expression. He wanted her, too.

She took a deep breath, wanting more than just his scent. "You don't know, do you?" She was certain of it. "You honestly think you're just a different sort of izzat."

Kirsty watched intently. Would it help Kirsty to know Elias was part human? Caroline didn't want to find out. She loved her best friend more than her own life, but right now she might kill Kirsty if she tried to get between herself and Elias. "You don't want to know, do you? You're happy in your ignorance while hiding your differences."

His expression was both offended and angry, but he smelled... desperate. "My mother is the only child of our King and Queen. She's pure izzat."

"And your father?"

"Izzen."

"Unlikely," she whispered, moving closer again. He didn't back away this time.

"Yes, he is," he said, his tone more assured now. "He fell through the Veil as a child. He's from another universe, but still izzen."

"You're wrong about his heritage," she said. "Or perhaps your mother's. One of your parent's isn't pure izzen." Elias backed another step, and like the predator she didn't want to be, Caroline followed.

"It's not possible for different species to interbreed."

Allyn cleared his throat. He seemed pale under his tan. "It might be possible. I never believed it. I heard something happened once before, but..." He glanced at Caroline. "It might be possible. Not randomly, but with the help of the Gods-"

"Not possible," Elias said. He smelled scared, the fear driving her growing desire as much as his scent.

"I know what I smell." She took his face between her hands, yet he didn't pull away as she gently drew his head down beside her own. Her lips close to his ear, she whispered, "Do you want to know?" She couldn't help taking another deep breath, the rush of need driving her heartbeat. As quietly as she could, so soft she doubted anyone could have heard, she whispered. "Last chance."

Very, very gently, she felt him nod. A thrill of excitement ran through her at the prospect of revealing his true origins in the hope it may lead to something more. It was all she could do not to take him to her room and make him beg for the word he wanted to hear. If they'd been alone, she might have. Her response barely a sigh, she whispered, "Human."

He jerked away, stumbling back. "No!"

His reaction hurt like physical pain. Nevertheless she tried to reason. "I smell it in every part of you."

"You're lying!" It was as if he'd suspected but refused to admit it.

She could see it in his eyes. He believed her, and he feared it. His revulsion carried strongly in his scent, and it made her angry enough to want to attack him. She clenched her fists, anger displacing desire. If he felt that way about his own heritage how would he feel if he discovered Kirsty's desires? Or her own. Protectiveness and hurt warred. "Is that so disgusting?"

"Now that is not appropriate," Allyn said. "Perhaps you'd be better off making your own way from here, Caroline."

She continued watching Elias, until Allyn's words finally cut into her thoughts. "What?" She turned on him. "You'd abandon me? Now?" Allyn didn't reply. "Elias?" she asked. Surely he wouldn't agree with Allyn.

The hurt in his scent and devastation on his face said he might. Oh Gods. She realised she'd just destroyed the foundation on which he'd built his life. Whatever his denials, he believed what she'd said, and it scared him. It meant he was mortal, like her. Barely minutes since she'd resolved to think before speaking, and she'd done it once more. Intense regret overwhelmed her. "I'm sorry, Elias. Your scent drives me to act and say things I shouldn't." She'd let her untamed instincts get the better of her.

She stepped back, realising just how badly she'd hurt him. "I'm so sorry, Elias," she repeated, unable to face his pain any longer. "You're right, Allyn. It might be best if you abandon me. I can't think properly when I'm around Elias. His scent..." If she waited until tonight and changed into a wolf, she could probably make it well into Fandelyon by dawn and then they'd all be safe from her and her horrid new nature. "Just promise me you'll get Kirsty home safely."

"By the Higher Realm, we're not going to abandon you," Elias said. He looked like he'd be happy to, and yet whatever drew them toward each other was clearly stronger than either of them. She saw her own needs reflected in his eyes.

She couldn't allow her curse to control her like that again. She had to leave them all. "I've caused more trouble than I can ever repay."

"We'll do what we can for you Caroline, but I'll need some assurances," Allyn said. He turned to Kirsty. "From you as well." Allyn didn't look angry or even irritated. He smelled... keen, of all things. Caution overcame her as she studied his expression. He wanted something.

Kirsty spoke a little too quickly. "Of course." She glanced at Elias, her eyes betraying her desire to spend more time in his company.

Goose bumps crept across Caroline's skin, suggesting magic was being manipulated, but she couldn't see the incandescent threads of power as she had the other night. She glanced from Allyn to Elias and finally Dobbin, but couldn't see magic from either of them. Dobbin frowned though, glancing from Allyn to Elias, while Elias gave Allyn a curious glance as if trying to work out what his mentor was up to. She still saw nothing. If it was Allyn, he clearly knew enough magic lore to hide whatever he was doing, if not the fact he was doing something. "I don't want to put any of you in more danger," she said, taking a half step away from Allyn.

Allyn accepted her words with a slight nod. "I'm offering my help, freely. Do you accept?"

She wanted to say no, but couldn't deny Kirsty a chance at safety. "Only if-"

"I won't accept conditions, Princess. If we're to escort you to Fandelyon with faspane searching for us, I need to know you'll do as you're told. There are too many risks now the faspane have caught up, and neither you nor Kirsty are skilled in the wilderness. This will be the most dangerous part of our journey. I'll expect you to obey me."

He smelled too eager and she couldn't help the caution warning her to walk away. "In what manner do you expect me to obey?" Caroline asked, her voice sounding slightly shrill. "I'm not a servant. I'm not going to wait on you."

"I need to know if I give you an instruction, you won't ignore me and get me or anyone else killed. A human kingdom is a very dangerous place for Elias and I, even skirting the edges. Worse with faspane dogging us. I need to know you'll do as you're told."

She looked at Dobbin for assurance. "I think it's an izzen thing," the shivra said. "Either way, he's got a point. Yer green, Kirsty too. Doing what yer told is merely sensible."

"You'll see us safely to Fandelyon City?" she asked Allyn.

"As close as we can manage."

She still hesitated. "What if-"

"No, Caroline. I'll ask nothing from either of you I'd be unwilling to do myself, but we can't take you otherwise. We've our own tasks, and my duties won't allow either of you to jeopardise it any further."

"So don't go observing any battles or rescuing stray humans," Elias muttered.

"What?" Caroline asked.

"It was a jibe at me," Allyn said.

"Oh." She glanced at Dobbin.

The shivra shrugged. "I've never known an izzat ta lead me wrong.

They're shifty sods, but if they commit ta something ye can rely on 'em." Allyn gave Dobbin an exasperated look.

Kirsty said, "I'm willing if you are, My Lady. It's only until we're home, after all." Kirsty's faith was almost enough to dispel Caroline's fears. Her only other choice was to risk travelling alone. Another week under Allyn's direction may be uncertain, but he had risked his life for her already.

"What if-"

"You have my terms."

She held her hands up in surrender. "Fine. I promise to obey you." A flash of white heat passed into her like the feeling she'd had when Kimbriel's gifts revealed themselves to her. Disorientated and dizzy, she almost fell.

"No!" Elias yelled. "If I'd known you intended that... Fool! You've broken a tradition older than yourself. You can't have two students. You've destroyed our bond!" Dobbin rushed to stand between the izzen, but neither moved.

"It was past time," Allyn said.

"I decide when it's time. It was supposed to be *my* choice."

Anger edged Allyn's voice. "You're supposed to make that choice as soon as you're capable, and you've been capable for years."

"I wasn't ready."

"I'm not a crutch. The bond ensures your safety, and mine. Consider this my final lesson. There's nothing more I can teach you."

The butterflies in Caroline's stomach fluttered in different directions as the implications sank in. She knew what Allyn had done. She felt it; sensed Allyn's presence like pressure in her mind. Kirsty's hand gripped hers and she jumped. Her friend didn't know what had just happened, but probably felt just as much need for assurance as Caroline did. Caroline squeezed back.

Elias's ears were actually quivering. "You planned this from the time we saw her, didn't you? Gave her hope and then threatened to cut her loose. When did you make that binding? I should have realised what you were doing when you activated something."

Allyn's face showed he wasn't proud of his actions. "It was necessary to protect our people. Noramgaell..."

"She doesn't even know what she's accepted!"

Allyn winced, actually winced. "She'd never have agreed, otherwise."

Caroline closed her eyes. "I think I do. I've become Allyn's student, just as you were." A week ago she would have trembled at the thought of how far she could fall. First lycanthropy, now magic, and she'd agreed to obey the sorcerer. Been deceived into it, but still. She tried to gather some resolve. "As soon as I can break your bond, I will, Allyn."

Elias spoke, "And I'll do everything I can to help her." How was it that Elias was siding with her after she'd hurt him so badly? Surely he should be gloating? "Fool. You're older than the faspane wars, yet have the common sense of a child."

"What are the faspane wars?" Kirsty asked.

"What's your plan, Allyn? Do you expect to return to Fandelyon City after we deliver the sword and demand to remain in her presence and teach her magic? The humans on this side of the Temern Straight fear magic. You're wrecking the poor girl's life." He sounded disgusted.

Allyn smelled... guilty, but it was more than that. He caught Caroline's gaze and flushed, shame and furtiveness in his scent. There was something more.

Quiet settled over the room, yet everything suddenly made sense. Whatever the intricacies of this destiny Marnier du Shae wanted for her, Caroline knew she'd been born for the purpose, and Allyn's mission was part of it. She knew it deep within her soul. Her *alimoth* flowers warmed in agreement as she raised her chin. "Allyn has a plan he hasn't shared."

Kirsty, Elias and Dobbin stared.

"He's not telling us something. Telling me." It was a guess, but Allyn's sent changed, confirming her suspicions.

"I've told you everything you need to know."

"I need to know more."

His inhumanly green eyes went cold for such a short time she wondered if she really saw it. He glanced at Elias, who returned a flat stare. "Fine. Kirsty, could you leave the room please?"

"Kirsty stays. I trust her," Caroline said.

"With your life?" Allyn asked. "With mine and Elias's? Dobbin's?"

"Yes." She felt warmth from her *alimoth* flowers again; something significant had happened. Kirsty seemed to have felt it too, judging by the way she gripped Caroline just a little harder.

The silence grew. "What I say doesn't leave this room. Swear it."

"I swear," she said.

"And you, Kirsty? Do you swear to obey Caroline?" Caroline felt the hair creep up the back of her neck. Goose bumps. Magic again. This time she saw a complex binding of energy spreading before Allyn like a gossamer web ready to catch its prey. She didn't know how, but she recognised the compulsion in the pattern, and saw the way it would become a part of Kirsty and hold her to her word.

Caroline squeezed Kirsty's hand tighter. "Kirsty, he's going to bind you to your answer. Think very carefully."

Allyn's jaw dropped and he stared at Caroline. "How?" he whispered.

Kirsty raised her chin. "Thank you. I understand. You have my oath, Allyn. I swear to obey Caroline." The gossamer web flared incandescent and fell around Kirsty, sinking into her flesh. Her friend stiffened and gasped.

Allyn frowned. "I believe you owe me some answers, Caroline."

"I believe you owe me some first."

His frown deepened. Was he thinking of using the bond to compel her? Would he make her reveal her discussion with Kimbriel? He took a deep breath. "How did you understand the compulsion spell?"

"I don't know Allyn, or at least not all of the answers you expect. I've been able to sense magic since I met you. Probably before, I guess. The night we rescued Elias, I saw Dobbin casting his darklight ward. I don't know why I could see it, but I could. I don't know how I knew what your magic would do just then, but I did." She didn't think it was Kimbriel's doing or Marnier du Shae's influence. Kimbriel hadn't given Caroline her gifts until after she'd seen Dobbin's spell, and she didn't feel anything from her *alimoth* flowers when magic was being cast.

Allyn and Elias shared a look while Dobbin pulled a chair nearer the fire and sat.

"Good enough," Allyn said. "Close to two decades ago, our oracles claim someone bargained their soul to the God of War in exchange for true immortality. His name is Phoenix and he'll rise to rule the faspane. Our seers say Phoenix has been stirring the faspane clans, trying to rally them. We believe he demonstrated his immortality recently and was reborn or resurrected in some way. Word spread and the clans are gathering."

"How does that affect me?" she asked. "You said I'm supposed to unite the human nations?"

"More than that, Princess. This war will define our universe and our place in it for the rest of existence. A united front among the faspane would outnumber shivras, humans and my kind together. What does that suggest?"

The gravity of it all forced a moment of whimsy on her. "That we shouldn't tease them?"

He gave her a look, but she thought she caught a hint of a smile underneath it. "Your kind could expect slavery. Dobbin's people the same. Mine, genocide. This is why I need you to learn about magic. You'll need every tool you can find."

"How do you plan to stop this Phoenix person if he gets reborn when he dies?"

"The shivras are forging a Gods-inspired sword we believe will destroy him. *The Sword of the Sun*. It's a weapon of pure fire which should destroy his body completely, preventing him rising from his own ashes."

"Believe?" The thought was ridiculous. "All this on a chance? What exactly do you expect from me? How is learning magic supposed to help?"

He shrugged. "Magic gives you another weapon, and you've an

affinity with fire. The faspane know a human will build an empire and stand against them and you have more power welling inside you than any human I've ever met, more than any shivra and even the strongest of the izzen. You stir *Quala Umitha* with your very presence, something only the Gods can touch at will."

Even if she got home she'd never feel safe. Her own people would kill her for what she was becoming. Had become. How often had she woken from a nightmare where she'd died by fire? "Sounds like a fairy tale," Caroline murmured. "A horrible one." She stared at him, waiting. "There's more, isn't there? What else? It isn't good, is it?

"Only Marnier du Shae's Champion can wield the Sword of the Sun. Why else would she gift you with an affinity for fire?"

She glanced at her alimoth outlines, something he didn't know about. "And?"

"Who else could survive such a weapon?"

30

———————

The massive stone door grated as it swung into a recess. Caroline walked into heavy morning mist behind Allyn. She took a deep breath of cold fresh air, mostly free of Elias's scent. As the chill began to seep through her clothes, Dobbin closed the cave's stone entrance using a small catch to the side. She held her cloak tight and shivered as icy dew chilled her bare feet, her boots lost in the simorath caves.

All around her the mist, or perhaps low cloud, clung to huge mossy pines like a drunken lover. Her own breath misted. A thrill of fear stabbed through her as she caught a whiff of something out of place. "Faspane," she said.

"Look out!" Elias shouted as he shoved her aside.

A bolt punched into her abdomen just above her hip and she crashed to the ground. Agony lanced through her. It felt as if the bolt had turned molten. Blinded by tears, she grasped the shaft, the reek of silver stronger than her blood. She pulled with all her strength, the barbless bolt coming out cleanly. "Oh Gods!" she gasped, dropping the bloody shaft from trembling fingers.

From the corner of her eye she noticed Elias raise his hand. She saw an intricate display of energy, and felt goose bumps. The intricate web of magic went incandescent as a blinding flash of light illuminated the trees from within. Caroline squinted, turning away.

"See them?" Elias asked Allyn.

"No, but it won't take long to reload that crossbow," Allyn said. Dobbin crouched in front of Caroline with his shield ready.

"Six inches higher and it would have hit her heart," Elias said.

Kirsty knelt beside her, but hesitated in reaching out in comfort, probably for fear of hurting her further. "Caroline?"

"We have to move." Elias grasped Caroline's free hand and hauled her upright. She gasped, her side exploding in pain and her legs barely holding her weight. "Can you move?" Elias asked, looking her in the eye to get her to focus.

Blood seeped through her fingers when she pressed them to the aching wound, mocking her supernatural healing abilities. "This might actually kill me," she whispered, weak and lightheaded. Her legs felt like they might collapse. "Oh Gods, please don't let me die before I get Kirsty home."

From the trees, a faspane called something in a harsh language. Caroline cringed as warm blood trickled over her hip. Allyn called something back in the same language. A quick conversation ensued.

"What are they saying?" Caroline asked, surprised at how weak her voice sounded.

Elias shushed her, his ears moving independently. She waited in pain and fear through the conversation until four faspane emerged from the fog, crossbows raised.

"Why haven't they killed us?" Kirsty asked. She looked so small and helpless that Caroline couldn't help but try and protect her with her body.

Elias spared Kirsty a glance. "They say they tried to kill Caroline cleanly, honourably. Now they're offering a challenge. Single combat. They want Caroline to fight one of them. It's got something to do with their honour."

"What?" Caroline asked, a new fear clutching her. "That's ridiculous."

Dobbin shifted his position, raising his axe slightly. "Aye. Even if she knew how to fight, she's wounded because of them," he growled. "Are they planning on waiting until she recovers?" The four faspane warriors stopped about twenty yards away. Dobbin stepped forward and raised his axe higher.

A bolt struck the ground at Dobbin's feet but he didn't react. It hadn't come from the faspane Caroline could see. She sniffed, but the stench of silver and her own blood overpowered everything.

"We didn't come to fight you, shivra," a thickly-accented female voice called from the forest. "If you charge, we'll kill the dark-haired girl first."

"Get behind me," Caroline said to Kirsty, trying not to betray her dread in her voice. Despite the pre-dawn gloom, Kirsty's fear was obvious. Bound to obey, Kirsty did as she was told.

One of the faspane stepped forward and drew his sword. Almost as tall as Caroline, his broken nose and scarred chin suggested he'd survived several duels. He spoke clearly despite his accent. "I apologise, Princess. If you'd been a warrior like him," he nodded at Dobbin, "then challenging you would show us both honour. Still, tradition demands I give you a chance now."

"Considering ye wounded her first, that's some sense of honour ye have," Dobbin said. He shifted his balance. Elias seemed ready to move too.

Caroline caught Elias's shoulder. "No," she said, unwilling to let any of them risk their lives for her again. She raised her voice, though fear nearly choked her. "I accept your challenge, faspane, so long as my friends are allowed to leave unharmed."

"Your Highness!" Kirsty hissed.

"Don't be stupid," Elias added, stepping in front of her, the move as unexpected as it was appreciated.

The faspane smiled. "I see why the Higher Realm chose you, girl. It's a shame we cannot resolve this through diplomacy."

Diplomacy? "We can!" she cried, suddenly hopeful despite the gaping wound in her side. "Leave us and I promise to turn away from my destiny." She'd never wanted it anyway, so it was hardly a loss. Her *alimoth* flowers went cold in warning. She ignored them.

The warrior raised an eyebrow at the unexpected offer. "Gods have a habit of forcing their will on people." He tossed his blade hilt first. It flopped to the ground before Elias.

Caroline stared. "You want me to use your sword?" It was long and two-edged.

"It would have been simpler if you'd died." He handed his crossbow to a shorter, thick-set companion and drew the man's sword. "The failure is mine, and I must finish it. We will fight, and you will die. One day, I hope your spirit will forgive me." It all seemed wrong. The faspane were supposed to be murderous assassins, not honourable warriors doing an unsavoury duty.

"Caroline," Elias said, still trying to stay between her and them. "We'll find another way."

She gingerly moved around him and retrieved the sword, gasping in pain as she bent. The weapon wasn't as heavy as it looked. "What other way?" she asked. She'd been lucky to survive this long. "Better they kill me than all of us." The blade reeked. The entire length was etched with strange symbols, which were filled with silver. She shuddered at the smell.

"Caroline-" Allyn began.

"There's at least five of them, Allyn, and only Dobbin's properly armed. Unless you've got some magic that can help, let me save your lives." He could use the bond to deny her this, but after a moment he looked away.

"He'll kill you," Elias said, fear in his voice.

She squinted into the pre-dawn fog shrouding the trees, wondering how many faspane there really were. She couldn't smell much besides silver; it even kept Elias's scent at bay. "Then I die and you all live. Maybe you'll find me in my rebirth." Thank the Higher Realm the threat was only to her. She raised her voice. "You have my terms, faspane. My friends leave here unharmed with a full day's grace."

"I agree to your terms, Princess. My companions will honour our terms. Fair?"

"Please don't," Kirsty pleaded. She smelled terrified.

"Agreed," Caroline said. "Dobbin?" If anyone might cause trouble, she figured it would be him and his huge axe. "Will you accept the result? For Kirsty?"

Dobbin's hand clenched the haft of his weapon as he glared at the faspane. They were easily beyond his reach, yet close enough they couldn't fail to miss him with a bolt, despite his shield.

"Fine, lass. Ye have me word," he said, sounding like he had to choke the words out. "But ye better kill the sod or I'll be looking fer revenge come dawn tomorrow."

"Kirsty?" No doubt her friend felt as helpless as she did. If it wasn't for the crossbows... She moved back and took Kirsty's hand, determined to protect her friend. She leaned close and whispered. "Kirsty, please obey the terms of the agreement. Don't make me force you." She felt Kirsty stiffen in response.

"That's not fair."

"I'm so sorry, Kirsty. But if it means you'll survive then I'll do whatever it takes." Her friend looked away, clearly upset.

Allyn grimaced. "May the Higher Realm protect you. I accept the terms."

"Elias?" she asked. His expression didn't hide his anger at the faspane and her decision. She had a feeling she couldn't trust his word, even if he accepted.

"It seems I've underestimated you, Princess. If I could see another way... Good luck. You have my word."

She watched his face for any trace of a lie, but he seemed sincere. "Thank you," she said. "Get Kirsty to safety." He nodded, but kept his eyes on the trees.

She hefted the horrible-smelling blade and limped toward the faspane, one hand clenching her aching side. At least the sword's hilt contained no silver. She doubted she'd be able to hold it if it had. Her pulse pounded double-time to her step, maybe triple. She tried to keep her eyes on her opponent's green ones, so like Allyn's. This was her fate, then. She didn't look back at her friends, people she'd come to care about more than her own life. Perhaps she'd get a lucky swing in.

"My Lady!" Kirsty called. Caroline paused, dreading the thought of Kirsty's expression. She couldn't look. Kirsty continued, "I don't believe the Higher Realm would bring us this far and not give you a chance. Have faith, My Lady."

Without turning, Caroline gave her friend a brief nod before moving forward, stopping a sword's length from the faspane. She almost put the point of her weapon on the ground to lean on, her side hurt so much. Blood still trickled from the wound, staining her new clothes.

"Do we just start?" Despite what Kirsty believed, she was going to die.

The faspane looked down, as if in shame. "The rules are what we agreed on. You may choose your weapon, but as you only have a sword..." he shrugged, finally looking up. "It was the only gift I could offer for such an unfair duel. Otherwise we begin when we're both ready. I'll give you a moment to pray to your Gods if you wish."

"Pray?" she asked, surprised again. "You'd respect my beliefs?" Would it do any good? If Marnier du Shae had placed her here, then why not give her something she could fight with? She stared at the silver-etched sword and a shiver of hope ran through her.

He glanced at her bloody wound. "I respect what you're doing, not the Gods. If you believe they're worthy of your devotion considering they've lead you to this moment, then pray."

If this was all part of divine influence, then perhaps Marnier du Shae had given her a chance. She turned the blade point-down and drove it into the ground. Pain shot through her side with the effort. "I'll fight unarmed," she gasped. "And I'll take that moment to pray."

He watched curiously, glancing between her and the weapon. "The moon is no longer full. You'll get no help from the curse." Clearly, he knew too much. Marnier du Shae may be helping her, but another God seemed to be helping, or perhaps manipulating, the faspane.

"You did me the honour of offering a fair fight. I grant you the same. I suggest you take up the second sword." She dropped her cloak to the ground and unlaced her shirt, gingerly pulling it off and dropping it to the ground along with the rest of her clothing. The cold bit into her exposed skin and made her bleeding wound ache. His posture lost some confidence.

"I'll take up that second sword," he said, drawing the weapon from the ground. His companions backed off, uncertainty on their faces.

Holding both weapons, he glanced from them to her, now defenceless. She could almost read his mind: he knew he could end it right then. Instead he straightened and nodded. "Should you defeat me, it is because faspane are honourable," he said. "The Higher Realm has ignored that for two hundred thousand years. No longer."

She inclined her head. "Should I defeat you, I promise to always treat your people with the same honour you've shown me. Perhaps our nations will find peace."

"We have peace now. The Higher Realm is drawing your people into this, not mine."

"Yet it's you hunting me."

A frown crossed his features. "If we have to destroy your people, the shivras, the izzen and the simoraths to regain what we lost and be free of the Higher Realm, we will."

She couldn't see how doing any of that would help his people. "What's your name?"

"I am called Zaramar. When you're ready, Princess."

"Thank you." She imagined the moon rising full on the horizon, and let its imaginary power consume her. It took longer than last time due to the silver-tainted wound, but heat and blinding agony eventually shattered her poise. She fell to the ground. It was a long moment before the pain passed and she could draw a breath again. Zaramar stared in fascinated revulsion. She stood gingerly on all four legs, the pain in her side only a little diminished. Changed, she could keenly sense the approach of dawn. She had to end this quickly.

He dropped the tip of one horrid, silver-etched sword toward her and raised the other, ready to swing down. The stench seared her nose and throat and made her neck ache, but she welcomed it as it meant she couldn't smell Elias.

She felt her strength rising and the raw power of a werewolf thrumming through her, her own magic fuelling the curse. She'd need that power to overcome silvered swords. She faced him and knew without doubt Marnier du Shae had given her far more than she needed to survive her journey home, if indeed the Goddess of Healing was responsible for her situation.

She bowed her head slightly, offering a genuine prayer of thanks to the Goddess. Zaramar nodded in reply, ready. She snarled, bunched her muscles, and sprang.

Zaramar raised one sword and swung the other, but he was too slow. Twisting to avoid the blades, she struck, tearing his throat out and landing beyond him. He fell backwards, both weapons slapping to the ground at the same time.

She bowed her head, for once feeling no bloodlust.

And then a woman screamed.

~

Elias almost backed away from the reddish-furred werewolf. Caroline had moved much faster than the werewolf he'd killed while saving her life - supernaturally fast. Hesitantly, he took a step forward in the hope she'd retained her sanity, but Caroline spun and snarled, her too-human green eyes in stark contrast to the dangerous animal she'd become. Corded muscle bunched, muscle that no ordinary wolf or even werewolf should possess. She was ready to leap.

He froze, watching her eyes as fear and the realisation of his own mortality held him in place. He was going to be killed by the one person he wanted to protect, and he didn't have a chance, even if she gave him time to draw his hunting knife. The curse clearly fed off her magic, making her incredibly strong and fast.

Just as quickly, Caroline turned toward several faspane running from the trees, one with a crossbow aimed at her. A female. Another warrior smashed the weapon from the woman's hands, but it didn't stop her. She drew a long, slender sword and ran at Caroline with a scream of anguish.

Elias reached for his dagger as Caroline snarled, ready to spring. He had no doubt after seeing her supernatural speed that she could take them all, but then she collapsed to the ground, convulsing as he body began to change with dawn. "Caroline!" he yelled with a different kind of fear as the powerful muscles under her fur contracted and she convulsed, her entire body shrinking.

"What's wrong with her?" Kirsty screamed.

"Dawn," Allyn said, raising his staff in readiness for a fight with the faspane.

Dobbin roared and ran to try and put himself between Caroline and the warriors, shield ready and axe raised, but the faspane woman was closer.

Elias drew his heavy dagger and raised it to throw. A big faspane warrior tackled the woman and drove her hard into the ground. Another forced her face into the pine needles and sparse grass, while a third pulled the blade from the woman's hands. She kicked and yelled, but they held her still.

"Enough," said one of her companions. "You know the rules."

"They don't apply to filthy animals like that," she said, her face pressed to the ground. "Let me go! She destroyed his soul! He'll never be reborn now."

Caroline's body seemed to turn liquid, reforming into that of a naked human girl. She moaned, only it seemed to be more in pleasure than pain. Elias hesitated, not sure whether to try and help Caroline or give her some privacy. With the exception of the woman, the other faspane warriors seemed to be honouring the deal.

Dagger still in hand, Elias glanced at Allyn, but his former teacher shook his head. "Keep alert, but do nothing."

Once they had the woman under control, the big warrior spoke in Faspaneth. "Zaramar was her husband. We apologise for her actions. She loved him too much, it seems." He glanced warily at Caroline's limp form, probably uncertain whether she could change back into a wolf if provoked. "By tradition, the girl keeps Zaramar's sword. May she use it with honour."

He removed the scabbard from Zaramar's body and dropped it

next to the dead warrior's weapon, before retrieving the other blade. Two warriors lifted Zaramar's body while a third forced his wife to go with them, still struggling and yelling abuse in Faspaneth.

The woman wrenched her arms free. Elias thought she was about to try and rush Caroline, but instead she stared murder. "I'll honour the deal, even if it's with a filthy, disgusting werewolf." She spat on the ground. "But after that, I'll find you and you'll never see me rip your heart out." She turned, walking away before the other warriors could force her.

Elias couldn't help but shiver at the woman's intensity.

As the group of faspane disappeared into the fog-bound trees, Caroline struggled to her feet and limped toward her clothes like an exhausted beggar. Kirsty rushed to help her dress.

She caught his eye and immediately looked away. He couldn't tell if she was embarrassed, or hopeful.

31

Tense and unsure the faspane would hold to their agreement, Elias led the party among towering pines, their wide trunks and rough bark covered in dark green moss, often growing as thick as a man's beard. Most of the pines would be thousands of years old. His head brushed a low branch of drooping needles, showering him with dew which found its way down the back of his neck and shirt.

It was a counterpoint to the memory of Caroline's warm fingers on his closely-shaved face, or his hopelessness at seeing her selflessly walk into a duel and what he'd thought was her death. He wanted to feel her touch again, glimpse her naked once more, and protect her all at the same time.

He needed to focus on the dangers, from both the possibilities of a closer relationship with Caroline and the more immediate threats surrounding them.

Either could bring a quick death.

He stopped and glanced around, turning his ears back and forth, but nothing seemed out of place.

"What's the matter?" Allyn asked.

"Just being cautious." He continued leading the small group.

The unwanted, sickly feeling returned to his stomach when he considered Caroline's revelation in the shivrad cave. Human. How could he possibly be part human? What did Allyn know about such a thing happening before? The royal line, his mother's side, was beyond reproach. Her very presence protected his people from the Gods' wrath, but his father's past was a mystery. Human.

He waited for Allyn to move up beside him. "What do you know about mixed bloodlines with humans?"

Allyn gave him a cagey glance. "Rumours. Queen Sellendria crossed the Veil into another universe in her youth. She said she met her soulmate there, as a human. If she'd given up her immortality and stayed with him, she believes they'd have been able to have children who would have been creatures of both worlds. Perhaps even immortal. She, though, would have died."

Could his own father be the product of another izzat finding a human soulmate? "Clearly, she didn't."

A broken cliff rose into the mist to the left while a steep climb among pines began about fifty yards to the right, making the pass a perfect channel for an ambush. They no longer followed a trail, but the area was sheltered and relatively flat.

"Allyn," he murmured as a new concern occurred to him. "You, Dobbin and I are warded against scrying. Caroline has that necklace which seems to do much the same thing. I assume you gave Kirsty something?"

Allyn's ears drooped. "I've been stupid..." He turned. "Kirsty, do you have any jewellery? Something with a gem or a crystal?"

"A gem," she said in her quiet voice. She pulled a fine gold necklace from under her dress, a small sapphire dangling from it.

Allyn examined the stone in the foggy gloom of dawn, the direct sunlight kept away by mist and the mountain's shadow. Chilling cold slid off the snow-covered heights above. The trees didn't grow much higher up the right slope, and barely at all on the cliff.

"It should hold a charge for about a week," Allyn said as he cupped the jewel in both hands. Elias felt the cool tingle of magic on his skin, almost the opposite feeling from sunlight. Anyone nearby who could sense magic would feel it, too.

He caught Caroline watching despite herself, clearly fascinated. Not only did she watch, but her eyes moved, examining the threads of magic as Allyn wove. She noticed Elias watching her and flushed before looking away.

"Dobbin, stay cautious," Allyn said, finishing. "When the faspane warriors report to their wizard he'll direct them this way, assuming he's got any skill with scrying."

"Aye."

They continued at a good pace until the slope grew dangerously steep, forcing Elias to cut a path back and forth across the mountainside.

He led them down rock faces and around trees bigger than they could all stand around and touch hands. The girls and even Dobbin moved much slower than he or Allyn could, with Caroline holding her wound the entire time.

As he jumped over a trickle of water, Caroline squealed behind him, the sound followed by a thump.

He spun, prepared to fight whoever had attacked her, but she sat on a jutting stone, one bare foot braced against a pine sapling. Allyn, between them, looked ready to grab her.

"Ow," she said, though the pain in her expression clearly showed she was hurting much worse than her simple word suggested.

"Your Highness?" Kirsty asked from behind while gripping tightly to the frond of a giant tree-fern, clearly undecided as to whether going to the princess would be more of a hindrance than a help.

"I'm okay. Bruised ego," Caroline said. She stood gingerly and brushed her damp backside with one hand, the other on her wound. The blood on her clothes hadn't begun to dry yet and was still being fed by a trickle of blood, the stain spreading.

"Dobbin, you'd better carry her," Elias said to hide the distress he felt at seeing her hurt. She'd probably slap him if he offered his hand.

Dobbin grinned back. "Aye. Lucky there's no other werewolves around. They'd be laughing at the clumsy new one."

Caroline flushed again, her pale skin making the smattering of freckles across her nose stand out.

"Dobbin slipped a few minutes ago, My Lady," Kirsty said quietly to Caroline, though not nearly quiet enough to keep it private. "He almost landed on me." She gave Elias a look, and he couldn't help a grin.

"Traitor," Dobbin muttered. "Next time either of ye need to be carried, and it seems often enough, remind me ta drag ye by the hair instead. Or ye feet."

"Elias too?" Caroline asked with a smirk.

"I wouldn't touch his manky feet. Guess yer on yer own, pixie."

The three stared at him expectantly, but he had the feeling that if he said anything he'd only give them a reason to properly unite. How had this become about him? Allyn raised an eyebrow, clearly amused and waiting to see how he'd find a way out.

He turned away. "We're wasting time," he muttered, the words heavy with defeat.

They continued down the mountain, picking their way around small cliffs and moss-covered trees and overhangs, the slow pace frustrating. A simple drop of ten feet was beyond the girls, and even Dobbin was struggling for breath.

"Elias," Caroline hissed, a sound of fear in her tone. "Faspane. They passed here late last night." She crinkled her nose, which looked surprisingly cute.

Elias climbed back to her position and examined the ground. There was at least one scuff mark.

She pointed from left to right. "They were moving across the slope, but I don't know which way they went." Caroline crouched low, sniffing again. When she looked up, there was something new on her face. He wasn't quite sure what. She flushed and looked away, almost as if in embarrassment. "You need a bath," she said.

"I need a bath?" He waited, but she didn't respond so he let it be. He examined the branches to the left of the path, a small one broken. "Someone definitely went by here. That way." He pointed.

"Two people. Their scents are distinct. I can even smell them over your stench."

He narrowed his eyes, trying to get a whiff of himself without being obvious about it. "I don't smell." Once again, Allyn appeared amused but didn't come to his rescue.

She flushed again, unexpectedly. Perspiration appeared on her forehead and her breathing seemed quickened.

Was she fevered? Did werewolves even get sick?

She returned her attention to the ground, as if she'd been caught with a hand among sweet pastries. "I think they passed a little after midnight."

"I only see evidence of one."

"There were two." She sounded flustered, yet the faspane were long gone.

Dobbin chuckled. "Elias. Please don't annoy the friendly werewolf. She bites if she gets annoyed."

"I believe there's more meat on you than on me," he replied, glad for a reason to break the unexpected tension.

Caroline tried to glare at them both, difficult when Dobbin was behind her. "But you smell so much better, Elias."

"I thought I needed a bath?"

She paled as if she'd been caught out in something. "Um, yes. You do."

Dobbin chuckled. "It's decided then. Let me know how pixies taste."

"That'll do," Allyn said, clearly suppressing a grin. "Elias, could you please scout ahead? Farsight's not going to help with the faspane hiding their auras from arcane Sight."

Elias nodded, glad for the opportunity to leave Caroline behind, yet the princess seemed disappointed as he stood. A part of him couldn't help but feel encouraged, while another part wanted to get away.

"I thought they were going to leave us alone until tonight?" Caroline said.

"Only the group we faced outside the cave. Your bargain didn't include any others."

∽

Caroline's heart continued pounding in reaction to Elias's lingering scent, leaving her with the horrid feeling she had no control over herself, and that he knew it and was taking advantage of the fact.

"No more talking if we can avoid it," Allyn murmured, breaking her concentration. "I'd rather slow the pace than rush and draw attention."

Overhead, a bronze-winged reba dragon the size of a horse circled above the trees, looking for early-season fruit no doubt. She caught glimpses of it through the foliage and wished she could fly away, never to return. Reba dragons were rarely seen within the Kingdom except when raiding orchards, and spooked easily, which was a good thing, considering their size.

Allyn crouched to examine the ground, fingertips spread wide. Magic washed outward in all directions.

"Are you hiding our tracks again?" she asked, recognising a pattern in his magic. It was ridiculously complex, unlike Dobbin's ward.

He finished what he was doing before looking up. "Was that a guess?"

"Yes."

He raised an eyebrow. "Yes. Let's go."

"I thought you were supposed to be teaching me magic?"

He paused, giving her a curious look. "Why so keen?" He seemed genuinely amused at her enthusiasm.

"Because I want to remove the hold you have on me."

The amusement disappeared and he dropped his eyes, clearly uncomfortable. "Now's not the time."

"Lucky they don't have any hunting dogs," she muttered. Following Elias's scent was like treading a paved road.

"Ye looking ta make some new friends?" Dobbin said. "Aren't we furry enough?"

She turned to tell him off, but he had a huge grin on his face which she couldn't help but match. "Did I mention I'm hungry?" she asked sweetly.

His grin got bigger. "That's me girl. We'll make a proper shivra of ya yet."

Caroline stayed with Kirsty and helped her friend down the rockier outcrops and along the most slippery places, her bare feet better than boots. A blunder could send them tumbling dozens of yards straight down, and Kirsty was fully aware of it, fear almost constantly in her scent.

The pain in Caroline's side slowly left as they struggled over and around fallen trees and rocks and through tree-fern fronds. She was careful not to push up against anything with her side in case she left a smear of blood.

After about an hour Allyn paused, one hand up. Her heart thumped with her own fearful surprise as Elias appeared out of the mist. How did he move so quietly? Could the faspane move like that too?

Elias held up four fingers and pointed off to her right.

She caught her breath as she listened, staring into the mist, the air mostly still. She thought she heard a footstep some distance away. Something else too, a boot scraping across an exposed root maybe.

Allyn pointed at Caroline and Kirsty before indicating a huge ghost oak, its winter-grey bark falling away in paper-thin strips to reveal white underneath. Surrounding the trunk was a thick undergrowth of young tree ferns, the fronds of the tallest spanning several yards and dropping downward at the tips. She nodded, grasped Kirsty's hand and pulled her friend in among the fronds, allowing mist and leaves to obscure them. Dobbin clambered into a clutch of shrubs a dozen yards away, making more noise than a horse trying to navigate a pottery merchant's shop. She assumed Allyn and Elias did something similar, although she couldn't hear them. For a brief moment she felt magic, but couldn't see who did it or why.

She put her arms protectively around Kirsty as she rested her back against the hard, dead fronds of the tree-fern's trunk. Her own breath sounded loud and Kirsty's even louder.

She closed her eyes, straining to distinguish the four sets of footsteps. Fabric snagged on something and pulled free.

She held Kirsty tighter as the faspane moved across the slope, no doubt hoping to cut across their tracks. Kirsty, eyes closed and very pale, smelled terrified.

The faspane came closer until footsteps sounded just a few yards away. Clothing brushed against leaves as a warrior bent low. She held her breath.

If it came to a fight, there were four armed and well-trained faspane against a shivra and two mostly unarmed izzen. In the daytime, Caroline would be a hindrance at best, and she hated feeling useless. Even if they won, she couldn't assume they would escape unharmed. Very bad odds.

The tracker moved past her ghost oak and its cluster of tree ferns with the skill of a predator, the three warriors following just as quietly. One of them paused. Could he see her through the fronds? Seconds passed, long and tense until the warrior continued on, giving her the chance to breathe again.

She kept still as their tread disappeared into the fog, retaining her hold on Kirsty for long minutes afterward until she heard Dobbin break cover, branches snapping as he slipped over and cursed under his breath. Hopefully the faspane were well out of earshot.

Trying to keep quiet, Caroline pushed through the damp fronds, Kirsty behind her. Allyn put a finger to his lips with a sour glance at Dobbin, who had the grace to look embarrassed. Caroline nodded and grasped Kirsty's trembling hand as they quietly followed Elias into the fog. Within minutes, Elias was scouting ahead.

They continued that way for most of the afternoon as they gradually made their way down the mountain, stopping only for a handful of nuts, a strip of jerky and some hard biscuits Dobbin carried in the pack under his shield. The fog never lifted, clinging to the mountainside like a wet blanket even when they'd descended almost as far as the lowlands.

Exhausted and with aching knees, Caroline put her hand on her lower back and straightened, stretching. The silver-inflicted wound had sapped a lot of her strength, but it had closed over and seemed to be healing well.

"How are you?" Caroline asked Kirsty. Her friend seemed exhausted.

"Fine, My Lady." Kirsty offered a small smile, though it was more a grimace.

Caroline raised an eyebrow. "Fine enough that Marnier du Shae's abbey is regaining some appeal?"

That drew a genuine smile. "Fond memories. Particularly the dawn bells."

They reached the base of the mountain and the Senbow River late in the afternoon. Caroline was thoroughly damp from the mist and wet foliage, and achingly tense with the possibility of running across more faspane. Just ahead, water roared through a huge gorge that divided the mountains from the lowlands, the sound almost too noisy to hear anything above. At least the fog had begun to break up, even if it remained overcast. The heavy clouds threatened rain.

Allyn examined the ground.

"Down river," Caroline said. Everyone looked at her. "Elias's smell goes that way."

About a mile down river they found a huge fallen tree across the river's gorge. Caroline stopped well short and the others stopped with her. She sniffed. "I smell silver. Blood too. Faspane."

Dobbin took the lead, shield and hammer ready. They stopped only when they got to the tree. Allyn examined a slip mark at the edge of the gorge. A hint of blood marked a stone nearby. "The faspane must have set a trap here. Elias foiled it."

"There's a body behind those rocks," Caroline said, sniffing. "Faspane. Elias's scent goes across the fallen tree. He's about half an hour ahead."

Allyn shook his head. "Tracking's no fun with a werewolf for company."

"Would you rather the company of a self-absorbed princess?" she asked.

Allyn grinned before walking across the huge tree, his step as sure as if treading a footpath despite the raging white water below. It had to be close to forty yards across, but the fallen ghost oak's trunk was still strong. Dobbin followed more cautiously, but the wood never shifted.

"Stay with me?" Kirsty asked. She smelled panicked.

"Of course."

Caroline walked behind Kirsty as her friend crawled across the mossy trunk, the snowmelt-laden river crashing underneath them. White water churned over boulders the size of carts, scouring the gorge's walls, parts of which were freshly exposed from a recent collapse. At least the trunk felt solid under her bare feet. Slipping was the biggest danger.

"Are you okay?" Caroline asked when Kirsty finally climbed off the trunk on the other side.

Kirsty nodded, pale and trembling. Caroline jumped to the solid ground of Fandelyon. The tension she'd been feeling for days seemed to melt. "You've got no idea how good that feels," she said. "We're in Fandelyon. Truly."

"Better not dally," Dobbin said. "The river may divide the lowlands from the mountains, but we're hardly in a city."

Forest quickly broke into tilled farmland, the spring crops already sprouting. Human smells wafted in the air like a wash of liquid lust, and she had a hard time quieting her newfound desires. They found Elias by the last trees, watching pigs in stone-walled paddocks.

"What now?" Caroline asked as sheep bleated in the next stone-walled paddock over. Her stomach growled. Mixed with the freshness of rain and the aroma of the Kingdom, Elias's scent enticed in all the wrong ways. She resisted an urge to move closer to him.

"We'll have to travel at night if we're to take you home," Elias said.

Dobbin snorted. "And what do ye propose we do by day? This is a human kingdom, not a flamin' forest, ya silly imp. They'll string ye up faster than the clansmen did."

Allyn's expression took on long-suffering look. "We've got faspane hunting us and a human kingdom ahead. Let's deal the most pressing problem first."

Caroline nodded. "Dobbin's got a point. My own father would hang me for associating with an izzat, particularly one with twitchy ears." She mimicked Dobbin's accent at the end.

Dobbin gave Elias a disappointed look. "She used ta be royalty. Now look at what ye did ta the lass."

"Me? It's your accent she's imitating."

"Back to the problem," Allyn said.

They were all quiet for a moment. "I know what to do," Kirsty ventured softly. She still looked pale and scared, though her scent was gradually returning to normal.

"Yes?" Allyn asked.

"Elias and Allyn, if you can find helms we'd be able to go directly to Fandelyon City. It's only your ears and Allyn's eyes that are obviously different. Some humans are as tall as you two, clansmen in particular."

Caroline offered Kirsty a smile of encouragement.

Elias shook his head. "Allyn would need a visor to hide his eyes, and he'd have to keep it down all the time. Risky. Our features are also a little unusual compared to a human's. I prefer stealth."

"Ya would," Dobbin said with a grin. "The tool of assassins, cowards and thieves."

Allyn gave Dobbin a warning look. "I can't think of anything else except a convincing illusion, and that's going to take time to prepare. A day at least. I doubt an aversion spell would be enough. With faspane about, it's more important to be out of the forest for now. We need somewhere to rest."

"Donele is about ten or fifteen miles north-east of here," Kirsty said. "Mostly east. We could find a room in a tavern and you could prepare there."

"Too far. It would take the rest of the day to get there, and if we travel after dark there may be no accommodation available. What else?"

"Kirsty, how do you know where Donele is?" Caroline asked. "I've got no idea where we are."

"I've seen maps of Fandelyon. We just came down the East Pass. With the Senbow River behind us and farmland ahead-"

"You remember that from a map?"

"Of course. Don't you remember the maps you've seen?"

"Not with that much detail."

Allyn said, "Kirsty, you can explain later if you like. What else can you tell us? Where's the next closest town or city?"

A faraway look came into her eyes. "Mossvale. It's smaller, but only about ten miles northwest. The lands between here and there are more populated though."

"Anything else?"

"Just small villages, mostly. There's a few temples dedicated to some of the Divine Lords and Ladies, but they're no good in... your company."

Although her eyes took in both Allyn and Elias, they lingered on Elias perhaps a little too long. Caroline took a deep, calming breath. If Kirsty wanted him she could have him. She just wished her own emotions would agree.

"Dobbin, how about you take Caroline and Kirsty to the next village and see if you can find a garrison. You can stay with the girls and help the soldiers escort them to Fandelyon City. A reward for saving Princess Caroline might be in order and a good excuse to remain with her. Caroline, you may need to insist he stays."

Dobbin rubbed his hands together. "More than happy ta accept gold."

"Gold's not the purpose," Elias said.

"Aye. But welcome, regardless," he said, grinning like a kid with a treat.

"You earned it," Caroline said. "You all did. Father will offer something substantial, I'm sure."

Dobbin's grin broadened.

"Dobbin can keep anything offered. If you get to the guard post this afternoon, how long before you arrive home?"

"A few days?" Caroline guessed.

Kirsty shook her head. "A week. Maybe more. The roads will be boggy."

Allyn looked unhappy at that. "Caroline, I don't suppose you want to grow fur and sprint home? It would save us all a lot of trouble. I'm sure Kirsty would be safe with Dobbin."

"Father would ask why, and how, I walked through the Kingdom alone. And naked. Besides, people smell like... food, when I'm changed. Even now, actually. It's hard just being this close."

He grimaced. "Fair enough. Dobbin?"

"Aye. Shouldn't be difficult so long as Caroline insists I remain with her."

"Done. Elias and I will shadow you. If we discover any faspane in the Kingdom we'll keep them from you if we can. Dobbin, when you leave Fandelyon City, keep to the roads and head for Delshere. We'll find you."

32

———————

It was almost an hour's walk through farmland to the nearest guard post, but being flat and reasonably dry it was easy compared to the mountains.

Caroline and Kirsty changed back into their torn dresses, though Caroline wasn't sure the condition of hers wouldn't attract more attention than the trews. It was loose on her now too, and hot, the wool conspiring with the late afternoon sun to bake her. After a few minutes she changed back. She'd rather suffer the embarrassment of wearing a man's clothes in public than be roasted alive.

The enticing aroma of human life grew stronger the deeper into the Kingdom they ventured, but with it grew the smells of industry, sewage and cooking. She wasn't sure if she was hungry or nauseous. The worst smell was the fields. They were so full of manure she wanted to puke.

Caroline peeled off her cloak and draped it across her shoulder, but without the hood the sun began to sting her face. She was tempted to put it back on.

"I feel like I'm drowning," Caroline said. "The air is thick with too many smells." Perspiration trickled from her temples. She took her cloak and held it over her head like a tent.

Kirsty kept her heavy cloak and hood on, clearly not prepared to risk sunburn, but perspiration coated her.

Dobbin removed his own cloak. He obviously didn't care about a tan.

Several farmers with long cotton sleeves stopped pulling weeds to watch them pass, lifting their broad-brimmed straw hats to get a better view of the newcomers. The unwashed human scents gave Caroline murderous desires, while he clothes made her feel less than ladylike. She wondered one of the farmers would trade Zaramar's sword for a hat and peasant dress. The sword weighed uncomfortably at her hip. Why hadn't she given it to Elias? He could have made much better use of it.

"Curious bunch," Dobbin muttered.

She couldn't blame the farmers for their curiosity. Shivras were uncommon, especially accompanied by two human girls, one with clannish red hair and wearing male clothing, and carrying an exotic sword. It would cause of months of gossip. Years, probably.

Her legs spattered with mud and the rest of her dripping perspiration, she ignored the farmers and entered a village of about two dozen homes.

No one ventured out, not even the single priest standing in the doorway of the tiny little temple dedicated to Loama du Rion, the Divine Lord that farmers asked to intercede for them. She pretended she couldn't see the divine marks in the shape of a sprouting seed on the priest's wrists, and yet he looked at her as if he knew she'd been marked too. She kept her wrists hidden.

"Social place," Dobbin commented as he frowned at a woodcarver's wares displayed outside one of the shops. The bench contained idols of Loama beside plates and bowls all carved from dark lowland oak and pale willow.

With her red hair and height, Caroline had probably been mistaken for a clanswoman and doubted she'd have been tolerated in the village without Dobbin's presence. Stoned or beaten perhaps. "Just keep walking."

Kirsty's stomach rumbled at the same time as Caroline's.

"Fancy eating a villager, too?" Caroline asked.

"That's not funny!" Kirsty actually sounded worried.

"Don't be silly. One won't be missed."

"Please don't joke about it." She looked genuinely upset. Smelled... fearful.

"Don't worry Kirsty. I'm not about to eat them. You smell far better."

"Caroline!"

Caroline paused. Kirsty never used Caroline's first name. "Sorry, Kirsty. Truly."

They found the guard post a few hundred yards past the village, close to the main road. It was a poorly-maintained shack big enough to house a few soldiers and a couple of stable hands. The stench of filthy bodies, rotten food, an open latrine and spilled ale identified the place as a hovel. Snoring almost rattled the door as they approached. "Are they asleep even before dark?" Kirsty asked.

"The roof's half rotten," Dobbin murmured.

"The place should be burned down," Caroline added, crinkling her nose. "I can smell four men inside and ten horses in the stables behind the barracks. The stables are putrid." At least now she knew why werewolves rarely lived close to human habitation. They couldn't stand the stench.

Dobbin scratched his beard. "Nothing like a respectful and enthusiastic welcome from one's people."

"They're drunk," Caroline said in disgust, trying not to let her embarrassment show. "They smell like ale."

"I doubt I'll ever get used to you saying things like that," Dobbin said as he thumped his calloused fist on the door. He got no response beyond a wisp of smoke drifting out the chimney. "Let's check the stables."

Caroline and Kirsty followed the shivra to the large stable doors. To the left, a fenced compound seemed in better repair, but she doubted the stables had been cleaned out in weeks. They reeked of damp, rotting straw. "There's no one inside," Caroline said. "Just horses." No human scent had been near the stable doors since the night before.

"Hello!" Dobbin called.

"Really," she added. "No one's been here for nearly a day."

"Poor horses," Kirsty said as Dobbin pulled the doors open.

Weathered and run down from the outside, Caroline gagged at the stench of mildew that rushed out. Rotting timbers had allowed the weather in, causing further decay. Insects buzzed lazily and an abundance of crawling things scurried from the disturbance.

"I think I'm going to vomit," Caroline said as nausea swept over her. She ran, but even fifty yards away she couldn't ignore the stench, though her stomach slowly settled. She heard horses reacting to Dobbin and Kirsty's presence, all keen for attention.

"The horses are darn lucky ta be in reasonable condition," she heard Dobbin say. "All ten could probably use a month in a green paddock, though. Let's saddle three and put this disgusting mess behind us. Kirsty, can ye grab me those blankets?"

It wasn't long before they led three horses from the stables, including a huge workhorse big enough to carry Dobbin. The horses stank of the stables, but it was a second-hand smell and out in the open, she could tolerate it.

She went to the smaller of the two horses Dobbin led, a black stallion with three white socks and a white blaze, but as she tried to mount him he flattened his ears and backed off.

"Uh, Dobbin. I don't think he likes me. Maybe he can sense..." She looked around to be sure no one was near. "You know."

Dobbin frowned at the skittish animal. "Aye. They seem to be tolerating yer presence, but that's it unless ya want hoof marks on yer face."

"But we can't have Caroline walking when we're riding. If Caroline walks, so do I," Kirsty said.

Dobbin glanced skyward. "Wonderful. Let's all walk to Fandelyon City." He paused, turning to Caroline, a challenge in his expression. "Of course, ya could try ta charm a horse. Charming's a trick izzen are good at, but I've used it a time or two. I think I can teach ya if yer willing."

"Certainly not," she said instinctively. She realised it sounded stupid the moment she said it. She was a werewolf and a sorcerer's apprentice, and she'd vowed to learn in order to get rid of the bond that bound her to Allyn. She'd free Kirsty from her oath as soon as she could, as well.

Dobbin shrugged and began turning away. "Yer probably not good enough ta do it anyway."

"I am so!"

A huge grin split his beard.

Caroline felt her face go red in embarrassment. "You knew I'd say that, didn't you?"

He winked. "I thought ya might. Are ye going ta back out now?"

She stared at the horses. Hadn't she already played with magic? "I suppose not. But you know how my people feel about magic. Using magic is evil."

"Only intentions are evil. Now, the stallion reacted the strongest, so that's the one ya want."

"I don't understand."

"It's simple. Ye can't charm any animal for long if it doesn't care either way. The stronger the emotion in the animal, the stronger the devotion if ye can charm it."

"Would that also imply a greater chance of failure?"

"Aye. But ye can always try with another."

Caroline wasn't convinced.

Dobbin handed the reins of the workhorse to Kirsty. "Take 'em over there, would ya?" The younger girl led it and the gentler mare to the shade of a nearby lowland oak.

"The other two don't seem so concerned by me."

"Ya didn't try to ride 'em."

She took a deep breath, trying to come to terms with what she was about to do. "Now what?"

"A charm's a simple thing, initially a contest of wills. If all ye want is cooperation for a short time, that's as far as ye need ta take it. In this case, ye'll need ta do more. First of all, make a connection using a touch of magic. Think ye can do that?"

"No."

"Ye can call on yer magic, right? If ye can see magic, ye can call it."

She still felt uncomfortable about discussing magic. "Okay. Maybe I did once."

He raised his eyebrows in surprise.

"I got curious," she admitted.

He bellowed a laugh. "Good. Just reach out with magic and ye'll create a connection. Once ye achieve that it'll become a contest of wills. Being a horse used to taking orders it shouldn't be much trouble, unlike a wild animal or a person. Just get it under control. Make it docile."

Her stomach tightened. In the mountains it had been an exciting test to see if she could call and manipulate magic. Something daring, yet still play. This wasn't play and it wasn't something she could dismiss or deny.

"Once ye achieve a connection ye can then try ta charm. Bridging's the easy bit."

"Bridging. Right. How do I charm it?"

"Ye have ta show the horse yer its friend. Ye need ta change its fearful emotions into something ya feel yerself for the horse."

"But I just want to ride it. I don't care about it."

He looked disappointed. "Then ye'll never master any worthwhile magic."

Offended, she tried to keep the sharpness out of her voice. "What do you mean?"

"Understanding magic is largely about understanding yerself. Ye can only give what ya have, and if ya have nothing ta give then ye'll get nothing back. It's the first lesson of magic."

"That's stupid."

Now he looked offended. "Is it? Really? Ta receive love ye must give it, as with friendship. To kill a man in combat ye must risk yer own life. Even a harsh word receives the appropriate emotional response. Everything in life is a balance, and the same principle is true of magic."

"So how will that help me with this horse?"

He looked like he was being forced to deal with a child. "Offer nothing yer unwilling ta give. If yer caught in a lie then the bond will be broken and never restored."

Seemed simple enough. "Got it. No deception. Someone should mention that to Allyn."

He nodded in agreement, a frown marking his forehead. "So ye agree with the principle then?"

Caroline pushed her curly hair back from her face. "Yes. It's just my upbringing. I can't help feeling like I'm doing something bad." She felt hot and sweaty at the thought of doing something she'd been taught was wrong. The thrill of her previous experimentation in the mountains was long gone.

"Have ye considered that the Gods who oppose Marnier du Shae foresaw ye, or something like this situation, and intentionally encouraged hatred of magic in order to stymie ye?"

"That would be a very long game they're playing."

"Aye. Two hundred thousand years' worth. Their game started when the faspane slayed the unicorn, or so Allyn claims.

"Two hundred...?" It didn't seem possible that they could spread their competition out for so much time or that she was expected to resolve it by defeating an immortal being with a magic-forged sword. "Marnier du Shae bet on the wrong girl."

"Aye."

"What?" She glared at him until his grin broke out, and she realised he was laughing at her predictability. "Sometime I really hate you, Dobbin."

"But ye love me more, right."

She couldn't help but grin back. "Aye," she said, mimicking his accent.

"Well then, get on with it. Charm the horse ye care nothing for."

"It's not that I don't care," she murmured. It just wasn't a horse she knew. She closed her eyes and felt for that lightening deep inside, and drew it forth. It tingled her fingertips, but disappeared when her fears rose up and she lost focus.

She took a deep breath, opened her eyes, and drew forth the energy anew. The horse backed a step, possibly sensing something even more amiss than a werewolf. Dobbin kept the reins tight.

She held out her hand and let magic ark between them. *First the bridge, then the charm.* She sensed it touch, felt the connection, and experienced the fear as the stallion reacted.

He fought her, but she pushed her will across the bridge and overwhelmed his mind in a moment. It was like slapping a child and she felt mean for doing it. The stallion's stance changed and he hung his head, defeated.

The vibrant connection between them felt almost physical. As long as she held it she could command him. A sudden, fearful thought occurred to her. "Is this what Allyn did to me?"

Dobbin's voice sounded distant – the magical bond drawing most of her focus. "It's a similar concept, but not the same. Now fer the hard part. Convince the stallion yer its friend. Ye need its consent ta create a true binding."

She was trembling with nervousness. "Its consent?" So this *was* what Allyn had done to her.

"Allyn or Elias could instruct ye better, but they're not here."

She felt the stallion's mind, docile under her will. She reached out, the sense of emotion just within reach. The stallion inwardly panicked at her blundering touch though its body didn't react. She felt his fear, the natural instinct to run.

Apprehensive herself, she pulled away. With her consciousness no longer threatening him he returned to passivity. Whatever she did to charm this horse it would have to be on an emotional level.

She reached out again, seeking something to work with. The stallion seemed to have no sense of freedom; it had lived its life as a servant.

She lightly caressed his emotions, searching until she blundered into memory. Its fears were based on fresh hunger and deeply buried pain.

It was tempting to use that, take its fear and drive it deeper, turn it to fear of her and make it so afraid of disobeying that its fear would override its instinctive reaction to her curse.

Dobbin's lecture cautioned against that approach. She couldn't see how using its fears would return to hurt her, but she wasn't willing to ignore Dobbin's advice either. He'd never given her bad counsel and only ever proved a friend.

And what if Allyn had used the same approach on her? She wouldn't just distrust him. She'd hate him and be seeking a way to get revenge. She didn't want to risk a horse throwing her at the wrong moment.

Ye get what ye give, he'd said.

She looked for something else, something she could connect with, and found a need for protection. It feared predators, its masters, and therefore her.

Caroline recognised her key in the very thing that kept her from riding the animal in the first place. She reached out with assurance, offering security, but the horse shied from the gesture. Gently, she pushed further into its emotions and saw the shallowness of her own offering. She had no idea how well an animal could understand, but it knew sincerity and its lack.

She would have to lie to herself, bury her real thoughts deep in order to have it believe something she didn't feel. She withdrew from the horse's mind, barely maintaining the bridge.

Or she could offer true sincerity. Make an honest commitment.

She reached out to the horse again, deeply yet gently. "I'll look after you," she promised, and meant it.

In an instant, bound within her own magic, she committed herself to protecting him. She exposed her own feelings, fears and hopes, and offered friendship.

The horse responded in kind, its sudden openness and trust filling her with hope. Mutual trust, respect and something higher passed between them, bordering on love. The depth of shared feeling overwhelmed Caroline. The stallion offered everything it had.

Their friendship forged itself in an instant, something Caroline fully accepted with everything it implied. She would never allow anything to harm him.

Her commitment was forged with her own magic as she bound herself to her promise. If necessary, she would die trying to save him. He was as dear to her as Kirsty or her own family.

As she released the bridge, a final sense of identity touched her. Clouds piled high and grey, trailing heavy rain driven by winds, and the sound of galloping. "Stormrunner," she whispered as she let the magic fade away.

Stormrunner stepped forward and she took his face in her hands. "I know you," she said, staring into his deep brown eyes. "And you know me." It was the most wonderful feeling she'd ever known.

She hugged him.

33

———

"Hey!" a man yelled.

Caroline spun, protectively holding onto Stormrunner. Two dishevelled soldiers barged out of the barracks with swords drawn, both red-eyed, unshaven, and partially undressed. Fortunately, both had their pants on.

"Told you I heard something," the grey-haired man said, blinking puffy eyes as he tried to look intimidating.

The second soldier, completely bald, had boots but no shirt and a big gut overhanging his belt. He shouldered the first man out of the way and pointed his sword at Dobbin. "Drop your weapons, shivra. Smiddy, go wake up the boys. We're going to hang 'em." He slurred a bit.

"You're going to hang the boys?" Dobbin asked as Kirsty took a step backward.

Smiddy glanced at Dobbin, "Huh?"

Caroline gave Dobbin a look. "I am Princess Caroline duFandelyon, eldest daughter of King Phillip duFandelyon. I command you to form an escort for myself and Lady Kirsty duPrey so we may travel in safety to Fandelyon City." She doubted she'd receive any real protection even if they escorted her right up to her father's face.

Both men looked at each other. "Of course you are," said the bald man. "I usually hate hanging women, but I don't mind this time. Don't like liars. Or clan girls." Stormrunner shifted his hooves restlessly.

Dobbin pulled his hammer free and removed the protective leather cover from it.

"Two of us, shivra. Drop the weapon." The man levelled his blade in Dobbin's direction. It wavered slightly.

Dobbin strode forward. Smiddy stood his ground, but the bald man backed a few steps.

"Jameson, don't you be running now."

Dobbin smashed Smiddy's sword from his hand and punched the soldier in the face. He hit the soggy ground and didn't move.

"Uh..." Jameson began. Two more thumps and he lay unconscious on the ground, too.

Dobbin returned his hammer to his belt. He didn't look in the least bit troubled. "We better get goin' before yer fine soldiers wake up."

Caroline felt herself blush. "Come on, Stormrunner. Time to find you a better stable."

"We'll take it easy," Dobbin said as they mounted and moved out. "The horses need some coddling." He looked like an adult on a child's pony, but the huge workhorse held up well enough.

With no trees to obscure them, they were forced to follow the muddy road, reaching the next village about a quarter of an hour later. Dobbin purchased grain and oats, three minced fruit pies and a loaf of bread, grumbling over the cost.

Caroline fed Stormrunner before taking her pie. She was tempted to ask Dobbin to buy her a broad-brimmed hat to keep the sun off her face, but judging by the way he grumbled over the money he'd already spent, she didn't feel comfortable asking. It was getting late anyway. The risk of sunburn was quickly disappearing.

They passed through two more villages over the next half hour, each no more than a few miles apart. Villagers and farmers stared at her, but she wasn't sure if it was the strange company, her unusual red hair, her sword, or the fact she wore shivra clothes.

They arrived at a larger town as dusk began to settle, a wooden wall surrounding it.

"It stinks," Caroline said, crinkling her nose. There was too much industry for her liking. It tickled her nostrils and made her want to sneeze.

"Is it safe enough to stay the night here?" Kirsty asked, eying the wooden wall.

"Banonvale," Caroline read the sign. "Safer than sleeping in a field."

A small castle overlooked the town from its vantage atop a small hill to the east, four squat towers and solid bluestone walls shadowed against the darkening sky.

"Something wrong?" Dobbin asked.

"No. Just the approach of darkness. Feels like I'm finally waking up."

"Perhaps we should go to the castle? Ye'll find a better welcome than this hovel of a town."

Caroline glanced at the torches on the castle's walls, trying to remember who owned it. "Let's not announce my presence to someone who may have betrayed my location in the mountains. Besides, the company of nobility can be stuffy."

"Ye've no true understanding of that statement," he said, doing a fair approximation of her own accent.

She pursed her lips, trying not to let him see her amusement. "No wonder you're always at it with Elias. Both of you go out of your way to irritate people."

He chuckled. "Aye lass, but at least yer learning to take a dig. I doubt he ever will. Come. We'll find lodgings tonight and perhaps seek help from the stuffy nobility tomorrow, if needs be."

They found lodgings above a rancid-smelling tavern filled with patrons, mostly farmers drinking ale. The men stared at them all as they entered, particularly Caroline. Even the three men playing fiddles opposite the hearth stopped their tune.

Dobbin paid extra for stewed vegetables, tender lamb shanks, and a cut of crusty bread each, and they sat in the corner away from the fire to eat, the fiddlers refusing to go back to their music in a clan girl's presence.

She overheard several whispering about giving her a beating if Dobbin left her alone. She was tempted to contrive the opportunity. Even if they did get the better of her, she was sure they'd regret it in the morning.

Regardless, she couldn't fill her stomach fast enough, eating like a peasant without caring who saw. She even finished half of Kirsty's shank.

The sun hadn't quite broken the horizon the following dawn when Caroline and Kirsty entered the stables. Dobbin was already there.

The stench of manure assaulted Caroline and she had to sniff to keep her nose from running, but at least the stable boy had cleaned the stables and spread fresh straw in the stalls. When the lad saw her he backed away as if she were going to choke him with her bare hands.

"I'm not a clanswoman," she told him irritably. "Why don't you stare at the shivra instead?"

Dobbin ignored the comment. He stood beside Stormrunner, tightening the stallion's girth strap. "Oy," he muttered at the horse. "Breathe out." He poked him in the ribs. Stormrunner released his breath and Dobbin finished with the strap. The shivra looked ridiculously large next to her horse.

Caroline rubbed Stormrunner's face. The stallion looked rested. "You wouldn't want me falling off, would you?"

Stormrunner snorted.

Dobbin grasped Caroline's shoulder, his meaty hand almost crushing it. "It's going to take at least three or four days from here to Fandelyon City, assuming the weather holds, and we can't afford to take as much as a single problem. Understand?"

"Of course," Caroline said.

"The roads are beginning to dry out," Kirsty said enthusiastically. "We should make good time."

"Good," Dobbin said. "The longer we travel, the more chance of something going wrong."

"At least the faspane are unlikely to attack us," Caroline said. She cocked her head at the sound of hooves. "Six horses," she said. "Chain shirts. You mentioned something going wrong?"

"Morning patrol?" Dobbin asked.

She kept listening. "They're coming this way."

"Do you think the soldiers at the guard post reported us?" Kirsty asked.

"Probably," Dobbin said. "Can't be hard to track a shivra and a girl with red hair in the lowlands."

It wasn't long before the horses stopped outside the tavern. Caroline heard two men dismount and enter.

"Better go greet 'em," Dobbin said, leading the way.

"I hope they're sober," Caroline muttered.

"Good morn', Sergeant," Dobbin said as he walked through the stable doors. Caroline and Kirsty followed.

The thick-set soldier turned, his expression as dark as his curly hair. Three more sat their mounts behind him. "It would have been, were I still asleep. I'm chasing some horse thieves. A shivra and two young girls, one clan born. Have you seen them?"

"The man's got a sense of humour," Dobbin said, raising an eyebrow at Caroline. "I'm impressed. Sober enough to sit a horse, too. Big change from the last lot."

"Hand over your weapons, shivra," the soldier said as the two who'd entered the tavern came out. "And the sword too, clan girl."

Other than her sisters and mother, Caroline couldn't think of another noble with red hair, so she would probably have to put up with *clan girl* for a few days. In a country where blond hair was prized and dark curly hair common, red singled you out as an enemy. She was lucky she had Dobbin with her. "I'm-" Caroline began.

"You're going to hang for stealing the King's horses and assaulting two of the King's soldiers."

Caroline put her hands on her hips. "Perhaps if those guards hadn't been drunk when I needed an escort, you'd have been sleeping now, Sergeant."

His eyes narrowed sharply at her accent.

She raised her chin. "Form an escort. You're taking us to my father."

"Nice imitation, but Princess Caroline perished in the mountains."

"I did? What of you, Lady Kirsty duPrey? Are you dead too?"

Her friend hid half a smile.

"You've seen my dead body, I take it?"

Dobbin cleared his throat, interrupting the soldier before he could speak. "Let's not antagonise the lad, Princess. Sergeant, perhaps ye should assume she's telling the truth. Hanging the King's daughter won't help ye live a long life."

The man looked them all over again, though he didn't seem any less unsure. "I'll let Baron Tennick decide. Surrender your weapons. We'll escort you to the castle."

Dobbin moved closer to Caroline, hand on his axe. "Sergeant, are ye prepared to risk injuring the King's daughter? The Princess is not going to the castle, she's going home, so ye can either try and force us or escort us to the King."

The man looked Caroline over again, eyes lingering on her curly red hair for a good long time. "Fine."

It was better than a fight, and definitely preferable to being hung. "Thank you," she said, a quiet doubt suggesting he'd given in far too easily.

The man looked Dobbin over. "Never seen a shivra ride before. Should be interesting."

Dobbin snorted. "Small things amuse ye then. Have ye checked inside yer trews lately?"

Caroline grinned as she mounted Stormrunner. Dobbin hauled himself into his saddle. His horse shifted his hooves to steady himself, though he probably weighed half again as much as Stormrunner.

"Lead on," Dobbin said.

They rode out the town gates as merchants were opening their stalls in the central market. She felt less at ease as dawn fully broke, her night-time strength ebbing, but her blocked nose began to clear as the town fell behind. The soldiers took up positions; two before, two flanking, and two behind. Caroline's instincts prickled. She exchanged a look with Dobbin, who nodded cautiously. Surrounded. She leaned closer to him. "Why did I ask for an escort again?"

"Better than a stretched neck?"

Louder, she said, "Dobbin, why don't you take the rear? I'm sure you don't need as much protection as Kirsty and I."

He touched his forelock. "As ye wish, Yer Highness."

The soldiers watched suspiciously as Dobbin pulled his horse aside and let them pass. "Nice crossbows," he said to the two rear guard men as he pulled in behind them. "Why do ye keep 'em loaded? Leaving them like that will warp the wood. Is this road so dangerous?" One gave him a look, the other ignored him entirely.

Dawn quickly became midmorning, the day's muggy heat rising up from the damp road and pressing in on them. Caroline watched the open fields as much as the soldiers surrounding her, but couldn't see or smell faspane.

The soldiers reeked of deceit. She could probably have headed off the problem by going to Baron Scott Tennick, but if he'd betrayed her in the mountains she might as well kill her friends. Just as bad, faspane could be anywhere.

She didn't smell any silver among the soldiers, so that was good, at least for her.

They stopped at a fair sized town called Marulan for a noon meal. Most of the peasants and merchants were sensible enough to wear hats or carry parasols, and looked askance at the strange group.

The soldiers didn't offer to share their rations and sat apart as they spoke quietly to each other, so Dobbin purchased fresh berries, bread and crumbly cheese, as well as two pounds of jerky. The place stank of open drains, rendering her sense of smell almost useless again.

While staring at a nearby smithy and pretending to be interested in the smith belting metal into a horseshoe, Caroline listened to the Sergeant whispering instructions to his men.

"We'll divide them," he said. "Once we have the girls, we'll use them to control the shivra. I doubt he'll risk them."

"Am I sunburned?" Caroline asked suddenly, no longer keen to hear more. She felt sunburned.

"Like a tomato," Dobbin said. "Kirsty's clearly got more sense than ye."

Caroline glanced at Kirsty, who'd draped her cloak over herself like a tent, though perspiration coated her face.

"Dobbin," Caroline murmured, deliberately not looking at the soldiers.

"Aye?"

"They don't believe who I am. They're going to cart us back for Baron Scott Tennick to hang us. The moment they move, get to Kirsty and keep her safe."

"And you?"

She shrugged. "There's only one weapon here that can kill me, and I'm carrying it."

They left, and as the afternoon wore on they passed through villages and farmland and scattered patches of trees. Fresh apprehension touched Caroline as they entered the largest stand of lowland grey oak they had yet encountered in Fandelyon, but she caught no scent of faspane. A few hundred yards into the forest's cool shade they crossed a wooden bridge over a wide rocky creek. The Sergeant turned his horse off the main road, following a narrow trail.

Caroline pulled Stormrunner up, causing the soldiers behind them to stop too. "Sergeant," one of the men called.

The leader stopped, glancing back with a smile. He wasn't good at smiling. "Come, Your Highness. This trail cuts out almost two miles of travel. We'll return to the main road just shy of Forecliffe."

"Really?" Caroline asked. The trail was little more than a path about a foot wide, crisscrossed by a tangle of roots as it wound into the trees. No horses had passed along it that she could smell, and no human had walked that way since the last rains. "This is not a shortcut travellers take. We'll stay with the main road."

"Aye," Dobbin agreed, his hand subtly unclipping the cover on his axe. "Looks like the sort of path kids might take to a swimming hole." He shrugged his shield so he could swing it from his back. Hopefully the soldiers didn't recognise the gesture for what it was.

This was it. Caroline glanced at Kirsty who swallowed, her scent betraying fear. Caroline's own stomach did a slow turn.

The Sergeant tried his insincere smile again. "It's a solid trail. It's just too narrow for carts."

Caroline gripped Stormrunner's reins. Should she act now, or wait for the betrayal to be sure? "We take the road," she said.

His smile disappeared. "We take the short cut." There was a huge *follow or else* left unsaid, echoed by his hand going to his sword's hilt.

"Yah!" Caroline yelled. Fear compounded the need to protect her friends as she kicked Stormrunner forward.

Stormrunner barrelled into the Sergeant's mount before she reared him and let him kick out, smashing links in the Sergeant's mail and throwing him off his horse. Caroline righted herself as Stormrunner dropped back down. Another soldier tried to unclip his crossbow from his saddle. She felt Stormrunner's muscles bunch as she directed him to turn and charge, chest-slamming the soldier's horse. The horse stumbled and the man fell with a cry.

Two soldiers faced Dobbin, but two others were already down. One had backed away and was aiming his crossbow, while the other held Dobbin off. "Go!" she yelled at Stormrunner, digging her bare heels in. The horse charged. The soldier with the crossbow turned with a panicked look on his face. She never saw the bolt and felt nothing but a thud in her chest before Stormrunner crashed into him. A little dazed, she ripped the bolt from her chest as she felt another thud.

Woozy, Caroline gripped she new bolt buried deep in her ribs, but her fingers slid off it. Surprised, she tried to grab it again, but somehow there was sky above her and a strange sensation of falling.

34

Caroline opened her eyes. It was dark except for a turned-down lantern in the corner of the room. The place stank of wood smoke, horses, ale and hard travel. An inn somewhere. She tasted it as much as smelled it, and cringed at the noise coming from the common room. She could smell Stormrunner too, which meant he hadn't been hurt, or at least not badly.

"That was bleeding quick," Dobbin said in his gravelly voice.

She turned her head, her chest extremely tender. It hurt to breathe. She lay on a pallet under scratchy wool blankets.

Dobbin sat on a stool beside her. "Ye must be getting used to this werewolf thingy."

She rolled her eyes. "Fine escort you are. Can't you keep me from getting stabbed, gutted, bitten or beaten for even *one* day? It's agony being around you. Honestly."

He chuckled. "Stop charging crossbow bolts then. Yer not invulnerable, ya know?"

She smiled back. "Are they likely to come after us?"

"We hurt 'em pretty bad. Only faspane to worry about now, so let's hope the izzen keep 'em off our trail."

Faspane. She reached out and took his hand. "Thank you, Dobbin. You're a true friend."

Kirsty slept on a nearby pallet. It must be late then. Caroline closed her eyes, feeling herself relax and drifting again.

Dawn woke her, a subtle tightening across her skin. She blinked, a little surprised she'd fallen asleep so easily. Dobbin snored with his back to the door, head lolling and his hammer across his lap.

Kirsty remained asleep. She'd never been one to rise early, not even at the abbey.

Caroline slipped out of the blankets and found her clothes washed and fresh-smelling. The deep ache in her chest hurt when she pulled them on, but the wounds were more than half-healed already. She could smell Kirsty's scent on the clothes and found the holes from the bolts already stitched.

"Thank you Kirsty," she whispered, but decided against wearing the shivra clothes, putting on her old dress instead. Stretching, she crossed to the shutters and pushed them open, allowing the grey light of an uninspiring, muggy day to enter the room. Heavy clouds had moved in overnight and the ground was soaked. By the look of the sky, there would be more rain today, but at least she wouldn't get sunburned.

Dobbin snorted, choked, coughed and then swore. He stood, weapon raised and looking bewildered.

She smiled as awareness crossed his face. "Good morning," she said. "Protecting me in your dreams?"

His expression turned sour. "Aye. Nightmare I'd call it. My apologies. I shouldn't have drifted off."

She kept her smile. "It's good you did. You might need to pull another bolt out of me later."

"Without yer help yesterday I'd certainly be dead, and Kirsty as well. Perhaps it's not me who should carry the hammer."

He seemed to be serious, at least about his inability to protect her and Kirsty. He pulled a pouch from inside his shirt and tossed it. "The money they carried," he said.

She managed to catch it, mainly because it and hit her chest where she trapped it. "Ow."

"Eleven coins," he said. "Six crowns, two halves and three half-royals."

She held the pouch out, unsure how she felt about robbing the men who'd tried to kill her. "Dobbin, I've never owned a coin in my life. Take them back." She was not about to throw them. She'd probably hit Kirsty, and Kirsty was nowhere near Dobbin.

He shook his head. "They're yers."

She glanced out the window. Farmers and traders were setting up stalls and many had begun calling to attract customers. "How much does it cost to purchase a crossbow?"

His bushy brows narrowed. "More than ye have there. Could have had some free ones yesterday. Why?"

"Because I can't use a sword and don't want to carry a weapon with silver etching." She glanced at the sword she'd won in the mountains. Even sheathed, it carried a dangerous tang of silver.

"Ye don't want to carry any weapon unless ye can use it. Good way to get yerself killed. Or me. That goes with crossbows too. Bloody useless. One shot and yer vulnerable. Better off running."

"What about a dagger? Something I could hide? Could you teach me to use one?"

"Why don't we leave that question until after ya see yer family?"

Thinking about her family brought feelings of regret, doubt, fear and uncertainty. What would she tell them? "I can't rely on you for much longer."

"Ah, so that's yer concern."

"I need to be able to defend myself, daytime as well as at night. Daylight makes me feel, well, human, weak and vulnerable compared to the night. Please teach me."

Dobbin dropped the haft of his hammer through the loop on his belt and slipped the cover over it, clipping it into place. "I'd be honoured, but it takes years of practice to get good with a weapon. What's more, we'll need to travel fast today."

She glanced over the market, admitting defeat. "Perhaps a new dress then?" Another possibility crossed her mind. "Dobbin, you have a spell to keep people away, don't you? I remember talk about it at your cabin."

"An aversion spell? I had a pretty strong one around me cabin, but ta be honest, me spells lack subtlety. Yer thinking about faspane, aren't ye?"

"Would an aversion spell keep them away?" she asked hopefully.

"Keep everyone away, though the izzat know a trick to target a specific group or individual. Their faspane wizard might be able to use whatever I teach ya to track us."

"Show me anyway?"

He looked surprised. "Yer begging to learn magic now?"

"Begging?" She arched an eyebrow. "No."

He grinned. "Well, it wasn't quite a grovel now, was it?"

She put her hands on her hips. "If I didn't love you so much Dobbin, I'd be inclined to thump you. I'm thinking about Kirsty. If I can use magic to keep her safe, then it's worth it."

"Not necessarily. It could light a beacon."

She sighed. "New dress first. Magic later." She glanced at the sword she'd won. "Would you mind selling that for me?"

"Of course."

It took a while to rouse Kirsty, but after a breakfast of porridge and honey in the noisy common room, the girls entered the market square. Everyone stared at Caroline, but no one seemed prepared to call her *clan girl* in Dobbin's presence, though a few met her eyes with hostility.

In the streets, she struggled to see over the parasols most of the wealthy women carried, and many of the men's broad-brimmed hats got in her way too. The poor made their hats from woven straw, scraps of leather, or stiffened cloth. She pulled her hood up and stooped as people stared, trying to blend in with the olive-skinned commoners.

Caroline had never actually purchased a dress before. Normally a dressmaker would come to her, take her measurements, and return with several dresses ready for fitting and alterations. She rubbed her nose. It was beginning to run. "This should be fun!"

She wanted to pull her hood off as the clouds were breaking and the day growing hot, but she'd already received enough glares today. There was little to be done about her height. Even among nobility, she looked over the heads of most of the men. At least pale skin wasn't so uncommon in such a large city.

"Breakfast was delicious," Kirsty said. "My favourite."

Caroline glanced slyly at her friend. "There wasn't enough human in it for my liking, and the honey was sickly sweet."

Kirsty gave her a worried look.

"I'm kidding!" Caroline said with a smile. "The honey was fine."

"My Lady, please-"

Caroline laughed and gave Kirsty a hug, cutting her off. Dobbin really was rubbing off on her. It was nice to feel relaxed again, even if she couldn't smell properly. A human city filled with normal humans. No faspane. It brought a sense of comfort and safety.

They wandered the paved market square and examined the traders' wares. The place reeked of industry, most of which gave her the sniffles. Sawdust and manure littered the streets. She turned away from the oily reek of a smithy tinged with silver, as well as tanners' products. In the opposite direction she could smell all manner of spring vegetables and more.

Something about human production didn't agree with her werewolf nature. She even shied away from the leather goods and woodcrafters' wares. The scent of oils and lacquers was overpowering.

Several people commented on her red hair even though she kept her hood up, while others pointed her out to their friends. She walked away every time, and dodged behind a carriage at one point.

"There!" Kirsty said, pointing. Half way down a street running off the market square, bolts of fabric rested at the front of a shop and dresses hung from the eaves.

Inside the shop, a small grey-haired woman with deep wrinkles smiled from behind a bench as she stitched a hem. She raised an eyebrow at Caroline, but didn't comment on her heritage. "After a new a dress, girls?"

"One each, already prepared as we need them this morning."

The old woman gave Caroline a second look as she spoke. Belatedly, Caroline realised it was her accent.

The woman walked around the bench. She was small, even for a Fandelyon woman, and barely came to Kirsty's chin. "I have something for your friend if she's not too choosy, but you're a foot bigger than most girls around here. Clan heritage will do that, I guess. Giants, most of 'em."

Caroline sighed. She knew how Dobbin felt.

After trying several dresses on, the only one that fit was plain brown and made of sturdy linen. Unfortunately, the hem was far too short, scandalously revealing her ankles and calves.

"Mother would collapse in horror," Caroline said.

Kirsty stood in a similarly-styled yellow dress, but long enough. Somehow, Kirsty made the peasant cut look elegant.

"You know I'm jealous, don't you?"

Kirsty turned away, trying to keep a smile hidden.

"You're laughing at me! Oh, that's not fair. Maybe I'll ask for the hem of yours to be taken up to match mine." She glanced at the shop owner. "How long will it take to lengthen it? Maybe give me some more room in the bust?" It was alarmingly tight.

"I have several dresses need doing today, but I can have it done by tomorrow afternoon."

Caroline tipped half the coins from her purse into her hand. "Is that enough to do it immediately?" she asked.

The old woman's eyes widened. "Yes dear, with two shawls as well."

"Good. We'll wait." After the woman took her measurements, she went looking for boots, finding a man's pair big enough to fit. Kirsty said nothing, though Caroline could see she wanted to. "I think I became a shivra over the winter," Caroline muttered.

An hour later they returned to the shop, Caroline's dress comfortably altered, though the length looked a little odd with the additional material. The woman had done a reasonable job to match it up, at least.

"Should we explore?" Caroline asked, wiggling her toes in her new hard-leather boots. She'd never been alone in a city before and it felt strangely liberating. "The city's no doubt safe enough."

"Your Highness?" a woman asked.

A thrill of fear coursed through Caroline. She found a young, pregnant woman regarding her, the quality of her dress and a piebald baja dragon on her shoulder marked her a noble. Commoners certainly couldn't afford a dragon as a pet. Few could, even nobles, as the creatures were so rare.

The young woman held a pretty white parasol over her head, although the clouds made it unnecessary. Caroline sniffed, but couldn't catch the woman's scent due to her blocked nose and the sheer number of people about them. "You are?"

The young woman touched her maid's arm. "Get me three lavender-scented candles." She pointed to a nearby candle shop and dropped a couple of coins into the maid's hand. The maid scurried off. "I'm Leasa duBerond, Your Highness. I married Quenton duBerond, Earl Mern's third son, last year." She looked Caroline up and down, but said nothing about her clothes.

"Leasa. Of course." She'd been a merchant's daughter, her pale skin and honey-blond hair a rarity among commoners. Caroline caught Leasa's hands and the baja dragon scurried under Leasa's hair to hide. "I hadn't heard you were pregnant. Congratulations."

Leasa smiled brightly. "Thank you, Your Highness." Her expression changed as she noticed Caroline's newly-dark eyes. Her voice dropped. "Are you well, Your Highness?"

"I've been sick, Leasa. A malady over the winter."

Leasa's expression became uncertain. "Everyone believes you dead or taken hostage. I assure you, Earl Mern was very shocked to hear the news of your disappearance. Are you in disguise?"

Caroline smiled, though her stomach churned with anxiety. "Yes, we were attacked. I only survived thanks to the help of a shivra who's now escorting me home, unannounced of course, in case there was a traitor. Perhaps I should have disguised my hair. Please don't tell anyone about me, Leasa."

"I'll say nothing, even to my husband."

Caroline let go of Leasa's hands, hoping to change the subject. "How far along are you? You don't look very big yet."

The parrot-sized dragon poked its head out of Leasa's hair, one eye watching Caroline. It hid again when she glanced at it.

Leasa's smile returned and she put both her hands on her stomach. "Well over half way, though the first pregnancy doesn't show as much as those that follow. It will be a summer baby. It's been kicking for weeks now. Would you like to feel? It's kicking now."

Memories of her own pregnancy almost shattered Caroline's composure. She felt her eyes fill with tears and struggled to keep them from brimming over. "I'd love to feel it kick," she whispered hoarsely, wishing she could run away. All the pain and hurt she'd tried to forget from the abbey returned like a slap to her face.

Leasa's smile widened. "Here," she said, taking Caroline's left hand and placing it low on her stomach.

The child inside responded obligingly, pushing against Caroline's palm. Caroline forced a smile, wondering what her own child looked like now. It was unlikely to have her red hair, considering its father had been so dark, but perhaps she'd given it other features. Green eyes or her height, maybe. She took a deep breath to calm her emotions, though she couldn't keep her tears away and had to wipe her eyes with her sleeve.

"Your child is going to be strong and healthy," Caroline said. "I'm very happy for you." She gave Leasa a big hug.

Leasa's head snapped back and her body jerked away, making Caroline stumble as she tried to support the pregnant woman's weight. Leasa crumbled, the smell of blood blossoming around her, blood tinged with the taint of silver. Caroline pulled back.

A crossbow bolt protruded from Leasa's right eye. Her other eye stared sightlessly.

Caroline spun. Thirty yards down the street atop a roof, someone ducked out of sight. Faspane.

Caroline yelled and ran in pursuit. At the building, she sprang onto a box and jumped for the upper-story window, catching it and pulling herself onto the sill. She jumped and caught the edge of the roof and pulled herself up in one motion, landing in a crouch. She sniffed. Faspane. Clear even with her blocked nose.

She charged over the roof and jumped the six yards down to the alleyway behind, the scent of the trail like a road, but she didn't need it. The faspane stood at the end of the alleyway, trying to load her crossbow.

Caroline roared with rage, bloodlust giving her all the strength she needed. The faspane dropped the crossbow and ran into a gap between two buildings. Caroline sprinted, her boots and dress hindering her as she ran through the alley and across the next street, narrowly avoiding a donkey-drawn cart before dashing into another alley.

As she burst from the other end the faspane jumped out from behind a wagon and swung at Caroline's head. Caroline ducked the blade and shouldered into her attacker, both crashing hard to the ground. Caroline pinned the assassin's sword arm and smashed her fist into the woman's face.

The woman's eyes lost focus. Caroline wanted to tear the warrior's throat out. Zaramar's mate!

"Leasa was innocent," Caroline said, pulling the dagger at the woman's hip and pressing the tip into her neck.

"Please," the woman whispered, absolute dread on her face. "Let me do it myself. I beg you. My soul..."

With a yell of anger, Caroline slammed the dagger into a cracked paving stone beside the woman's head. Killing her wasn't enough. "Leasa didn't get a chance to say please."

"Please-"

Caroline made a fist, arm raised. "Tell your friends to begin praying to whatever Divine Lord or Lady they believe will help, because tonight I'm coming for them." She leaned closer. "And I'm going to kill you last."

She grabbed the assassin's sword from the cobbles as she stood, determined it would never be used again. She drove it deep between two stones beside the dagger, and then put all her strength against the hilt. The sword bent and snapped, the hilt and a few inches of blade coming clean away in her hand. She tossed it at the faspane.

The woman lay still, either too scared to move, or too hurt. Caroline put her foot on the dagger's hilt, pressing sideways until the blade bent. It didn't snap like the sword, unfortunately.

"Run!" she said, trying not to think of Leasa or her baby. "Enjoy your last day if you can."

The woman climbed to her feet, blood running from her nose and dribbling over her lips. She ran.

By the time Caroline got back to the inn Dobbin was ready with the horses, Kirsty was with him.

"Let's go," she said before either could question her. "Faspane are here. We need to find Elias and Allyn."

She pressed her face against Stormrunner's neck and tried to let his familiar scent ease the tension from her. He snorted, glad to see her again.

She had to end it tonight, had to make sure the faspane would never threaten her again.

35

———————

"Something's wrong," Allyn said as he stared intently at the bluestone walls of the small human city.

Elias raised his head. A slight haze of wood smoke hung on the air. They were perhaps two miles away on a rise, his view obscured by the rustbush shrubs they were hiding among. "More wrong than your prized student's game of pincushion last night?" Elias asked. Sitting against a low stone wall, he'd been trying to get comfortable since dawn. Branches pressed against his face and he'd already snapped several off, dropping them to the ground.

This was the only place within sight of Forecliffe's walls that kept them reasonably well hidden, and any traffic to Fandelyon City had to pass within sight.

"The bond remains intact," Allyn replied.

"Can you sense anything specific?" Elias asked, surprised at how relieved Allyn's statement made him feel.

"Only that she's angry. Murderously so. You seem worried."

Elias cleared his throat, trying to look nonchalant. "Why would I be concerned?"

"Perhaps it's something to do with a certain raven-haired Lady that keeps the Princess's company? She has eyes for you."

That caught him by surprise. "Kirsty? That's... Why would you think I'd be interested in a human?"

"What is it then?"

"Nothing," he said too quickly. "We can't seem to stay close enough to help."

Grazing sheep bleated nearby as a cold feeling came over Elias, his wards reacting to the presence of faspane. He glanced warningly at Allyn as he raised a finger to his lips for silence, but by the sorcerer's expression he already knew.

There was nothing but sheep and goats between them and the town, so the faspane had to be behind them in the trees. Tense, Elias got to his knees and peeked over the stone wall. No movement among the trunks.

He sprang over and dropped into a crouch, ears forward. No sound. The faspane had to be within a couple of hundred yards for his wards to react. Allyn dropped to the ground beside him, his staff charged with deadly force, the magic giving Elias gooseflesh.

Elias unsheathed his knife and ran to a large grey oak. He drew magic and cast an inattention spell on himself before running to the next tree. Another sorcerer would sense the magical resonance, but it was still the best option.

The forest remained ominously calm, not even a breeze rustling the leaves. He wished Caroline were here. She could have sniffed out the faspane. He could only smell manure and trees.

Keeping low, he dashed to another tree. If he closed his eyes and concentrated he could probably glean a direction, but the distraction might also encourage a crossbow bolt through his chest. Better to stay alert.

A stick snapped deeper into the trees, the sound sending a thrill of tension through him. He peeked past the tree trunk, and then dashed to the cover of a bushy grey oak sprouting from a stump.

Allyn ran to the tree he'd just left, the sensation of his magic marking him out.

Heart thumping, Elias made his way through the trees, but even when he stopped at the place where he thought the faspane might be, he found nothing but untouched earth.

A bow twanged.

He dropped flat, rolled to the side and back onto his knees with his knife ready, but a gasp behind him caught his attention.

A faspane woman staggered from a clump of bushes, her crossbow triggering before she fell on the weapon, snapping the crosspiece. A yard-long arrow protruded from her stomach, the fletching made of black feathers. She rolled to her side, blood spreading through her woodland leathers.

Elias darted to a lowland grey oak and pressed his back against the smooth bark, looking for the bowman. No doubt they'd mistake him for a faspane too. It was quiet except for a whimper of pain from the faspane woman. There was no sign of whoever had released the arrow.

"Good morning, Elias," called a youthful, cheery female voice from high in the branches.

Shock almost staggered him. "Your Majesty?" His Queen, his *grandmother*, was here? The risk!

Elias caught Allyn's eyes and saw disbelief there too, but his old teacher shook it off and ran to the fallen faspane. Elias backed toward him to provide what little protection he could in case there were more about. They were at a severe disadvantage even with the Queen protecting them, but they had to finish the warrior or their wards would continue to react to her.

Allyn rolled the wounded woman onto her back and drew her dagger. "Gods! She's a child." Allyn hissed. "I doubt she'd be nineteen."

Allyn helped the girl grasp the blade and position it over her heart, his hands around hers. She grimaced, looking both grateful and scared, and far too young. Elias looked away.

She tried to speak, but only stuttered.

"May your rebirth be swift, and in your new life may your soul find immortality," Allyn said in Faspaneth.

"Thank you," she gasped, before Allyn helped her drive the blade home.

Elias turned back as his wards settled. There were no other faspane about. "She's barely old enough to have earned her sword," he murmured.

"Your Majesty?" Allyn called, looking around.

Queen Sellendria dropped to the ground fifty yards away, bow in hand. She slung it across her back and strode over to them, inspected the girl, pulled her arrow free and cleaned it on a cloth she drew from her belt.

The arrow's feathers had come from a siren, and the magic distilled in them ensured they never missed so long as she could see her target.

Elias didn't think he'd ever seen his grandmother in fighting leathers before.

Tall and youthful, she moved with grace. "Elias."

He belatedly dropped to one knee, head bowed. Allyn did the same.

"It's far too dangerous for you here," Allyn said, his voice almost angry. "Why have you come?"

"I'm being careful," she said. "Stand, Elias. You too, Allyn."

They did.

Her violet eyes regarded Elias speculatively. "I hear you've found the likely human Champion. Is it true?"

Surprised by her knowledge, Elias hesitated, but Allyn nodded. "Yes. Princess Caroline. How did you know?"

"Do you really believe you were both needed to get the sword?"

Allyn closed his eyes as if something finally made sense. "I thought it was too close to Elias's test."

"Then clearly it's no coincidence why I'm here now. Allyn, you will continue to Delshere alone. Elias, you must return home. Your task here is complete. The Champion is safe with Allyn."

"My test?" Excitement and fear made his heart thump harder. "But... my bow's lost."

"Then you must work harder to win. Ternise completed her

apprenticeship yesterday. You must test each other as soon as possible."

"I need time to enchant another bow. A few weeks to find-"

"No. The Gods won't allow it."

"But-"

She stared at him until he dropped his eyes.

"Would you dare insult me, or your teacher? The Gods accept no excuses." He heard an accusation of cowardice in her tone.

He flushed. "I... It's not. I mean-"

"Tradition dictates your immediate return."

"But... I need a weapon." Whatever weapon he chose and enchanted had to be made specifically for the test. He glanced sidelong at Allyn, silently begging for help, and found none. "I'm only seeking a slight delay. With the Council's approval you could intercede with the Gods."

Allyn cleared his voice. "It is within your jurisdiction, to ask, Your Majesty. A short delay-"

Sellendria's delicate ears dropped back. "Allyn, need I remind you what happened the last time I asked the Gods to intervene on my behalf? Helping Elias would be seen as a favour. I can't risk that again."

Allyn dropped his eyes. "I apologise."

Elias watched them, curious. What had she asked for?

"You're of my bloodline Elias, my second heir. This is your time to be tested. You must fulfil your duties."

"But how can I be considered worthy enough to face Ternise without a weapon? Asking for a small delay can only honour her."

"The Gods don't grant favours lightly, Elias. Invoke them yourself if you're foolish enough. I guarantee you won't like the response."

"You'd allow me to invoke the Gods?" Elias asked.

Sellendria made an exasperated sound. "You're of my bloodline. I can't stop you, but are you really prepared to try? Any favour granted will cost you dearly."

Elias hesitated. "It's more than just the bow. We have a task."

She must have caught something else in his voice as she frowned. "Allyn, leave us please."

Allyn stiffened. "As you wish. Your Majesty." He sounded insulted.

When Allyn was out of earshot, his grandmother unclipped a necklace she wore with two charms on it. One charm appeared to be a bow, the other a quiver. "These were given to me a long time ago." She detached the tiny bow from the necklace and it flashed into a full-sized longbow, strung and ready to be used.

Elias leaned back in surprise. "What magic is this?"

She held it out to him. "I would never have sent you unprepared. This bow's owner never took the test, though he created it for that purpose."

Elias stared, but didn't reach out.

After a moment she let her arm fall to her side. "There's another reason you don't want to return, isn't there?"

"Caroline," he whispered before he thought about it, and nearly swore. He'd been going to say *the Silver Well.*

"Caroline? The human Champion?" she asked. She watched his eyes, clearly curious.

He turned away. "*Potential* Champion, Grandmother. She's vulnerable." That might be enough. "She needs our help."

The Queen gently caught his jaw with her free hand and lifted it until he met her gaze. It was almost as if she were looking into his soul. Her eyes suddenly widened. "No!" she whispered, dropping his jaw and taking a step back. "No! How could the Gods do this after everything they've already demanded of me?" Her hand clenched tight around the bow, her own slung across her back.

"What?" he asked.

"You're in love with her," the Queen whispered.

"No! That's not it. She's..." How could he explain it? "Our souls are connected somehow."

Sellendria closed her eyes as if trying to understand. "She can't be your soulmate. Your soul is newly made."

His soul was newly made? "But-"

"Would you defy the Gods to be with her?"

"Of course not. I know my duties. She'll be reborn. I can wait."

So softly he barely caught the words, she whispered, "Would you die to protect her?"

He found himself unable to deny the possibility. "I don't know."

A hint of a smile touched the corners of Sellendria's mouth, making him wonder what she was thinking. There was certainly no malice in her voice. More of a tease.

"The Gods must hate me," he whispered. Why else would they make Caroline human?

With a flick of her wrist the bow returned to the size of a charm. She reattached it to the necklace and put the necklace back on. "The Gods rarely share their plans with us."

"Huh?"

"They reward those who act selflessly. That's why we're tested, why the weaker of us give up our lives in the hope the stronger may better serve our people. It's cruel, but would you rather see our way of life gone and izzen reduced to the likes of humans or faspane?"

"No," he whispered. "But Ternise is my friend, Grandmother. We grew up together."

"When I went for my Test, I was paired with a boy called Daen. I had my sword. He, like you, favoured the bow. For seven weeks we hunted each other through our forests. A dozen times each of us nearly killed the other. In the end I surprised him, but he tested me to the edge of my skills, to the edge of my life, and he almost took it. To do anything less would have been an insult to the Gods and to me, but he made sure I was worthy of my place among our people. I thank him for that every time I pray, and I thank the Gods for giving me such a worthy opponent. I expect nothing less from you, or from Ternise. You will go to your Test and you will make sure Ternise is worthy of serving the Gods and our people, or she you, and neither of you will give the other any quarter."

"I understand, Grandmother. I didn't mean to shame you, or insult Ternise. Give me the bow and I'll leave."

She placed a hand on his shoulder. "Be honest with me. Do you believe you'll best serve our people and the Gods by staying, or taking the Test?"

"I don't know," he whispered. "My emotions may be distorting my judgement." He swallowed. "Grandmother, why would the Gods give me a mortal soul twin, or whatever she is? Why taunt me like this? Am I simply to act as her guardian, or do they intend more?"

She surprised him by smiling. "It's a family tradition."

Family tradition? It took him a moment to realise what she meant. *"Grandfather* was born a mortal in a previous life and you loved him then as well as in his current life." It must have been incredibly painful for her to watch him die and then wait centuries or millennia for his rebirth.

"It was a long time ago, Elias. It took me a while to admit I loved him, even to myself. When I did, I risked everything for him." She met his eyes. "How could I deny you the same choice? Does she understand your feelings?"

"She's usually trying to kill me."

She laughed, genuinely. "Give her time, Elias."

"It's wrong. She's mortal."

"Yet your souls are immortal. I'll ask the Council to grant you leave to finish your task. Should they agree and the Gods concur, you may remain, but be aware, there will be a price."

"Thank you."

"Do not leave this place until you hear from me. We're too far away for a message to reach you without knowing your location."

"Yes, Your Majesty."

She called magic as she reached into a pouch at her belt and pulled out an eagle's feather. The feather burst into the shape of an eagle made of light. She leaned close, whispered into its ear, and drew on more magic. The bright bird doubled in size and doubled again, and then launched itself into the air, leaving a faint trail of residual energy in its wake.

Sellendria glanced at him. "She'll reach the Council in a few hours. You should have your answer by dawn."

Ghostly wings flashed out from the Queen's wingbuds, each wing twice the length of her body. Elias stepped back, allowing her room.

"Oh, and Elias?"

"Yes?"

"You need another shave." She winked.

With a light spring her spirit-wings drove her skyward after the eagle, her body breaking through the leaves above while her ghostly wings passed through as if the trees weren't there. In moments she was gone.

He touched his jaw, fingertips brushing the stubble just coming through. He thought he'd kept that a secret from everyone, but she hadn't been surprised at all.

How long had she known?

36

The drizzle began midmorning and only got heavier.

Caroline couldn't stop shivering. Kirsty shook worse. At first it had been muggy, but then the rain turned cold. In typical shivrad fashion, Dobbin ignored the cold and wet, though his cheeks were flushed pink above his beard.

Caroline wished she'd let Elias teach her how he avoided getting wet. No doubt she'd be a lot warmer, and Kirsty too if she could share the magic.

She kept herself distracted with the anticipation of tearing the faspane apart, limb from bloody limb. Her rising bloodlust and imaginings might have disturbed her a week ago, but not now. Now she was looking forward to it.

Although she tried to appear calm, inside she seethed and longed for nightfall so she could go hunting. She found herself thinking about the morning she'd faced Zaramar. If a warrior ready for her had no chance, then what trouble could the rest represent?

The roads quickly became boggy, and for long stretches they had to walk the horses, getting themselves covered in mud, much of which the rain refused to wash off. Sheep and goats huddled in the fields and farmers kept indoors. Caroline's mood darkened.

She wanted to warn Elias off or else get as far from him as she could so she wouldn't endanger him, yet they made very little progress, perhaps just five or six miles by early afternoon, and she never saw him. She had a sense of Allyn, but the bond was too new to work out anything more.

"There's an inn ahead," Dobbin said as they approached a village. "I say we wait the bad weather out."

She wiped rain from her eyes, shielding her face with a hand to see ahead. "What if faspane are watching us? They had no trouble sneaking into a fortified town. A simple village would make us even more vulnerable. Let's keep going."

"Perhaps, but if they were following closely I doubt they'd have left us alone this long. Besides, they know where we're going. They only need to watch the roads between here and Fandelyon City. We could stumble into a trap if we keep going."

Caroline's mood sunk further, and further again as she noticed how blue Kirsty's lips were and how her friend shivered uncontrollably. "We'll wait it out. Tonight I'll fix our faspane problem."

"Do you think that's wise?" Kirsty asked through chattering teeth, both fear and concern in her voice.

"No," Caroline said. "But it's better than being ambushed."

An hour later they found themselves settled in a small room with four sleeping pallets and little else. Dobbin pushed two together for himself. Caroline sensed her mood rubbing off on her friends, so she tried to get Dobbin talking.

"Know any weather magic?" she asked as they sat cooped up on their beds following a hearty meal of salted fish and fresh greens. "Maybe bring out the sun?"

Caroline had finished a second helping of freshly-baked fish and hadn't felt so full in days. The dark-haired locals, farmers for the most part, were taking advantage of the poor weather to get together and drink ale in the room below. The sounds of their talk grew louder the more beer they drank. One man plucked at an instrument, tuning it.

Dobbin snorted. "Try a priest, or maybe ask fer wings so ye can fly above the clouds."

"There's a thought," Caroline muttered, trying not to glance at the marks on her wrists. "Do you suppose there are were-eagles? I'd rather have been bitten by one of them."

"Bitten? By an eagle?"

Kirsty scent became infused with curiosity. "Dobbin, can magic make you fly?" There was an intense note of longing in her voice, surprising Caroline.

He shrugged. "Not shivra magic. I've heard rumours some izzen can fly, but izzen aren't normally forthcoming about their magic."

"Really?" Kirsty asked, her scent infused with enthusiasm. "You're not just teasing us?"

"No, lass. Perhaps Allyn's new student will find out one day." He glanced slyly at Caroline. "I have it on good authority that the izzen King and Queen have wings." He winked.

"Really," Caroline said dryly. "Do they have feathers, too?"

He shrugged. "Maybe. Never met 'em."

"Dobbin, how exactly did your cabin's wards work?"

"I guess I could explain. Perhaps even show ye. Like a good deal of magic, it's all about misdirection and assumptions. Me cabin's wards got people ta see what they expected. The less likely something is to be in a place, the easier it is to hide it."

"So it's easier to hide something out of place?"

"Aye. If ye went into a bedroom ye'd expect ta see a bed, right? Very difficult to hide that. Ye could better hide a snake or pot because it's not what yer expecting."

She listened to him talk about the principles for half the afternoon, even trying a few minor wards to hide mundane objects in the room. She then tried her new skills on Kirsty.

"Anything?" Caroline asked. Kirsty had found the bowl and spoon without trouble, but now looked confused.

"Everything seems to be in its place," she said, walking around the small room, examining things. "Candles, our gear and cloaks. What did you hide?"

"Nothing," Caroline said with a grin.

Kirsty put her hands on her hips. "Tell me!"

"Tomorrow."

Kirsty sighed and sat on her pallet, and squealed. She jumped up and turned, but her expression was curious.

"Can ye see it now?" Dobbin asked.

She shook her head and knelt beside the pallet, gingerly reaching out and stopping when her fingers found something. She ran her hand over it and laughed in delight. "Dobbin, it's your hammer. I can see it now."

Caroline smiled, just as enthralled and feeling a whole lot less guilty than she'd expected. Kirsty tried to lift the huge weapon, but couldn't do more than lever up the haft. Caroline found Dobbin watching her with something akin to disbelief. "What?" she asked.

He shrugged. "Just impressed. Kirsty should have seen the hammer when she touched it, but didn't until she felt its shape, despite knowing something was there. Ye've got a knack, lass."

Guilt and pride warred. She sided with pride.

She sensed more than noticed the evening fall. Her black mood returned. Although she wasn't particularly hungry after the noon meal, she didn't want to transform on a half-empty stomach.

"Ye still planning on slaughtering faspane?" Dobbin asked, a hint of disapproval in his voice.

"I only intend to ensure our safety." She'd calmed down a lot since Leasa had been killed, but rage still simmered.

"It's not about revenge, then?"

She met his eyes. "Revenge stops bad things repeating."

"Or makes them worse."

"Only if I die." She tried not to remember Leasa's head snapping back as the bolt killed the innocent young woman. "But better I die trying to kill them, than risk anyone else dying in my place, including you two." She stood. "I'd better get prepared."

～

Despite his wards repelling water, Elias shivered. He finally stopped pacing and put his back against a huge willow as dusk chilled the already-cool air. Cold water dribbled down the back of his neck and he futilely pulled his hood forward. He needed to renew his wards. They were growing too weak to be effective.

Heavy drops spattered his head and shoulders, dipping from branches. It was the best shelter they could find, a stand of willows by a fast-flowing creek. The drooping braches hid them and kept some of the rain away, but not enough. After the better part of a day his wards weren't helping much at all.

"We need to do something," Elias said. He moved away from the tree and began pacing, his shivra-sized hood slipping back again. He doubted a human would be able to see much in the gloom, but he could. The problem was, he couldn't see Caroline. She could be forty miles up the road by now, well beyond his ability to help.

"Make a suggestion," Allyn said. "Our Queen said to remain here. Would you defy her? Ignore the Gods and your test?"

"No," he said with resignation. He wouldn't defy the Gods for anyone.

"I'm sure Dobbin is capable of protecting Caroline for one night. Do you trust him?"

Elias gave Allyn another look, wishing he dared speak of his true feelings and concerns. "So we do nothing? You, at least, could go."

"I could, but she'll be in a town somewhere, warm and comfortable in a decent bed. What would I do but what I'm doing now? At least this way we'll both get some sleep. If you honestly think the faspane are going to ambush her tonight, I'll lend you my staff and wait for the message myself."

Elias glanced at the weapon. Hidden within the wood was a crystal holding a full measure of magic. Elias could use it to charge the weapon with deadly power, much deadlier than he could put into a normal weapon at short notice. For a few minutes after activation it would be enough to kill almost anything it touched. Using it like that would drain the crystal quickly though, and it would take a decade to recharge naturally.

"We promised we'd keep her safe. I feel like I'm reneging."

"A week ago you wouldn't have cared."

"I would have cared," he said. Now he cared *about* her, not just the promise to shadow her to Fandelyon City and keep her safe from the faspane. She'd proven an ally, someone who would risk her life for him. Give her life, really. If the Gods were testing, her she was passing. He, on the other hand, would likely be punished if he went to her, by his Queen and the Gods.

"What would you do if you found her?" Allyn asked. "Other than my staff, we've no offensive magic, and nothing that can find faspane beyond a couple of hundred yards. She can look after herself for a night."

He knew Allyn was leading him to reach the most sensible conclusion, yet he resented it. It didn't help that his former teacher was right. Unless he intended to disobey his grandmother, he had no right to do anything but stay here tonight.

It was still a struggle. "You should have taught her a few spells, shown her how to set wards to detect faspane, at least."

"Force her into it?"

"She has to obey you."

"And have her hate me for the rest of her life? She resents me enough already. She'll learn when she wants to, just as you did. Regardless, I've had no time to teach her anything."

"You should have made time. Taught her while we were walking. What if the faspane come for her tonight?"

"Then Dobbin deals with it, or she turns into wolf and deals with it herself. Take the staff or leave it be."

Elias crossed his arms, shivering, and sucked water from his upper lip. He tried to agree. "She's probably nice and warm in a common room somewhere, tucking into a decent meal. The worst danger she'll risk is Dobbin accidently sitting on her." He tried to make himself believe it. He really wanted to.

Somehow, he knew it wasn't likely to be that easy for her.

37
———————

"Filthy clan girl," an old man whispered as Caroline pulled open the inn's door to leave.

She hesitated, but confronting them wasn't worth the angst. Barefoot, she left the inn wearing the clothes Kirsty had adjusted for her in the mountains. She'd already stuffed herself with a double helping of roast pork, in the hope of tempering her bloodlust.

Other villagers watched her leave, openly curious, but she didn't care so long as they all remained inside.

Cold rain struck her face as she pressed her back against the inn's door. She squinted, the cold biting. Her nose was mostly clear and there seemed to be nothing out of place; rain, wet sheep and cattle, tilled earth and manure, wood smoke and other muted scents of human habitation.

She struggled through mud past a dozen two-storey homes to the edge of the village. A weather-worn sign proclaimed the place to be Featherwood. Beyond the village stretched farmland and orchards. Most of the fields were stone-walled with the rocks that generations of farmers had dug up or scavenged from ruins. A few looked like they may be marble, which would date them back to the time Mistapol ruled here.

Homes dotted the farmland, the escaping light from their shutters letting her know the lay of the land.

She walked a few hundred yards further down the road, the cold wind carrying a salty hint from the Temern Strait. She jumped the stone wall into a field of spring vegetables, her toes squelching into the mud. She didn't recognise many of the sprouting plants, not being a farmer, but none seemed ready to pick for market.

She stripped and folded her clothes, taking time to pack them against the wall with a rock on top. It would hardly do to walk naked into the village at dawn if the wind scattered them.

Wet and wind-chilled, she ran a fingertip over the fine stretch marks given to her by childbirth. They were marks Leasa would never have the chance to earn, and just like Caroline she'd never get to hold the baby either.

Hurt flared fresh and sharp, but she didn't want to charge into a trap and die or kill innocent people. She had to be smarter as well as deadlier than the faspane.

When calm again she took a nervous breath and imagined the moon large and full, rising above the horizon, and willed her body to change.

She gasped in agony and collapsed, the power of the curse shattering her composure for long seconds. When she could breathe again she was laying on her side in the form of a wolf, wind failing to ruffle her damp fur. Everything ached.

She struggled to her paws, shook the mud away and set off toward Forecliffe, wary of an ambush. She stayed within the fields and tried to avoid any place Elias may have taken shelter, even avoiding the ruins of an old castle.

Dogs barked when she came too close to sheep they guarded, but neither the sheep or dogs smelled as good as the farmers in their homes. As tempting as it was to investigate the human smells, she hunted deadlier game tonight.

Cutting across the paddocks took much less time than struggling with horses along muddy roads, and it wasn't long before the walled town of Forecliffe rose before her. She began a wide circle of the place, keeping her nose to the ground as often as in the air to catch stray scents. As she came around to the south side she caught a trace of her enemy, the same female assassin who'd entered the town.

Caroline's hackles rose. Anger and hatred resurfaced. She hoped the woman was scared. If not, she would be soon.

She followed the scent south, wary of a trap, stopping to listen and watch every few hundred yards. The assassin's trail quickly met up with three others. She examined the area and found their scents going south and west, the west being the freshest. The rain dulled the trail, but not enough.

With the wind behind her, she began tracking them again, a few minutes later crossing the main road and continuing on toward the western mountains.

Barely a mile on, the group of faspane merged with another of the same size. Eight now. She growled. They wanted her dead and they knew she was coming. It only made sense they'd assemble into a fighting force.

She continued more cautiously through farmland and small areas of woods, across several swollen streams and around hills, keeping to cover whenever possible.

At one point, she caught a hint of familiar scents. Allyn and Elias. A flare of desire and bloodlust caught her so she sprinted in the opposite direction, not breathing again until she had to. It was enough. She picked up the trail again somewhere to the west of Elias, where the faspane eventually turned north toward Fandelyon City, the wind now coming from her right.

It didn't take long before another group of seven faspane joined with the eight she was tracking, all continuing north before turning northwest. She followed cautiously, ears up and listening.

Five or six miles northwest, they changed direction again, this time almost directly east, into the wind. She stiffened at a hint of human blood on the air and cautiously padded forward, nose high.

Featherwood! The trail led directly there. Fear rose toward panic at the thought that her friends were in danger. She sprinted ahead, caring nothing for caution now. It was a trap, certainly, but Kirsty and Dobbin were the bait and it was her own doing. The faspane must have stayed downwind and watched her leave, knowing it would take time for her to circle back. And now the trap was set.

Her stomach tightened with tension as she neared. She smelled more blood and the scents of fear and pain. She couldn't budge the deep pit of despair in her stomach. The homes were quiet and little light escaped the shuttered windows and doors. The quietness made her fear even more. There were too many human smells mingled together with faspane to tell where anyone might be from a distance, or even who was still alive.

As she approached, faspane scents crisscrossed the ground, deliberately trying to confuse her. She snarled. She wanted to chase them down and tear them apart, one by one, but now they had Kirsty and Dobbin. Her stupidity sickened her. Worse, she smelled enough silver to kill her dozens of times over.

Kirsty abruptly screamed, the pain-filled sound coming from the tavern.

Tensing to charge, she caught sight of a faspane on the roof of the first house.

Click.

Heart hammering, she dodged a crossbow bolt as a warrior stood up from behind a stone wall, sword raised. She changed her stride and leapt, taking him down and tearing his throat out.

Bloodlust flared, fresh and joyous. Three more strides and she leapt to a cart and onto the single-storey shingle roof, the faspane there trying to reload his crossbow. She crashed into him, breaking his neck as they tumbled off the roof. She hit the ground running, the taste of flesh driving her desire for more.

She reacted to movement at the side of the two-storey inn and dodged another bolt. A second bolt from the rooftop beside the inn nicked her hind leg, but she ignored the searing burn of silver and ran at the faspane on the ground. She knocked him back ten feet as she struck, and tore his arm off as they landed.

She spun as he screamed. The shutters burst open in the bakery beside the inn. She squinted at the light, but it wasn't bright enough to obscure a faspane inside, aiming a crossbow at her. She dodged as he released the bolt, the silver tip punching painfully through her ear.

With the thrill of her hunt growing stronger she leapt through the window, but he'd already dodged to the side. She caught movement and killed someone, a human hostage, then killed the other warrior as he drew his sword.

Several people screamed and tried to run for the stairs. Her instincts to chase rose up. She ran them all down and killed them, too. They tasted much better than the faspane. Human.

She wanted more. She could smell plenty of them.

Kirsty stumbled and crashed shoulder-first into a stool. She sprawled as it clattered to the ground beside her, grazing her palms on the ale-sticky floorboards. Someone screamed in agony amid the wind and rain outside, the cry cutting off abruptly.

"Please leave here!" Kirsty cried as she pushed herself half up, her shoulder aching. "She's killing people. If you have any honour then draw her away from here. Save yourselves." One of the faspane stared at her, his expression uncomprehending. She looked to another of the three. "Please, they're just villagers and farmers. They've done nothing to you." She glanced at Dobbin who lay unconscious across the room, wishing he would wake. There was nothing she could do to help him or the people Caroline was killing.

The narrow window across from her was too far to reach, its glass pane heavy with grime and impossible to see through, but if she could distract the faspane and get outside, she may be able to calm her friend and stop the slaughter.

A farmer caught her attention, drunk by the look of his eyes, and gave a slight shake of his head. Maybe he wasn't as drunk as he appeared. His grey curly beard was long enough to scrape across his chest.

She took his advice and curled up against the wall, her forearm aching from where the warrior had twisted it to make her scream earlier. Her opposite shoulder now hurt as well after hitting the stool and she still tasted blood from where she'd been backhanded when the faspane had burst into the tavern.

She checked on Dobbin from where she was. He was breathing, but she suspected if they lived through this he'd have an awful headache in the morning. She took a deep breath and mustered enough courage to try again, staring at each of the faspane in turn and hoping to look confident. "My Lady will kill you, you understand? Flee while you have a chance. I won't scream or give you away, I promise."

She glanced at the farmer who gave her another signal to be quiet. She ignored him. The barman, sitting a few feet from the farmer, tried to glance her way, but blood ran across his face from a cut above his left eyebrow and he had trouble focusing.

One of the three faspane gave her a curious but uncomprehending stare. She focused her attention on the one with the crossbow. "You understand, don't you? She's going to come in here and kill you. Holding me will only increase your danger. Leave by the rear door. Help yourselves. Help the villagers."

The faspane frowned before turning his attention back to the inn's door, his crossbow ready. She couldn't tell if he understood or not.

She began crawling toward Dobbin where he lay amid broken tables, one of which had two snapped legs so it rested above him like a lean-to. The faspane with the crossbow looked up.

"No," he said. The one who'd thrown her levelled the tip of his blade in her direction. He was much closer. She stopped, slowly leaning her back against the wall again. It didn't seem to matter what she said or did, they wouldn't listen or let her help her friends.

She glanced at one of the villagers, dead in a pool of his own blood a few feet from Dobbin. He'd been stabbed in the guts earlier when he'd tried to fight back. There were half a dozen more bodies, though many of the men who'd been here earlier had long gone home, fortunately. The dead were farmers, not fighters, though they'd tried to resist.

"Please-"

"Shush girl," the bartender said, a hand on his forehead and his eyes closed. "You're making matters worse. Just shush, please, and some of us might survive."

The one with the crossbow caught her looking at him, the firelight from the hearth giving him a harsh expression. A cruel grin crept across his lips. "Maybe your dog bitch kill you first when she come, huh?" He pointed the weapon at her. She held her breath, certain the three faspane no longer needed her or the locals as hostages, but he quickly returned his attention to the door as wood splintered somewhere in the village.

A high-pitched voice cried out several homes away. A woman's voice. No, a child's. The cry ended quickly.

Kirsty closed her eyes with a shudder, trying not to cry or vomit. She wanted to do both. Caroline needed to see a familiar face, smell someone familiar. Several more screams broke through the patter of rain and gusting wind before everything went dangerously quiet again.

The faspane with the crossbow frowned at her. She cringed as he aimed his weapon at her face. "Shivra no help you. Werewolf no help. Die tonight. Yes?"

"You die tonight," Kirsty said, raising her chin and almost daring him to release the bolt. "Caroline's my friend. She'll kill you and save me."

He grinned. "You friend no friend now. Insane. We kill or she kill. No else."

The sound of someone being savaged cut him off. Kirsty wished the warrior appeared even a little scared. The third faspane who'd remained quietly in the corner clicked, his fingers and made several gestures. The one who'd shoved Kirsty to the ground moved over to her, caught her by the hair and hauled her upright.

"Ow," she cried as she stood, trying to get to her feet as quickly as possible. This close the faspane stank of sweat and wood smoke.

He let her hair go and gripped her wrist, twisting. She screamed, then he forced her arm straight and made her double over as he lifted her wrist high behind her, almost shattering her shoulder. She could barely gasp.

"Ow-ow-uh," she whispered as he relaxed his hold slightly, tears blurring her vision.

She managed to move a little and ease the pain, but it hurt far too much to attempt to pull away or escape his grip. He shifted his weight and she thought he was about to release her, but he lifted her arm once more. She screamed until he twisted her about, pulling her close and pressing the flat of his sword against her neck.

"Please," she whispered, fighting down panic. "Go now. Leave us alone and she might let you live."

He raised the weapon slightly, forcing her to stand on tip-toes or allow the blade to cut into her jaw. Determined not to let him use her against Caroline, she breathed in short sharp gasps, hoping for inspiration, but she could barely think past the blade under her jaw. Everything outside had gone quiet except for the wind.

Blood trickled down her throat and she realised she'd been cut without feeling it. She tried raising her chin but it only forced the back of her head to press harder against the warrior's leather-clad chest.

The faspane holding her said something in his own language and the one with the crossbow moved slightly, his weapon staying on the door. Seconds passed. She finally began to notice the pain from the cut under her jaw, a stinging ache that grew worse each second, exacerbated by the blade still at her throat.

"*Aketh dei ortas,*" the faspane behind her said. "*Orta. Aketh!*"

The faspane near the door glared at the warrior holding Kirsty, but conceded with a slight nod at whatever demand had been made. Sword out and ready, he tentatively reached out and grasped the handle.

The door exploded off its hinges as Caroline burst through,

tearing the arm off the faspane in a spray of blood before twisting to dodge a bolt as if she'd known it was coming. Her claws scratched the floorboards as she spun and leapt sideways with impossible agility. She crashed into the faspane who'd released the bolt. He screamed in pain as she caught him by the shoulder and violently shook him until he went limp and silent.

"*Amaarth*!" said the faspane warrior who held Kirsty. He pulled her closer.

Caroline dropped the body and turned her attention to the warrior holding Kirsty, and Kirsty swore she saw insanity combined with cunning.

The faspane's body, which she'd just savaged, struggled for air as if failing to realise it was already dead. With clear cunning and calculation, Caroline ignored the warrior holding Kirsty and turned back to her dying prey. She opened her jaws wide and crushed his throat.

"No," Kirsty said, fearing her friend had completely lost herself. The werewolf, turned toward the faspane still holding Kirsty as she licked the blood from her maw. "Go," Kirsty whispered to the faspane behind her. "Leave now and I'll try to calm her. She trusts me."

Caroline appeared even larger than the last time Kirsty had seen her as a wolf. She snarled, and Kirsty wasn't sure if it was directed toward her or the faspane.

The blade pressed tighter against Kirsty's throat, a low growl making Kirsty fear her friend may be lost forever. The huge werewolf leapt and the faspane's grip disappeared. Dragged along with them, Kirsty slammed into the bar and crashed to the floor.

"Caroline!" she cried as she staggered to her feet, the barman staring in shock and remaining still. "Don't!"

By the time Kirsty stood it was already over. Caroline leapt to the top of the bar, her blood-soaked muzzle drawing into a snarl as her insane green eyes fixed on Kirsty.

"Stop," Kirsty whispered, lifting her hand so the werewolf could get a better sense of her scent. She wouldn't hurt her best friend. "Caroline, it's over. We're safe now. You saved us."

A low growl escaped the werewolf as it exposed its huge teeth.

"Caroline?" Kirsty said with the first inkling of fear, trying to keep her eyes on her friend. "Caroline, it's me, Kirsty. You remember me, don't you?"

She held her hand out once more, hoping her friend would catch her scent, but instead the werewolf's muscles tensed.

38

———

Elias jerked awake, his heart racing. He'd fallen asleep on his watch. Thanks to cloud and rain he couldn't easily tell what time it might be, but there was enough light to suggest it was already past dawn. He squatted with his back against a kissing tree, named for its small heart-shaped leaves. It took him a long minute to calm his pulse. Anyone could have approached and slit their throats while he dozed.

His former teacher sat hunched with his back to a willow, his wet woollen hood keeping the worst of the rain off his head. Neither tree proved effective at keeping the drizzle away. Elias briefly closed his eyes and took a deep breath, wishing for calm but finding none.

He stood and stretched, his uncomfortably damp. A simple spell using the element of fire quickly warmed him and his clothes. He was still uncomfortably damp. Even if the rain stopped, it would take his wards hours to force out the remaining water.

The piercing cry of an eagle broke the stillness, a tinge of magic in the sound. Finally. Elias squinted as he tried to see through the leaves, dreading the news and desperate for it.

Allyn pushed his hood back, his hair plastered to his face as Queen Sellendria's huge eagle burst through the leaves and back-winged to land at Elias's feet. The magical creature stared at him in the unnerving way only birds of prey could.

"Well, get on with it," Allyn said.

Elias frowned at his mentor, but nevertheless reached out. Magic discharged in a stinging flash of energy.

"Return with the sword or not at all,' Queen Sellendria's voice echoed in his mind.

All that remained of the eagle was a single feather, water beading on it. Elias met Allyn's eyes. "I'm to return with the sword, or never return."

Allyn nodded. "There's always a price when asking concessions of Gods and rulers. I'm surprised it wasn't more onerous."

An hour later, Elias and Allyn stopped at the ruins of an old castle a mile or so west of the village of Featherwood. In a haze of drizzle, they picked out a scene of devastation. A long, piercing wail reached them, followed by another, both ineffectively hushed.

Elias felt sick as he realised he witnessed the results of a slaughter. What had at first appeared to be damp lumps on the ground became ripped and dismembered bodies.

Humans wandered about, some in a daze, others just standing and staring, while more sobbed or consoled or tried to restore some form of normality. Few seemed game enough to approach any of the faspane bodies, some of which had been dragged to the edge of the village.

"What did she do?" Elias asked, shock evident in his whisper.

Those people capable of it began the horrible task of restoring their village. They pulled mourners away and moved bodies from the streets and homes, placing the human dead in the smithy. Farmers came in from the fields, quickly leaving to return with wives and older sons and daughters to help.

Some of the people seemed so shocked, they just stood in the rain, staring. A youth, no older than fourteen, took a workhorse from a nearby farm and rode down the road toward Forecliffe, its hooves flicking up clods of mud.

"She really is as deadly as she thinks she is," Allyn whispered. "I felt her hatred and anguish last night, but never expected this."

"Surely even werewolves aren't capable of such a massacre? If they were, a single werewolf would kill hundreds, possibly thousands of people every year."

"Her magic feeds the curse, but I had no idea..."

Two men carried a bloodied body from a house, one arm swinging loose as if only a small shred of flesh kept it attached. Elias couldn't tell if it was human or faspane.

"We should never have let her live," Elias whispered, thinking back to the mountains. "How could the Gods expect us to protect her from herself when she does this?" He wasn't sure if it was his own fears speaking or his honest opinion.

"We've no idea what really happened," Allyn said.

"It doesn't outweigh the devastation she's caused. No werewolf should have been able to do what she's done even with magic fuelling their strength. She might have got a few of them, but even a werewolf's supernatural speed shouldn't have allowed her to so freely massacre a well-armed ambush."

Allyn didn't respond. When Elias looked, he was surprised to see pain on his former teacher's face.

"Her emotions are coming through the bond?" Elias asked. It shouldn't have surprised him. "Is she suicidal?" The thought concerned him more than he cared to admit.

Allyn took a deep breath. "No, but it wouldn't take much to push her that way. I'm not entirely sure she'll recover. Last night..." He trailed off, face pale.

"You should have said something! We might have been able to help."

"No. She'd have killed us too."

Humans carried another body out of a home, laying it with a stray leg like a macabre puzzle. It appeared to be a child no older than ten.

An old man, perhaps the grandfather, stared blankly as if he expected to wake up soon. Eventually, a girl Caroline's age put a blanket around the man's shoulders and guided him away. He didn't resist.

Elias couldn't disguise the accusation in his voice. "Why didn't you use the bond to control her?"

For a fraction of a second he saw anger in Allyn's eyes and almost stepped back, regretting his words. "I tried."

"That's impossible." He'd seen the magic bind her. She'd accepted it. She couldn't have defied the bond, which left only one other possibility. "Did she break it?" He hoped she did. It was wrong of Allyn to have claimed her as his student without informing her of the process.

"There was nothing left of her to control. She lost herself. There was nothing to control."

That was a very frightening thought. "If she can shrug the bond... What happens next time? What if it's us she comes after?"

"I don't know. She's not a normal werewolf."

"What werewolf is normal?"

39

———

Caroline woke at dawn as she changed back into human form, but she stayed where she was, warm and comfortable under a blanket while rain pattered lightly on the shingled roof. As painful as turning into a wolf was, returning to her natural shape was like stretching after a long sleep.

She didn't remember crawling to bed in her room above the tavern, or even... She crinkled her nose at the reek of ale and... blood and gore.

"Oh no," she whispered, fear gripping her. She sat up. So much slaughter and she'd enjoyed it. She rolled to the side of the bed and vomited until she could do nothing more than dry retch. It wasn't enough.

Kirsty and Dobbin weren't in her room. The door was off its hinges, busted inward. She clenched her fists around her blanket, heart hammering as memories refused to uncloud. What had she done? She couldn't remember it all. She wiped the corner of her mouth with the back of her hand, the reek of vomit suffocating. She spat, trying to clear the taste from her mouth.

Faspane. She'd hunted them. At least at first.

She pushed her curly hair from her face, struggling to remember the sequence of events, but the scent of human and faspane blood mingled in the damp air and distracted her.

She's killed faspane, certainly, and humans. Villagers. "Oh Gods," she whispered. How many?

Trembling, she left the bed and put on her dress, the sickly feeling growing worse when she noticed devastated sounds in the village - people crying, many in denial. The scent of fear and shock carried in the air like a knife pressed to her stomach.

The entire village grieved with an eerie dread that threatened to burst into anger and violence. Weeping competed with people trying to console one another and cries of open devastation.

Others shuffled about aimlessly, the sounds of their footsteps mixing with the patter of rain on the roof. Paralysed with guilt and the fear of facing anyone, particularly Dobbin or Kirsty, she froze, unable to make herself leave the room.

Dobbin's heavy footsteps made the decision for her. He began up the staircase, the tread slow and deliberate. Hesitant.

She hadn't killed him, at least. She wanted to weep in relief.

The floorboards creaked alarmingly as Dobbin stopped just beyond her sight outside the broken door. She heard him take a deep breath before he ducked through. He didn't seem surprised when he saw her. Only sad. Dried blood caked his left temple from a blow and both his eyes were black from a broken nose.

She rushed to him, throwing her arms around his hard waist to press her face against his shirt.

"What did I do, Dobbin?"

He should have been angry. She couldn't begin to count the people she'd killed, all as innocent as Leasa had been. Her own people.

"Yer not going to want to leave the room fer a while." He disengaged her arms and guided her back to the bed, his huge hands on her shoulders. He forced her to sit. His scent told her there was more weight to his words than he wanted to voice.

"Dobbin-"

"They surprised us," he said, his voice edged with grief and pain.

"They beat me unconscious to make sure I wouldn't make trouble. I only woke to the slaughter this morning."

"What about Kirsty? Is she okay?"

His scent changed at Kirsty's name. Anger. Pain. Sorrow.

"Not Kirsty. Please Dobbin." She stared at him as tears began to blur her vision, but he wouldn't meet her eyes. "Oh Gods, I killed her, didn't I? Please say I didn't."

"Just stay here for a while. Okay?" He pulled the sheets and blankets off the other pallet, bundling them in his arms. He carried them toward the doorway.

Caroline began to shake and struggled find the courage to speak again. "Dobbin. How many people?" Not the question she wanted to ask.

He leant against the splintered frame as if his own weight were too great for him. "Fourteen faspane and nineteen humans, including eight children. We're not sure how many farmers yet, but ye ventured into the farmland as well."

She couldn't hold back the tears, but did her best not to look away. He frowned. "Don't ye care at all, lass?"

"Of course I care," she whispered. She wiped her tears away. "You've got no idea." Kirsty. And eighteen innocent villagers. More.

She cleared her throat to speak again as the knowledge brought memories back to her. "I'm horrid. Oh Gods, I remember staring Kirsty in the face now and not knowing her at all. She wasn't scared." It was more than she wanted to remember. "I killed her."

More tears stained her cheeks. "I can't return home, Dobbin. How can I face Kirsty's family after what I've done? You should kill me so this never happens again. Surely you carry some silver, hidden from me?"

His bruised face and blackened eyes betrayed his own disappointment, but he didn't seem to have the energy to be angry with her. She wanted him to yell at her. To hate her. His pity hurt more than his anger ever could.

"Stay here lass. Don't come down." He left the room.

She wiped more tears away. She waited until she heard his

footsteps leave the tavern, but even then she hesitated to rush down stairs and find her friend's body. More disjointed memories surfaced, torturing her. She'd nearly ripped Kirsty's leg off before throwing her across the room like a toy, the small girls bones cracking as she hit the wall and slumped, unmoving.

Caroline wanted to do what she'd promised herself days ago and beg Allyn to kill her. Allyn owed her that much, at least. And yet, she didn't want to die. She needed to make amends. She began to follow Dobbin, hesitating at the door. She wasn't sure she had the courage to leave the room. It took her one slow step after another before emerging in the common room.

Tables were overturned, chairs and crockery smashed, and the scent of fresh blood and fear clung to the room like a wall of despair. Kirsty's blood hung above it all. Unique. Familiar. Caring. She could almost taste the lingering scent of Kirsty's trust in the air.

Dobbin walked in, but didn't see her standing in the shadows near the stairs. He knelt beside a body under a blanket on the far side of the room. "I'm sorry lass," he whispered as he pulled the blanket back.

Kirsty, her eyes staring, didn't move. Caroline retched.

Dobbin turned, angry. "I said to stay up stairs!"

She raised her chin, spitting bile but determined to face the consequences of her actions.

"I had to see." Now she knew how impossible she would become during the next full moon. Dobbin turned his back on her and closed Kirsty's eyes. His stiff posture said more than words ever could.

"I'll be burying her shortly. Ye can say yer goodbyes then."

"You fear me, don't you?" Caroline asked. "I'm a creature of nightmare. Worse, because I know what I am and can't control myself."

"We all fear ye," he said in a near-whisper as he gently brushed dark hair from Kirsty's face. "Except her, perhaps, at least until the end. She was the best of us. She never seemed apprehensive of you, even at your worst. Perhaps that's why she's dead."

Caroline dropped her eyes, wishing she were somewhere else. "I have to leave. The werewolf in the mountains was far enough from everyone that it couldn't do much harm. I'll go that way if you need to find me."

If she couldn't find the courage to kill herself, then she should do the same as the poor creature who'd turned her into a beast. "I need to leave Fandelyon."

"Ye need to get ye home," he said. "The Higher Realm has plans for ye which don't involve hiding like a coward."

"I'm not a coward!" she said, feeling like one anyway. "I have to protect the people I care about." She lowered her voice. "I have to protect you, and I can't imagine doing this to my sisters." Kirsty's face seemed so peaceful, almost as if she were asleep.

Dobbin wiped his brow with the back of his arm, slowly, as if very tired. "Fandelyon City's probably the only place ye'll be safe from doing harm over the full moon. There'll be dungeons under the castle to hold ye. Judging by yer work last night I think ye'll need 'em."

"You really are scared of me, aren't you?" She'd hoped it wasn't true, but it was in his eyes, his scent. She glanced around the room, looking for one of the faspane's silver-etched swords, but they were gone. Taken. Running herself through with one would solve a lot of problems.

His scent changed to guilt. "It takes a lot of power ta do what ye did last night, lass. Yer not a normal werewolf. Ye killed fourteen faspane, all armed and ready for ye, and I doubt they had a chance. That's enough ta put some concern into a shivra."

"Dobbin-"

He held up a hand. "The surviving villagers have a lot of questions, but they're not looking at us ta answer 'em. I'll help 'em bury their dead this morning and we'll leave soon after."

"I should help."

He paused, and this time a little anger entered his scent. "Aye, perhaps ye should. Oh, don't expect a meal. Ye killed the innkeeper."

She felt her chin quivering. How many more abhorrent acts could she perform before the Divine Lady of Healing cast her aside. How much would it cost everyone around her? Dobbin drew the blanket back over Kirsty's face before leaving. Marnier du Shae's divine markings remained on her wrists, the Goddess's divine light almost too bright in the gloomy room. Caroline wanted to scratch them away.

"How can you still favour me, Divine Lady, when I've done such horrible things? You should despise me. Cast me from your light."

Despite the words, she knew it was beyond the Divine Lady's power to withdraw her light once offered. The decision was Caroline's now. Surely the Goddess must have foreseen this possibility when she'd marked Caroline at the abbey, even with eleven other Gods attempting to influence events to their own favour. Unable to abide the accusing presence of Kirsty's unmoving body under the blanket, Caroline left the room.

Outside, drizzling rain had washed away some of the blood on the cobbled steps before the doors and smeared it down the walls across the street. The smell was enticing, and all the more sickening because of it.

The villagers reeked of anguish and fear, their scents causing her pain she deserved. A calm, eerie air of shock and disbelief stretched across the village like a fog. It would take decades of rain to wash it away.

Caroline pulled her hood over her head, wishing she could wash away their anguish. A few villagers and farmers were already trying to repair the damage she'd caused to their homes. A couple of men were moving human bodies to a vacant building. Others replaced shingles, fixed windows and doors, or dragged faspane bodies into the rain.

Sobbing came from far too many homes, some of the crying from children whose parents she'd murdered.

"The Higher Realm has turned away from us," she heard one grey-haired woman whisper to another. She caught Caroline's eye and looked away just as quickly, determined not to let a stranger see her grieve.

Through a gap between buildings, Caroline spotted Dobbin

helping villagers dig graves to the east. She wanted to help but couldn't find the courage.

Three women were stripping the faspane bodies of weapons and anything else of value, no doubt to be sold to pay for some of the damage. Other villagers remained inside their homes, the sounds of people scouring blood off walls and floors grating on Caroline's nerves. Distantly, horses plodded up the road, their hooves making wet, sucking sounds in the ankle-deep mud.

Eventually, six Divine Servants from Forecliffe rode into the village on tired-looking horses. Even if it wasn't for the yellow robes they wore she'd have recognised the four healers from Marnier du Shae's local temple. Two others in blue robes served the Divine Lady Toram du Grah, Mistress of Weather.

Guiltily, Caroline glanced at her wrists and made sure they were safely hidden, but if she recognised them as Divine Servants, they'd certainly recognise her. She slipped inside the tavern's door, preparing to duck out of sight if any of them looked her way. She couldn't face Divine Servants today. Or ever again.

Commoners began crowding the priests and priestesses as they dismounted.

"My daughter is dead!"

"Has the Higher Realm abandoned us?"

"Will you perform the burial rites?"

"Is my husband's spirit within the Higher Realm? Is he ready to be reborn soon?"

"What do we do now? Please help us."

"Should we burn the izzen?"

Their heartbreak drew more tears to Caroline's cheeks. She moved back into the common room, her heel cracking against a broken clay mug and sending it skittering across the room to bump into the wall.

Someone moaned. Caroline froze, spinning and staring at the blanket as if she expected her friend to pull it back.

Nothing. No movement. No sound. Someone had survived and she needed to help them.

The moan had come from Kirsty's body.

She'd imagined it, of course. Her guilt was torturing her. Kirsty was dead. She's seen her staring eyes. Wishing otherwise wouldn't change the fact.

Kirsty coughed, the blanket moving. Caroline stumbled away in fear and shock as the blanket returned to stillness. Uncertain whether she was going crazy, Caroline took a hesitant step forward, hand out.

Kirsty tore the blanket away and took a deep breath as if she'd just surfaced from a drowning. She coughed and then blinked, squinting as if the gloom were too bright for her.

Caroline remained frozen in place. "Kirsty?"

Kirsty rolled onto her side, coughed again, and looked around as if she didn't know where she was.

"Kirsty? I... Kirsty?"

Kirsty followed the sound of Caroline's voice, her eyes finally focusing. "Princess?"

Caroline's chest almost burst with relief. "Oh Gods!" She rushed to her friend and pulled her into a hug. "You were dead. I saw you dead." Caroline released Kirsty so she could see her face and try to believe the miracle. Kirsty frowned at Caroline in confusion, her long raven hair dishevelled and her brown eyes bleary.

"Where are we?"

"Kirsty? Do you remember anything?" For her friend's sake, she hoped she didn't.

Rather than shrinking back in fear or disgust, Kirsty caught Caroline's hands as her expression changed. "Yes. Marnier du Shae was watching over me."

"If a Divine Lady or Lord had been watching, I'd have been struck down before it began."

Kirsty turned her wrists over. There was nothing there. "Oh. I thought I'd been marked."

Caroline touched Kirsty's wrists and felt a tingle within her own mark, divine light reacting to divine light. "I think perhaps you might have been, though I see nothing.

"She *blessed* me, Princess. I think last night was a test for us."

"But I killed you." Caroline tried to pull away, but Kirsty gripped her hand.

"I stood in the Higher Realm and spoke to Gods. Rhonda was there. She returned me to you."

"I don't understand."

"When Rhonda died it wasn't to save you. She did it for me. A life for a life. Marnier du Shae foresaw last night. She used Rhonda's sacrifice to return me. Allyn was right. Noramgaell approaches and the Divine Lady needs you as her Champion. She returned me as a favour to you."

Caroline closed her eyes, struggling with the concept. "She knew this would happen even before I left? She's been manipulating me since I arrived at her abbey."

"No! She wants your love. Your devotion. She wants you to willingly accept your role as her Champion. But more than that, she wants your faith. Trust in her Princess. She'll reward you. I promise."

Belatedly, Caroline reached for Kimbriel's gift to try and lift the curse from Kirsty, but found nothing within her friend. The curse had never taken hold, because Kirsty had died.

She didn't want to consider the meaning. Instead, Kirsty's divine light, though hidden, would remind Caroline of this night the rest of her life. It was another punishment, but better than the alternative.

Kirsty reached out and touched Caroline's cheek, and this time there was hurt in her eyes. "She said she expects you to turn away from Her guidance once more. She told me to say things will be worse if you do." Kirsty glanced at Caroline's wrists. "You should have told me you'd been blessed."

A fresh wave of guilt assaulted Caroline. She had to resist pulling her hands back. "At least you deserve a blessing. I don't."

"Of course you deserve it."

"I have a confession."

"Another secret?" More hurt entered Kirsty's scent.

"I went to Marnier du Shae's abbey to have a child."

The confusion on Kirsty's face was almost comical. "But you're not married. How can you have a baby?"

Caroline didn't know whether to laugh or cry at Kirsty's innocence. "It can happen."

"Where is your baby? Oh... It must have died! I'm so sorry." Against all expectations, Kirsty hugged Caroline.

Caroline gently untangled herself from Kirsty's embrace. "I had to give it up. That's why Marnier du Shae marked me, to punish me for going to the abbey under false pretences." In the distance she heard more horses approaching. Men wearing chain armour.

"The Divine Lady would never do such a thing. She heals, not punishes. She marked you for a good reason. She loves you."

"It would be nice to think so. No more secrets Kirsty. I promise."

"No more secrets," Kirsty agreed.

"We should leave. Soldiers are approaching."

"Wait," Kirsty said. "There's another secret between us. Well, not a secret, but... The Divine Lady told me something else last night. She said something you should know."

"What?"

Fear flushed Kirsty's scent. "She asked for my forgiveness. She said I have worse trials to endure and I may not survive them. She said they'll be your fault unless you follow her path."

Taken aback, it took Caroline a moment to respond. "What trials?"

"I don't know, but no Divine Lady should be asking for forgiveness. I think something terrible is going to happen to me."

"It did. Last night." Caroline struggled to find words to fill a new silence. "How bad is your leg? Can you walk?"

Kirsty flexed it. "Fine. It's as if I was never harmed."

"Maybe I should return to the abbey and accept Divine Service," Caroline murmured. "High Priestess Tarine could keep me from doing more harm."

Kirsty took Caroline's hands. "No. You need to go home. I'm certain of it."

∼

Caroline watched Lord Bravis duLevi ride in with a full complement of soldiers. Even from a distance, he reeked of his breakfast of boiled eggs and oatmeal, and plenty of it judging by his girth. His long blond hair hung limp with dampness, sticking to his jowls in thin strands.

Caroline stood outside with Kirsty, tense with fear and self-loathing, and wondering what to do. It was far too late to saddle Stormrunner and leave unnoticed.

The procession came to a stop in the middle of the village, none of the horses spent. Lord Bravis obviously didn't consider the decimation of one of his villages important enough to rush.

"Shivra!" called one of the soldiers as he and Lord Bravis dismounted. The remaining soldiers did likewise to the creak of leather and clink of mail.

Dobbin glanced up from the grave he stood knee-deep in, just beyond the edge of the village near a small shrine to the Divine Lord Loama du Rion. He threw a too-small pick on the ground and raised a hand to his forehead to block out the drizzle. "Aye?" His gravelly voice carried, even though he had to be a fifty yards away.

The soldier strode toward him. "Several messengers from the village claim an attack by izzen last night. They say something killed them all, a pack of wolves perhaps. Were you here?"

"I was," Dobbin said, climbing out of the grave and meeting the soldier half way. "But one of the izzen belted me over the head first thing." He pointed to his black eyes. "I knew nothing more until dawn."

Another soldier casually glanced at Caroline, and did a double-take. "My Lord!" he called. "Lord Bravis!"

Caroline didn't know the soldier, but even with her hood up he obviously recognised her.

Lord Bravis duLevi glanced her way and his eyes widened. It had been nearly two years since she'd seen him, but she knew him well enough that he couldn't fail to recognise her.

His boots made sodden sounds as he approached, walking as if she were a spirited horse readying to bolt. The last time she'd seen him, she'd only been a little taller than him. Now she easily looked over his head.

"Princess Caroline? I heard you were dead." The words were hesitant, uncertain. "Your Highness..." His second chin quivered as if he didn't seem to know what to say next. He studied her eyes, probably trying to remember what colour they'd been before.

She smelled no deceit in his scent, only honest surprise. Caroline sighed, giving in to the inevitable. "My guard was betrayed in the mountains, My Lord. I thought it best to return home anonymously."

Surprised villagers began whispering along with the soldiers, the word quickly spreading. People came out of houses to gather around. Some of the villagers were even brave enough to reach out and touch her for luck. Others stood back, farmers from the tavern who'd snidely called her a clan girl yesterday afternoon.

"I must get you back to your father," Lord Bravis began. "I-"

She knew exactly what the man was thinking. She could smell his greed just as easily as anyone could see it. She'd make it hard for him. "I'm sure there'll be a healthy reward you can use to help the people of this village recover from the disaster that befell them," she said loudly enough for everyone to hear.

"Yes, yes, of course. My thoughts too," he said, petty irritation in his eyes. A couple of the villagers began looking hopeful.

"I'll return to this village as soon as I'm able to so I may see for myself how much assistance my father's coin brings to the people here."

His expression went flat, but he was too much of a politician to let any more show. "We'll welcome the generosity of your time," he said, reeking of annoyance.

After far too many questions, she found herself with an escort of fifty soldiers. A rider was sent ahead to Fandelyon City to deliver the good news to the King and Queen. She wondered if her mother's instincts for knowing things would have warned her already.

Her sisters would be relieved and perhaps even her brothers. She may be the last in line to the throne due to being born a bastard, but she was still the oldest of her siblings. Her brothers had always been threatened by that, though it was shown through spite rather than any genuine fears.

"There's nothing like returnin' from the grave," Dobbin said grimly in a quiet moment, staring at Kirsty with clear shock and unasked questions.

"Unlike the villagers here," Caroline murmured, wishing she could offer the survivors something more in compensation than a vague hint that Lord Bravis might help. Tears blurred her vision without warning. "Dobbin I..."

The shivra drew her into a hug. "I understand." He released her, bending close. "Kirsty...? How...?"

"Later," Caroline promised.

She soon found herself mounted on Stormrunner and on the muddy road again, dreading the thought of returning to the last place she wanted to be to fulfil a destiny she didn't want. As she passed the last house in the village she caught a fresh whiff of human blood.

On the back of the stone wall of the house a message had been written above the corpse of a little girl, in her blood.

Ware your family.

A lmost three days later in deep darkness, spitting rain and gusting wind, a complement of the King's Guard met Caroline and her exhausted companions and escort outside Fandelyon City's walls.

Kirsty leaned in close to Caroline. "This is a faspane trap. They know where you're going."

"I agree." She could smell faspane already. Some of them had managed to get into the city. "Don't relax until we're safely inside Kirrilee Palace. Perhaps not even then."

Caroline couldn't help but think of her siblings, all unaware of how her Gods-granted destiny threatened their lives. She squinted at the flickering watch-fires on walls above the huge open gates. Her stomach churned at the smell of humanity washing through the gap.

Her family were inside those walls. She was certain the faspane intended to make her pay in her family's blood, if they couldn't get hers.

"I have no choice." She could almost feel the tendrils of her unwanted destiny ensnaring her. She had to find a way to escape it. Home was the last place she wanted to be.

She drew back her sleeves, staring at the unformed *alimoth* flowers. "If you let them kill my family," she whispered to the Goddess who'd marked her, "You'll never have my devotion. Never."

40

Two-story houses loomed over them, shod hooves ringing out in an otherwise wet, dark and oppressively silent city. Caroline felt trapped as her father's soldiers led the way through the city. Very little light leaked from the windows of the stone-walled homes and businesses, but when they passed through the circular Boulevard of the Higher Realm, each temple had dozens of lanterns illuminating the way. The light was almost blinding after the darkness of the rest of the city.

Despite her fears they eventually reached the wide Avenue of Temples leading to the palace. If the faspane were going to attack, now was the time. Huge statues of Gods loomed over them at regular intervals before their own temples, all in some pose of miracle-creation or benevolence.

She sensed Marnier du Shae's temple inviting her in so she could rest in safety on holy ground, the statue of the Goddess almost watching her pass. *Alimoth* vines grew in massive stone boxes, the plants kept trimmed and full of bell-shaped flowers. She turned away, focusing instead on her sense of smell, but the flowers' perfume called to her nonetheless.

She caught traces of faspane in the Avenue of Temples, their scents diluted with time and rain. No doubt they'd been scouting places to ambush her. Where they were hiding she couldn't guess. Down side streets and behind the Avenue of Temples lay closed shops, the keepers abed in their homes above. Nothing moved on the roofs or down alleys.

The palace, when she finally saw it, seemed a dark and ominous shape against the bleak sky.

They entered the quiet market square before the palace gates. She watched for movement, trying to peer past the marble statues of ancient heroes left over from the time Mistapol ruled these lands. There were too many places someone could hide. It would only take a single silver-dipped bolt to kill her. The sound of shod hooves rang out on the flagstones, crying for attention as well as any hawker could.

She caught Kirsty's hand for comfort and then regretted it. It made Kirsty a target, too. She tried to let go, but Kirsty held on tightly as if she needed the contact. Caroline felt no safer after they entered the palace grounds, even when stable hands took Stormrunner after she dismounted. She could still smell hints of faspane. Servants stood waiting for her in the entryway.

Inside, it was too bright. Oppressive heat assaulted her as she walked into the palace's grand entry, decorated with huge carved columns and alcoves capable of hiding assassins. The warmth stung her cold cheeks and hands, but did little to ease the tension in her shoulders.

Wood polish, fragrant candles, and hundreds of other scents filled the warm air, carrying a hint of faspane from distant parts of the palace. Faspane were inside. They'd probably entered through servant's doors.

Maids surrounded her like a swarm of bees, and Caroline tensely endured their attention. A short maid whose frizzy hair refused to remain bound placed a towel in Caroline's hands. Others hurried her and Kirsty into an antechamber, helping them strip and dry off.

It seemed like years since she'd had to endure this sort of attention, but it had been less than one. Warm dry dresses were pulled over their heads. Caroline's was far too short and tight across the shoulders and chest. Wood oils, dust, cleaning suds, smoke and people confused her sense of smell, keeping her edgy.

"Your parents must be excited," Kirsty whispered.

Caroline's stomach did a slow roll. So much had happened, so much she didn't want to admit to or take responsibility for. Like the village. She had no idea how much they would know, particularly her mother.

"No doubt," she whispered back.

When she left the room she found Lord Bravis still in the grand entry, probably expecting to take Caroline directly to the King.

Caroline caught master Xaramin's arm. "Where are my parents?" she asked as he directed the maids. He was an exceptionally dark-skinned man who usually assisted the old Castellan, Lord Aramier.

Fluent in four languages, he'd once been a slave in one of the kingdoms across the Temern Straight, but had ran away from his master and gained passage to Fandelyon. He'd been employed in the kitchens, but had been assisting Lord Aramier for nearly five years now.

"The Queen is readying herself, Your Highness. We weren't expecting you until tomorrow. I cannot speak for the King." He spoke with a noble-born accent he'd managed to perfect.

His words only made her more nervous. What would she see in her mother's eyes? Relief? Reproach? Fear?

"If you're ready, I've prepared some refreshments."

Caroline and her growing retinue followed him to an even warmer room, but despite a delicious-smelling spread of cheeses and dried fruits, she was too nervous to taste any. She tried to keep her fears buried, but thoughts of assassins stalking her and her family kept her wary.

The room's heavy doors finally swung inward and she stiffened at the sound. Even with her back turned, she recognised her mother's scent. She wasn't sure she wouldn't have preferred faspane.

"Caroline?"

Taking a calming breath, Caroline turned. Her mother regarded her from across the room in a long black dress, her expression and scent giving little away. Her long red hair was held back in a simple braid. It was hard not to mistake the clan heritage, the red hair, dusty green eyes, and height. What Caroline hadn't expected was the tiredness around her mother's eyes and the carefully guarded formality.

There was no mistaking that look. Her mother knew what had happened in the mountains. "Yes Mother. I'm back." For now.

Caroline crossed the room and formally hugged Queen Lynn, holding her tight until she realised her mother couldn't breathe. She relaxed her grip and stepped back, looking down to meet her mother's eyes. They'd been eye-to-eye when she'd left.

Queen Lynn smelled ordinary. She wasn't appealing at all, which was a nice change. "It's so good to see you, Mother," Caroline said as formally as she could, curtsying.

"You've grown," Lynn said.

"Clan ancestry, I believe. I blame you." That almost got a smile. Caroline pushed damp hair from her face, wondering how many other changes her mother noticed. Lynn seemed to have trouble looking at her newly-dark eyes.

"Come. We'll talk in your father's chamber."

"You look tired Mother. Bad dreams?" Caroline asked.

Lynn hesitated before giving a single nod and lowering her voice. "Nightmares about a wolf."

A thrill of fear ran through Caroline. "Have you discussed these dreams with Father?"

"He's a busy man."

Lord Bravis cleared his throat as he broke propriety and approached. "Your Majesty?" His second chin wobbled with each step.

Resignation coloured Lynn's scent. "Lord Bravis. Please forgive me for not acknowledging you earlier. I truly appreciate everything you've done for my daughter."

Caroline should have been thankful it was Lord Bravis who'd stumbled across her. Many other nobles might have tried to take advantage of her vulnerability.

Bravis smiled, though it was clear from his scent that he'd expected her attention earlier. "Of course, Your Majesty. I would be similarly overcome in your place."

"You must be keen to gain an audience with my husband to explain your invaluable part in my daughter's safe return." He looked like he was readying to boast about it as Lynn put a hand on his shoulder. "May I ask you to delay your request until tomorrow? As you can appreciate, it's already late and we have much to discuss with our daughter. I have rooms organised for you."

He smiled again, though he smelled put out. "Of course, Your Majesty. Until tomorrow."

"Thank you. Come Caroline. Kirsty, you too." Lynn hesitated when she caught sight of Dobbin standing across the room. It was a critical look more than one of surprise. She'd definitely known what to expect.

Caroline took the initiative. "Come with us Dobbin. I'm sure there'll be a reward."

Her mother raised an eyebrow, but didn't gainsay her. "Yes. Please Master Dobbin. My daughter insists."

Caroline followed her mother into a dim corridor, their footsteps echoing on the hard stone. Breathing through her nose to catch any scent of faspane, she found nothing more than she had upon entering the palace. They were here somewhere and had been for days, but she had no idea where or how many. There were simply too many smells competing for her attention.

Lynn stopped walking as the servants closed the doors behind them. "You look surprisingly well, Caroline." She glanced at her daughter's stomach.

What did she expect to see there? The baby she no longer carried? Caroline suppressed hurt and placed a hand on Dobbin's forearm. "Mother, I'd like to formally introduce Dobbin of the Five

Peaks." He took up a lot of space in the corridor, his head almost brushing the wooden roof.

Lynn smiled. "Many thanks to you, Dobbin, for assisting my daughter."

"We can talk safely before Dobbin, Mother. I owe him my life. Kirsty too. I've kept no secrets from them."

Kirsty nodded, but Lynn frowned. "None?"

Caroline glanced pointedly toward the guards. "None."

Lynn followed her gaze. "Wait at the end of the corridor, please." They both eyed Dobbin's weapons suspiciously, but did as asked. Lynn turned back to Caroline. "Tell me everything." She smelled fearful. Only now, away from the scents of food and people, could Caroline tell that the fear came from concern. "You've changed, Caroline. I can see it in your eyes, and not just their colour."

"You heard we were attacked?"

Lynn grimaced as if the thought pained her. "Yes. Oh, Kirsty, your brother Jared is safe at home in Conrandese. Captain Bastion bought him out of the mountains with seven other men. We don't know if anyone else survived, but King Phillip has sent men into the mountains to look. I am very sorry about Rhonda and Jonathan. We'll miss them both."

Kirsty paled. "Jonathan? I thought..." She put her face in her hands.

Jonathan was dead? He'd been fine the last time she'd seen him. Caroline pulled Kirsty into an embrace. "I'm so sorry, Kirsty." She rested her chin on the top of her friend's head. "This is entirely my fault." And it was, a chain of events that began with her asking a boy to her rooms nearly a year ago.

"Oh dear," Lynn began. "How insensitive of me. I assumed you knew."

Kirsty pulled away from Caroline. "I'm fine. Thank you for informing me, Your Majesty." She blinked to clear her eyes, sniffling slightly.

Caroline took one of Kirsty's hands. "Kirsty, anything I can do..."

"Aye, lass. Me too."

"Mother, do you have any idea who attacked us on the road?"

Lynn shook her head. Prospects of war, both civil and beyond, hung heavy. "Perhaps this conversation should wait for your father."

41

———

The old Castellan, Lord Aramier, was waiting outside the King's chamber at the rear of the throne room, blinking red, watery eyes. Caroline stared. He seemed to have aged a decade over the winter, his face grey and his cheeks sunken. He even smelled sick.

"Are you well, Lord Aramier?"

He bowed his head slightly. "Of course, Princess."

The throne room carried the reassuring smells of oiled wood, incense, dust and people. The vaulted room was wide and deep enough to seat nearly five hundred people, with long wooden high-backed benches only slightly more comfortable than the stone floor they rested on. She'd sat on them often enough to know.

At the back of the throne, marble shields hung high on the wall, one for each of the twelve Gods. Marnier du Shae's was currently the highest as it was designated her Prime Year. The familiar guilt flared at the sight of the *alimoth* flower, which almost exactly matched the ones on her wrists.

The room was so familiar, it should have set her at ease. But Caroline hadn't felt so uncomfortable since the last time she'd awaited a private audience with her father, when she'd had to explain the circumstances of her pregnancy.

Lord Aramier bowed shallowly to Queen Lynn. "The King awaits you in the left antechamber, Your Majesty."

"Thank you, Lord Aramier."

Aramier struggled to pull the heavy red curtains aside, the fabric seeming to weigh more than him. Caroline itched to help, but held back for fear of insulting him. The alcove behind the curtains smelled of steel and men. It seemed smaller than she remembered.

Two broad-shouldered guards stood on duty, neither formally at attention nor slouching, but as they caught sight of Dobbin, one gripped his sword's hilt and stepped forward. The other rested his hand on his pommel, but remained where he was.

"I'm sorry, Master Shivra," the first guard said, "But we can't permit you to carry weapons into the King's presence." He glanced at Queen Lynn, perhaps wondering why she'd permitted the shivra to carry the axe and hammer this far.

"When's a shivra ever threatened anyone ye know?" Dobbin grumbled, but complied, almost throwing the man off balance as he handed over his hefty weapons.

He swung his shield off his back and held it out, too. The guard had to put Dobbin's weapons on the ground to take the three-foot wide shield, though it looked small on Dobbin.

Caroline fought a bout of butterflies. All this time she'd thought only of getting home, but rarely about arriving or what she'd say.

Kirsty caught her forearm with a gentle squeeze. "I'll be with you," she whispered.

Gods, was she so obvious?

Lord Aramier knocked and then pushed the heavy door inward. Warmth rushed out, filling Caroline's head with her father's scent, musky and sharp and almost as unappealing as her mother's. The room smelled entirely of him. If it wasn't for Kirsty's staunch support, she might not have been able to follow Lord Aramier in.

Half as wide as the throne room and cluttered with furniture, books, maps and papers, there was still enough space for quite a few people. Three padded red velvet chairs loosely faced the fireplace.

Shelves stacked with books lined the opposite wall. Several thick, leather-bound books were open on a low table.

King Phillip stood with his back to the fire, dark brown eyes quickly moving to Dobbin and then Kirsty before darting back to Caroline.

Dobbin bowed. Caroline barely managed a curtsy.

Dark curly hair and deep brown eyes were traits more common to the lower-born, but somehow she'd never thought of her father that way. Having spent so much time travelling she couldn't but help realise his ancestry must have come from commoners, a carefully guarded secret.

Lord Aramier bowed his way out of the room. Phillip continued to watch her as if trying to discern what had happened in the mountains simply by reading her features.

"Father?" she ventured, not daring to try a whole sentence.

His expression held back any thoughts she might have gleaned, and his scent didn't change either, though she could smell a certain sense of relief. What had her mother dreamed while Caroline had been away? How much had she told him?

He looked older. There were strands of grey in his dark hair and deeper lines in his face. She wanted to rush across the room and hug him, but doubted he'd approve, at least not with company.

"Sit," Phillip finally said as he moved behind his desk to sit in his stuffed chair, lifting his boots to his desk. He had the air of a man trying to appear casual.

Her tension renewed itself at his nonchalance. She perched on the edge of one of the room's velvet chairs, the heat from the fire flushing her cheeks.

"Tell me about your adventures, Caroline. We likely have a traitor in the Kingdom, or perhaps Kenmoore or Yaleem are behind this. What more do you know?"

A safe topic to begin with, she realised. "Nothing, Father. It could be either."

Phillip raised one finger to his lips. Caroline found the familiar gesture worrying. "Then tell me what happened." Not so safe.

Her mother took the moment to slip past and seat herself beside her husband on a stiff-backed chair. He acknowledged her presence with a touch.

"What happened after your escort was ambushed in the forest by the izzen? Do you know who attacked you?"

Caught off guard, she realised he meant faspane, not izzen. "We escaped into the forest, Father. And no, I've got no idea who they were."

"And then?"

Intuition told her he knew more than she was planning on telling him, and she wasn't sure what to do about it. She glanced at her mother and saw guilt there. Lynn may not have told her father everything she'd dreamed, but certainly more than she'd acknowledged earlier.

"Kirsty, a soldier and I became lost. We found a clearing and waited, hoping my escort would find us." She looked down to hide her discomfort. "Faspane, I mean izzen, attacked." She gestured toward Dobbin. "Dobbin says they call themselves faspane. Later, I awoke in Dobbin's cabin. He saved us, Father."

King Phillip nodded in Dobbin's direction, though his expression, even his scent, suggested he didn't believe her. "My thanks, shivra. May I ask what you were doing in my mountains? Your people live to the north, not south."

"Yer Majesty, I merely live off the land. Or did, I should say. The faspane burned me cabin, forcing us to flee."

Genuine surprise crossed Phillip's expression. "You escaped the izzen, again?"

"Faspane, Father."

He gave her a look which suggested she remain quiet for now.

Dobbin shrugged, but Caroline smelled his sudden spike of concern. "They came as I was preparing ta take the Princess and Lady Kirsty over the passes. Fortunately, I had a hidey hole under the floor with a tunnel ta safety. That was all that saved us. By the time me cabin was ash, we were well away, half way up the first pass. It gave us a good lead."

Phillip watched the shivra with a look Caroline knew well. He didn't believe it. "How is it, even with a good lead, you kept ahead of izzen? From what I hear they're fiends in the wild. Escorting two noble-born ladies would have slowed you considerably."

Caroline began feeling very uncomfortable. Even Kirsty shifted her feet.

"Yer Majesty, either they thought us dead, or if they pursued I can only assume the snakeheads hindered 'em. We stirred a nest in that first pass and barely escaped with our lives. Perhaps they distracted or killed off the izzen, for our journey remained trouble free after that."

Caroline caught her mother's assessing gaze, the comprehension beginning to show in her eyes as if she were putting the pieces of a puzzle together. The finger went back to Phillip's lips. There were no servants in the room, and that worried Caroline even more. Her father planned to talk about things he didn't want overheard, things only her mother could have told him.

"Caroline. I am not a man who accepts less than the truth. I've seen too many people try it, people much more skilled at hiding things. What *else* happened in the mountains?"

Someone knocked on the door and she jumped. Lord Aramier brought in a tray of heavily salted ham and cheese, which he placed on a small table in the centre of the room. Caroline took a slice of ham, silently thanking Lord Aramier for the distraction.

"Old fool." King Phillip muttered as Aramier left. "I keep telling him to make someone else run around for him, but he seems to think he can do it all himself." His tone held a fondness his words tried to hide. He returned his attention to Caroline. "Well?"

She played with the ham without eating it, her stomach too upset. "I'm sorry Father. I ordered Dobbin not to speak of it. There is more, but I honestly don't think you want to hear it."

She saw her mother look away, shaking her head slightly as if she could deny the dreams she'd had.

"I expect to hear everything, Caroline."

Kirsty's hand on her back offered encouragement and support.

Caroline needed it. She glanced at her mother for assurance and caught an almost imperceptible nod in return. She definitely knew, and thought it best to be honest.

If she couldn't be honest with her parents, who then?

She took a deep breath and let the words come out in a rush. "The night we were ambushed, I was attacked by a werewolf."

Coals collapsed in the fireplace, the sound unnaturally loud in the silence. Caroline dared not look up. Dobbin muttered something, but not loud enough for anyone to hear but her. She thought she caught the word 'foolish'.

"And?" her father asked.

Caroline gathered her courage. "Dobbin took its head off with his axe."

"Aye," said Dobbin, brooding. "Nasty creature it was, too. Would never have got near if it weren't already distracted."

She silently thanked him for backing her up so well. Lynn turned away, her expression one of hope dying. She might have dreamed about some of the events that had happened, but it was Caroline who made them real. Lynn touched her stomach as if expecting blood, reminding Caroline of when she'd been half-gutted. If her mother had dreamed of that as well...

"I fought the curse with all my strength, Father, and won. I'm sane, and alive. I drove it back, caged it and buried it deep." She spoke fast, trying to get the words out before anyone could stop her. "Please tell me you understand?"

"And the village where Lord Bravis found you?" Her father asked, coldness in his voice. "Did you do that?"

She closed her eyes, the painful memories riding on a wave of remorse. "Yes," she whispered, almost too quiet to be heard. "The faspane, the izzen, set a trap. It was horrible. I lost control." Her bloodlust began to rise up at the thought, and for a brief moment she wanted to do it again.

Phillip's shoulders slumped and he rubbed a calloused hand over his face, exhaling hard. He appeared tired. "I should order you beheaded tonight and your body burned. Please give me a reason not to. Right now, I can't think of one. Both the law and the temples agree."

She couldn't keep the shock and hurt from her voice. "Father, I'm your daughter!"

"Do you honestly think that will save you? Or me and your mother, if I let you live? How can I possibly hide this from the Council of Divine Prelates?"

The Divine Council... she pulled her sleeves back, forgetting for a moment they couldn't see the marks. "Send for a Divine Servant, Father. I've been marked by Marnier du Shae."

"Ye've what!" Dobbin asked.

Phillip dropped his feet to the floor, his expression suddenly hopeful. Even her mother looked up in surprise. "We have options to consider."

"Father. The faspane. They're here, in the palace. They'll hurt people to get to me." Her throat almost choked up at the thought. "They want me dead because of-"

"Master Dobbin!" her father interrupted. "I grant you as much gold coin as you can hold in your bare hands, doubled, so long as I have your oath of silence on the matter."

Dobbin nodded. "Ye have it, Yer Majesty."

"One problem solved," her father said under his breath. He raised his voice. "Lord Aramier will see to your reward along with rooms for the night. You may retire."

"Thank ye, Yer Majesty." Dobbin bowed and left. Outside she heard him retrieve his shield and weapons. His heavy footsteps retreated.

"Kirsty, tomorrow morning you will leave for your father's city of Conrandese. I will dispatch a rider to announce the news of your safe arrival at dawn. You too will give me an oath of silence."

Kirsty glanced at Caroline, her expression unhappy. She smelled devastated. She must still have held hopes of finding a way to return to Elias.

Phillip continued. "Please wait outside, Kirsty. I wish to speak privately with my daughter."

Caroline grabbed Kirsty's hand before the younger girl could move. "Kirsty, stay with me."

Phillip paused while her mother caught her breath, eyes wide and darting between husband and daughter. Kirsty tried to free her hand, but Caroline held tighter.

"Did you just countermand me, Caroline?"

Her heart pounded, but she nodded. "Kirsty's bound to me by oath. We have no secrets. None, Father."

He narrowed his eyes at Kirsty. "There's a strength about you Caroline, a lack of fear at consequences. I don't like it. It's more than a curse."

She met his eyes. "I grew up, Father. I had little choice after you sent me away and forced me to give up my child."

He set his jaw and anger showed in his eyes. He took a long, slow breath. "Go to your chambers and take Kirsty with you. Lord Aramier will find rooms for Kirsty once he has seen to the shivra."

"But the faspane-"

"Now!"

Trying not to let her hurt show, she stood and walked out. What had he intended to say in private? "A moment, please," she murmured to the guards. "I'm weary." Under the guise of gathering her thoughts, she closed her eyes and listened.

"What will you do?" her mother asked, her voice muffled through the door. Kirsty and the guards probably wouldn't be able to distinguish their voices, let alone what they said.

"I don't know, but I can't let her continue on as if nothing's changed. We need to hide her secret and protect her as much as protect our people from her. We need to contact Marnier du Shae's Prelate and have her enter the temple as a novice. That should give her some protection."

"It's more than religion, Phillip. I know you can see it. She's as stubborn as you, only she's still young enough to think she's just as wise."

"You know I can't allow her to walk among our people. By the

Higher Realm, it took all my strength to face her without betraying any doubts. If I'm uncertain of her, what does that bode for others?"

Seconds passed and Caroline began to wonder if they'd realised she was listening, until mother spoke again. "We can't afford a hint of a rumour," Lynn said, her voice stressed with concern and fear. "Even if Marnier du Shae's followers protect her, there's eleven other Gods. Their Prelates won't accept it."

"For the moment, I'm more concerned about Kirsty. The shivra I will see out of this Kingdom and into the Shivrad Mountains. He will not break confidence."

"And Kirsty?"

"She's young. Maybe a royal command and the fear of the Higher Realm will be enough. In the morning I'll ask High Priest Canthor to give her a lecture on keeping oaths and the consequences to her soul if she fails to do so."

"You should post a guard on Caroline's door."

"And have her realise the palace is her dungeon? No. Leave her the illusion of freedom."

"Let's go," Caroline said.

Her father didn't trust her, not at all, and her mother had lied about what she'd told him. Her stomach churned.

Nervously sniffing the air for faspane, she led Kirsty toward her rooms. "When you get to your own room, bolt the door. There are faspane here."

Kirsty suddenly looked worried. "How?"

"I can smell them. Be cautious."

Lord Aramier met them at the stairs near Caroline's room and took Kirsty to a guest chamber. Caroline cautiously pushed open her bedroom door. The musty smell of disuse escaped despite the unexpected warmth from a small fire dancing merrily in the fireplace and the familiar scents of her maids. When sure no one else was there, she slammed her door shut and drove the bolt home, and then pulled her clothes chest up against it.

What was she supposed to do? She couldn't protect herself or anyone else and even her parents didn't believe the danger they were in.

When no inspiration came, she stripped and crawled under her luxurious sheets, leaving her clothes before the fireplace. Heavy winter blankets weighed on her as she curled up, but sleep didn't come for hours, despite exhaustion.

What was she going to tell her sisters?

42

———

E lias gingerly placed his left foot on a fallen branch, holding his breath as his weight squished the wood into the muddy ground. The faspane didn't react. If the warrior turned, though...

Water dripped from Elias's nose and jaw as he carefully shifted his weight and placed his right foot on a soggy clod of fresh spring grass. He was so close he didn't dare blink. He was close enough to touch, and thanked the raid for providing noise and cover.

He was also being stupid, and all for a human girl who had absolutely no understanding about why they were attracted to each other or how her mortality would kill him if he gave into it.

He should be in Delshere now, preparing to collect the *Sword of the Sun* and return it to his people. More than likely, it would go to Caroline, but until she was confirmed as Marnier du Shae's Champion, the izzen would hold it.

The faspane shifted his weight and Elias tensed, but his quarry merely rested his shoulder against a tree, his hand casually flopping to the hilt of his sword. Taking a moment to steady himself, Elias raised his hunting knife, ready to strike.

The warrior turned like a viper.

Elias swung, the hilt cracking sweetly against the faspane's temple. The warrior collapsed sideways to the muddy ground, his hand still grasping his half-drawn sword.

Heart thumping, Elias blew water from his nose. "That was far too close," he murmured, his words barely audible.

He took several deep breaths to calm himself, hoping no other faspane were nearby. None came at him, but it didn't make him feel safe. There were six sleeping rolls hidden under the nearby bushes as well as several backpacks. They could return at any moment, or they could already be inside the city.

He slipped his knife away and hauled the warrior up and across his shoulders. "By the Higher Realm, you're a heavy sod," he muttered.

He adjusted the faspane's position as he moved off, trying not to let his feet sink into anything that would leave an obvious impression. Stepping from roots to fallen branches and rocks, he trusted to the gloom and rain for concealment. At least the rain would hide his passage.

He was struggling with fatigue as he approached another copse of trees a few miles away. Once hidden within them, he was too tired to let his burden down gently and simply dumped the warrior to the soggy ground. The faspane didn't move. Elias rolled his shoulders to relieve the tension, stretching his back.

As quickly as he could, he removed the faspane's sword and other weapons, tossing them across the clearing. He drew his hunting knife and cut off the warrior's vest and shirt, tearing them into strips and binding the warrior's feet before gagging him.

"I might as well be raising a newborn, the amount of sleep I'm getting thanks to you lot," he said.

He hauled the unconscious warrior to a young tree, shoved his back against the trunk and bound his hands behind it. The warrior remained slumped, head down. Elias pushed the faspane's head back, but he wasn't part of the group who'd witnessed his fight with Thule or even one of the few he'd seen at the ambush in the mountains. There could be hundreds searching the mountains and lowlands for Caroline.

Elias shook cold water from his hair, listening for any sign he'd been followed, but heard nothing past the pitter-patter of rain.

He reactivated the wards that would alert him to the presence of faspane and they flared immediately, but hopefully only in reaction to the warrior he'd caught. He watched the trees as he touched the warrior's face to get a stronger sense of his aura, and then reset his wards, excluding the warrior before him. The wards settled down immediately.

He remained alert even so. Their wizard might have given some of the warriors a charm to nullify their auras, as well as hide them from farsight, making it difficult or even impossible to detect them.

He pulled his damp cloak's hood over his head and settled down to wait under the shelter of leaves. After an hour the rain eased and finally stopped, yet it was close to dawn when Allyn returned with his hair slicked back from the rain. He raised an eyebrow at the sight of the slumped faspane. "You've done much better than me," he said.

Elias glanced at the warrior. "I was lucky this one moved at the right time or I'd have missed him too. I'd forgotten to renew my wards last night and they only reacted when I got within about a dozen yards."

"He's awake," Allyn said.

"His breathing changed about half an hour ago. He probably assumed someone was watching and didn't want to give up his only advantage."

"His shoulders must be aching, slumped forward like that. Do you think he'll tell us what they're up to or should we kill him now?"

The faspane's breathing quickened slightly, but he gave no other response. Elias smiled. "I'm pretty sure he'd rather it be by his own hand."

Allyn raised his voice. "Noble warrior, want to talk? If not, I'll open your arteries and let you bleed out."

The faspane jerked, straining against his bonds. When he failed to break them he glared, making threatening noises around his gag. His jade eyes stared hatred.

"I think he has something to say," Elias said.

"I think he'd rather kill us."

The warrior began struggling again, making more muffled noises. Allyn crouched beside the struggling faspane and drew his hunting knife, placing the edge under the warrior's chin. The muffled abuse stopped. "If you yell, I'll slit your throat. Understand? No rebirth."

The faspane gingerly nodded. Allyn cut the gag away and then pressed his blade against the warrior's neck.

"If you kill me, my clan will never stop until you're dead, you and your people."

"Who's going to tell them?" Allyn asked.

Elias moved closer, crouching. "How do you plan to kill Princess Caroline?"

"Silvered weapons, of course. Our wizard has the Sight. He knows what she is."

"That's not what I meant," Elias said. "Princess Caroline is already inside the city. How to you plan to get to her?"

"She's dead already."

"She lives," Allyn said. "How do you hope to kill her?"

"Are faspane in the city already?" Elias asked. No response. "I'll assume that's a yes. Think he's got more to say?"

"Yes, but I don't think we have to worry about anyone hiding in her room. She'd smell them. Mind you, there's plenty of other ways to ambush someone."

Knowing there were faspane in the city troubled Elias in an entirely unexpected way. "How many?" Elias asked.

Allyn pressed the blade hard enough to draw a line of blood. The faspane met Allyn's eyes. "Only one."

"At least ten, then."

"If they come at her at once, particularly during the day, she'll never survive. I have to warn her. Perhaps I can find a way to contact Dobbin. I'll find a helmet or hat to disguise my ears."

"Be careful. The humans will kill you just as quickly as they'll kill him."

Elias grabbed his pack and the faspane's sword.

"I'll try and make sure no more slip into the city," Allyn said. "I'll take care of this one, too." The faspane's eyes widened.

"You wouldn't dare kill me. My soul-"

"I haven't killed one of your kind since the war ended, and I'm not going to change that now."

The warrior looked confused. "What war?"

"The Faspane War. You call it the Millennia War."

"That was more than twenty thousand years ago!" the warrior said with something akin to awe in his voice.

"And I still have nightmares."

43

The sun was barely above the horizon when Elias stopped before *The Trapper's Prize* in Fandelyon City's main thoroughfare, a shop within sight of the palace. Nervous in the vicinity of so many humans, he moved cautiously, watching as many of them as he could.

"Filthy clansman," he heard someone say.

A well-tanned youth sneered at him while the boy's friend sniggered. They must have mistaken him because of his height. A little ahead, one of the city's guardsmen watched Elias, not the youths.

A stone thumped into his shoulder and he clenched his teeth. Children giggled. The day's warmth was beginning to lift the fragrance from the city's open sewers, one more thing to endure among humans.

Elias fidgeted at the heavy strip of cloth across his forehead which bound the top half of his ears. It was extremely annoying not being able to move them, like having an arm or leg splinted. At least the cloth kept his hair from his eyes. Fortunately his eyes weren't emerald or jade like other male izzat and faspane, and with his ears hidden he could pass as a human, if not a local.

His wards hadn't reacted to the presence of any faspane yet, but that didn't mean they weren't in the city. The wards were only good for a couple of hundred yards, and buildings would reduce that. Another stone thumped into his back followed by the sound of more laughter.

The guardsman watched on, so Elias did nothing. The recent rains had washed most of the sewage from the city, but the humans were busy replenishing it with each bucket of muck thrown into the streets. The day promised warmth, and therefore a worse smell.

Something in *The Trapper's Prize* caught his eye. Furs adorned makeshift benches at the front of the shop, but it was the longbow just inside the door that drew his attention.

Taking the opportunity to avoid a confrontation with the children or guardsman, he entered the shop and picked up the weapon, examining the workmanship. The shine on the tightly-bound leather grip suggested the bow had been well used. Plain but sturdy, he flexed it several times before looking it over again, checking the wood for any faults. Plenty of marks, but it had been maintained well enough.

"A good longbow, that," the shopkeeper said. "Served me well for quite a few years."

Elias turned his head to listen to the man properly. The shopkeeper had grey hair and had let himself go soft, but seemed happy enough with his lot.

"Perhaps," Elias said cautiously.

"Would suit you well," the shopkeeper added, squinting as he looked up. "You've the look of a man who knows the mountains. A little young to know all the tricks, but you've got the look regardless. Clan born, are ya? Pretty rare to see clansmen here."

Quivers of arrows hung from the rafters and a dozen more bows rested across pegs on a wall. There were several sheathed swords behind the counter and an array of knives and other weapons.

"No, I'm not a clansman," Elias said, trying to match the man's accent. "I can't afford the bow either." He didn't have any money.

"I'd consider a trade," the man said, moving back to indicate his other wares. He had a slight limp, perhaps the reason he'd taken up shopkeeping.

Elias replaced the bow. "Unfortunately I've got nothing of value."

"That sword you're carrying is worth some coin."

Elias touched the hilt of the weapon he'd taken from the faspane. Better a sword than no weapon at all. He drew the blade. "It's worth a lot more than an old bow," he suggested hopefully. He had no idea about the cost of either and his sword looked like it had been passed down for a couple of generations.

The shopkeeper shrugged. "Perhaps, but I've got to make a living. I'm a trader, after all. I don't do anyone out of coin as it's bad for business, but if I don't make a profit I've got no business at all."

Elias handed the weapon to the man for inspection. "Perhaps you could make me a better offer then?" He wouldn't have the chance to enchant a new weapon before returning home, but any longbow was better than a sword.

"Well," the shopkeeper said, examining the blade. "Quality steel, certainly. Where did you say you bought it?"

"It was a gift from an old friend."

"I've never seen etching like this. Looks like it's been filled with silver and polished back. The silver's tarnishing, is how I can tell. Is it writing? I don't recognise it."

Elias glanced at the words in Faspaneth, a family and clan name. "I don't know, but I've seen it's like in other swords from across the Temern Straight." A blatant lie, but he hoped the shopkeeper wouldn't know any different.

The man raised his eyebrows. "That so?" He looked over weapon again, examining it thoroughly. "Solid, despite the exotic etching. Good balance. Well used. Perhaps I can revise my offer? Why don't you examine my other bows? Take your choice if that suits. I'll even throw in a quiver of arrows." He didn't look up from the sword.

Certain the man was getting the better of the bargain, Elias examined the other longbows, ignoring most before picking up the only one made of ghostwood. The man pursed his lips, obviously unhappy with Elias's choice. "You certainly know your bows. That's the best I've got, but I still believe it's a fair trade. Do we have a deal?"

"A deal, so long as you can provide me with an oiled sleeve to wrap it in. Can't have the weather get to it." Elias removed the sword's sheath and handed it over before taking a quiver and slinging it over his back.

"You're pushing our friendship," the trader said with a wry grin, "But I can go that far." He put out his hand. Elias gripped it. "Done then."

A few minutes later, Elias stood before the front of the shop, holding his unfamiliar new bow while examining the palace walls and the rising towers beyond. Caroline was somewhere in there. Dobbin and Kirsty, too. Possibly faspane. The youths who'd thrown stones at him had gone.

A young woman, perhaps seventeen or eighteen, stopped beside him. Probably quite beautiful among humans, she was small and as pale as any noble in these parts, with long blond hair. She obviously kept out of the sun as much as possible.

"Looking for the princess too?" she asked with a bright enthusiastic smile, her hair cascading down her back as she glanced up at him. Six or seven inches shy of his shoulder, she seemed to have no inhibitions about talking to a strange man. Her confidence suggested she might be the bastard child of a noble.

"Princess?" he asked.

A conspiratorial look crossed the young woman's face. "Didn't you hear? Princess Caroline is said to have ridden in from the mountains last night." She pointed to one of the higher windows. "That's her room there. See, the shutters are open. Haven't been for the better part of a year now."

Elias caught a flicker of movement within. Red hair. He cursed the cloth pinning his ears. He couldn't listen properly like this. A guard moved into view within the room, pausing before the window and lifting his visor before raising a naked, silver-etched blade in his hand.

Faspane.

"Can't be," he whispered, staring in shock. "Call for help!" he said to the blonde girl, but she'd gone already.

He glanced back to the window. "By the Higher Realm," he swore, sprinting for the palace gates.

44

———

Caroline woke at dawn, still tired. And yet, she was home.

The palace didn't smell as bad as she'd thought it would, her nose only a little blocked. She smiled, and despite feeling trapped found herself at ease for the first time in the better part of a year. Her parents still loved her, though their love was clearly a problem. They'd do what they thought best for her, just as they'd sent her to the Sisters of Mardier du Shae to have her baby.

She stared at the roof for perhaps an hour, trying to get more rest, but eventually gave up and threw her covers back. She used a basin of cold water to wash the sleep from her eyes and then pulled on a chemise and woollen dress from the chest she'd dragged to the door.

The heavy wool felt like a luxury after days of travelling through rain, tight though it was. She frowned at the short hemline. She hadn't worn it since early last winter, but it would have to do for now.

Pushing open the room's shutters, she found the day bright and sunny. "Typical." She'd barely had a clear day since entering the Kingdom. The city smelled fresh from the rains, but full of people. She hoped she'd get used to that particular smell soon.

She pulled a warm woollen cloak over her shoulders, close-woven and thick, and found her favourite leather boots. They were too tight, but she'd almost forgotten how good it felt to be warmly dressed. Not that she would need warm clothes for much longer, probably not even today. Summer in Fandelyon was scorching.

Rather than call a maid, she brushed and braided her own hair, finishing as a timid knock sounded on her door.

"Who is it?"

"Me, of course!" came a child's voice.

"Daniella!" Caroline squealed. She dragged the chest from the door and slid the bolt aside, pulling the door open.

Princess Daniella, her long red hair recently brushed and bound but somehow still dishevelled, crashed into her with a huge hug. "Caroline!"

"You've grown," Caroline said, holding her baby sister tightly. "I can't believe how big you are."

"Of course I'm grown. I'm six now."

"So you are," she said. "And I was away for your birthday. I'm so sorry."

"That's okay. Mother said we could have another party."

They sat on Caroline's bed. Daniella's features had changed and one of her front teeth was missing. "It's a good thing you're younger than me. Everyone would think we were twins otherwise." She held out a long lock of Daniella's escaped curly hair to demonstrate.

Daniella laughed, but then her face turned serious. "Mother and Father thought you'd died in the mountains. I'm very glad you didn't." She looked absolutely serious about it. "I cried."

Caroline pulled her close, trying not to cry herself. "I've had some big adventures, muffin. I'll tell you all about them some time." She squeezed her sister again. "How'd you like to help me pick some jewellery for the day?"

"Can I wear some?" Her tone suggested she already knew the answer.

"Of course you can."

Daniella's face lit up at the unexpected boon. Caroline brought her jewellery box to the bed and put it in Daniella's lap. "You pick."

Daniella opened the box. The reek of silver stung her nose and sinuses. Caroline slammed it closed, gagging. The smell lay thick on the back of her throat. "Oh Gods, that's horrible."

"What?" Daniella asked, leaning away as if box might hurt her.

Caroline forced a smile. "Nothing muffin. Maybe you'd like to take the box back to your rooms? You can wear anything in it you like."

"Anything? Oh, thank you!" Daniella hugged her again.

No jewellery, then. She tried to remember what else might be made of silver around the castle. She'd never paid any attention before. The cutlery, certainly. That would be awkward. Maybe some of the mirrors and plates. Candleholders.

Someone shifted their weight outside her room.

Oh! Father must have set a guard on her door. Furious, she stalked to the door and yanked it open. As expected a guard stood there, dressed in a tabard and helm. "You tell Father-" The sting of silver burned her throat as she noticed the man's dagger was drawn. "Faspane!" she hissed, his scent hidden by the silver.

She staggered back as he swung, missing her by an inch. Another swing nicked her arm, the cut burning like ground-in salt. Daniella cried out as Caroline stumbled to the bed post, thumping her hip on the rose-carved wooden post.

The faspane threw the blade and Caroline ducked, too slow. It slammed into her left shoulder, burning like a poker.

She cried and tumbled to the floor, unable to breathe from the pain. The silver burned as if the blade had been heated in a forge. She couldn't even whimper. She struggled to stand and barely staggered to the far wall, leaning heavily.

"Caroline!" Daniella ran for her, but the faspane backhanded her little sister out of the way. Caroline flushed with rage as Daniella hit the bed post and bounced off, crashing to the floor. She staggered half a step forward, but the assassin put his hand on his sword's hilt.

"Please don't hurt Daniella," she begged. "She's just a little girl."

The warrior moved toward Caroline, forcing her back past the open shutters to the corner of her room.

"I right be wait come dawn," he said in an accent so thick she had trouble understanding him. "You helpless be."

Desperately, Caroline grasped the dagger buried in her shoulder and pulled with all her strength. She cried in agony, the sound barely a whimper, but the blade came free. She collapsed to her knees, half a breath away from passing out.

Her blood reeked of silver and her shoulder felt as if the weapon were still embedded. "I'm supposed to be safe here. I just want to be safe." Tears wet her cheeks as the bloody dagger slipped from her fingers.

The faspane raised his visor and pulled the helm off to reveal jade eyes. His expression went from cold resolve to sympathy. "I are, am, sorry. No honour in killing like this." He drew his sword, his eyes reminding her of Allyn's. "May soul find best life in rebirth."

Grasping the hilt of the bloody dagger, she sprang at him, driving the blade deep into his stomach. They crashed to the ground together and Caroline cried out, her shoulder jolting so painfully she almost blacked out.

Desperate to avoid a deadly response, she struggled to her feet, but the faspane remained on the ground, his expression shocked.

Blood trickled down the inside of her dress and soaked the fabric. She couldn't move her left arm at all and held the freely-bleeding wound with her other hand, trying to quench the blood. The entire room stank of silver. Blood and silver. "Daniella?" she called. She wanted to go to her sister, but didn't dare leave the faspane. If she could pull out a dagger and use it, so could he.

The assassin's breath came in short gasps as he gripped the hilt, but gave a small cry of pain without freeing the weapon.

"Failed," he whispered, perspiration on his face. His fingertips slid off the hilt. "Kill me then. Send my soul to oblivion."

"Why won't your people leave me alone?" she said. "I didn't *choose* any of this."

He took several shallow breaths. "Bring magic to humans. When war come, that enough reason."

She didn't resist the fury that swept over her. "I'll kill every one of you they send for me."

His eyes finally found hers. "The price we pay to take back what Higher Realm stole." His hand strayed toward his sword.

She picked the weapon up by the hilt, careful not to touch any silver. He gave her a slight nod, almost as if giving her permission. Angrily, she raised the weapon.

Someone gripped her wrist.

Caroline spun in shock, wrenching her hand away and turning the blade to swing.

Kimbriel stood there, seemingly unconcerned by the threat of violence. Her long blond hair cascaded over her shoulders.

"What are...? How?"

"Perhaps you could do me a favour?" Kimbriel asked, her hair hanging to her waist.

Caroline stared into the woman's eyes, her youth belying wisdom far older. The memory of her gifts returned unbidden. "Of course."

Kimbriel glanced at the faspane. "Let him do it himself. There's a dagger on his belt. Take it, help him grasp it, and help him drive it home if necessary."

"I don't understand."

"The faspane have mortal souls, remember? He needs to take his own life or his soul will be extinguished. It's not your place to consign it to oblivion."

Caroline finally understood the fear in his face, the hidden terror. He'd expected her to extinguish his soul? Her bloodlust disappeared. She knelt beside him and lay the sword down, pulling the ceremonial dagger from its sheath.

The slender, steel blade looked horribly sharp. He watched her as she placed the hilt in his palm and wrapped his weak, sweaty fingers around it.

"Thank you," he whispered.

She helped the faspane position the knife above his heart. "May your pain be over swiftly, and may your soul find immortality in your next life," she said.

She felt an answering response in her *alimoth* flowers, almost as if she'd intoned a blessing. Caroline glanced back at Kimbriel, but the woman was gone.

Under her fingers the assassin's calloused hand tightened around the blade, but she could feel he didn't have the strength to drive it home. She put her weight behind it and it slid between his ribs much too easily. He stiffened and gasped, but his expression never changed as his breath released and life left his eyes.

Her whole body began shaking. Without the emotional distance lycanthropy brought when she changed form, she broke into tears.

"Daniella?" she called, running around the bed.

Her youngest sister lay slumped on the ground, unconscious. She picked her slight weight up despite the pain in her shoulder, noting the marks on her sister's face. She gently touched the bruise on her sister's cheek before realising the little girl wasn't breathing.

"Daniella?" She cupped her sister's good cheek. "Daniella!"

She couldn't see through her tears as she put her ear to Daniella's chest and listened for a heartbeat that wasn't there.

Caroline sat on the wooden floor and pulled her sister's body close, her back against the bed. The faspane would pursue her anywhere and kill anyone who got in their way. Even a child in the heart of her home wasn't safe. She shouldn't have returned home.

For a blinding instant she regretted her compassion for the warrior who'd killed her sister. She glanced skyward. "Is this punishment?" she cried, thinking about all the people she'd slaughtered in the village.

What if they killed her parents or another sibling next?

As she sat there rocking Daniella's body back and forth, what she was going to have to do became clear. She had to protect her family and friends and that meant she couldn't hide behind the palace's ineffectual walls.

There were only two options she could see, and she didn't like either of them.

A maid found her like that some time later, tears running freely down her cheeks, but grim resolution in her heart.

45

"Explain, Caroline," King Phillip said, his voice raised. "Why are izzen killing *my* family in *my* palace?" He may have kept his voice measured, but he smelled both furious and devastated.

"Faspane," she whispered, looking down to hide her tear-red eyes while pretending to study the rug beneath her. She had no idea what else to say.

What would he do now? Banish her to another abbey? The plans she'd made a few hours ago were already in ruins. She'd never be free of his scrutiny now.

Her entire arm throbbed along with half her chest and neck. Freshly bandaged, blood still seeped through the dressings and had begun to mark her new dress. The silver taint marring the wound gave it a disgusting smell. A brief memory of Daniella excitedly entering her room almost brought her to tears again. She barely held them back.

Her father crossed the room and pulled the door open. "Fetch Lady Kirsty and the shivra Dobbin. Also, bring the big fool who tried to barge his way into the palace. I want to know if he's involved."

Big fool? Her father's fury was beginning to show and she

couldn't blame him. His youngest child was dead and Caroline was partly responsible.

She kept her eyes down. "I'm trapped," she whispered. The truth of her situation was very clear now. Marnier du Shae intended to use the faspane to clear Caroline's way to the throne. Her brothers and sisters would die. What of her mother? Kirsty? The guards and servants who tried to protect her? How many of them would also die before she could be crowned Queen? She had to leave, now, yet she wasn't sure how to escape unnoticed.

"Are you going to explain all this to me, or shall I force it from Kirsty and your shivra friend?"

She kept her eyes down. There'd be extra guards now, making her decision to leave far more difficult.

He raised his voice. "What are izzen doing in my palace?"

She flinched. "Faspane," she whispered. "And I've already told you. They want me dead because of a stupid belief."

The door opened and her mother's perfume flooded the room. The Queen rushed to Caroline's side and knelt, pulling her into a hug. Caroline winced, her shoulder throbbing anew. Her mother had been crying too. She could smell it, even though her nose was half blocked from the reek of the city.

"What happened?" Lynn asked, holding Caroline close.

King Phillip grunted. "That's what I keep asking."

"Caroline?" Lynn took Caroline's cheeks between her hands and made her look at her. "Tell me."

The door opened again and Kirsty slipped through. The guard closed it behind her. Kirsty looked around apprehensively before curtsying and making her way to Caroline's side. She gasped when she saw the blood seeping through Caroline's dress.

"My Lady?"

Phillip cleared his throat. "Kirsty, why would an izzat... a faspane attack my daughter?"

Kirsty glanced at Caroline as if looking for direction.

"Kirsty?" King Phillip repeated. "You answer to me, not Caroline."

"I-"

Caroline sniffed. "Father, she answers to me."

Phillip's expression hardened. "Even if that were true, you answer to me, Caroline."

What could she possibly tell him that would make sense? "I have to leave," she said, just loud enough to be heard.

"So you are keeping more secrets, as if being cursed wasn't enough. Explain everything. Now." His tone was quiet, but all the more menacing for it. "And no more nonsense about a destiny."

She thought he smelled betrayed, his scent mixed with anger and fear. She supposed she'd feel the same way. The door opened again and she smelled... Elias!

She couldn't stop herself looking up, releasing a relieved sigh when she saw a strip of cloth hiding the top half of his ears. His hands were chained behind his back.

Caroline reeled as his scent filled her head. Everything was falling apart.

"Elias?" Kirsty asked in disbelief.

Caroline could have choked her friend right then.

"Elias," Caroline acknowledged for her father's benefit. He looked almost entirely human with his ears hidden.

Elias showed no surprise at Caroline's wound, his eyes darting from her shoulder to her face. He actually seemed relieved. "I was watching out for you," he said. "I saw a faspane through a window and stupidly ran to help. I didn't think. I don't know how many more there are in the city."

Two guards pushed Elias further into the room.

Her father considered that for a moment. "And why are these faspane trying to kill my daughter?" It was clear from his voice that he had doubts.

"I don't know, Sire. They've been chasing Princess Caroline since her retinue was attacked in the mountains."

"I see. Explain your part in this, Elias."

When Elias hesitated, one of the guards clipped him over the back of his head. Caroline stood and glared at the guard, drawing her father's attention. "It makes no difference, Father. If they're prepared to attack me here, then my only choice is to leave."

"What?" Elias asked. She didn't have to smell his surprise to understand it. He'd risked his life several times to ensure she had a chance to fulfil her destiny. To turn her back on it was an insult to him and Allyn.

"I'm sorry, but I can't stay," she glanced pointedly at her parents.

Elias's jaw tightened and his eyes narrowed.

"Caroline, be quiet. Elias, I asked you for an explanation," King Phillip said.

Elias glanced at Caroline as if trying to gauge what had already been said. "Perhaps that's a story for your daughter." There was anger in his tone, and it surprised her how much it hurt. "She seems to know best."

Phillip stepped forward. "I expect to hear it from you."

Caroline sat back, wishing she were anywhere else. "Father, Elias was only trying to help me. Let him go."

"It's true, Your Majesty," Kirsty said. "It wasn't Dobbin who saved Caroline from the-" she glanced at the guards. "People pursuing us. It was Elias."

Queen Lynn stood and moved to her husband's side. She smelled as if she'd been betrayed too. Caroline was surprised she could smell anything over Elias's scent.

Phillip pointed to Elias. "Well?"

When Elias hesitated, one of the guards clipped him across the back of the head again - dislodging the cloth hiding his ears.

Phillip's eyes widened and her mother gasped.

King Phillip backed away as he pointed to Elias. "Secure that thing in the dungeons. Lady Kirsty and my daughter are to be escorted to their rooms. I don't want either leaving."

"Your Majesty," the guards said in unison. One of them grabbed Elias and dragged him out of the room.

"And why hasn't that shivra arrived?"

The other guard hesitated. "His rooms are empty, Your Majesty.

We're searching the grounds for him, but he may have left the palace."

Fury fleetingly crossed King Phillip's face, the scent of his anger like a haze in the room. "Hurry up."

A guard escorted Caroline back to her room, a man by the name of Jahnson. The blood had been scrubbed from the floorboards but its taint and the stench of silver remained, softly overlaid with Daniella's scent. Caroline lay on her bed and closed her eyes, wishing she could see some way out of the mess. Of all her sisters, Daniella had been the first to smile, the first to laugh, and the first to forgive.

Her door opened to admit a young maid carrying a tray of food. Of peasant stock or possibly from across the Temern Strait, she was beautiful and nearly as dark-skinned as Lutasicus. Caroline had seen her before, but didn't know her name. She carried porridge, bread, butter and honey. As the girl placed the tray on the end of the bed, Caroline recoiled at the sharp smell of silver cutlery still wrapped in a napkin. "Thank you," she said.

The maid glanced sharply at her. She probably remembered Caroline as a spoiled brat. "Milady," she murmured with a curtsy, and left. A guard closed the door behind her.

Despite the stench of silver, Caroline's stomach growled. Unthinkingly she pulled the napkin free and picked up the knife to spread butter. She dropped it with a curse. Her fingers stung.

"Rotten silver," she muttered. She used the napkin to pick up the silverware and wrap it tight again before taking it to the door. She slid it under, caring nothing about what the guard thought. She dribbled honey onto the porridge and used the crusty bread as a spoon, bending low over the tray so she didn't have to use her throbbing fingers to pick the bowl up.

How was she going to get Elias out of the dungeon? Where had Dobbin gone? With luck, he'd be out of the city by now. She had to do the same before her father made more plans of his own.

She was tempted to leave Kirsty behind where she'd be safe, but she'd promised.

Her door banged open and Stephanie, the oldest sister after Caroline, came in. The normally gentle girl slammed the door, leaning against the heavy wood and breathing hard. Her red hair was so dark it was almost brown, and she was also the only one of her sisters to inherit their father's brown eyes. She looked Caroline over, smelling frightened and upset.

"What did you do?" Stephanie asked. "Father's planning on throwing you into the dungeons!"

46

"I have to leave," Caroline said as she unlaced her bodice and pulled her bloodstained dress from her shoulders. The blood had stopped seeping and the wound smelled cleaner, but the bandages were thoroughly bloodied.

Stephanie helped her remove the dress and chemise, letting them drop to the ground. Almost as tall as Caroline, Stephanie's brown eyes and darker hair made her distinctive among the sisters.

"Father said you'd been hurt, but I didn't realise it was so badly."

Caroline's supernatural healing was beginning to work, so it wouldn't matter that the bandages needed replacing. She removed them with Stephanie's help. "It bled badly. The wound wasn't deep."

"Mother says you're a werewolf."

Caroline pulled sharply away. "What?" she said a little too sharply as she stared at her sister.

Stephanie stepped back, uncertainty and caution filling her scent. Almost whispering, Stephanie said, "Mother said some other things, too."

Caroline finished unwinding the bandages, tossing the bloodied mess on the coals in her fireplace where they quickly flared up, providing much-needed warmth. "I have to leave, Steph." The fire consumed the bandages. Examining the wound as best she could, it seemed to have closed over, though the silver was certainly slowing the healing. It was very tender and badly bruised around the cut.

"She wants me to help you."

Caroline paused again. Her whole life her mother had always known what she'd been up to, and sometimes even what she'd planned to do. "Mother said that?"

Stephanie's pale cheeks flushed. "Not quite. She told me what you and Father intended and walked away."

"I wonder if she knew what you'd do?" Caroline dug through her clothes chest, picking the plainest riding dress she could find before struggling into it. Stephanie helped her lace the bodice. "You didn't have to come to me," Caroline added. "You could get in a lot of trouble."

"So could Mother. I don't believe you're a werewolf. I wouldn't care even if it were true."

Images of torn and dismembered people came to Caroline, along with a disturbing longing to do it again. "You might," she said quietly.

She pulled on her cloak and approached the door. Despite beating the curse, it was difficult to remember when she hadn't healed so readily. It seemed almost normal now.

"Stephanie, would you mind standing by my bed please? Face the window."

Uncertainty entered Stephanie's scent again, but she did as asked. Concentrating, Caroline drew magic, and using the skills Dobbin had taught her she cast an inattention spell over herself. It wouldn't last for more than a few minutes, so she had to be quick.

"Steph, please stand still for a minute. I'm hoping the guard mistakes you for me and I can slip past. Draw him into the room if you can. I'm sorry to use you like this, but I have to leave."

Stephanie smiled over her shoulder. "Mother told me, remember?"

Caroline nodded, hoping the quick enchantment held. "Guard!"

Boots shifted outside the door as the man pulled it open. "Your Highness?" he asked, looking directly at Stephanie.

Caroline shifted her weight, preparing to slip past, as Stephanie turned. "Please come in."

"Princess... Stephanie?" He glanced at Caroline as she moved. "Wait, you can't leave, Your Highness. I'm sorry."

Caught. With no other inspiration, Caroline punched him in the face. He stumbled back and dropped his spear, clutching his nose. Caroline winced. "Ow!" She'd never punched anyone before. She must have done it wrong because it hurt.

The guard stared in shock as his fingers came away bloodied. "Wha... Why did you do that?" His clogged nose made him sound like he had a cold. "I think you broke my nose."

Broke it? She hoped not, but she could almost taste his blood in the air, which brought on a dangerous desire to bite him.

She ran over and hugged her shocked sister. "Never doubt Mother," she whispered. "And don't follow me. I love you. Tell Mother she has my thanks, and tell our sisters how much I wanted to see them."

Before Stephanie could say anything, Caroline lifted her skirt and ran out of her room. "Milady?" the shocked guard called as he ran after her, doing his best to get in front of her and block her way. Blood dripped through his fingers as he held his nose high.

She stopped. "I'm sorry about your nose," she said, meaning it. Hitting him wasn't something she would have done before the curse, or at least, she didn't think it was. It seemed to be influencing her more than she knew.

"Your Highness, the King says you're to be confined to your rooms. You must return."

She was taller than him by a good three inches, so she moved uncomfortably close, making him look up at her. "Tell Father I will *not* be confined to my rooms."

"What? But, Milady-"

"Get out of my way before I tell Father you..." What? "You hurt me. I've got so many bruises you couldn't deny it." She had to force guilt away to keep standing there. Hating herself for treating him so badly, she added, "I swear I will."

He hesitated, but the conflict kept him quiet. She took the initiative and walked around him, continuing toward the guest wing. He began to follow, but stopped after a few steps. She didn't give him another chance to catch up. Lifting her skirt again, she ran.

Several curious guards stared as she hurried through the corridors and down a flight of steps, but none challenged her. How long before that changed? She entered the corridor to the guest rooms, and then stopped. Something smelled out of place. Fear crept into her as she sniffed.

Faspane. One she recognised. It was the woman who'd killed Leasa.

Caroline ran, but found a young guard standing outside Kirsty's door as if nothing were wrong. He stood straighter when he saw her. Caroline stopped before him, trying to look intimidating as she stared down at him. "Father has requested Lady Kirsty's presence. Open the door."

Zaramar's mate must have stopped when she saw the guard and retraced her steps. Either that, or she was setting a trap and wanted Caroline to follow. It only made Caroline more determined to get Elias out of the dungeons and leave the palace.

"Your Highness? I received no such orders."

"I'm relaying them." She moved closer, crowding him.

He hesitated, backing away. He finally nodded and pushed the door open. "Of course, Your Highness."

Kirsty was sitting on the bed, looking dejected until she saw Caroline. "My Lady?" She stood and ran to Caroline, hugging her hard enough to make her shoulder ache. Caroline allowed herself a huge sigh of relief as she hugged back.

"Are you ready to go?" Caroline asked.

"Ready? Yes." Kirsty gave the guard an uncertain glance before she grabbed a warm cloak hanging on the hook beside the door and threw it around her shoulders.

Both disappointed and relieved, Caroline wanted Kirsty to be able to choose her own path almost as much as she wanted her to return safely home, but making her stay would be treating her no better than the way her father wanted to treat them both.

"What's your name?" she asked the guard.

"Kevan, Your Highness."

"Kevan, please escort us to the dungeons."

Elias paced his cold cell, wondering how long it would take before someone came to drag him to the gallows. Light from a lantern outside the heavy bars let him see there was no escape unless he could tunnel through stone or pick locks.

Another prisoner moaned in a cell further down, clearly in pain.

His cell was clean at least, including a bucket in the corner for wastes, but it was no compensation for the lack of open space. He examined the heavy lock again, but even if he knew how to pick it he had nothing to use but straw.

Still, it was better than staring at the oppressive stone walls. There was enough room to pass a bowl of food underneath the bars, not that he'd seen a bowl of anything yet, even water, but the floor was stone and there wasn't enough space to get more than his forearm through.

He kicked the door in frustration, the metal rattling. He wanted to kick himself for his rash act; thrown in a dungeon because of a human girl. He leaned his forehead against two of the bars, the metal cold. Did he dare try escaping, or should he wait and hope the King would release him because he'd saved the man's daughter? Perhaps he could fake illness and try to overpower his guards? The likely consequences of failure weren't inspiring.

But then, neither was staying.

Magic could make him stronger and faster, but not strong enough to bend steel or dash past a guard unnoticed, should they open the door. Even if he got through the cell door, there was a locked gate at the end of the corridor, guards beyond it, another locked gate, and finally the door out of the dungeons. That didn't include a castle and a city to get through with men hunting him the entire time.

Still, he had no choice but to try. Perhaps if he used magic to temporarily blind someone... or try and charm a guard.

He should be able to charm a guard and apply an aversion or inattention spell on himself. Assuming the charm worked, the secondary spell should keep anyone from looking too closely when the guard led him out.

It would all depend on how bored the other guards were and how much effort it took to maintain the bridge between himself and the charmed guard. He'd have to pick his target carefully. Someone weak-willed.

He sat down and began to prepare the spells. The door at the end of the corridor rattled and squealed open on hinges overdue for oil. Two sets of echoing footsteps approached, and the door slammed closed. Cursing the timing, he calmed his breathing as he listened to the footsteps.

They stopped outside his door. His fears rising, he released a sigh and let his spells dissipate unformed.

"Oy, you. Elias. Get up," the guard said. "The King wants to speak with you."

Did he dare try the charm without a secondary spell prepared? Was there any chance at all with two people? He doubted he'd be able to charm both, and wasn't sure even one would work. He stood as they unlocked and shoved open the door. It clanged against the wall.

The guards entered. The first man was short like most humans in this region, but broad and barrel-chested. The second was almost as thick-set, but considerably taller, almost Caroline's height.

"Take that cloth off your head," the shorter guard said. "The King don't like deception," the man said, moving close enough to grab at it.

Elias dodged, but the man's fist drove into Elias stomach. He doubled over, winded, and a second punch caught him across the jaw. He hit the ground hard, struggling to breathe.

"Get up, izzat."

Hoping to avoid a kick too, Elias struggled to his feet, barely able to breathe.

The guard shoved him hard against the wall, half spinning him so he thumped his cheek on the stone. Before he could recover, the man yanked the strip of cloth away.

"Filthy izzat." He drove his fist into Elias's side.

Elias collapsed to the ground. Gods, the man could hit. He threw the cloth at Elias. "Let's hang the bastard now," the taller guard said.

Struggling to breathe, Elias leaned on the wall to get back to his feet.

"We'll need ta be hanging this one from his door, Denny. Make it look like he did it himself." He spat at Elias, but missed by a couple of feet.

Denny crumpled without warning, and as the other man turned in surprise a massive fist punched him in the face, throwing him bodily back into the cell.

Dobbin ducked under the door.

"Dobbin!" Elias gasped. By the Gods, he'd never been so relieved to see the shivra.

"Ye had enough relaxing?" Dobbin asked. "I can come back tomorrow if ya like. I'm sure these lads will appreciate more time with ya."

"I'm happy to leave." He grabbed the strip of cloth he'd been using to hide his ears.

"Good, cause ye've been released. A couple of the other lads let me in. Pack yer gear, pixie, unless ye prefer the comforts of cold stone." Dobbin held up a note with the royal seal on it. "King's orders. Yer weapons and gear are outside." He pointed at Elias's ears. "And keep yer foldaways covered, just in case. Most of 'em only heard a rumour, they don't know for sure. I'm sure they'll have something ta disagree with if ye put 'em back on display. We'll tell the lads outside these two are dealing with a rowdy fellow further down. Might give us enough time ta get ye out of the city."

Elias staggered forward but Dobbin held up his palm. "Ye can kiss me later."

47

"My Lady, you said the King wanted to see you." Kevan appeared suspicious, his scent changing to reflect it.

Caroline tried to cover her hesitation as she thought of a suitable lie. "He wants to see all of us, including the man caught trying to barge into the palace this morning. Hurry now. Father has less patience than me."

She marched out of the room and turned toward the stairs, giving Kevan no option but to follow or try to physically restrain her. He wasn't likely to do that without the King's direct authority.

He quickly got ahead of her to lead the way.

"Be cautious," Caroline whispered to Kirsty. "There are faspane about."

Aaron, the younger of her twin brothers, walked into the corridor from the stairs. "Caroline?"

His thick brown curly hair, much like their father's, was brushed and trimmed, and his clothes similarly perfect. He looked her up and down with a sneer. "I heard you were confined to your rooms."

"It's nice to see you too, Brother Spare. Tortured any animals lately?" His scent was as sour as his features.

The sneer deepened. "You got fat."

"Kevan, meet us at the bottom of the stairs please." The man nodded and moved as quickly as he could without running, smart enough not to get between royal siblings in conflict.

Aaron leant against the stone wall with a cocky expression. At twelve, he had begun using a full-sized sword at practice, and his strength had grown with its use. At thirteen he'd been much stronger than her despite the age difference, and used it whenever he could. His petty shoves and punches had often left her bruised.

Before she'd left for the mountains he had booted her so hard in the rear she could barely sit her horse without wincing. She doubted he'd have acted any differently had he known she'd been pregnant. He'd filled out considerably since then too, heavy boned with broad shoulders from his clan heritage, and as tall as many men already. He was going to be a huge adult one day.

She considered ignoring him and continuing down the stairs, but he'd only take it as a challenge and follow. He'd grown over the winter, but she'd grown more. "What do you want, Spare?"

His jaw clenched at the nickname. He grabbed her left wrist with his right hand and twisted, or tried to. She held firm, the ache in her shoulder renewing itself. He was strong, but lycanthropy made her stronger. A look of surprise crossed his face, quickly followed by the scent of anger. His teeth showed and he put all his strength into it, but she still held.

"Do you have any idea how much I detest you?" she asked. She caught his neck with her free hand and squeezed.

He dropped her arm and grabbed her right wrist in both his hands, but she pressed him against the stone wall before he could break free. If he'd been a full-grown man, she doubted she could do as much, but he wasn't. She gripped harder until he stopped making noise, both his hands desperately trying to pull her away.

For the first time in human form she felt true bloodlust rising, a terrible desire to tear someone limb from limb. "Not as much fun when it's you getting hurt, is it?" she asked, scared at how much she was enjoying herself.

"My Lady?" Kirsty said, concern in her tone.

Aaron kept struggling, unable to speak.

Caroline shifted her grip and with all her strength pushed him up the wall until he was eye-to-eye with her. "Don't *ever* touch me again. Understand?"

He gave the barest hint of a nod, his fear an acrid stench all over his skin.

"That goes for our sisters and brother too."

She let go and he dropped to the ground, coughing. As well as fear, there was a good measure of hatred on his face. She hoped she hadn't made a mistake.

Leading Kirsty, Caroline met Kevan at the foot of the stairs and followed him again, catching the scents more faspane in the lesser-used corridors. "Be wary," Caroline said to Kirsty. "The faspane are planning something. I can smell at least a dozen of them in the palace." She sniffed again. "And smoke, too. Cloth burning. It's distant, though."

Elias's scent seemed to be everywhere as they neared the dungeons. Her heart beat quicker, even though the stale air reeked of dampness and the filth of unclean bodies and excrement.

Kevan pounded on the heavy door until a peep hole opened from the inside. Caroline bent down so she could see through. "My father wishes to speak to the prisoner, the one called Elias. Open the door."

The man's eyes opened wide. He seemed about to ask a question, but instead closed the peep hole. His footsteps disappeared into the dungeons. Distantly she heard muffled words.

Caroline caught Kirsty's hands and pulled her away from Kevan. "In the corridor outside your room, I smelled the faspane who killed Leasa," she whispered.

"What?" Kirsty said, too loud.

"Shh! I thought I'd killed her at the village, but either she got away or she wasn't there when I arrived. Be very careful. We need to get away before they come for us."

Kirsty glanced at the guard, perhaps grateful he'd been watching her room. "Why would she come after me?"

"Because she knows I'd try and rescue you."

Kirsty looked wounded. "You can't risk yourself."

"Of course I can. The further away we get from them, the safer everyone will be."

Footsteps finally returned and another guard reappeared behind the peep-hole. "Your Highness?"

Caroline went back to the peep hole. "Yes?"

"The prisoner, Elias. He's gone. The King released him not long ago." He appeared curious, as if waiting for an explanation.

"He's gone?"

"Yes, Your Highness," the man repeated. "The shivra collected him. Had a signed order with the King's seal on it."

"Dobbin had orders from Father?" That made no sense. "Thank you. Back to your post."

The peep hole closed a little too quickly. "You too," she said to Kevan. "Come on, Kirsty." Somewhere in the corridors above, a scream sounded. Caroline paused, heart hammering.

"Did you hear that?" she asked Kirsty.

"No."

"We have to go. Now," she grabbed her friend's hand. "I think whatever the faspane are going to do is happening."

Kevan hurried to catch up. "Your Highness? I should take you to your father."

"I'm safe enough in my own palace," she said. Hopefully he hadn't heard the scream.

"You were attacked this morning, and your sister..."

Caroline stopped. She took a deep breath and pushed the grief away. "Fine, then. Lead the way." If they ran into faspane, she would need the help.

She'd find another way to get rid of him and escape the palace.

Dobbin thumped his head on a low beam with a solid *thunk*. "Ow!"

"Good thing you're small for a shivra," Elias said with a smirk. "You'd have hit more beams otherwise."

Dobbin grasped his head as he gave Elias a look. "That bloomin' hurt."

"Sounded like it. We'd better find some wax to stop up your ears. Can't have your brains leaking out."

Dobbin frowned. "Doubt I've got any left."

Elias gave the shivra a grin as he tried to cover his tension. They'd been gone from the dungeons for far too long and Dobbin seemed intent on leading him through the entire castle. "Have you worked out where we are yet? I swear we've been through this corridor already."

"That way," Dobbin said.

Elias followed him down another quiet corridor under the palace, the shivra almost doubling over to get though a door which even Elias struggled under. At the sound of footsteps, Elias slapped Dobbin on the arm and they ducked into a room stocked with bags of oats, dried fruit and sacks of grain. There was no dust, suggesting it was regularly used. Clay jars and other ingredients lined the shelves. Dobbin had to half crouch just to stay in the room.

"Something's going on," Elias said. "There's a commotion in the palace."

"You think they're looking for us?"

"No. Something else." Elias glanced around. "Another storeroom," he said with false enthusiasm. "I assume the exit's in here?"

Dobbin gave him a sour look. "A wine cellar might have dulled yer tongue."

Elias pulled the top off an unsealed clay jar to discover dried apple slices. He grabbed a handful as footsteps went down another corridor. "So," he began as he bit one. "How'd you steal the orders to free me?"

Dobbin poked his head out of the room. "They were genuine."

"If they were real, why are we sneaking around?"

"Because the guards saw yer ears, ya dopey pixie, and others heard about 'em. I'm only being cautious."

Elias chewed. "You stole the orders, didn't you?"

"Ye could go back to yer cell if ye'd prefer."

"Who'd you bribe?"

"Ya really think I'd waste good coin on an overgrown sprite?" He led the way past several more storerooms and up a flight of stairs to ground level. Elias followed, wishing he had the nerve to unbind his ears so he could listen properly. There was a hint of smoke in the air.

They passed close to the kitchen, the waft of roast meat and baking pastries more tempting than his dried apple slices. Dobbin led him up a set of servants' stairs and along another corridor, ducking into an alcove as two guards rounded a corner.

"You've no idea where we're going, do you?" Elias whispered.

"I know exactly where we're going," Dobbin said in a hushed voice. "I'm not certain about the relationship between there and here."

"How'd you even find the dungeons?" he whispered. "I swear you're the only shivra in the world without a sense of direction."

"Someone led me there," Dobbin conceded, looking embarrassed.

"We really need to get out of this palace." When the guards passed, Dobbin led him down several more corridors to a dead end. Elias ground his teeth in frustration. "I bet you could find the treasury."

Dobbin gave him another look, but it was tinged with a hint of desperation. He clearly felt the need to get away, too. They found another set of servants' stairs and surprised two maids gossiping on the landing as they went down.

"Ladies," Dobbin said as he squeezed past the surprised women, one young, the other middle aged.

Elias paused as he was about to pass. "Would you mind telling us the way to the stables?"

The older of the two looked from Elias to Dobbin and back. "Turn right at the bottom of the stairs, master huntsman. Follow the corridor and take the last door on your left. It leads to the rear courtyard. Stables are on the far side."

Elias touched his forelock. "Thank you."

At the bottom of the stairs, four guards stood at the far end of the corridor to the right. "Oh, for the..." Dobbin muttered, going left until he found another staircase. "Down?" he asked aloud.

"How should I know?" Elias asked. "All I've seen is the throne room and the dungeons.

"Up, then."

Elias heard a scuffle, and curiosity got the better of him. He slipped past the shivra and followed the noise down.

"Up! Up I said, ye silly git."

48

____

Caroline and Kirsty followed Kevan, ascending the stairs to the basement level and leaving most of the dungeon's musty reek in the corridor below. The scent of smoke was stronger. Swords clashed somewhere distant.

Her heart beat hard. It had to be faspane.

Just ahead, three liveried servants were setting up with buckets of soapy water, one already mopping the stone floor before the staircase. Another of the men looked up, his eyes widening with surprise when he saw Caroline.

Caroline sighed. She was leaving a trail anyone could find. How long before her father heard? She ignored the men in the hope that the less she said, the smaller the rumours, and moved toward the staircase at the opposite end of the corridor.

A mop handle clanked against the stone before the distinct sound of a dagger whispered free of a scabbard. Two more daggers followed.

"Run!" she yelled at Kirsty, who stumbled to a stop as she looked around for the danger. The servants charged. Kevan backed away, confused, but nevertheless raised his spear. Half panicked, Caroline shoved Kirsty toward the far stairs as one man went for Kevan and the other two came at her.

The gleam of silver etching reflected in lantern light. They knew her for what she was.

Kevan jabbed his spear at the first man. "Run, Your Highness!" he yelled, but the other two were already on Caroline.

Instinct took over and she kicked low, catching the first man in the knee. He collapsed with a cry of pain, his blade flying from his hand and clattering loudly to the stone floor. The other shoved past and swung wildly at her, missing.

Thank the Higher Realm they were servants, not guards or soldiers.

She stumbled back as he raised the blade high, dagger plunging. She barely caught his wrist with both her hands as she tripped and fell, his weight driving her hard onto her back. She held the blade inches from her chest, her wounded shoulder flaring in pain.

The man grimaced and put his weight behind the dagger, forcing it toward her heart, his onion-breath washing across her face.

"Help!" she screamed, pushing back with all her strength.

Unlike her fight with her brother, this man was larger, stronger, and had his full weight behind the dagger. She cried out as her wounded shoulder tore. Blood warmed her skin, but she refused to let go. If she did, the blade would plunge into her heart.

The veins in her attacker's neck stood out and the blade moved an inch downward. She pushed back, but the weapon dropped another inch, touching her dress and piercing the bodice. The reek of silver burned her sinuses.

She barely held the blade there, her arms shaking.

"Please!" she begged him, but saw no sympathy in his eyes. His face was going red with effort.

The tip of the blade cut into her skin. "No. Please! I beg you." She struggled to hold his weight for another heartbeat. Two. Three.

Her shoulder gave out as the man's eyes widened. He stiffened and collapsed across her, his hands slipping from the hilt as she twisted the blade flat against her bodice. His weight crushed her as he lay atop her, unmoving.

Trembling, she couldn't do anything but breathe and didn't notice the tears blurring her vision until she saw Kirsty beside her, her friend's face paler than parchment. Caroline tried shoving the man aside, but she was shaking so badly she didn't have the strength.

"My Lady?" Kirsty asked. "Are you okay?" A knife protruded from the dead man's back, the scent of blood and silver strong. A hint of blood marked Kirsty's sleeve.

Caroline took a shuddering breath. "Ye-yes. Thank you, Kirsty." Caroline caught movement behind Kirsty. "Look out!"

Kirsty spun, backing in fear from the man Caroline had kicked hobbled toward them. Caroline desperately shoved the dead man's weight off her, fear giving her strength.

Staying on the ground, she twisted around and kicked out again, catching his other knee. He cried out and fell, his dagger falling to the floor. Caroline got to her feet and kicked him as hard as she could, her boot catching his jaw. He lay still.

"Elias!" Kirsty cried.

"Elias?" Caroline whispered, spinning.

Kirsty ran and threw her arms around Elias with enough force to make him stagger back. Near-blinding jealousy flared as her friend held tight.

Elias disengaged Kirsty's arms, appearing embarrassed, and when he caught Caroline's eyes his face flushed red. She felt guilty relief that he didn't seem to want more from Kirsty. Whatever it was between herself and the half-izzat, it went both ways.

Caroline tried to hide the petty, self-satisfied feeling. Kirsty had just saved her life. If her friend wanted Elias, Caroline was determined to give her the chance. Looking into Elias's eyes though, she knew her friend was doomed to heartbreak.

Kirsty ran back and dropped to her knees as she hugged Caroline. Anger and jealousy still simmering, Caroline had to force herself not to stiffen or push Kirsty away. Elias's scent finally reached her, making her heartbeat quicken.

"I couldn't let him..." Kirsty glanced at the man she'd killed and shuddered.

Dobbin cautiously walked up behind Elias, a hand on his

uncovered hammer. "We heard the scuffle," he said, frowning at the bodies. "I think someone's lit a fire in a storeroom outside the palace. Guards are rushing there."

"Which means they won't be here," Caroline said. She got to her feet with Kirsty's help, still fighting jealousy and trying not to feel anything less than grateful. "Thank you," Caroline whispered again.

Dobbin put his hand on Elias's shoulder. "We should hurry," he said in his gravelly voice.

Caroline took Kirsty by the shoulders and held her back slightly. "Anything you want Kirsty, if it's in my power, it's yours." She couldn't help a longing glance toward Elias.

Kirsty followed her eyes, stirring a fresh wave of jealousy. "You already gave it to me when you kept your word."

Gods. Why was she jealous? She didn't even like Elias in that way. She just... wanted him. Fighting down her own petty emotions, Caroline pushed Kirsty in Elias's direction. "Go with him, Kirsty."

"What?" Elias asked, backing a step, his expression caught between confusion and betrayal. Dobbin looked just as surprised.

"Without you?" Kirsty asked, shaking her head. "You have to come too!"

"Don't you see Kirsty? They're paying palace servants to kill me." She had to force herself to speak the next words, and they were bitter. "If I come, they'll hunt you all to get to me."

"No," Elias said. "You're both staying here."

"I can't stay, and I can't go with you," she whispered.

"You have to stay. It's your Gods-granted destiny."

Moaning intruded. Kevan. He sat against the wall, his left arm bleeding profusely from wrist to elbow. The man who'd attacked him lay in a pool of his own blood, Kevan's spear through his neck.

Caroline ran to the young guard, bloodlust rising at the smell of his wound. It was only mildly tempered by the aching scent of silver. Kevan grimaced as she knelt beside him, his olive skin pale.

"Thank you," she said, swallowing saliva and holding back a desire to bite him.

He tried to smile. "I'll be fine, Your Highness. You're safe. I did my duty."

She gripped his arm above the wound and he sucked in a breath, the focus returning to his eyes. Despite the pressure, blood still flowed. "I need a cord, a belt or a strip of cloth."

"Dobbin and I must leave," Elias said. "I'm sorry Caroline, but your father will throw me back in the dungeons if he catches me again. I doubt Dobbin will fare any better."

"You're using this man as an excuse to leave me behind?"

He pursed his lips. "If I have to."

Kevan gritted his teeth as she pressed harder, his blood making her hands slick. She'd seen another wound like this. A boy in the training yard had gashed his leg open just as badly. They'd tightened a cord above his knee and it saved his life, but his leg had to be cut off.

"I think you're going to lose your arm," she whispered.

Kevan smiled, though it was more of a grimace. "I'll brag about it."

"I wish you didn't need to."

"The pixie's right," Dobbin said as Kirsty handed Caroline a servant's corded belt.

Caroline looped it around Kevan's arm above the gash, pulling it tight.

He gasped in pain.

"I'm sorry."

The blood flow eased. She allowed herself a deep breath and almost swooned. The wound was so fresh, the scent so overwhelming, she found herself imagining what his flesh would taste like.

Kirsty crouched on the opposite side to help. "Please go with Elias and Dobbin, Kirsty."

"Not without you," Kirsty said. Her eyes begged Caroline not to order her away.

A guard ran down the stairs, sword drawn. Elias and Dobbin tensed as the man saw Caroline and the dead servants. He rushed over, sheathing his sword on the way.

"Princess Caroline, your father is looking for you."

"This man needs help," Caroline said. She recognised the new guard's face, but didn't know him.

"There's fighting. Some of our own attacking us."

"I'll find somewhere to hide if you can look after this man for me," she said with a nod toward Kevan. "I have loyal companions. They'll protect me."

The new guard glanced at Dobbin and Elias, then their weapons.

"With our lives," Dobbin said.

The man nodded. "If you trust them, so do I. Find somewhere safe, Your Highness. Don't emerge until you're sure the fighting's over."

Elias held his hand out. "Quickly. This might be your only chance."

She grabbed his hand, her own slippery with Kevan's blood, and he hauled her to her feet.

There was too much blood in the room, and mixed with Elias's scent she was having trouble concentrating.

Kevan spoke. "I feel strange," he murmured. "Cold."

"You're a hero, Kevan. You saved my life."

"Hurry," Elias said.

Kevan's wound continued to seep blood.

"I'm sorry, Kevan," the new guard said as he tightened the cord. "I don't think we can save your arm."

"I'll get help for Kevan," Kirsty whispered, glancing regretfully at Elias. "But Princess, you need to leave."

"I made a promise to take you with me."

"You have to leave."

"Caroline?" Her father's voice.

Caroline stiffened, all her plans unravelling at the sound her father's footsteps. "Not now," she whispered.

49

———————

King Phillip stormed toward Caroline from the far end of the corridor, four guards marching behind him in pairs. Four more came down the near staircase, blocking any chance at escape.

"Not fair," Caroline murmured.

She stood, trying to rub the wet blood from her hands. The small cut in her breast ached, pulling painfully as she moved. The guards fell back as King Phillip approached, his boots thumping on the floor while he glanced at the bodies. He frowned at the fresh blood on her bodice and hands and seemed caught between fury and relief. His lips moved, as if he couldn't decide what question to ask first.

Caroline sighed, too tired to be afraid of consequences. "Our own servants tried to kill me, Father. If it wasn't for my friends and this guard..." She indicated Kevan, who appeared barely conscious, a lot of his own blood soaking into the floor.

King Phillip's scent went sharp with anger, yet he caught her in a fierce hug. It felt strange, being taller than him. "Why do they want you dead?" he whispered.

Gingerly returning the hug, she said, "I told you, but you wouldn't listen. The faspane paid these servants to kill me. How many more they've corrupted I can't guess, but if I stay they'll keep trying. I can hear the commotion in other parts of the palace. They're looking for me, aren't they?"

He stepped back, determination showing. "This is my palace. My Kingdom. I will not tolerate their presence." He glared at Elias who backed a step, picking his longbow up off the floor.

Caroline took her father's calloused hand with her blood-covered fingers and raised his knuckles to her lips. "Father, if I stay you'll die. You, and all my siblings." It hurt just to consider the thought of being responsible for their deaths, even Aaron's.

He pulled his hand away. "I'll hang anyone who tries to harm you." He glared at Elias again. "That izzat first."

"That won't help."

Click!

Fear hammered and she twisted her father aside just in time. The bolt slammed into her shoulder, punching through the muscle near her neck like a knife through cloth. She staggered and dropped to her backside with a gasp.

She knew the marksman. Markel Loftus. He'd guarded her dozens of times. He had the grace to look guilty even as he drew his sword, his eyes on her father. The men with him drew their swords.

Caroline called out to the only power she could think of that might save him. "Divine Lady!" They were so badly outnumbered she had no chance without divine help. "Please! I need you."

"Look out!" Dobbin's axe clashed with another blade - the four guards behind them had taken advantage of the distraction. A man with a bolt trained on Elias turned it toward Caroline instead. Petar Mikai, another man she'd once trusted.

"Please, Divine Lady! Anything you ask is yours if you help me save my friends and family."

The *alimoth* flowers on her wrists flared with a light so bright she couldn't see. A channel opened to something buried deep inside her soul, a direct connection to the Goddess who'd marked her, creating a moment held in time by the Goddess's will.

"Marnier du Shae," Caroline whispered, touching her forehead to the ground. "Divine Lady."

"Daughter." The words echoed as if spoken from a distance, another Realm, yet they were almost too loud to hear. *"It's time to accept the path I've prepared for you."*

"But if I walk your path, my family will die. Please, don't ask this."

"All destinies are linked."

"I beg you to take my life and let them live instead."

"Then who will walk your path? Who will make your sacrifice?"

"Many would beg for the honour."

"I can't alter the balance without consequences and concessions. If you wish to alter your father's path, you must forfeit your own life. What other sacrifices would you make for your siblings?"

"Please don't ask this of me,"

"I've given you everything, daughter; magic, power, and even some knowledge of your fate. I protected your child and bargained with other Gods to secure your life. All I ask is your faith."

"But I don't want this fate. Please, let me save my family."

"To save your father now and alter the course of the future, I would have to awaken your affinity with fire. To awaken yours is to awaken those of your sisters, and none of you are prepared. Would you have them suffer so your father can live?"

Her sisters have affinities? "Anything, Divine Lady. They'd choose to save our father, as I would."

"Yet the decision is yours, not theirs. What of your brothers?"

"I'll accept anything else you ask. Anything. Just let them live. Please."

There was a long pause. "As you wish. Your choice is sealed."

Fresh fears rose up. "What else do you demand of me?"

Agonising heat flared throughout Caroline's body as fire ignited within her soul. She screamed until she had no more breath.

"For your third sacrifice, you must soon pass your affinity with fire to your sister, Stephanie, the next time you meet. She will suffer in your place."

Caroline fought back tears as her soul became an agony she couldn't assuage. "Stephanie must endure this to save our brothers?"

"Give her your ruby faeriestone. She was your only sister born without a gift. Her fate, like yours, is now changed."

Caroline's soul burned, and now she had to give that same pain to her sister? It felt like holding her hands too close to a flame, to the point of blistering, and being unable to pull away. "May I know what you mean by giving my life to you?"

"It means you will die for my purposes when I choose. You will recognise the time. If you fail to willingly accept it, Fandelyon will be razed and your family obliterated."

Caroline's *alimoth* flowers flared. When the bright light faded, she found her father, Elias and Dobbin struggling to hold back eight men. Kirsty crouched by Kevan, protecting him as best she could with her body.

A crossbow released, aimed at Caroline.

"I'm fire," she said.

Flame surrounded her and engulfed the silver-tipped bolt. Molten silver spattered against her skin with a searing hiss.

She growled, directing all her anger into the silver. Liquefied metal flew back at the man, spraying across his face. He screamed and fell, writhing in agony.

The man to his left aimed his crossbow at her, but she liquefied the bolt before he could release it.

He yelled, dropping the burning crossbow.

He tried to draw his sword, but Caroline heated the metal white. The man screamed as his leather scabbard ignited.

Standing, Caroline wrapped the man in flame and he fell writhing, the stench of his burning flesh filling the room. Markel Loftus dropped his sword and tried to run, but she caught him in flame too. He screamed as her fires consumed him and he tumbled to the stone, rolling around in agony before laying still. "Traitor."

The final guard stood his ground, but let his crossbow fall from his fingers before he lifted his visor.

Faspane!

Hatred flared so sharp she let out a vicious snarl. Heat rose around her, making the air waver.

"Caroline! Don't!" Elias called, shielding his face from her heat. The sounds of struggle behind her had vanished.

It took all her strength not to destroy the faspane in that instant. "Take your dagger and thrust it through your heart or I swear I'll kill you before you can move."

He glared, his hand straying toward his sword's hilt.

"Do it or you'll never be reborn." The air between them became blisteringly hot. Elias, Dobbin and her father backed away while Kirsty turned her face, yet she still used her body to shield Kevan.

The assassin held his defiant pose for a moment, and then did as commanded. He drew an ornate dagger from his belt. Glaring hatred at her, he whispered several words in his own language, positioned the blade, and with a single thrust collapsed to his knees before falling face-forward and driving the blade deeper.

Breathing hard, Caroline let the heat vanish from the air as quickly as she'd brought it on.

Kimbriel had seen this, her *affinity with fire*. Caroline could feel it now, burning inside her soul, an ache she couldn't touch. It wasn't magic, but some other innate ability the Divine Lady of Healing had awakened, and it hurt as if it were consuming her from within.

Worse, it was a pain she would soon have to pass to Stephanie. Her other sisters would be enduring something similar already, each affinity hurting them somehow.

"What have I done?" she asked, uncertain she had made the right choice. She staggered, weak and tired.

"Caroline," Elias said. "The other four were all faspane."

"Please forgive me my choice, Divine Lady," Caroline whispered, almost wishing she could undo it. Almost. And yet, her father was alive, her sisters would survive, and her brothers' fates were their own again, none of them tied to hers any longer.

She held out her wrists and felt a strong sense guilt as she watched her *alimoth* flowers fill in, sealing her to the bargain she'd made with her Goddess who now owned her soul. At least Marnier du Shae hadn't abandoned her. For that, she was grateful and would die willingly.

Her father let the tip of his sword fall to the stone floor, staring at her. Kirsty's expression was one of wonder.

Tangles of sweaty red hair fell past Caroline's face, escaped from her braid. "Do you see now, Father? They want me dead because I threaten them. If I'd chosen to stay, you'd be dead, and your other children would soon follow." She wasn't entirely sure about her sisters, now they'd been revealed to have affinities too, but that was only a guess. If they could be passed on, then perhaps they may have died. "How many more people would die because of me?"

"No." Despite the fear on his face he still seemed to want to protect her. "I won't let you leave."

She loved him for it. She pointed to Kevan, his head slumped in unconsciousness. "He saved my life, Father, and hopefully I saved his. He's a loyal man. Honourable. Treat him well."

An idea suddenly came to her. She approached Kevan and placed her right wrist against his forearm.

"Please, give me a small miracle, Divine Lady. I have nothing left to sacrifice, but he kept me safe. Please help him."

She waited, but she didn't feel any blessing through the *alimoth* flowers.

Kirsty knelt beside her and grasped Caroline's hand. "Divine Lady," she whispered. "You once asked me to forgive you. Whatever your plans for me, I accept them without reservation. I ask nothing in return, but if you choose I'd like to share in this man's suffering so that perhaps his burden can be lessened."

Kirsty gasped as a wound slowly opened in her left forearm from elbow to wrist.

She whimpered, stiffening in pain as blood began to ooze from the deep cut.

Elias ran to her side, bandaging the wound closed with torn livery, while Dobbin handed him more strips. Caroline watched tensely as blood seeped through the bandages, but by the time Elias tied them off the blood eased to almost nothing.

As Elias tied the last knot, Kirsty passed out. Elias caught her, and Caroline couldn't help another jealous twinge.

Hoping she was doing the right thing, Caroline carefully removed the cord stopping the blood reaching Kevan's arm. A thin line of fresh blood seeped through is wound, but that was all.

"Kirsty did it," Caroline said. "By the Divine Lady." Without doubt, she knew the Divine Lady of Healing had chosen the wrong person for her Champion. It should have been Kirsty. She deserved Elias. Hopefully, he'd come to recognise it.

"Caroline," her father began. "I can't allow you to leave."

"Why would you want to stop me Father?" she asked, exhausted enough not to care about her tone.

"I can help you." He sounded so earnest, she wished it were true.

"Then help my sisters. They'll need you. Watch over Phillip too. He'll need your guidance to be as good a King as you.'

"And Aaron?" It wasn't so much a question as a criticism.

"Aaron looks after himself, but he needs guidance. He's petty and spiteful, but not bad at heart." She approached him, kissing him on the cheek. He didn't flinch. "I love you Father, but we have to go. Please don't try to stop us."

"I forbid you to leave."

She left him standing there, her soul ablaze with a pain she couldn't express in words. "Stephanie, I'm so sorry," she whispered as she walked away from her father. After a moment's hesitation, she heard Elias's soft tread behind her, burdened with Kirsty's weight. Dobbin's heavy boots were loud by comparison.

"Caroline!"

She paused. "Father, you can't stop me." She held out her hand and flame flared twelve inches high above her palm. "Marnier du Shae gave me the power to save you, and the only way I can ensure that is to leave." And die at her bidding. "Goodbye, Father. I love you too."

～

Still shaken, Elias followed Caroline with Kirsty cradled in his arms, the small group attracting more stares than he felt comfortable with. All it would take would be for the King to order his guards to apprehend them, and Caroline would be faced with a difficult choice, considering what she could do now.

He followed her through the corridors, anxious for far too many reasons. Stray wisps of hair had escaped her braid, some sticking with perspiration to her neck, a strange thing to notice as he tried to make sense of the power she'd been given.

Using it, apparently, cost her. She looked exhausted.

Whatever her Goddess had given her wasn't magic. He'd have felt that. It could only mean some kind of a bargain had been struck in the Higher Realm, a payment of some kind.

But then why was Caroline leaving her home? How could Marnier du Shae allow it?

He followed the princess out of the palace proper through a servants' entrance, emerging into a sun-drenched courtyard swept mostly clean of manure, though still reeking of it. The sounds of fighting in other parts of the palace had ceased, although the corridors were still touched with smoke.

With relief, he found the stables directly across the yard, the side door closed. Trying to ignore the tension he felt, Elias pointed, though it was difficult with an unconscious girl in his arms. "That way's north, Dobbin, in case you're curious."

"Shut up." Dobbin's cheeks flushed above his close-cropped blond beard. He had a splash of blood across his face from where he'd hit a faspane with his axe.

Elias held back a grin of relief at the expected answer. "What's our plan?" he asked. "Find a guard and ask which way to Delshere?"

Dobbin gave him a look. "I took one wrong turn, that's all. Just one."

Caroline gave them both a look over her shoulder that suggested she wasn't in the mood for their banter. Elias did his best to ignore her.

"Lucky we've got Caroline to lead the way," Elias murmured more quietly. "Stables can be tricky to find. Particularly those ones over there."

Dobbin stopped in front of him. "How'd ye like me to drop ya down the first well we find?"

"You want a well? Hold on and I'll ask someone for directions."

Dobbin clenched his fists. "If ye weren't holding that wee lass..." The shivra looked like he might actually punch him.

"Easy. I'm jesting. I'm sure you know where all the wells are."

"Please! The pair of you!" Caroline said, hands on hips as she glared at each in turn.

Elias walked around Dobbin to the stable's side door. Theatrically, he shifted Kirsty slightly in his arms and touched the handle with a fingertip. "Do you think we should find a maid to show us how it opens?"

Dobbin closed his eyes and took a long, deep breath.

Caroline stopped beside Elias, leaned close and spoke softly. "I know you two are just having fun, but my soul is on fire. Literally. Please, not now."

Her soul was on fire? What had the Gods done to her? Had he mistaken her gift for another curse?

Dobbin moved up behind them. "Keep it up pixie," he said. He reached past Elias and pulled the door open.

Someone stood on the other side.

Caroline jumped back, fire igniting around her. "Watch out!" Elias said, stumbling away from the heat radiating from her. Dobbin moved back too.

A woman stepped forward.

"Mother?" Caroline asked, the heat abruptly vanishing.

Queen Lynn's eyes found Dobbin's. "Did you get lost?" She asked. She appeared genuinely curious.

50

————

Caroline stepped back, expecting guards to follow Queen Lynn from the stables. Her mother hesitated, reaching out, but then dropped her hand. "Caroline, your father doesn't know I'm here. I wanted to say goodbye."

Caroline looked around. "How did you know I'd be here?"

Elias stared, mystified. The Queen slipped by Elias and tentatively embraced Caroline. After a moment's stiffness, Caroline returned the hug, the fire in her soul momentarily quenched at her mother's touch.

"You need to stay with them, Caroline. They can help you. They're your family now."

Those were the last words she wanted to hear. "Mother, I can't."

"You have to." Lynn glanced at Kirsty, and the look sent a chill through Caroline. What did her mother know about Kirsty's fate?

"I have to go my own way, Mother. My presence puts everyone in danger."

With a fingertip, Lynn touched the ruby necklace Caroline still wore. "A friend gave me that when I became pregnant with you, though I didn't know I was pregnant at the time. She made me promise to pass it on when I thought you were old enough. I made that decision when you got yourself with child, but that doesn't mean you're old enough to ignore me."

Caroline turned away, shamed at the unwanted reminder and freshly hurt by the loss she knew she'd never completely leave behind. There was no accusation or anger in her mother's voice, but it stung nevertheless. "Mother, I-"

"I'd have liked to have held your baby."

Memories of her pregnancy and the baby she'd never seen rose anew, and she struggled to force the pain back down. "Please don't remind me. Not ever. It hurts too much."

"I'm sorry," Lynn whispered. "We've only just lost Daniella and now I'm losing you. Another child to hold..."

"Please, Mother," she said. She wiped her eyes with the back of her hand. She couldn't afford to think of her baby. The child wasn't ever going to be in Caroline's life.

Lynn took a deep breath. "Tomorrow, we lay your sister to rest. It scares me to see her so still. It scares me equally, knowing you're leaving."

Caroline tried to hold her chin up. If she didn't leave now, more people would die. "Mother-"

"We're both being forced down paths we'd rather were different. I need you to make me a promise."

This was something she could do, some way to part company and not regret it. She took her mother's hands. "What?"

"Promise me you'll stay with your friends."

"Of course. I mean, no! I'll put them in danger, like Daniella. Father nearly died minutes ago and only intervention from the Higher Realm saved him." She backed away. "Everyone's better off if I make my own way." And die at Marnier du Shae's command. Would she even have the courage to accept it when it came?

Lynn caught Caroline's hands, squeezing. "Caroline, your fates are linked. I can feel it. Promise me. Stay with them."

Caroline glanced at Elias and Dobbin. They turned away as if they had something much more interesting to look at on the nearby wall. "What if they die because of me? No one should be burdened with my company."

"What if Kirsty dies because you're not there to protect her?"

How could she tell her mother she'd already killed Kirsty once?

"She needs you. Promise me you'll keep her safe. You know I dream things and I know you do too, sometimes."

"Rarely."

"For me, it's almost every night. Last night I dreamed you left Kirsty and she suffered horribly for it. Stay with her. Please."

Caroline dropped her eyes, a cold shiver creeping over her as she remembered Kirsty's words after she'd returned to life. The Goddess had asked to be forgiven. If Caroline could prevent that need, she would. "I won't abandon her. I promise." But only Kirsty, she added silently. She hadn't promised anything more.

"Thank you. I love you." Lynn kissed Caroline's cheek before breaking away and hurrying across the empty courtyard, her long blue skirts brushing the cobbles. She didn't look back.

"Yer mother's got the Sight," Dobbin said. "Let's hope she's not about ta change her mind about freeing Elias."

"Mother freed Elias?"

"Aye." He shook his head as though sad. "I can't understand it either."

That almost drew a smile from her. "We must go. Father's not a man to let people defy him. He'll try to stop me once he regains his composure."

Determined not to lose more tears over leaving her family, she raised her chin and entered the cool, shingle-roofed stable. The overwhelming reek of manure, dust and straw half-choked her.

Dust motes wafted in the sunlight by the door, but at least these stables didn't smell of rot like the ones she'd found Stormrunner in. She may have puked otherwise.

She sniffled, unable to pick out Stormrunners's scent above the reek. "The less time I spend in the stables, the sooner I can go back to hating Elias's scent."

"What's wrong with my scent?" Elias asked. He appeared as much curious as hurt.

"It makes me want to kill you. Or worse. Hurry up."

"Worse? What could be worse?"

She flushed with embarrassment. "See if you can wake Kirsty while Dobbin gets her horse." She walked along the stalls, looking for Stormrunner. She desperately wanted to hug him. It surprised her how much she'd come to depend on her sense of smell. Without it, she felt blind.

There were huge double doors at the midway point on her left, and another small door at the far end. Stormrunner stuck his head over the last stall's door on the right. She smiled. "It's good to see you, too," she said as she walked up to him, rubbing the soft spot on the end of his nose and placing her cheek against his.

Something moved behind him.

She froze. Stephanie stood near the stone wall, someone behind her with a knife at her throat. Her sister's brown eyes begged Caroline for help. Smaller but wiry-strong, Zaramar's mate glared hatred from behind the young princess.

The woman made a shushing noise and signalled Caroline to enter the stall.

When a glance back the way she'd come failed to catch anyone's eyes, Caroline did as instructed, closing the door behind her. She placed a hand on Stormrunner's neck to ensure the fire she felt rising inside her stayed at bay. If she lost control, the entire stables would go up.

Her fourteen-year-old sister trembled. Caroline mighn't have wanted her father's guards in here a minute ago, but now she hoped they'd hurry up.

"My husband didn't deserve to be killed by a Gods-cursed creature like you. He was an honourable warrior."

"One of you was."

The woman's violet eyes narrowed. Stephanie squeezed her eyes shut and whimpered as the knife pressed harder. "Murder my sister and you'll never get a chance at rebirth."

The woman lifted a fine chain over her head, and even in the stable the acrid tang of silver burned Caroline's throat. "My husband gave me this." She threw it at Caroline's feet where it half disappeared in the straw. "Put it on."

"No."

"Put it on or I'll open your sister's throat."

Stephanie whimpered. With Caroline's affinity with fire rising on a tide of hatred, she struggled to contain herself, unable to think of a way to use it without hurting Stephanie or destroying the barn and killing all the horses.

This was her price for saving her father, then. He would live and she would die, and Stephanie would inherit her affinity with fire. A good trade.

Caroline pulled her ruby necklace free. "I'll do as you say," she told the faspane woman, her fingers painfully tight on the ruby. "I promise. Just allow me to give this to my sister to remember me by. After that, I'll do whatever you ask."

The faspane pulled Stephanie back slightly. "A faeriestone?"

"A keepsake," Caroline said quickly. "My mother gave it to me."

The woman stared at the jewel for a long moment, but finally gave a brief nod. "Fine, but then you put my necklace on."

Caroline held the ruby out. "Take it, Steph. It's yours now."

Stephanie froze as the blade pressed hard against her skin.

"Careful, little Princess," the woman said. It sounded absurd considering Stephanie was bigger.

"It's okay, Steph. Take it."

The younger girl reached out with trembling hands. Her fingers touched Caroline's as she took the ruby. Caroline barely hid a gasp of pain as her affinity tore free, the faeriestone acting as a conduit. It felt as if her soul had been ripped out, too.

Stephanie's eyes widened, and in a heartbeat they went from brown to dusty green. Comprehension and disbelief spread on her face. "I'm fire," she whispered, awe in her voice, but moments later the awe was lost to a grimace of pain.

"I'm sorry, Steph," Caroline whispered.

The faspane woman's blade scraped against Stephanie's skin. "Put the silver necklace on. I want you helpless when I kill you."

Caroline crouched and grasped the silver necklace. "Ow." She dropped it. Reaching out again, it was all she could do not to pull away. She let out a small whimper as she held it up, her fingertips blistering as she dropped it over her head, her hair cushioning it at the back of her neck.

"Against your skin."

Hands shaking, Caroline slipped the necklace down the front of her dress. It burned into her. "Gods!"

"Move your hair out of the way," the woman said. "I want all of the chain against your skin."

Caroline managed to lift her hair up, allowing the necklace to burn into the back of her neck. "Let Steph go," she whimpered, tears streaming from her eyes as her knees buckled. "I'm helpless."

The faspane woman jerked sideways as an arrow cut chips from the stone wall behind her and bounced to the ground.

"Stop!" Caroline cried. "Elias. Don't interfere. She'll kill Stephanie."

"Throw your bow aside izzat!"

"Elias, do as she says!"

Caroline tried to stand, but the silver chain was burning into her skin like wire hot from the forge. She could barely talk.

"Who do you value more, izzat? Your Champion or her sister?"

"Caroline?" Elias asked.

"Let her kill me," Caroline said. "If she's honourable she'll let Stephanie go," Caroline said.

"What?" There was real shock in his voice. "Never."

"It's my destiny," Caroline said. "I sacrificed my life to Marnier du Shae. I die today."

The faspane sneered. "I might prefer killing your sister more than you now."

"What?"

Stephanie whimpered as the knife broke her skin. A trickle of blood welled and ran in a line to her dress.

"Don't worry, Champion, you'll have time to say goodbye. I'll open her veins so you can watch her bleed out while you regret killing my husband."

If only she still had her affinity with fire... "Steph," Caroline whispered. "You're fire."

"Wha...?" Comprehension bloomed on Stephanie's face. "I'm fire." The blade in the woman's hand went red hot. She screamed and dropped it, but kept a grip on Stephanie. She cried out again as her other hand caught fire. Elias released an arrow and it took the woman in the eye.

Stephanie ran to Caroline as the woman slid to the straw against the wall.

"The necklace," Caroline said in too much pain to feel more than a moment of relief. "Get it off me."

Stephanie grabbed the chain and pulled, snapping a link to tear it free. Sharp pain flared as skin ripped away, but Caroline didn't care so long as the silver was gone. She caught Stephanie in a hug. "Thank the Divine Lady of Healing you're safe."

Caroline pushed her sister back as Elias pulled the stall's door open. Stephanie's dusty green eyes stared back, the exact same shade her own used to be.

"We have to get you to a healer," Stephanie said, her voice shaking.

Caroline grasped Stephanie's hands. "I'll be fine now. I promise." Stephanie helped her up, despite the doubts on her face.

Elias caught Caroline in a bear hug, lifting her off her ground. "I thought she was going to kill you."

Caroline stiffened. "Elias. Please."

"But-"

"Kirsty loves you. Let me go. Please."

"But... You feel it. I know you do."

She almost wished she could undo her bargain with Marnier du Shae. She wrapped her arms around him, his scent strong enough to taste. "Maybe in my next lifetime. I'm to die soon, so it shouldn't be long."

Stephanie cleared her voice. She was staring at Elias as if he were a simorath. "Caroline?"

Grateful for the distraction, Caroline broke from Elias and hugged Stephanie. "I have to go, Steph, but you're going to be okay." She didn't dare look at Elias. "Come, we'll talk outside." She took Stephanie's hand and led her from the stall.

Stephanie stopped as they reached the warm sunlight at the stable doors. "What do you mean you're going to die? Where do you have to go?"

Caroline led her a little further from the stables, hoping the fresh air would clear her head. "Keep your secret, Steph, and help our sisters do the same. You've all been given affinities by the Higher Realm. They won't be easy to endure, but you'll have to."

"I've never been this frightened. I hurt inside. Everywhere. All at once."

"The Divine Lady of Healing will look after you." Caroline gently pushed one of Stephanie's sleeves back, but found only normal skin there. "Marnier du Shae hasn't marked you?" She checked to make see if her own markings were still there. They were.

Dobbin led Kirsty's horse and his own from the stables, eyebrows lifting when he saw Stephanie. "We taking yer whole family now?"

Kirsty, following unsteadily, appeared curious too.

"Stephanie was helping us kill assassins, that's all."

"Assassins?" Dobbin asked, reaching for his hammer as he looked around for danger.

"Look after our family, Steph. You're fire, remember? If anyone hurts you, you can stop them."

Stephanie grimaced as if the reminder brought the ache in her soul to the fore. "It hurts. A lot."

"I know, and I'm sorry. There wasn't another way." Trying to appear strong, she waited for Elias to bring Stormrunner to her, and mounted astride as a man would.

A churn in her stomach told her the bargain she'd struck with Marnier du Shae wasn't the right choice. "You're alive. That's what's important."

"I'll look after our sisters," Stephanie said. "I promise."

"I know you will."

As Dobbin and Kirsty mounted their horses Elias moved to jump up behind Caroline, but she gave him a warning glance. "Kirsty's lighter," she said. "Perhaps you should ride with her." It nearly killed her to say the words.

He seemed to want to argue, but stalked over to Kirsty's horse and sprang up behind her instead, strung bow in hand.

"What?" she asked a little too sharply.

"Allyn isn't going to be happy," Elias said as Kirsty kicked her mare into motion, shod hooves clattering on the sun-warm cobbles. "He's invested a lot into getting you home. He'll be offended. The Gods too."

"If a Divine Lord or Lady wants me to fulfil some destiny, they should have the courtesy to ask, not push. Allyn too."

"It's an honour to serve the Gods," he said.

"I disagree." The divine markings on her arms suddenly itched, but she didn't care. "Last chance to stay, Kirsty."

Kirsty leaned back against Elias. "I know my place, My Lady." She seemed happier than Caroline had ever seen her, despite the bandage on her arm. "I always have."

Elias gave Caroline a flat look before turning away.

"Say goodbye to nice clean stables and regular meals," she said to Stormrunner as she scratched his neck. "We won't be coming back. I won't, at least." The horse raised his head and snorted at her touch. "You could pretend to be unhappy," she said as she gave him a rub.

With only Stephanie watching on, Caroline guided Stormrunner toward the palace gates and a future blissfully devoid of foresight.

EPILOGUE

Kimbriel stood atop Kirrilee Palace's northwest tower as Caroline, Elias, Dobbin and Kirsty guided their horses through the palace's huge gates. Every step the princess took reverberated into the future as time itself realigned to accommodate her choice.

Seething at Caroline's unexpected success in avoiding her fate, Kimbriel could do little but watch.

Everything had pointed to the girl remaining. Her father should have died today, and in a few weeks her brothers and sisters as well, leaving her free to ascend the throne.

No longer.

Everything was ruined now the Goddess had condemned Caroline to die. There was nothing to do but try and influence the next Champion, whoever that was. Certain the other Gods were already preparing new ways to affect events, it could be decades before Kimbriel would be able to navigate their whims.

She withdrew a necklace from under her dress and held it up. A clear diamond faeriestone dangled from a chain much like the ruby faeriestone Caroline once wore.

It had captured Princess Daniella's affinity with spirit when she'd died, and now it belonged to no one. Kimbriel wanted to crush the diamond into dust, she was so fed-up with the petty whims of Gods.

"Caroline was strong enough to take you to Noramgaell!" she yelled at the sky, half expecting Marnier du Shae to rebuke her. "Why let her defy you?"

It's not wise to antagonise Gods, Kimbriel.

Kimbriel spun. No one was there, but she knew who spoke. Marak du Tren, God of War. "I don't bow to Gods."

Where's my war, Kimbriel?

She held her temper. "How can I give you a war when the challenger refuses to stand?"

The Goddess of Healing is not a fighter. You'll have to lure her into battle.

"I've done everything you've asked and more. I want my reward."

Earn it. Give me Noramgaell. His presence disappeared.

Kimbriel clenched her fist around the diamond faeriestone. The affinities gifted to some of Lynn's daughters had been a down payment of sorts, gifts to humanity for being drawn into Noramgaell. They should be forfeit now that Caroline had turned away. And yet, they weren't. It suggested Marnier du Shae had new plans.

The other three sisters all wore faeriestones too, on the assumption their affinities would be caught when they died. That wouldn't happen now. Not for decades, at least.

Struggling to find some hope, Kimbriel looked into the future. Very few people surprised her, but Caroline had, and the consequences could take centuries to repair. Perhaps Caroline's sisters would pass their Gods-granted gifts to their own daughters. She might only have to wait another generation or two before a new Champion arose from the same bloodline.

A vision of a draken flickered in the near future and Kimbriel's heart thumped with hope. How far into the future she couldn't tell, but less than a human lifetime.

She traced the unexpected glimpse back to the present. Surprisingly, it stemmed from Caroline's decision today. It was too early to tell, but Caroline's actions may have assisted her plans more than confounded them.

"What purpose has your Goddess given you now, Princess? How will your death advance her cause?"

Kimbriel concentrated, but couldn't see through the chaos to safely influence anything. What was clear was that the sooner Caroline died, the sooner Kimbriel could guide events back toward Noramgaell.

"Do what you can for now," she reminded herself.

Kimbriel asked a Permission. When granted, she shifted herself to a small clearing beside a creek. "Hello, Allyn,' she said.

Allyn spun, staff in hand. "Kimbriel?" He didn't look as shocked to see her as she'd expected.

"You failed, sorcerer. Caroline turned from her destiny. Marnier du Shae has bound her to death now."

His face paled. "She can't have."

"The Goddess of Healing needs to find a new Champion. You must ensure Elias arrives at Delshere so he's prepared. Do not interfere again."

"Interfere?"

"You foolishly bonded Caroline, which set her on the path to rebellion."

"She had to learn."

"Your influence caused her to defy her Goddess."

"But Caroline has so much potential!"

"Had potential, Allyn. No longer. Her mistress is almost finished with her. Take her to Delshere, but tell her nothing of the citadel's wards. Can you do that for the sake of your people?"

He clenched his jaw. "The wards will detect her lycanthropy and the shivras will kill her for it."

"So they shall."

"But-"

"Stop interfering. Do as your Queen commanded and take her grandson to collect the sword. Let him fulfil his destiny and let Caroline fulfil hers. Her fate is beyond us now. Once Caroline is gone we can begin working toward Noramgaell again. Hopefully the Goddess of Healing finds a new Champion we can influence."

He glared. "I'll do what's best for my people, of course."

"So will your Queen. Remember that before you interfere again."

Far to the north, she sensed Phoenix sitting on ruined battlements well above a faspane village. She asked another Permission and shifted herself across the distance to sit beside him.

"You look younger after your rebirth," she said.

He jumped in surprise. "Please stop doing that." His voice was equally youthful.

"Your demonstration worked. The clans are beginning to unite behind you."

He looked her over, his ice-blue eyes narrowing. "Playing with humans again?"

She smiled. "Is this better?" She shifted form.

"Yes, although you look more izzen than faspane now. There aren't too many blonde faspane. *And* you look no older than a girl barely grown into adulthood."

She gently held his cheek in her palm. His skin was soft like a newborn's. She gave it a gentle caress before letting her hand drop away. "I like blonde. And small. And young. People underestimate me far more easily."

"How *are* things among my opponents?"

"Elias will soon take up the *Sword of the Sun* and seek out the Silver Well."

Phoenix turned away, staring over the fields below the crumbling battlements. "I'd rather he didn't. That sword can kill me."

"He won't find the Silver Well otherwise, and you need the Power of Ages to shatter Delshere. Only Elias can close the circle I've opened."

His voice gained an edge. "You've the power of a God. *You* could take me to the Silver Well. *You-*"

"I can't foresee the consequences of my actions. You wouldn't even have your regenerative abilities if Marak du Tren hadn't demanded it of me."

"But-"

"When you discover the Silver Well, and you will, you'll cast Elias *and* the *Sword of the Sun* from this universe. This is what Elias was born for. I've seen it."

"And the Princess?"

"All you've done is push her deeper onto a path that will cause trouble. Leave her be."

"I had to try and kill her. She's the most powerful human alive."

Kimbriel laughed at his ignorance. "Attempting to kill her was pointless. You've achieved nothing but delays. Caroline feared everything her Goddess gave her and you merely pushed her to renounce it all."

"Fear can be overcome."

Kimbriel sighed. For some reason, she liked the young princess. "It makes no difference now. Marnier du Shae has forsaken her."

He smiled as he considered the ramifications. "So we begin anew?"

"Yes, as you'd hoped. Perhaps one of Caroline's future nieces or nephews will make an acceptable Champion, although the Goddess of Healing is rarely so obvious. Perhaps I'll be able to force events."

"Let the Goddess find her own Champion." He returned his gaze to the fields.

"You need Noramgaell to bring resolution to the faspane, and for that the Goddess of Healing needs a Champion. The sooner she selects-"

"Are we likely to see another Champion so potent?"

"Not for generations, if then. I suspect it took Marnier du Shae millennia to concentrate so much power into a single human. She's unlikely to try the same again. Whoever you face will have other advantages, but most likely no magic."

"Comforting." He stared out over the fields, his smile broadening. "Thank you, Mother."

Thank you for reading Divine Prey.

I hope you enjoyed the story as much as I loved writing it.

If you have the time, please consider leaving a brief review on Amazon, your blog, or wherever else you think people might appreciate hearing about it.

Reviews are the best way to spread the word about stories you like.

If you want to be the first to hear about my upcoming novels, short stories and other offers, please **subscribe to my newsletter.** As a bonus, you'll get several of my short stories for free.

The following chapter is from Epicentre, a Veil of Gods novel set thousands of years before the events of Divine Prey (here on Earth, now).

EPICENTRE

Epicentre

A Veil of Gods novel

Coming soon

Grace smiled and closed her eyes as a wave rushed up the beach and washed around her ankles, the subtle hints of lifeforce in the water making her body ache for more. As the wave slipped back out cool wet sand oozed between her toes, a pleasant distraction from her sunburn. With her lifeforce nearly spent she couldn't afford the energy to heal. Not until she drowned someone.

Hundreds of people were bodysurfing, swimming, and jumping the waves, but she only needed to drown one today. Grace pulled her blond hair over her shoulders as another cool wave washed around her feet, sinking her deeper into the sand.

Her claws, normally hidden when in human form, began to protrude from under her fingernails as her needs grew stronger. She had to choose a victim before she lost control and took someone she couldn't live with.

Hating herself just a little for giving in to her needs, she began humming, the subtle enchantment disguised by crashing waves and yelling children. She reluctantly pulled the temporary affliction of her feet from the sand and began meandering along the beach, determined not to let the water draw her into a killing frenzy.

Several young men eyed her as she strolled and she made herself smile at one, a tall, skinny, awkward-looking kid about sixteen or seventeen, but he turned away in embarrassment. She couldn't help her sense of relief that he didn't fall for her. Still, if she spoke to him she could easily lure him into the ocean.

A few yards ahead a boy of three or four squealed in delight as his father chased him into the waves. Grace almost swooned at the rush of the child's lifeforce when the next wave struck her feet, and not just his. Hundreds of people were begging her to drown them. She made herself continue humming, widening the effects of her enchantment. A teenage girl, maybe fourteen, fell under her spell.

The girl pushed sun-bleached hair aside and bit her bottom lip invitingly as Grace strolled past. She had two friends with her though, either of which could cause a problem unless Grace took all three.

A few yards further along a toddler with brown skin and black curly hair spooned wet sand into bucket his father was holding. She felt the father's will crumble under her enchantment, but didn't dare look at him in case he left the child and tried to follow her.

A swarm of small children ran across her path to escape a wave, dodging around a tanned, muscle-bound guy carrying a boogie-board into the water. The guy did a double-take as he saw Grace, but made an effort to turn and follow a pre-teen girl who looked enough like him that she couldn't have been anyone else's child - his parenting instincts overriding her enchantment.

Another wave washed around her ankles, trying to tease her concentration away and draw her back to the ocean's embrace... and a killing spree. Killing indiscriminately felt so callous and... inhuman, and she didn't want to forget she'd once been human herself.

Another wave struck, the lifeforce tingling her skin and

sharpening her breath. Determined not to fall prey to her own needs, she left the water's edge for the hot sand, grimacing as her feet lost their natural toughness from exposure to the water.

Almost entirely human now, sand ground painfully into her uncalloused soles and clung to her feet and ankles, giving her a pedicure she didn't need or want.

Maintaining her enchantment, she continued to search for a victim who wouldn't weigh as heavily on her conscience. Humans ran about, lazed, read, and generally had fun. Some watched her, several young men staring openly now, but their instincts, or perhaps doubts, kept them from approaching.

Eyes followed her, heads turned, and a few mouths fell open as she meandered across the beach. She suspected that if she walked into the ocean now, at least half a dozen people would follow.

An older man slathered in poorly rubbed-in sunscreen did a double-take as he glanced her way. Quickly ensnared by her enchantment, his eyes wondered to her bikini-clad breasts, but then his face flushed red when he noticed her watching and he turned away, his embarrassment enough to break her hold. She could have lived with taking him.

Humming still, she continued her slow walk, both hoping and fearing she'd attract the right person. Many people stared openly now as she strolled past, one couple even following from a distance. Grace hesitated when she saw Maria on the sand ahead. Her sister's dark hair cascaded to her waist, the slight breeze moving it as she anxiously watched Grace, clearly determined to help if needed.

A toddler ran into Grace's leg and bounced off, the little girl landing on her rear in the dry sand.

Grace stopped humming. "Are you okay?" she asked as the toddler looked up with surprised blue eyes. A child of her own might have appeared much the same if Grace had had the opportunity while still human.

Sand clung to the little girl's hands and legs as she stood. "Uh-huh," she said before offering a gorgeous smile. The child's parents didn't seem to be nearby, catering to Grace's darker instincts. This close, Grace could feel the child's lifeforce emanating from her body like mist from dry ice. "You need to go," Grace whispered hoarsely.

An old, almost buried instinct to keep the toddler safe welled up in her, but it was fleeting and hard to cling to when her need to survive was growing so strong. She wanted to walk away, but her own needs ensnared her as much as her enchantments had caught the people on the beach.

Grace smiled back at the little girl, sensing herself approaching an edge she couldn't back away from. "Hush little baby," Grace found herself singing, the old nursery rhyme coming unbidden.

Her body ached with need and desire as her claws protracted and her canines lengthened and pushed hard against the insides her lips. Today more than any other day in the past few decades she had to kill someone. She wished it didn't have to be such a gorgeous child.

"Mamma's going to buy you a rocking bird..." Rocking horse? Mocking bird? She couldn't remember, not that it mattered. Slowly, deliberately, she reached for the child who watched her as if in a trance. "Are you lost?" she asked in the same sing-song voice, lifting the little girl up.

The toddler stared, wide-eyed and unblinking now, her will completely washed away by Grace's voice. "How about I help you find your mother?" Grace continued. She smiled at the little girl. "Would that be good? I saw her in the water, taking a swim."

"Uh huh," the girl murmured, still staring.

"I think that would be best," Grace continued as she turned toward the foamy waves.

"Oh, there you are!" a young woman cried, running over to snatch the girl from Grace's arms. The woman was pregnant with her next child, maybe half-way there.

Grace's enchantment shattered like a stomped-on sandcastle. She clenched her fists to hide her claws as the woman became her new focus for murder, reluctantly letting the mother keep the toddler.

"She's a beautiful girl," Grace managed, almost grinding her teeth.

The woman smiled. "Thanks. If only she had a leash. I swear I only turned away for a second. Come on Tiani. No running off again, okay? You could have drowned and I'd never have known."

Grace's instincts made her tremble as the woman left with her victim, but she forced her needs down until her canines receded. It took a full minute more before her claws did the same.

"That was stupid," Maria said from behind, her tone annoyed to the point of anger.

"I-"

"You could have drowned the toddler before her mother even realised she was missing!" Despite centuries without seeing her homeland, Maria still retained her Italian accent.

"I was nearly there Maria."

"Two days, Grace. Just two left. I can feel you slipping away." Maria touched Grace's pearl-encircled sapphire necklace with a single fingertip, the necklace matching the one Maria wore. "You should kill more often. It makes it easier. You can't always rely on disasters to carry you through the years."

Grace tried to smile, but her charms were completely wasted on her sister.

Maria's dark brown eyes watched her, full of concern and love and fear. "You're going to have to pick someone. The less you think about it the easier it will be."

Grace watched the humans enjoying the day's warmth. "Easier? The only time it was easy was when you made me and I was in the throes of transformation. I didn't even know what I was doing."

"Pretend that's today."

Grace stared at the soft sand, a torn piece of dry seaweed crushed under someone's footstep. "Dying once was enough."

Maria placed her hand on Grace's shoulder. "You didn't die. Of all the victims the sea should have claimed that night, I kept you alive."

"Yes, I died. We can't we have children Maria. Living people have children."

"You're my daughter! My sister. My love."

"I'm nothing but your creation."

Maria stiffened as hurt and anger collided on her features.

Grace instantly regretted the words. "Your my best friend and the person I love most in the world, but I'm not your daughter. My mother died in England a century ago," she said softly.

Instead of the expected outburst, Maria's eyes filled. "You're not human Grace, and neither am I. We kill humans. We have to."

"Not all magical have to creatures kill for lifeforce. Most just take what they need to survive, like vampires."

"Never compare yourself to them! We're magical. They're barely supernatural... Never mind. You're the only thing in the world I care about Grace. The only thing. Don't ever belittle that. I love you more than my own life. I even defied our sisters to create you."

Grace couldn't meet Maria's eyes. "I'm sorry. It's just... I hate this part. If I didn't have to kill there'd be nothing to hate about this life." That, and her inability to have a child of her own, but she kept that to herself as she toyed with her necklace, the slight tingle of stored lifeforce it still held doing little to make her feel better.

Maria's expression softened. "Would you rather I'd let you die that day? Would you change that if you could?"

"I just wish..." Wish what? That she could kill without feeling guilty? Did she ever really want that? "I really hate this part."

"Sometimes you have to kill to survive, Grace. All life struggles in one way or another, and we're part of that. We keep the balance by taking the injured, the unlucky, and the stupid." She glanced around the beach. "And sometimes we take those who don't deserve it. It's how life works."

"I know."

Maria took Grace's hands. "How about I help you pick someone? That way you can blame me and you won't have to feel guilty."

"I'll still feel guilty."

"Maybe a little less guilty?"

Grace couldn't help a tiny smile. "Maybe just a little."

Maria pointed to a balding man walking toward the water. "How about him? He's old enough to have lived well, and by the look of that mole on his back he isn't going to survive much longer. Nothing to feel guilty about. Right?"

Grace watched the man for a moment, but he didn't go deeper than his knees. If he feared swimming beyond his depth then no enchantment would likely lure him further.

"A decent rip would be handy about now.'

"You've got it easy little sister. In the old days we had to wait for a shipwreck or creep into a village at night and steal a child. Some of us died that way." She got a distant look in her eyes, but it disappeared almost as quickly. "Nowadays there's plenty of people in the water. Just pick someone swimming alone and drag them under. Better yet, stalk a surfer. No one will notice if they don't surface for a while after a spill, and by then you'll have another year to chance upon a disaster and top up that necklace."

Chance upon a disaster? It sounded so cold.

Maria squeezed Grace's arm. "How about that boy?" she said, pointing with her free hand. "He's out way too far, and no one's near him." She raised an eyebrow. "What kind of parent lets a kid that young swim out so deep on his own? Looks like he's getting into trouble, too."

"He's not in troub... oh."

"C'mon!" Maria began dragging Grace toward the water.

"Okay, okay!" Grace said, hating herself for listening. She could do this. It would be far too easy to drown the boy, and after that she wouldn't have to think about it again for a year. Wincing as the sand ground into her feet she walked down to the water and sighed in relief when a cool wave washed soothingly against her shins, toughening her skin.

The touch of water brought on the familiar need to change forms as well as the comforting sense of Maria's enthusiasm and love.

Grace struggled to hold onto her human shape as she walked deeper into the ocean, the waves crashing into her thighs.

The beach was shallow for the first twenty steps or so, but there it rapidly dropped off. A wave crashed against her waist and it was almost too much to hold her human form. She clenched her teeth at the next wave and barely managed not to revert. She wouldn't last through another.

Looking around to be sure no one was watching too closely, she dived under and slipped off her bikini bottoms. As the ocean welcomed her, her body shuddered in near ecstasy. She held on for another second just to prove to herself that she could, but then her legs fused into a long, powerful tail.

A single flick and she was away, powering under the waves faster than any human could hope to swim, the bottom half of her body elongated and shaped like a dolphin's, the end of her tail a fan over two feet wide.

Her hair washed out behind her, the golden sun-streaks tinged with green and blue now, while her skin changed to the mottled colour of the sandy bottom to help her blend in.

Better to take the boy quickly before she had time to talk herself out of it. She cleared the breaking surf and swam deeper, scaring schools of fish in all directions.

Few humans were brave enough to swim beyond the waves, but the lack of sand under their feet didn't deter them all. Only the fact they weren't the preferred prey of anything in the ocean made it even remotely safe for them. Anything except a mermaid.

Grace stopped and faced the shore as a swell moved over her, the water there almost luminescent with lifeforce. She could absorb the lifeforce, but it was like drinking from a morning mist. She need much more than the ocean could ever give to her.

Hopefully the boy had grown some sense and retreated into the relative safety of the group, but it only took a few seconds to find the small pair of legs pumping beyond the reach of sand, his body bobbing up and down with the surface movement.

Staying close to the bottom, Grace drifted nearer, allowing her instincts to crowd her thoughts and dissolve her human desire to nurture and protect the child. If she relaxed completely she'd risk taking more than just the child though, but she couldn't do it while thinking entirely rationally either. She might drown a dozen people before regaining her senses.

She felt Maria's presence on the beach, her sister's feet in the water and her emotions calm and assured, but focused. There was no obvious danger then. Her disappearance under the waves hadn't been noticed, not that it would really matter - people would forget soon enough. Magical creatures could never have stayed hidden otherwise.

Hopefully Maria had managed to collect her bikini bottoms. Clothes were hard to come by when you were naked and broke. With her tail moving up and down she eased nearer, wary of people close enough to see the boy disappear. She didn't want searchers in the water if she lost control.

She waited until the boy drifted a few yards closer to her, and as a swell moved between the boy and the nearest person she darted in behind him, drove her shoulder against the back of his knees, grabbed his ankles and took him under.

He didn't react for a moment, but then thrashed and kicked. She dug her claws into his skin and flicked her tail, driving her shoulder down and forcing him deeper.

The boy's desperation became blind panic, but she held his ankles hard against her chest.

Having drowned herself once, she hated inflicting the same fear on someone else and cursed herself for forgetting to sing, but his panic was completely beyond her enchantments now. His arms struggled wildly for the surface while he tried to kick free, but it didn't take long before his strength waned.

She loosened her grip and turned his limp form in her arms.

He seemed so small, sandy brown hair floating about his face. He blinked, smiled, and mouthed the word, 'Mum', and then his eyes rolled back.

The word felt like a knife in her stomach and Grace's instincts failed her.

Grabbing the boy by the shoulders, she shot up at an angle, breaking through the surface just beyond the breakers.

She pinched the boy's nose and blew oxygen into his mouth, but he remained limp. She flicked her tail and pushed toward shore just behind a wave, and as she reached the first person she drove her tail downward and felt sand.

"Quick," she said, pushing the boy into a well-tanned woman's arms. "I think he's swallowed some water."

The woman hesitated as she came to terms with someone appearing in front of her holding a limp boy, but then she took the child. "What happened?"

"Just get him to shore! Go!"

Grace held back as the woman spun and desperately struggled toward the beach, all the while trying to keep the boy's head above water. Several people came to help as Grace took the opportunity to slip under a wave and shoot away like a terrified porpoise.

AFTERWORD

I hope you enjoyed the opening chapter of Epicentre. If you want to be the first to hear about Epicentre's upcoming publication date, special offers, or any of my other works, head over to my website and subscribe to my blog and my newsletter: http://chrisandrews.me.